The Tour of Do
In Search of the Picturesque

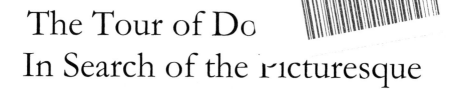

By William Combe

A Critical Edition for Readers of Jane Austen

with illustrations by Thomas Rowlandson and others

Edited by

Ben Wiebracht, PhD

Madeline Ayer	Isabella Romagnoli
Aidan Bekendam	Annika Ross
Jacob Bryant	April Wen
Ferris Haukom	Silas Wesner
Mayuko Karakawa	Noelle Wu
Edithe Lam	Ethan Yun
Sabine Mazzeo	Nicolás Zepeda
Rathan Muruganantham	Jiayun Zhang

PIXELIA PUBLISHING

The Tour of Doctor Syntax in Search of the Picturesque. A Critical Edition for Readers of Jane Austen

First Edition

Copyright © 2024 Pixelia Publishing

All rights reserved. Subject to the exception immediately following, this book may not be reproduced, in whole or in part, in any form (beyond that copying permitted by Sections 107 and 108 of the U.S. Copyright Law and except by reviewers for the public press), without written permission from the publisher.

The editors have made an online version of this work available under a Creative Commons Attribution-Noncommercial-Share Alike 4.0 International License. The terms of the license can be accessed at creativecommons.org.

Accordingly, you are free to copy, alter, and distribute this work freely under the following conditions:

(1) You must attribute this work to the editors (but not in any way that suggests that the editors endorse your alterations to the work).
(2) You may not use this work for commercial purposes.
(3) If you alter, transform, or build upon this work, you may distribute the resulting work only under the same or similar license as this one.

ISBN: 978-1-7370330-5-9
Published by Pixelia Publishing
pixeliapublishing.org
Cover design: Jiayun Zhang
Cover image: "Doctor Syntax Losing His Way," Thomas Rowlandson
Frontispiece: "The Revd. Doctor Syntax," Thomas Rowlandson
Map 1 (p. xlii): "The Tour of Doctor Syntax in Search of the Picturesque,"
    Madeline Ayer, Mayuko Karakawa, Ethan Yun
Map 2 (p. 326): "Battle of the Books," Madeline Ayer
Font: Garamond

Forgotten Contemporaries of Jane Austen

Volume I. Bath: An Adumbration in Rhyme

Volume II. The Tour of Doctor Syntax
In Search of the Picturesque

Drawn by Rowlandson.

THE REV.^D DOCTOR SYNTAX.

To Dean Wiebracht

for showing me the magic of words

CONTENTS

A WORD TO THE READER

The Tour of Doctor Syntax in Search of the Picturesque was the great comic hit of the Regency, and it continued to be widely read and enjoyed throughout the nineteenth century. After that impressive run, well over thirty editions in all, it quietly fell out of print. Today, it is read only by specialists.

We believe it is time for this forgotten bestseller to be remembered. Thanks in part to the explosive growth of the Austen community, interest in Regency popular culture is at an all-time high—not only among scholars but students and general readers as well. This edition of what was, by some measures, *the* most popular poem of the Regency is designed to serve all these groups.

Students will find this book much easier to use than most critical editions. Our annotations are informative, jargon-free, and, just as important, effortless to find. Simply glance to the right: the note will be in the margin or on the opposite page, neatly parallel with the text. We do make an exception for terms that appear several times. In those cases, we gloss the word the usual way the first time it appears, and mark it with an asterisk thereafter. All words marked with an asterisk are in a glossary at the back of the book.

For scholars and specialists, this volume offers many new insights into the poem, supported by a great deal of original research. To give just one example, we identify in our notes, for the first time, the central reference of the allegory in Canto XXV—the climax of the poem. The biographical essay, meanwhile, breaks new ground in our understanding of Combe's life—including with the discovery of an early play by Combe that had been assumed lost. Finally, the text of the poem has been painstakingly edited for accuracy and correctness; see the Note on the Text for our methodology.

For readers, students, and teachers of Jane Austen, this volume contains still more. Many of our annotations draw connections between the poem and Austen's life and work. If you wish to know what this poem might have to do with a particular Austen novel or character, we recommend that you consult the Austen Index at the back of the book. As part of the introduction, you will also find an essay on the picturesque that puts Austen, Combe, and the great popularizer of the picturesque, William Gilpin, in conversation.

Doctor Syntax, from the beginning, was meant to be *seen*, not merely read. All thirty-one of Rowlandson's aquatints are reproduced here in full color, as are the fifty-two wood engravings of the Victorian illustrator Alfred Crowquill. Fifty-eight additional images sprinkled throughout the text—caricatures, paintings, engravings, and drawings—further allow the modern reader to picture the world that Doctor Syntax and Jane Austen shared.

"William Combe, Author of Dr. Syntax," William Daniell,
after a portrait by George Dance, 1854.
National Portrait Gallery.

Stipple engraving of Jane Austen, after a portrait by
Cassandra Austen, 1870. National Portrait Gallery.

ACKNOWLEDGMENTS

This book, as the title page indicates, is the work of many hands—sixteen students at Stanford Online High School and their teacher. But many others contributed their time and expertise to this project as well, and we wish to thank them here.

Author and speaker Brenda Cox sparked this project with her article "Comical Dr. Syntax and Jane Austen" for *Jane Austen's World*. She was also our guide to all things clerical throughout the project—both in class, which she made time to visit, and out of class via email.

Anne Fertig and Elizabeth Shand helped blaze the trail for our work with their online edition of *The Tour of Doctor Syntax in Search of the Picturesque* (doctorsyntaxblog.wordpress.com), which they created while they were graduate students at UNC Chapel Hill. Their visit to class was equal parts illuminating and inspiring.

Matthew Payne, Rowlandson's biographer, helped us sort out the provenance and context of several of Rowlandson's original Syntax drawings.

Christopher Ridgway, Head Curator of Castle Howard, clarified several points regarding Frederick Howard, 5th Earl of Carlisle, who appears in the poem as Doctor Syntax's patron.

The Jane Austen Society of North America supported this project in both large and small ways. We especially thank Jennifer Weinbrecht and the other organizers of the 2024 Annual General Meeting for inviting us to share our work with the JASNA community in Cleveland, and for providing the funding to make that possible. Additional thanks are owed to the Ohio North Coast region of JASNA for their generous financial support.

The Bowes Art and Architecture Library at Stanford was an invaluable partner throughout this project—hauling up its vast collection of early *Doctor Syntax* editions from the locked stacks whenever we asked (and we asked *a lot*), and making high-resolution images of the Rowlandson plates. We especially thank librarians Katharine Keller, Amber Ruiz, and Andrea Hattendorf.

Kate Snyder, a senior at Mount Holyoke College with a very bright future, generously lent her talents as a researcher to this project. Our account of *Doctor Syntax*'s origins in the Biographical Essay is based on her work.

ACKNOWLEDGMENTS

The Morgan Library in New York City and the Yale Center for British Art kindly allowed us to view their wonderful collections of original Doctor Syntax drawings. We also thank the YCBA for putting so many of their images in the public domain. This allows small publishers like ours to create richly illustrated books without being crushed by licensing fees.

John Crichton, owner of the Brick Row Bookshop in San Francisco, discovered the lost manuscript of Combe's play *The Flattering Milliner*, and Stanford librarian Rebecca Wingfield acquired it and made it available to scholars. Their work, and their generous willingness to discuss it, allowed us to fill in a major gap in Combe's biography.

The team at Pixelia Publishing—Tom Hendrickson, Anna Pisarello, John Lanier, and Christine Gosnay—provided valuable feedback on the manuscript and helped in many other ways.

Michelle Wiebracht offered candid and insightful comments on the manuscript. She also made high-resolution images of the wood engravings by Alfred Crowquill which are included in this volume. The lead editor of this book, who has the profound good fortune of being Michelle's husband, is especially grateful to her for her unwavering encouragement and support, even as this project grew far beyond the scope he originally envisioned for it.

Dean Wiebracht, the lead editor's father and dedicatee of this book, was another major source of encouragement, as well as a sharp-eyed copyeditor. The parents of the student editors also deserve thanks for their moral and practical support.

Stanford Online High School has provided crucial financial and institutional support to Pixelia Publishing and the projects it has undertaken, including this one. We especially thank Head of School Tomohiro Hoshi and Business Director Josh Carlson, as well as the entire Business Office.

Speaking now as Wiebracht, my fellow teachers in the English Division deserve thanks for, among other things, answering questions on eighteenth-century culture and history (David Nunnery), offering close, detailed feedback on the manuscript (Kristina Zarlengo and Jason Morphew), and simply being willing to chat about this project (all and sundry). I have never known a more inspiring or supportive professional community.

Last but not least, we thank Vic Sanborn, founder and editor of the blog *Jane Austen's World*. Vic saw the value in these kinds of public-facing student-teacher collaborations before I knew how to articulate it myself. She has been a supporter, a guide to the Austen community, an ever-available expert, and a friend. Her blog has also been an indispensable resource. Both of the texts I have edited and published with students were first brought to my attention in its (virtual) pages.

FORGOTTEN CONTEMPORARIES OF JANE AUSTEN

AN INTRODUCTION TO THE SERIES

The 2005 film adaptation of *Pride and Prejudice*, starring Keira Knightley, had a special ending for its American release. The scene takes place on a torch-lit balcony at Pemberley. Presumably it is the wedding night of Elizabeth and Darcy. No longer bound by the formalities of courtship, husband and wife are in a moderate state of dishabille, seated cross-legged and facing each other. They banter about what Mr. Darcy will call Elizabeth now that they are married—whether "goddess divine" or "my pearl" or, Darcy playfully suggests, "Mrs. Darcy" when he is feeling cross. No, replies Elizabeth; he may only call her "Mrs. Darcy" when he is "perfectly and incandescently happy." Darcy then murmurs "Mrs. Darcy" no fewer than five times as he kisses her brow, her cheek, her nose. The camera never moves from the lovers; instead it zooms in closer and closer, until their faces fill the frame as they lean in for one last, perfect kiss.

This, on the other hand, is the ending Jane Austen wrote:

> With the Gardiners, they were always on the most intimate terms. Darcy, as well as Elizabeth, really loved them; and they were both ever sensible of the warmest gratitude towards the persons who, by bringing her into Derbyshire, had been the means of uniting them.

Those who have only read the novel once may need to be reminded who the Gardiners are. In short, they are Elizabeth's favorite aunt and uncle: a likeable, intelligent couple, but certainly minor characters. And yet, here they are at the curtain call, sharing center stage with the hero and heroine themselves. Take the final chapter as a whole, and the stage becomes more crowded. We learn how the Darcys deal with their difficult relatives the Wickhams. We learn that Elizabeth is fast friends with her new sister-in-law, and that the Bingleys have settled near Pemberley. Even Kitty, the most marginal of the Bennet sisters, gets a paragraph: apparently she lives with the Darcys much of the year.

The difference between the two endings boils down to this. In the 21st-century ending, the one meant to appeal to modern American tastes, the central couple is alone, perfectly fulfilled in each other. Their faces dominate the screen; their names echo in our ears. In Austen's ending, the central couple is integrated into a community. Their lives are interwoven with other lives—so much so that the final sentence focuses not on the Darcys' love for each other (though that is present, a steady undercurrent), but on their love for, of all people, the Gardiners.

This series—*Forgotten Contemporaries of Jane Austen*—strives to see Austen in the same way that Austen herself saw Elizabeth and Darcy: not balconied, not high up and alone, but at ground-level and in a broader context. It will do this by recovering some of the Gardiners of her literary world: writers whose work receives little attention today, but who can nevertheless enrich our understanding of Austen and her novels.

In selecting works for this series, we are guided by three criteria.

- First, the work cannot be available in any other modern edition. In a series focused on minor writers, this is not much of a limitation: there are thousands of titles from Austen's time buried in university archives and academic databases that have been neglected for decades if not centuries. This series, of course, can recover only a tiny sliver of that material, but a sliver is better than nothing—much better, if it piques readers' curiosity about what else might be out there.

- Second, the work must treat subjects that directly concerned Jane Austen and are prominent in her novels. In the case of *Doctor Syntax*, the key connection is the aesthetic idea known as the picturesque. To modern readers, that word often means little more than "scenic" or "quaint," but in Austen's day—and in Austen's novels—it was much more charged. When her characters talk about landscape beauty, they are often implicitly talking about other things as well— politics, religion, the place of the individual in society, and the balance between reason and emotion. *Doctor Syntax*, the most popular picturesque satire of the Regency, is just as engaged in these conversations. Readers will come away from it better equipped to appreciate Austen's own commentary on the picturesque, one that ripples through her oeuvre and informs some of her most celebrated scenes.

- Finally, while we do not presume to be publishing forgotten masterpieces, the work must have merit in its own right. We are interested in recovering the Gardiners of Austen's era, not the Mr. Collinses, and we are confident that the reader will find a Gardiner in William Combe. *Doctor Syntax* has a further claim to republication in the extraordinary popularity it achieved during the Regency. Any reader curious about the "middle of the market" in Austen's day—the kinds of books enjoyed by regular literate people—would do well to make the acquaintance of the good Doctor and his faithful mare.

At the core of each volume in this series is a richly annotated text. Whereas most critical editions relegate the notes to the foot of the page or the back of the book, we opt for a side-by-side layout, which makes notes much easier to find. In our commentary, readers will find not only historical and cultural context, but images and connections to Austen's works as well. Each volume also includes a biographical essay and a contextual essay. The biographical essay tells the story of the author's life, showing parallels with Austen's life and work along the way. The contextual essay introduces the reader to a key genre, debate, or literary trend with which the work is engaged, and explains how it figured into Austen's career as well.

We are launching this series with a varied audience in mind. Academics will value the rigorous and original scholarship that is the foundation of these volumes. Lovers of Austen, whether associated with academia or not, will appreciate the direct links we draw between the texts and authors we feature and Austen herself. Finally, teachers and students, particularly high-school students, will be inspired to know that the volume they are reading was researched, designed, and edited in large part by other high-school students. Indeed, one of my hopes for this series is that it challenges the narrow assumption that only university faculty and graduate students are capable of making original contributions to literary scholarship. It simply isn't so. These volumes, produced in full collaboration with my students at Stanford Online High School, are proof that high-school English students belong in active scholarly conversations—not just as listeners but as speakers.

Ben Wiebracht, Series Editor
Stanford Online High School
Stanford University

BIOGRAPHICAL ESSAY: WILLIAM COMBE (1742-1823)

Readers of Jane Austen often wish she had lived to write more. After several early frustrations, she finally broke through in 1811 with the publication of *Sense and Sensibility*. By the middle of the decade, she was writing a new novel almost every year. Sales, if not blockbuster, were good. Her publisher, John Murray, was one of the best in the business; and Sir Walter Scott, the most famous novelist of the day, had written a glowing review of her works. The future for Jane Austen was bright, but that future, as we know, never arrived. Jane Austen died on 18 July 1817, less than six years after publishing her first book. It is impossible not to wonder, as Virginia Woolf did, about "the novels that Jane Austen did not write."[1]

No one, probably, has wondered that about William Combe. If any writer of the nineteenth century had time to "glean his teeming brain," it was him: he lived to the age of eighty-one at a time when the life expectancy was less than half that. Indeed, his career as a published writer, which began somewhat late at the age of thirty-three, was longer than Jane Austen's entire life—and it was a time of almost uninterrupted productivity. From 1775 to 1823, novels, satires, and political pamphlets poured from his pen. He wrote numerous works of history, churned out endless letterpress for illustrated books, dashed off a play in one night, and, as the first editor of the *Times*, filled hundreds if not thousands of newspaper columns. Late in life, he discovered a remarkable talent for comic verse, the fruits of which you are holding now, just as Austen did over two hundred years ago. His first biographer, John Camden Hotten, called him "the most voluminous English writer since the days of Defoe"[2] and that may have been an understatement. He may have been the most voluminous English writer, period.

It seems safe to say, then, that most literate people in the early nineteenth century would have read something by Combe. Austen was one of them. She wrote in 1814 that she had "seen nobody in London yet with such a long chin as Dr. Syntax."[3] Only a few of those readers, though, knew the identity of the author. Like Austen, but for different reasons, Combe never signed his name to any of his published works. It wasn't that he was modest or shy; on the contrary, many of his contemporaries remembered him as a lively dinner guest and an engaging conversationalist, always ready with a story. Nor was his work scandalous or dangerous to be associated with: he was conservative in his politics and generally wrote for the middle of the market. Instead, Combe's anonymity was all about class. In society, he preferred to present himself not as a successful author, but as an independent and, indeed, rather idle gentleman. To understand this duality, which defined Combe's life and career, we need to pay a visit to a neighborhood in London called Cheapside, where Combe was born.

CHILDHOOD AND EDUCATION

In the eighteenth and nineteenth centuries, Cheapside was populated by middle-class merchants and shopkeepers. Combe's father was an ironmonger and his mother the daughter of a West-Indies merchant.[4] His family was well off, with one house in town and another in the country. His future, too, was secure. As an only son, he was set to inherit his father's wealth and, if he wished, his thriving business. But despite these blessings, his early years were not without trouble. His mother died when he was just five, which may explain some of his difficulty forming healthy relationships with women later in life. Some time after that came a different blow, less sudden but still deeply impactful. This was the realization that he was not the son of a gentleman.

Readers of *Pride and Prejudice* likely know why not: Combe's father, despite his prosperity, was in trade. The same is true of Elizabeth Bennet's uncle, Mr. Gardiner. Mr. Gardiner is a wealthy man, intelligent and educated, but, at least for some, that does not outweigh the fact that he lives in Gracechurch Street, "near Cheapside" and "within view of his own warehouses" (I.8; II.2). This has consequences not just for the Gardiners, but for the Bennets as well. Darcy is not trying to lob an insult, but merely state a fact, when he says that the Cheapside association "must very materially lessen [the Bennet daughters'] chance of marrying men of any consideration in the world"—that is, gentlemen (I.8).

In other ways, though, the novel blurs the dividing line between the gentry and the trading classes. No one seems to question the right of Bingley and his sisters to marry among the gentry, and yet they come from trade as well. The Bingleys get a pass for two reasons: they have been given elite educations, and they have been left sufficient money to support a genteel lifestyle. In Austen's England, it was not always possible to buy your own way into the gentry, but you could, with enough money and some tact, usually buy your children's way.

William Combe's father seems to have had such hopes for his son. When the boy was ten, he was sent to Eton College, the most prestigious public school in England. Robert Combes (as the name was spelled then) knew that his son would receive a classical education there, one of the passports into genteel society, and, just as important, that he would acquire the polish and manners of a gentleman. If anything, his plan succeeded too well. Combe left for school and never looked back. In adulthood, he not only hid his association with the mercantile world, but defined himself in opposition to it. His first published work, *The Philosopher in Bristol*, deplores the coarsening effects of trade and industry, which stifle the feelings and "entirely absorb and overwhelm the intellectual powers." He grants that tradespeople are useful and necessary, but nevertheless, "I thank my propitious stars, that I am not a man of trade!"[5]

HIGH LIFE AND LOW LIFE

Perhaps it was for the best that Robert Combes did not live long enough to see himself and his world so emphatically disowned by his only son. He died in 1756, when Combe was fourteen. Combe, now deprived of both his parents, was left to the care of his godfather and his father's business associate, William Alexander. Perhaps at Combe's request, Alexander arranged for his ward to take up residence at the Inner Temple, one of the Inns of Court, in order to study the law.

The law was considered a genteel profession, so the campaign to make Combe a gentleman was still alive, but the law also paid, and Alexander knew Combe would need to make some money of his own. His father had left him £2,500 ($360,000)—a very good sum to begin adult life with, but not enough to sustain the lifestyle of a leisured gentleman. Edward Ferrars (SS) lives that lifestyle for as long as his mother is willing to support it, but when he is left to shift for himself with nothing but his legally inherited £2,000 ($288,000), he knows he needs to find work.

The problem with sending Combe to the Inner Temple was that it was all too easy for him *not* to work. At that time, a large number of the Temple's residents were law students in name only; in reality they were simply men about town, making the fashionable rounds while living on family money. While this was all well and good for wealthy heirs, it was not a feasible course for a young man like Combe who needed an income. But with a small fortune at his disposal, a keen desire to live the fashionable life that many of his Eton schoolmates were embarking on, and no parent to rein him in, Combe was prepared to ignore that reality. He soon left his chambers at the Inner Temple and made, instead, a grand entry into the *beau monde*, turning heads with his fine manners, his good looks, and, most of all, his free spending. He showered money on horses, carriages, clothes, a trip to France, and a fashionable residence in the West End of London. Friends took to calling him "Count Combe" or "Duke Combe" on account of his magnificent style.[6] While Combe certainly made a splash, one also senses a touch of amused scorn in those faux-aristocratic titles. If Combe was seeking to prove that he was a gentleman, he was clearly overdoing it.

What had gone up inevitably came down. When Combe's money ran out in 1769 or 1770, he disappeared from society as suddenly as he had entered it, living who knows how. Decades later, his friends would tell stories of discovering the one-time dandy working as a waiter at an inn or serving as a private in the army (according to one account, the *French* army).[7] It is impossible to know how many, if any, of these tales are true, but what is certain is that Combe had learned a valuable—and expensive—lesson. If he wanted to live like a gentleman—indeed, if he wanted to live at all—he would need to work.

But what work could he conceivably do? The law and the military were no longer options: to enter those professions as a gentleman, one needed money, and Combe had spent all his. To become a clergyman, he would have needed a degree from Oxford or Cambridge, which he did not have. The medical profession, at least the genteel tiers of it, required a university degree and additional training. There was, however, one path left to him—a narrow one that would require more brains and hard work than Combe had yet demonstrated, but that at least did not require ready money. He could be a writer.

DEBUT AS A WRITER

We do not know when Combe first hatched the idea of pursuing a literary career, but we can make an educated guess. In 1764, during his years of fancy living, he formed a friendship with one of the most popular writers of the day, Laurence Sterne, author of *Tristram Shandy* (1759-67). Sterne is probably best remembered today as a comic writer, but in his own day he was celebrated for promoting "sensibility"—refined and morally elevating emotion. His *Sentimental Journey* (1768), which Austen read, suggested that to live wisely and virtuously, we need only cultivate fine feelings. Austen takes direct aim at that idea in her first published novel, *Sense and Sensibility*.

Combe's four-year friendship with Sterne had a profound influence on him. As a young man taken under the wing of a famous writer, he probably imbibed a good deal of the latter's sentimental philosophy. More important for his future career, though, he developed an uncanny knack for imitating his style. For the rest of his life, the Sternean mode was one Combe could fall into at a moment's notice. A contemporary later wrote that, whenever Combe was short of content for the *Pic Nic*, a paper he edited in 1803, he would "sit down in the publisher's back room, and extemporize a letter from Sterne […], a forgery so well executed that it never excited suspicion."[8] For the time being such exertions were unnecessary, as he had not yet burned through his patrimony, but he must have known it was disappearing quickly. Perhaps Combe was already planning, if he ever spent his way out of society, to write his way back in.

When Combe re-emerged in Bristol in the mid-1770s, then, it was not as a man of fashion but a man of feeling. Having scraped together some ready cash, he paid a local publisher to bring out his first book, called *The Philosopher in Bristol* (1775). It was not a work of philosophy in the modern sense, but rather a collection of affecting anecdotes and sentimental reveries—all from the perspective of a sympathetic friend of humanity, precisely Sterne's pose in his *Sentimental Journey*. Combe's goals are to call "forth the finer affections of the human breast" and in so doing to "improve and meliorate our nature."[9] Elsewhere, he was even more impassioned: "if I could, but for a moment, possess those keys which unlock that sacred treasury of virtuous and tender sentiments;—Oh heavens!—how little should I envy the most celebrated names!"[10]

The gushing sentimentality of *The Philosopher in Bristol* is unlikely to find much favor with modern readers. But tastes were different then and the book was a modest success. A reviewer for the *Westminster Magazine* wrote that "*The Philosopher in Bristol* amuses, instructs, and even draws a sigh from the generous heart," though he added that the author "is not equal to Sterne."[11] Qualified applause was still applause, and Combe was pleased enough with the reception of his first book to write a sequel shortly after, as well as a long topographical poem called *Clifton*.

His productive season in Bristol concluded with a golden career opportunity: Combe was invited to write the afterpiece to a performance of *The Merry Wives of Windsor* being put on by Samuel Reddish's company of actors. It was to be the company's final performance in the city, and John Henderson, one of the leading actors in England at the time, was playing Falstaff. A packed house was guaranteed. If Combe's play went well, he would not just be the toast of Bristol for a few evenings. Given the company's stature, he might have a chance to write for the London stage itself.

For his afterpiece, Combe wrote a one-act farce called *The Flattering Milliner* in which a clever shopowner, Mrs. Blond, thwarts the attempts of a rakish baronet to seduce one of her employees. Maybe Combe had a bit of Cheapside pride after all, or maybe he was simply sticking with the theme of Shakespeare's *Merry Wives*, which also sees an upper-class philanderer outwitted by middle-class women. In any case, it is an amusing piece of work and an early testament to Combe's literary range.[12]

For one reason or another, though, *The Flattering Milliner* flopped. A reviewer for *The Morning Post* reported that the crowd suffered through the play in a kind of stupor, punctuated by occasional "sighs and groans."[13] It must have been a stinging blow for the aspiring writer, and one that probably hastened the end of his short season as the local bard of Bristol. A few weeks after the performance, he shook the dust of the city from his feet and returned to London, where he promptly set about finding a publisher for a new edition of *The Philosopher in Bristol*. The manuscript of *The Flattering Milliner*, meanwhile, was stuffed into some dark drawer or trunk: it was one of the only things Combe wrote that he never sought to publish.

MARRIAGE AND EARLY SUCCESS

Combe's return to London brought him back to the scenes of his childhood. Paternoster Row, the center of the London publishing industry, was directly adjacent to Cheapside and about a three-minute walk from the house where he grew up. But Combe, as he took himself from one publisher to the next, was determined to present himself not as the ironmonger's son but as a literary gentleman and a man of feeling. The hard-nosed booksellers of the Row were probably unimpressed, and Combe likely had some rejections. He may have put something of the experience into Canto XXII of *Doctor Syntax*, in which the learned clergyman, manuscript in hand, is forced to endure the coarse contempt of the money-minded bookseller Vellum. In the end, though, Combe managed to get his *Philosopher in Bristol* back in the press, while also picking up a few odd writerly jobs. But he was still hesitant to commit fully to the life of a professional writer. Tossing off the occasional work of high sentiment (and reaping the consequent financial rewards) was consistent enough with his genteel posture; but grubbing day in and day out at the behest of this or that publisher was another matter. Perhaps there was another way to obtain a gentlemanly income.

In the end, an opportunity did present itself, though Combe had to set his better principles aside to take it. Francis Conway (Viscount Beauchamp) was preparing to marry, and that meant he needed to dispose of his mistress,

Maria Foster. Combe, who knew Beauchamp from Eton, was single and needed money. The two men came to an agreement: Combe would marry Maria, and in exchange Beauchamp would settle an annuity on her. Combe held up his end of the bargain, marrying Maria in May 1776, but Beauchamp, apparently, reneged. Combe was now considerably worse off than before—no richer, and with a wife to support as well. He had been hoodwinked.

In circumstances such as these, there was no maintaining the lofty pose of the man of feeling. Instead, he got revenge, unleashing a blistering satire called *The Diaboliad* (1777) which was certainly the most painful public skewering of Beauchamp's life. The premise of the poem is that Satan is retiring from the throne of hell, and wishes to appoint a sufficiently evil successor. A handful of English lords and politicians apply, Beauchamp among them—all making their case for why they should be chosen. Beauchamp, cringing and stammering, argues that he is utterly selfish, cruel to his wife, cowardly, and comprehensively base. Satan readily agrees, but still refuses to grant him the throne of hell because Beauchamp's vices are just too pathetic. He is looking for a robust, red-blooded sinner, not a sneaking, snivelling wretch like Beauchamp: "Such minds as thine,—Observe the truth I tell! / *Find neither Friends on Earth,—nor Friends in Hell.*"[14]

The Diaboliad certainly provided Combe with a release for his anger, but more importantly, it proved to be a smash hit. The image of the English elite engaged, quite literally, in a race to the bottom appealed to the public's taste for acidic and irreverent humor. Imitations of *The Diaboliad* quickly appeared, and Combe capitalized too with an expansion and a sequel. At least for the moment, Paternoster Row was at his command, and over the next few years he published satirical books and pamphlets at a furious clip, while also developing a formidable reputation as a scourge of high society. The sentimental philosopher of Bristol had become, as one reviewer put it, "the poet laureate of hell."[15]

What became of Maria Foster, now Combe? Her story is a sad one. Around 1780, she experienced an onset of mental illness and shortly thereafter she was confined to a private asylum in Plaistow, where she would spend her remaining years. This asylum was acquired in 1798 by a gardener and fruiterer named Stephen Casey.[16] What conditions were like before his acquisition we cannot say, but after it, they appear to have been grim indeed. By 1804, Casey was already advertising his establishment as the cheapest in the London area, and letters indicate that he sometimes charged as little as 10s ($72) a week.[17] Such low rates would have secured only the meanest care. Poor food and lodging, however, may have been the least of Maria's worries at Casey's asylum. Commissioners from the Royal College of Physicians who inspected the facility described it as one that they "regret they have not the power to suppress."[18] In addition to the generally "miserable" accomodations, they noted that it was impossible to reach the men's bedroom without passing through the women's; and they were shocked to find, at the top of a staircase that they were told led nowhere, a room fitted with chains and staples. To add to all this, by the early 1810s, if not earlier, Casey was regularly admitting patients who had been acquitted of crimes such as attempted murder, theft, and treason on grounds of insanity.[19] Such was the home of Maria Foster Combe for much of her life, until she died in 1814.

LITERARY CHAMELEON

Back in London in the late 1770s, Combe's career was at a crossroads. He could continue to fillet the upper classes as a satirist, which would pay the bills and ensure a measure of literary celebrity, or he could try to regain his posture as a leisured gentleman of letters. He chose the second path. He stopped signing his work "by the author of *The Diaboliad*," and instead started to write under the guise of other, recently deceased writers. First he channeled his old mentor Sterne, bringing out a collection of *Letters Supposed to Have Been Written by Yorick and Eliza* in 1779. (Yorick and Eliza, as the public knew, were Laurence Sterne and his platonic beloved Eliza Draper.) The next year, after the death of the infamous "bad Lord Lyttelton," Combe obligingly wrote his letters, too. The year after that, he wrote an epistolary novel called *Letters of an Italian Nun and an English Gentleman*, which he boldly declared to be "Translated from the French of J.J. Rousseau." He even started a series called *The Royal Register*, full of court gossip, which he attributed to King George III himself!

These productions have earned Combe some scowls from modern critics. Among Sterne scholars in particular, who have spent decades trying to weed out Combe's imitations, our author is *persona non grata*.[20] But Combe was not seeking to deceive anyone. Contemporary reviewers were neither fooled by Combe's imitations, nor were they outraged by them. They saw them instead as literary exercises, to be read *as if* by Sterne or Lyttelton or Rousseau, and to be judged on the accuracy of the imitation. Opinion was divided, but most of them thought Combe's imitations were skillful.[21] The frustrations of modern scholars, who still debate the authorship of this or that letter, have only validated that judgment.

By the mid-1780s, Combe had been publishing consistently for ten years. Most of his works had sold well, and a few—in particular *The Diaboliad*, the Lyttelton letters, and *The Royal Register*—had been hits. He was earning more than enough to pay for his wife's care while also supporting a respectable "bachelor" lifestyle. But respectability was never enough for Combe; only unqualified gentility would do. Once again he lived beyond his means, and, with no family to come to the rescue, he met the usual fate of unconnected eighteenth-century spendthrifts. One of his creditors took him to court for non-payment of debt, and shortly after that he was committed to King's Bench Debtors' Prison.

WRITER-FOR-HIRE

Debtors' prison must have been a severe blow to Combe's pride, but it did not overwhelm him. Combe was the kind of person who always kept his head in the bad times (and generally lost it in the good ones). Once, when down on his luck, a friend asked how he could bear the humiliation. "Fiddlesticks!" he replied, helping himself to a nonchalant pinch of snuff, "A philosopher can bear anything."[22] It helped, too, that despite the King's Bench's imposing exterior, with 25-foot walls topped with spikes, life inside was not as bleak as one might suppose. For inmates with a little ready cash, there were breweries, coffee shops, wine rooms, and other amenities. Private quarters could be had for a consideration as well. For some, the greatest hardship was the enforced idleness, but Combe, who always had some plan in the works, could easily avoid that. In the present instance, he apparently convinced his primary creditor, John Palmer, the Comptroller-General of the Post Office, to agree to his release. In return, he offered the services of his pen. Palmer introduced Combe to the publisher John Walter, and Combe, once again gainfully employed, set about making amends. In 1787 Walter brought out a new edition of Adam Anderson's monumental 1764 *Origin of Commerce*. The edition had an additional, fourth volume which brough the history up to date, treating in detail the economic reforms of Prime Minister William Pitt. That fourth volume was entirely the work of William Combe, and it included a gushing appendix praising the post-office tenure of—whom else?—the man who had put him in debtors' prison, John Palmer.

Combe's career was full of improbable successes, but his continuation of *The Origin of Commerce* has to rank among the most stunning. There was every reason to expect this work to be a hack-job. Here was a man, fresh out of debtors' prison, whose writerly experience up until that point had consisted of sentimental effusions and satirical smack-downs. He was told to write a continuation of one of the most respected works of economic history, and, at the same time, to puff the achievements of a man with little claim to inclusion in such a book. Based on Combe's glowing praise of Pitt, he probably had additional instructions to butter up the Prime Minister. He was to write this work in weekly numbers, giving him little opportunity to organize the whole and no ability to revise with the benefit of hindsight— and at the same time he was to supply Walters' press with a variety of other material. It is hard to imagine less auspicious conditions for the writing of good scholarship, and yet that is exactly what Combe produced. The work was hardly perfect—Combe has a tendency to serve up long, undigested quotations in order (one suspects) to hit his weekly quotas.[23] But, as reviewers universally acknowledged,[24] it was competent, and under the circumstances, competence was a major achievement. Once again, Combe had reinvented himself. He had begun with works of sensibility; now, after a sobering stay in debtors' prison, he would write works of sense.

In particular, the government's sense. With *The Origin of Commerce*, Walters and Combe had proven their value to the Pitt Ministry, and in 1788 they were both duly rewarded with government pensions; Combe's was a handsome £200 ($28,800) per year. That money, though, came with strings attached. Combe was expected to wield his pen in defense of the ministry and its positions—its prosecution of the war with France, its "not now" approach to political reform and, perhaps most dicily, its high taxes. He did just that, producing a steady stream of vigorously written political pamphlets and articles from the late 80s to the mid 90s. Combe, a staunch conservative, probably did not need to bend his principles much in order to fulfill this role. As far back as *The Diaboliad*, he had attacked Charles Fox, the leader of the Opposition, and no one was paying him for that. What irked him later about his work as a pamphleteer was the fickleness with which he was treated. He was cut off suddenly in 1796, brought back in the early 1800s, and then dismissed just as abruptly in 1806. The final installment of his pension was never paid. Combe wrote later that to treat him thus, William Sturges Bourne, the Secretary of the Treasury, must have had "the most perfect contempt for me."[25]

Combe, who usually had several irons in the fire, did not limit himself to government propaganda during this relatively prosperous season. He published another volume of "original" Sterne letters, this time sprinkling in a few authentic ones which he had in his possession, often with additions and adaptations of his own—all to the enduring anguish of modern Sterne scholars.[26] The task of sorting the wheat from the tares continues to this day. He also brought out a new satire called *The Devil upon Two Sticks in England* (1790-1), full of vignettes of London life. It ran through six volumes and was another success: his obituarist recalled that the book "was as popular as any in its day."[27] His works during this season were miscellaneous enough, however, that no one could have known he was the author of them all. Combe preferred it that way. He liked to be known as a man of letters, but not one who had to write for a living. He had a habit, in fact, of sneaking his name into the list of subscribers for works he himself had written, even when he had every right to put it front and center on the title page. Apparently, he had rather appear as a gentlemanly patron of literature, mixed up in a list of esquires and lords, than as a professional author.

RIVER TOUR AND SECOND MARRIAGE

In the early 1790s, a project came along that offered the best of both worlds—handsome remuneration and access to the best society. John and Josiah Boydell, jointly one of the premier publishers in England, wanted to bring out an illustrated book celebrating the picturesque beauties of the major rivers of Great Britain, and in particular of the great estates along their banks. The Boydells had engaged Joseph Farington, one of the leading landscape artists of the day, to furnish the illustrations, and they turned to Combe to supply the letterpress. As part of his work, Combe was to make a tour of the Thames, stopping at various manor houses along the way to contemplate the scenery and write his impressions.

These were happy days for Combe. Backed by the august names of Boydell and Farington, he was a guest of honor everywhere he went. His hosts were pleased to have their houses and grounds featured in such a deluxe work, and they were delighted, as were most people who met Combe, with the writer's manners and talents. Indeed, George Simon, 2nd Earl Harcourt, seems to have been a little nervous to meet, as he put it in a letter, a man of Combe's "literary eminence."[28] Combe's grateful memories of this time may explain why, in *The Tour of Doctor Syntax*, the bedraggled hero meets with nothing but hospitality from the gentry and the aristocracy. They always insist that he spend the night at their house, and they always press him to stay longer the next morning. No doubt Combe wanted to believe that a man of learning like Syntax (or like him) would be recognized and welcomed as a gentleman wherever he went, regardless of the condition of his purse.[29]

For the moment, though, Combe's own purse was in a thriving state. The Rivers project alone had earned him over £500 ($72,200), close to what Jane Austen made from all her novels, and he was being paid for other work as well. His government pension further eased his circumstances. But as always with Combe, fortune led to folly. He began to keep a horse—a costly and unnecessary luxury for a Londoner—and, even more recklessly, he "married" again.

The new object of Combe's affections was Charlotte Hadfield, the sister of the artist Maria Cosway. The two eloped in January 1795, when Combe was fifty-two, and announced their marriage shortly after. In a legal sense, of course, they were not married, since Maria Combe was still alive. But by this time, few people remembered that fact,[30] and Combe and Charlotte were able to pass as man and wife without scandal—though not without expense. We know Combe purchased an expensive harpsichord for his new bride, and we can assume he hired one or two more servants. At the same time, his income suffered a series of heavy blows. The Boydells had fallen on hard times and decided to cancel the remaining volumes of the Rivers project. The government stopped his pension in 1796. The war with France was going poorly and the economy was in decline, which meant commodities like books were in less demand. Combe's debts mounted, the creditors descended, and on 4 May 1799, he was taken back to the King's Bench. Charlotte left for Ireland and she and Combe never lived together again.

The largest claim against him was brought by Stephen Casey, owner of the asylum where Maria was locked up. His claim was for £193. 10s ($27,864), about four years' worth of expenses.[31] Combe, it seems, had stopped paying for Maria's care shortly after his elopement with Charlotte, even before his finances went south. The world had already forgotten, and now her husband apparently chose to forget, that such a person as Maria Combe existed. Casey's bill, read out in court, was an inescapable reminder that she did.

NEWSPAPER EDITOR

For the rest of his life, Combe would live under the shadow of the King's Bench, though not always within its walls. His present stay was about ten months, after which he was allowed to live "within the rules," that is, the vicinity, of the prison. Technically, he was not supposed to leave the area of Southwark without the express permission of the Marshal, but these rules were not rigorously enforced and Combe, provided he did not flout them too egregiously, could typically go where he needed to in London. Still, his freedom from this point on was precarious—a privilege that could be taken away at any moment.

Combe's next major engagement was as a newspaper editor—no surprise given his professionalism, versatility, and rapidity. Back when he was working for John Walters, he had provided copy and perhaps a degree of oversight for the *Daily Universal Register*, which became the *Times*, but he was not the head of the operation. In 1803, though, he was given the head job at a new paper called the *Pic Nic*. The paper's main claim to fame was that it published genuinely independent theater reviews at a time when most papers accepted fees (or bribes) from the major theaters. Combe himself authored a fair number of these reviews, while also supplying an array of other content for the paper. His miscellaneous talents were ideally suited to the role.

The *Pic Nic* lasted only two months, but those two months set Combe up for an even more important role—the full editorship of the *Times*, now under the management of John Walters II, the son of his old employer. Walters likely admired Combe's work for the *Pic Nic*, since he, too, refused to take fees from the theaters. Combe proved to be a steady hand at the helm. He wrote many of the leading articles himself, essentially becoming the voice of the paper, while also supervising Walters' staff of writers. Combe did not preside over a period of explosive growth for the *Times*, but he does deserve credit for keeping the paper alive and respected during some of its earliest and most fragile years. Without his sound management, one of the most respected and widely distributed newspapers in the world might be nothing more than a footnote in the history of journalism.

Combe's work for the *Times*, however, required near-daily violations of his terms of release from the King's Bench. Eventually, his long leash ran out and he was met during one of his excursions by the Marshal and his assistant, who, in a manner not to be refused, offered to escort him back to his old quarters within the walls.[32] So began his third and longest stay in debtors' prison.

Combe's imprisonment necessarily brought an end to his work for the *Times*. It may have felt like the end in a larger sense, too. He was approaching his seventieth year and he was hopelessly in debt. Would he live to see the outside of the prison again? Even if he did, would he still have that access to polite society which was so essential to his self-worth? Would the publishers still seek out his services, or would he have to trudge back to Paternoster Row, hat in hand, to beg odd jobs? When his health failed and he could no longer work for his bread, would any of his friendly acquaintances come to his aid? After all, while liked by many, he had not made any really intimate friend; that would have required a dangerous level of openness—a confession, perhaps, of the dark truth that he was the son of an ironmonger. Combe had successfully hidden the facts of his birth; now his death threatened to be equally obscure.

But Combe, it turned out, had one last act in him. During his final imprisonment, which lasted four years, this "elderly hack"[33] would write a poem that would eclipse in popularity not only anything he had written before, but anything that ANY poet then living had written—or would write for the next ten years. The early 1800s were one of the golden ages of English verse—but the greatest popular success of that splendid era did not come from Wordsworth or Coleridge, Shelley or even the famous Lord Byron. It came from the ironmonger's son, King's Bench regular, and self-made gentleman, William Combe, Esq.

THE BIRTH OF DOCTOR SYNTAX

The turning point came when a man named Rudolph Ackermann visited Combe in the King's Bench and offered him a job. Ackermann was a German immigrant and nationalized English citizen who had risen from a carriage designer to one of the leading publishers in London. His Repository of Arts, located at 101 Strand, was a cynosure of the fashionable world. There you could find original artwork, high-quality paints, and the latest products of Ackermann's press. Printed illustrations were his specialty. Ackermann commissioned work from some of the finest artists in the country, and his team of engravers and colorists were widely regarded as the best in the business. Ackermann had also recently expanded into illustrated books, which meant that, luckily for Combe, he was on the hunt for good writers.

The first project Ackermann entrusted to Combe was well within the writer's wheelhouse. Ackermann needed letterpress for the third volume of *The Microcosm of London*, a lavishly illustrated homage to the capital. While Combe was working on that, Ackermann sought his help with another endeavor. He was planning to launch a new periodical called *The Poetical Magazine* that would combine full-color prints with original poetry. Would Combe write verses to accompany some of the prints?

Many of those prints, as Combe wrote later, were miscellaneous—made up of "views of interesting objects, and beautiful Scenery" (p. 2 of this book). But Ackermann had in mind a series of prints as well. In his possession was a curious set of drawings which he had recently purchased from the great caricaturist Thomas Rowlandson, another regular contributor to his press. They featured a scrawny clergyman on a rawboned nag, traipsing about the country in search of picturesque sights, but mainly running into various scrapes and mishaps. He laid them out for Combe there in his King's Bench quarters, and thus the writer and the character who would make his fortune were introduced.[34]

Those drawings form such an essential part of this book that a short digression must be allowed to treat their origin. The story goes that in the summer of 1808, Rowlandson took a tour of Cornwall with his friend Mathew Michell, in part to seek inspiration for a new comic character. Rowlandson had in mind a sort of hapless tourist, but he was struggling to visualize him. Michell magnanimously offered his own ample self as a model, but Rowlandson objected that he was too fat—a "walking turtle," in fact—and therefore totally unsuitable for a traveling character. Upon his return, while dining with the actor John Bannister, he described his difficulties, and his friend suddenly burst out:

> I have it! […] you must fancy a skin-and-bone hero, a pedantic old prig in a shovel-hat, with a pony, sketching tools, and rattle-traps, and place him in such scrapes as travellers frequently meet with,—hedge ale-houses, second and third-rate inns, thieves, gibbets, mad bulls, and the like.[35]

Bannister called for paper to brainstorm the image, and Doctor Syntax was born.

Rowlandson warmed quickly to the character. To Bannister's suggestions, he added a projecting chin for the ages and, as ballast, an ill-fitting wig with an outrageous occipital bulge. The two together form an unforgettable profile. Rowlandson sketched the character in one comic misadventure after another: shipwrecked, chased by a bull, tumbling into a lake, startled from his horse by a beached whale. At some point, probably in early 1809, he sold most or all of the drawings to Ackermann. Ackermann wished to run a selection of them as a series in *The Poetical Magazine*, but there were challenges to that plan. Except for a few discernable episodes, Rowlandson's drawings were in no particular order, and many of them, for reasons of propriety or probability, were unpublishable. Ackermann needed help to work them into a coherent story.

In the end he and Combe reached an unusual arrangement. Ackermann would decide which drawings to publish in each issue, and Combe would write the accompanying verses, devising a larger story that would both incorporate the drawings and fill in the gaps between them.[36] For whatever reason, though, Ackermann decided to make his selections one issue at a time—thereby making his writer's task a good deal harder. Combe wrote in his Advertisement (pp. 2-3 in this volume) that when "the first print was sent to me, I did not know what would be the subject of the second," and so it continued for two years until the work was complete.[37]

That work was initially called *The Schoolmaster's Tour*. It ran from 1809-1811 in regular installments, and was probably responsible for whatever success *The Poetical Magazine* enjoyed, for the magazine closed shortly after the tale concluded. According to William Pyne, Ackermann likely would have let *The Schoolmaster's Tour* rest in peace, were it not for the encouragement of his neighbor, John Taylor, who edited *The Sun*. Taylor urged Ackermann to bring out the poem as a book, confident that it would "suit the public taste," and Ackermann decided to give it a try.[38] Interestingly enough, Combe seems to have had doubts. In his Advertisement to the book edition, retitled *The Tour of Doctor Syntax in Search of the Picturesque,* he disclaimed any "parental fondness for the work," and declared that it "would have been no more thought of by me" but that Ackermann had "his reasons for risquing a republication of it"—hardly a ringing endorsement!

DOCTOR SYNTAX'S RECEPTION

Despite Combe's misgivings, the success of the book was instantaneous and stunning. Two editions the first year; three more the year after; nine by the end of the decade. *Doctor Syntax* flew off the bookstalls so fast that Ackermann could hardly keep it in print: the copper plates used to print the illustrations kept wearing out and new ones had to be etched. Possibly for this reason, Ackermann also sold copies of the poem without the illustrations at half-price. One contemporary suggested that "no poem perhaps has experienced so extensive a sale."[39] Our best estimate is that the book sold 20,000 copies in the 1810s—remarkable for any work, outstanding for a poem, and absolutely unheard of for a hand-colored, illustrated book.[40] We can be confident, too, that there were many more readers than buyers—for the book, priced at one guinea ($151), was not cheap. One character from an 1819 tale declared that she borrowed the poem to read it, since "Such extravagance I cannot brook, / As to give a guinea for a book."[41]

But the popularity of *The Tour of Doctor Syntax* cannot be measured in sales alone, or even in readers. The character of Doctor Syntax transcended the pages of his own book and became a cultural icon. Before long, spinoffs extending the Doctor's adventures in one way or another began to appear. They take the roving don to Paris and London;[42] they add new characters to the Syntax universe such as the portly Doctor Prosody;[43] they recruit Syntax for various political and religious causes.[44] Other books appeared that announced themselves to be "in the style of *Doctor Syntax,*"[45] and still others that claimed to be *by* him.[46] Indeed, scholars likely do not know all the spinoffs that this work generated. In the course of making this book we stumbled upon another that had gone unnoticed in previous lists: a curious pamphlet called *The Battle of the Trees* in which the staunchly Anglican Syntax must contend with a group of Methodists sowing confusion in his parish.

Then there was the merchandise. Syntax figurines, Syntax plates. Syntax hats, wigs, coats, and snuffboxes.[47] Syntax fishing poles that collapsed into walking sticks.[48] Even a Syntax board game.[49] And that list is far from complete.

One could continue in this vein for quite a while (there was a racehorse named Doctor Syntax; there were Syntax pantomimes on the stage, etc.). The question is, why? What was it about the hard-visaged and quixotic clergyman, determined to make his fortune as a travel writer, that so captured his age?

THE COMBE-ROWLANDSON COLLABORATION

It became popular in the twentieth century to assert that the success of the book was wholly owing to Rowlandson's plates. One scholar even proposed, without evidence, that people bought the book "only to look at the pictures and never seriously bother[ed] with the poetry itself."[50] But that view does not stand up even to cursory scrutiny. Contemporary reviews of the book praised the poem, and barely mentioned the plates.[51] Victorian editions of *Doctor Syntax*, meanwhile, often dropped the Rowlandson illustrations altogether. From the late 1830s to the late 1860s, the wood engravings of the caricaturist Alfred Crowquill were preferred. Beginning in 1838, many editions included a preface sketching the biography of Combe; there were no biographical prefaces for Rowlandson. Nearly everyone in the nineteenth century, in short, considered the author, not the artist, to be the work's primary creator.

Yet the Victorian erasure of Rowlandson also misrepresents the work. At its core, *Doctor Syntax* was a joint endeavor, combining the best talents of both men. Rowlandson brought the humor. The raw comic energy of Doctor Syntax, the earthiness, the occasional rascality, the accident-proneness—that is all Rowlandson's doing. What Combe added were the things Rowlandson was never very good at: moral wisdom and sensibility. Combe's Syntax often shows real insight into human character. He is sociable and kind. He launches into moral reveries that, if rather stereotypical, have a certain old-fashioned charm. He takes his clerical ministry seriously and wishes to help the poor. He is no "pedantic old prig," but a genuine scholar. In short, Rowlandson created Syntax to be a laughingstock; Combe transformed him into a laughingstock who also inspired affection and admiration. As he put it in Canto VII, "tho' the jest of all he knew, / Yet while they laugh'd they lov'd him too" (VII.61-2). It was precisely this balance of the ludicrous and the sentimental that contemporaries praised. As the *Monthly Review* put it,

> As we attend the Rev. Divine in his rambles in search of the Picturesque, he grows in our good opinion, and the ridiculous traits

in his figure and character do not hide the excellence of his heart; so that, when we are constrained to laugh, we are forced to esteem.[52]

What contemporaries saw as a harmonious blend, however, was not the result of harmonious cooperation. On the contrary, Combe and Rowlandson never met in the course of the project, and Combe, for his part, spent much of the poem working *against* what he perceived to be Rowlandson's drift. To Combe, Rowlandson's irreverent drawings looked for all the world like a "satire upon the national clergy," and he resolved, in his verses, to "turn the edge of the weapon which [he] thought was levelled against them."[53] His transformation of Syntax into a kind-hearted dreamer may have been his way of doing just that. The challenge lay in making the illustrations, largely completed before he joined the project, play along.

Take "Doctor Syntax Loses his Money on the Race Ground at York" (p. 110) as an example. Rowlandson clearly intended Syntax to have lost a bet: he says so verbatim in a caption he added to an early draft of the image.[54] But since conscientious clergymen do not bet, Combe took the plate in a different direction. In the poem, Syntax isn't gambling at all. Instead, a fellow racegoer falsely *accuses* Syntax of losing a bet, hoping to intimidate him into paying up.

An even better example concerns the plate "Doctor Syntax & Dairymaid" (p. 209). Rowlandson's original caption read, "The Doctor makes strong Love to Kitty over a Bowl of Cream and endeavours to enforce his old friend Madam's Doctrine on Plurality of Wives."[55] He intended the scene to form part of a sequence in which Syntax would fall in love with a girl named Kitty Cowslip, attempt to seduce her, and fail—and he worked up drawings for each stage. Combe, who wanted nothing to do with such bawdry, instead gave the scene a Sternean spin. In the poem, it turns out that Syntax isn't ogling or seducing the dairymaid; he is consoling her, the same way Yorick consoles Maria in *The Sentimental Journey*. He was passing by when he heard the sound of weeping, and he stopped to see what was wrong. In this way, Combe transforms the most compromising plate in the book into a shining example of Syntax's benevolence and sensibility. No doubt this is one of the moments he had in mind when he wrote in his Advertisement that "though on a first view of some of the prints, it may appear as if the Clerical Character was treated with Levity, I am confident in announcing a very opposite Impression from a perusal of the Work" (p. 3 of this book).

For the biographer of Combe, *Doctor Syntax* has an additional interest, because Combe, usually so private, seems to have poured much of his real self into the character. Syntax, for example, shares Combe's fundamental view on religion: that virtue is the best guarantee of happiness both here and hereafter.[56] He shares Combe's opinions on the theater: the criticisms he lodges in Cantos XXIII and XXIV are nearly identical to ones Combe had made years earlier in the *Pic Nic*.[57] Combe's disappointments as a government pamphleteer crop up rather out-of-the-blue in Canto XXIII, as does his misspent youth.

Perhaps most profoundly, Combe seems to have externalized in Syntax some of his anxieties about his origins in trade. Syntax has a number of run-ins with tradespeople who treat him with contempt on account of his poverty, ignoring or ridiculing his claims to respect, in particular his deep learning. When Combe was given the opportunity to add a canto for the book edition, he devised an even more spectacular clash between learning and trade. He had Doctor Syntax dream a "Battle of the Books," in which the Greek and Roman classics, much prized by the scholarly Syntax, fight the forces of trade, represented by various commercial documents. The battle takes place at the intersection of Cheapside and Old Jewry—barely a stone's throw from Combe's childhood home. When the classics win, Syntax feels vindicated, reassured that "Learning will give an unmix'd pleasure, / Which gold can't buy, and trade can't measure" (XXV.500-1). The astounding success of *Doctor Syntax* may have felt like a vindication for Combe, too, of his decision to leave the world of trade for the world of letters.

LATER YEARS AND DEATH

Syntax and Combe both had opportunities to cling to the consolations of learning amidst poverty, but in the end learning did pay. Syntax makes a cool £300 ($43,200) on his book, which only took him a month or two to write. Combe, meanwhile, did even better. After *Doctor Syntax*, he was a made man—Ackermann's star writer—and the publisher made sure he was properly taken care of. Ackermann may have helped facilitate Combe's final release from debtors' prison, which occurred in 1812. Rather than a fixed salary or a percentage of sales, he gave Combe access to a special account from which her could draw whenever he wanted, but which he did not in fact own—a clever device to shield Combe's earnings from his creditors. Combe was thus able to live in comfortable and secure circumstances for the rest of his days. In exchange, Combe continued to churn out books for Ackermann at his usual rapid pace. He wrote letterpress for a series of illustrated books in the vein of the *Microcosm of London*. He teamed up with Rowlandson on a pair of works that, while not the equal of *Doctor Syntax*, are still quite worth reading: *The English Dance of Death* (1814-16) and *The Dance of Life* (1817). So as not to leave the market for Syntaxiana entirely to his imitators, he and

Rowlandson also joined forces on three sequels: *The Second Tour of Doctor Syntax, in Search of Consolation* (1820), *The Third Tour of Doctor Syntax, in Search of a Wife* (1821), and *The History of Johnny Quae Genus* (1821-22), which treats the adventures of Doctor Syntax's adoptive son. Combe wrote more from 1812-1822—his *seventies*—than most of his peers did over their entire careers. And it all sold: the Regency public was always willing to open its wallet for "the author of *Doctor Syntax.*"

Eventually, old age did catch up with Combe, but not before he had left prison and enjoyed the most productive and, in all likelihood, the happiest decade of his life. The money worries were over. His literary fame was at an all-time high and (which may have meant more to him) he was once again a sought-after dinner guest. Ackermann was not just a good employer but a true friend to Combe:[58] the writer was always welcome at his table and at the polite *conversazione* Ackermann held at his Repository of Arts—just the sort of learned, genteel company Combe relished. When Combe died on 19 June 1823, he was remembered as a sociable gentleman of letters who was friends with "so many people in every rank of society, that it seems hardly necessary to draw his character. [...] He knew others as well as he was known to them."[59]

But just how "known" was he? Neither his obituarist nor, apparently, anyone else then living, even knew where Combe was born. They did not know he already had a wife living when he married Charlotte Hadfield. They probably did not know half the things Combe wrote. Modern scholars have filled in some of those blanks, but we, too, struggle to see behind the social mask that Combe almost never let slip: his real feelings, his deepest values, are often a matter of speculation.

There is a curious story about Combe that when he was a private in the army, a company of actors decided to help him purchase his discharge by putting on a benefit performance. He had already roused much curiosity with his knowledge of Latin and Greek, unheard of in an enlisted man, and he promised to give an address after the performance during which he would disclose his true identity. The performance was given and Combe took the floor. He teasingly ran through the various theories; then, with masterful showmanship, he commenced the grand reveal. "Now, ladies and gentlemen, I shall tell you what I am. *I am—ladies and gentlemen, your most obedient humble servant.*"[60] With that, and with a sweeping bow, he left the stage. He had shown himself a gentleman, and that is all he would show. He left the stage of life, too, with his secrets intact. The author of the Regency's most popular poem remains, by his own design, something of a mystery—our most obedient humble servant, William Combe, Esq.

[1] Woolf, 261.

[2] Hotten, v.

[3] Letter to Cassandra, 2-3 March 1814. In the line before, Austen sent her love to her five-year-old niece. Perhaps "little Cass" was enjoying the tale of Dr. Syntax, too, and hoping her aunt would meet him during her travels!

[4] Much of the information on Combe's life in this essay comes from Harlan Ware Hamilton's *Doctor Syntax: A Silhouette of William Combe, Esq.* (Chatto & Windus, 1969)—the authoritative biography of Combe.

[5] *The Philosopher in Bristol* (Bristol: G. Routh, 1775), 108, 31.

[6] See Bentham, Vol. X, 61; and Campbell, Vol. I, 41n.

[7] Campbell, 42n.

[8] H. Smith, 20.

[9] *The Philosopher in Bristol*, 16.

[10] *The Philosopher in Bristol, Part the Second*, 12.

[11] *Westminster Magazine* (Sept. 1775), 466.

[12] This play, which was lost for over a hundred years, actually came to light in the course of the project which produced this book. Two members of the research team wrote an article on the manuscript's discovery and the significance of the play in Combe's career. See Ben Wiebracht and Rathan Muruganantham, "The Flattering Milliner, Lost Play By William Combe, Discovered," *Notes & Queries*, Vol. 70, No. 4 (Dec. 2023), 282-6.

[13] *The Morning Post, and Daily Advertiser*, No. 903 (18 Sept. 1775), 1.

[14] *The Diaboliad*, 16.

[15] Hamilton, 97, quoting from *The Gentleman's Magazine* (April 1778).

[16] L. Smith, 99.

[17] HO 17/92/85: Petitions Rh-Rl; Joseph Bonney. 1824-1825. MS Crime and the Criminal Justice System: Records from The U.K. National Archives. These records can be found in the database *Crime, Punishment, and Popular Culture: 1790-1920*, from Gale. Within the file cited above, see especially a letter from John Orridge to Robert Peel, 8 Jan. 1825.

[18] *Report: Pauper Lunatics in Middlesex*, 156.

[19] See note 17 above. In addition to HO 17/92/85, files HO 17/102 and HO 17/112 also describe tranfers of so-called "criminal lunatics" from prison to Casey's asylum.

[20] As the editors of Sterne's letters rather saltily put it, Combe "is a figure to whom Sterneans owe a great debt of *ingratitude*" (*Letters*, xlviii).

[21] Hamilton, 113-32.

[22] Campbell, Vol. I, 45n.

[23] For example, does the reader really need all 34 articles of the Dutch-American Treaty of 1780 copied out verbatim? (*Origin of Commerce*, Vol. 4, 305-12)

[24] See, for example, *The World* (25 June 1789) and the *Monthly Review*, Vol. 2

(Aug. 1790), 376-82.

[25] This passage is from a letter reproduced in *The Gentleman's Magazine* (May, 1852), 469-70.

[26] *Original Letters of the Late Reverend Mr. Laurence Sterne, never before published* (London: Logographic Press, 1788).

[27] *Monthly Magazine* (July 1823), 567.

[28] Quoted in Hamilton, 188.

[29] One of the many too-good-to-be-true tales that circulated about Combe involved just this sort of discovery. The story goes that after he spent his inheritance, Combe was forced to enlist as a private in the army. One day, an officer happened upon him reading the Latin poet Horace in the original, and thereupon realized that "Private Combe" was no common soldier, but a gentleman. In another version of the story, Combe is discovered reading Aeschylus in the Greek, an even more dramatic proof of his learning. (Campbell, Vol. I, 46n; H. Smith, Vol. I, 19n)

[30] Early biographical sketches of Combe are dimly aware that he had a wife before Charlotte Hadfield, but no one seemed to remember her name or what happened to her. The anonymous editor of the 1838 edition of *Doctor Syntax* simply wrote, "Of his first wife little is known" (v). No doubt that was how Combe preferred it.

[31] This is assuming Maria's keep was around £1 per week—the low end of the range for non-pauper patients (L. Smith, 174).

[32] Hamilton, 235.

[33] Payne, 282. Modern scholarship often refers to Combe as a "hack."

[34] Pyne, 222.

[35] Adolphus, Vol. I, 291.

[36] Pyne, 222.

[37] Contemporary reviewers were rather in awe of Combe for writing so well under such bizarre and adverse conditions. One declared that Combe could "claim a higher degree of merit than almost any other poet of the age" for "vanquishing" such a difficulty. *Critical Review* (May 1813), 542.

[38] Pyne, 222.

[39] Pyne, 222. A few other poems may have outsold *Doctor Syntax*—Byron's *Corsair* (1814) apparently sold 10,000 copies in a single day—but by other measures, *Syntax* outstripped even that sensation (see below in the body).

[40] This estimate is not based on how many editions the poem sold, because there was no standard number of copies per edition at that time. Rather it is based on how many times the copper plates wore out. A copper plate at that time could make 2,000-3,000 impressions before it was rendered unusable (Hackwood, 203). Across the nine editions of *The Tour of Doctor Syntax in Search of the Picturesque* that were published in the 1810s, four sets of plates were used; one can tell simply by looking at the various editions of the poem. If we assume that each set produced 2,500 copies, then 10,000 copies of the

poem were sold with the plates. If another 10,000 half-price, plateless copies were sold, then the total sale was 20,000.

41 *The Rich Old Bachelor*, 80.

42 *The Tour of Doctor Syntax through London* (London: J. Johnson, 1819); *Doctor Syntax in Paris or a Tour in Search of the Grotesque* (W. Wright, 1820).

43 *The Tour of Doctor Prosody, in Search of the Antique and Picturesque* (London: 1821).

44 *The Political Doctor Syntax, a Poem* (London: Grove and Co., 1820); Peter Porcupine, *The Methodists Unveiled!! The Battle of the Trees, or, Doctor Syntax at his Living* (London: J. Johnston, [1816]).

45 *The Rich Old Bachelor: A Domestic Tale in the Style of Dr. Syntax* (Canterbury: Ward, 1824).

46 *The Life of Napoleon, a Hudibrastic Poem in fifteen cantos, by Doctor Syntax* (London: 1815); *The Wars of Wellington, a narrative poem [...], by Doctor Syntax* (London: 1819).

47 Hotten, xxvii.

48 "Piscatoribus Sacrum," *The New Sporting Magazine*, Vol. VII, No. 34 (May 1834), 34.

49 Currently held at the Wilson Library, University of North Carolina, Chapel Hill (catalogue number: PR3359.C5 T68 1830).

50 Rousseau, 353.

51 The four most important are those in the *British Critic*, Vol. XL (July 1812), 56-9; *Monthly Review*, Vol. LXX (January 1813), 50-9; *Anti-jacobin Review*, Vol. XLIV (May 1813), 490-500; and *Critical Review* (May 1813), 542-49.

52 *Monthly Review*, Vol. LXX (January 1813), 51.

53 *Letters to Marianne*, vi.

54 The caption read, "The Doctor goes to the York Races and betts [sic] on the Wrong Horse." Recorded in Gully, 185.

55 The drawing with the caption is in the possession of the Yale Center for British Art: https://collections.britishart.yale.edu/catalog/tms:6436 (last accessed 12 Aug. 2024).

56 In *The Philosopher in Bristol*, Combe wrote, "I cannot but think that the happiness of this world, and the next are nearly connected together;—and that religion conducts us to them both" (84). Syntax makes a nearly identical point: "For thus to virtuous man 'tis given / To dance, and sing, and go to Heaven" (XVII.274-5).

57 See especially *The Pic Nic*, No. 1 (8 Jan. 1803), 18-24, where Combe complains about the bad effects of overly large theaters on the quality of the acting. Compare to *Doctor Syntax*, XXIII.472-493 and XXIV.80-87.

58 Timbs, Vol. II, 206. In the "Advertisement" to *Doctor Syntax*, too, one detects a deep gratitude on Combe's part toward his last and best employer.

59 *Monthly Magazine* (July 1823), 567.

60 Campbell, 46.

CONTEXTUAL ESSAY:
THE PICTURESQUE

Austen is sometimes remembered as a bit of a homebody. We can easily picture her, as a girl, holed up in some corner of Steventon Rectory, scribbling away; or as a mature woman, composing at her treasured mahogany writing desk in the drawing room of Chawton Cottage. But there was another side to Jane Austen. Throughout her life, she was also a lover of the great outdoors—trees, fresh air, and most of all, beautiful views. In fact, in the "Biographical Notice" that introduced Jane Austen to the world, her brother mentioned as her first literary influence, not a novelist or poet, but a travel writer—William Gilpin. "At a very early age," writes Henry, "she was enamoured of Gilpin on the Picturesque; and she seldom changed her opinions either on books or men" (*Pers.* 330). Austen, as we will see, did change her opinions on Gilpin and the picturesque somewhat, but the love of landscapes that he helped quicken did indeed last her entire life.

William Combe was another unlikely lover of the picturesque. Although he spent the vast majority of his life in London, he wrote a great deal about the beauties of the countryside, and he never turned down an opportunity to take a tour: the summer of 1792, during which he traveled the full length of the Thames taking notes on the scenery, was probably one of the happiest seasons of his life.

Combe, though, is best remembered for a *satire* of the picturesque, and Austen, too, made fun of picturesque theories and discourse time and again in her work, sometimes at the expense of her beloved Gilpin. What were these two picturesque aficionados up to with this mockery? Were they rejecting the great landscape theory of their day, or were they reimagining it?

WILLIAM GILPIN AND PICTURESQUE THEORY

The writer who did most to define and popularize the idea of the picturesque was William Gilpin. A clergyman and schoolmaster, Gilpin developed his ideas over the course of several tours which he took in the 1760s and 70s. According to Gilpin, a view is picturesque if it would look well in a picture (Gilpin himself was an avid sketcher of landscapes). Henry and Eleanor Tilney (NA) show themselves to be faithful disciples of Gilpin when they view the country around Beechen Cliff "with the eyes of persons accustomed to drawing," and discuss "its capability of being formed into pictures" (I.14).

So what, according to Gilpin, made a good picture? Not the familiar elements of beauty such as smoothness and symmetry. Instead, the essence of the picturesque was roughness: "make it *rough*," he once declared, "and you make it also *picturesque*" (TE 8). For this reason, jagged cliffs and rugged mountains were more picturesque than rolling meadows. A wild heath was more picturesque than an orderly garden. A ruined castle or abbey was more picturesque than a well-appointed, modern manor house.

The picturesque love of roughness was part of the late-eighteenth-century "return to nature." As Gilpin put it, "the picturesque eye abhors art; and delights solely in nature: [...] art abounds with *regularity*, which is only another name for *smoothness;* and the images of nature with *irregularity*, which is only another name for *roughness*" (TE 26-7). By art, Gilpin does not mean the fine arts. His meaning is closer to "craft"—anything created by human skill and ingenuity. That is why the picturesque was so closely associated in the period with travel: you had to leave the orderliness of human society to

IS DOCTOR SYNTAX A PARODY OF WILLIAM GILPIN?

It has become common in contemporary criticism to say that "Doctor Syntax is a parody of William Gilpin." Scholars sometimes point, as evidence, to the fact that Syntax, like Gilpin, is a clergyman and schoolmaster, but that is a rather weak connection. As the poem is constantly reminding us, there were vast inequalities in the clerical profession: Syntax is an impoverished curate who strongly resents the fact that other clergyman have it so easy. He would have seen William Gilpin's situation as a well-off vicar as the exact opposite of his own. Another reason why it is problematic to see Syntax as a caricature of Gilpin is that Gilpin actually exists in Syntax's world separately, in his own right. Syntax says at one point that Gilpin was able to make his fortune with his picturesque writings, and he hopes to do the same. It would be strange to have the actual Gilpin—and a satirical figure representing Gilpin—in the same work.

That said, the poem certainly does satirize Gilpin's ideas. At times Syntax espouses them in a ridiculous manner; and at times he directly criticizes them. But to reduce Syntax to a caricature of Gilpin is to miss the uniqueness of the character. Syntax, like all great comic characters, is an original.

find it. The picturesque tourist, like Doctor Syntax, was always on the move, looking for new scenes. The surprise and variety of discovering one view after another was part of the delight. As Gilpin put it, when traveling there is no "greater pleasure, than when a scene of grandeur bursts unexpectedly upon the eye" (TE 44). Words like "burst" and "abrupt" thus became important parts of the picturesque lexicon. Julia Bertram is enraptured by a "fine burst of country" during the drive to Sotherton (MP I.8); while Elizabeth Bennet and Emma Woodhouse both admire the "abruptness" of the views around Pemberley and Donwell Abbey. These are experiential words—they do not describe the landscapes themselves so much as their effect on the moving eye or the moving body.

The picturesque, then, was more than an aesthetic category; it was also a thrilling type of experience. Today, we often associate the word with "quaintness" or "prettiness," but in Austen's day the picturesque was grand and exciting; it was about travel and discovery; it was an escape from the humdrum rhythms of daily life. "You give me fresh life and vigour," cries Elizabeth when her aunt invites her on a picturesque tour to the Lake District (PP II.4). Elizabeth, stuck in a small market town, visiting the same people and dealing with the same frustrating family, leaps at the opportunity to journey north and forget it all amidst "rocks and mountains." It is the same with Doctor Syntax. Trapped in a dead-end job and regularly harassed by his ill-tempered wife, he too seeks liberation and a fresh start (as well as a windfall in the form of book sales) by embarking on a tour.

PROBLEMS WITH THE PICTURESQUE

There is no doubt that Gilpin awakened new interest in the English countryside, but his theories did not go uncriticized. He could be quite doctrinaire in his picturesque views—rather ironic, given that so much of the delight of the picturesque lay in its spontaneity. Some of his "rules" seem arbitrary indeed—for instance, that a group of three cattle is picturesque, but not a group of four (OCW, Vol. II, 258). Elizabeth playfully refers to that rule when she tells Mr. Darcy and the Bingley sisters, upon being invited to join them for a walk, that they are "charmingly group'd [...]. The picturesque would be spoilt by admitting a fourth" (I.10). Elsewhere, Gilpin made the strange pronouncement that a fisherman in a boat is picturesque, but one on the bank is not (OCW, Vol. II, 45): Combe has some fun with that quibbling distinction in Canto XIV.

Gilpin's ideas about ideal landscapes became so particular, in fact, that he began to doubt whether nature, unaided, could really produce them.

"Seldom," he wrote in a late essay, "does she produce a scene *perfect in character*"—that is, consistently and thoroughly picturesque (TE 164). More and more, he began to promote the *"imaginary* view, formed on a judicious selection, and arrangment, of the parts of nature," since such a view, he thought, "has a better chance to make a good picture, than a view taken in the whole from any natural scene" (TE 128). If the artist did happen to be sketching directly from nature, they should feel free to enhance it: "This ill-shaped mountain may be pared […]. Upon yon bald declivity […] may be reared a forest of noble oak. […] On a gentle rise, opening to the lake, and half incircled by woody hills, some mouldring abbey may be seated" (OCW, Vol. I, 119-20).

Passages like these are the target of one of Combe's more memorable parodies of Gilpin. Ambling along absentmindedly, Doctor Syntax finds himself lost in the middle of a featureless landscape, with nothing but an illegible guidepost to interrupt the monotony. At first Syntax laments his lot: "How could I come, misguided wretch! / To where I cannot make a sketch?" But then he remembers Gilpin, and all difficulties melt away: "I'll do as other sketchers do— / Put anything into the view." A pond becomes a stream, and gets a bridge to boot. A group of donkeys is promoted from the background to the foreground. A plain is transformed into a "shaggy ridge," and voila!—Syntax has *"made a Landscape of a Post."* Syntax considers his revisions to have been well within reason, for "tho' from truth I haply err, / *The scene preserves its character"* (II.90-145).

But there were more serious problems with Gilpin's ideas, too. At times, he took his principle of "roughness" to absurd or perhaps even unethical extremes. In one of his books, for example, he writes enthusiastically about the beauty of dead trees: "What is more beautiful […], on a rugged foreground, than an old tree with a *hollow trunk?* or with a *dead arm*, a *drooping bough*, or a *dying branch?"* (FS 8) To find such beauty in plant decay was already somewhat eyebrow-raising, but more concerning was Gilpin's seeming indifference, at times, to human thriving as well. At one point he rather loftily declared that it is not the business of the picturesque "to consider matters of utility. It has nothing to do with the affairs of the plough, and the spade; but merely examines the face of nature as a beautiful object" (FS 298). In a different book, he made the point even more emphatically:

> Moral, and picturesque ideas do not always coincide. In a moral light, cultivation, in all it's [sic] parts, is pleasing; the hedge, and the furrow; the waving corn field, and the ripened sheaf. But all these, the picturesque eye, in quest of scenes of grandeur, and beauty, looks at

> with disgust. It ranges after nature, untamed by art, and bursting into
> all it's irregular forms. [...] In a moral view, the industrious mechanic
> is a more pleasing object, than the loitering peasant. But in a
> picturesque light, it is otherwise. [...] [T]he peasant lolling on a rock,
> may be allowed in the grandest scenes; while the laborious mechanic,
> with his impliments of labour, would be repulsed. (OCW, Vol. II,
> 44)

Such language was alarming. To appreciate the beauty of a picturesque scene, was it really necessary to cultivate a callous indifference to the practical good of real people—especially people less well off than the middle- or upper-class tourist? Did the picturesque observer really have to view fertile fields, providing food for a whole community, with "disgust," and shut their eyes to the shocking sight of a person working?

Combe didn't think so. He has Doctor Syntax fall into all kinds of reveries and speculations,

> But none arose which did not tend
> Poor human nature to befriend;
> None but were aptly form'd to prove
> The firm support of social love. (XXII.91-4)

Austen, too, objected to Gilpin's views on the disconnect between moral and picturesque ideas. Edward Ferrars (SS) is almost certainly channelling his author's views when he says that a fine country "unites beauty with utility" (I.18). He continues, making several direct references to Gilpin's theories:

> I like a fine prospect, but not on picturesque principles. I do not like
> crooked, twisted, blasted trees. I admire them much more if they are
> tall, straight and flourishing. I do not like ruined, tattered cottages. I
> am not fond of nettles, or thistles, or heath blossoms. I have more
> pleasure in a snug farm-house than a watch-tower—and a troop of
> tidy, happy villagers please me better than the finest banditti in the
> world.

Marianne is shocked at Edward's "lack" of taste, but in fact, she is the one with the deficient view. Throughout the novel, her sentimental creed, in its selfish narrowness, mirrors Gilpinesque orthodoxy: both have a tendency to focus too much on the feelings and perspective of the self, and to disregard others. The debate between Edward and Marianne, then, isn't merely about landscapes and aesthetics, but about aligning the good with the beautiful, the individual with the community, and, of course, sense with sensibility.

In critiquing the picturesque, however, Edward falls into excesses of his own. He tells Marianne that he knows "nothing of the picturesque" (obviously untrue), and goes on to give this rather dull-souled speech:

> [R]emember I have no knowledge in the picturesque, and I shall offend you by my ignorance and want of taste if we come to particulars. I shall call hills steep, which ought to be bold; surfaces strange and uncouth, which ought to be irregular and rugged; and distant objects out of sight, which ought only to be indistinct through the soft medium of a hazy atmosphere.

If Gilpin's picturesque "disgust" at farms and meadows is absurd, Edward's yawning indifference to rugged hills and misty distances—undeniable landscape beauties—is not much better. Elinor, in fact, suspects that it is all a pose, and that

> to avoid one kind of affectation, Edward here falls into another. Because he believes many people pretend to more admiration of the beauties of nature than they really feel, and is disgusted with such pretentions, he affects greater indifference and less discrimination in viewing them himself than he possesses.

The scene ends, then, with a rejection of extremes, but without a clear articulation of the middle ground. Edward gestures at that middle ground with his line about uniting beauty and utility, but his overly pragmatic descriptions do little to evoke beauty, just as Marianne, a true Gilpinite, is unable to appreciate utility. The passage creates a demand for some sort of synthesis.

A NEW PICTURESQUE

Austen achieved that synthesis most fully in the last novel that was published during her lifetime—*Emma*. Emma is visiting the estate of Mr. Knightley, and happens upon a beautiful view:

> It was hot; and after walking some time over the gardens in a scattered, dispersed way, scarcely any three together, they insensibly followed one another to the delicious shade of a broad short avenue of limes, which stretching beyond the garden at an equal distance from the river, seemed the finish of the pleasure grounds.—It led to nothing; nothing but a view at the end over a low stone wall with high pillars, which seemed intended, in their erection, to give the appearance of an approach to the house, which never had been

there. Disputable, however, as might be the taste of such a termination, it was in itself a charming walk, and the view which closed it extremely pretty.—The considerable slope, at nearly the foot of which the Abbey stood, gradually acquired a steeper form beyond its grounds; and at half a mile distant was a bank of considerable abruptness and grandeur, well clothed with wood;—and at the bottom of this bank, favourably placed and sheltered, rose the Abbey-Mill Farm, with meadows in front, and the river making a close and handsome curve around it. (III.6)

One can see Gilpin's influence in this scene. The view is a surprise, bursting suddenly on the eye. The steepness of the hill and the "abruptness" of the bank are both forms of picturesque "roughness." There is even something ruin-like about the low stone wall and pillars which, at an earlier stage of planning, were supposed to face the house.

This ideal picturesque view, however, culminates not in faraway mountains or some other expression of the sublime, but in that least picturesque of features: a farm! Nor is the Abbey-Mill Farm just any farm. It is the home and livelihood of Robert Martin, the man Emma deems an unsuitable match for her protégé, Harriet Smith. Emma's objection is class-based, but it also resembles the beauty-utility divide at the heart of Gilpin's picturesque theories. Robert Martin is a practical man: he raises fine sheep, speaks about cows, and, by way of courtship, brings Harriet walnuts. Emma thinks Harriet was born to grace a higher sphere, removed from the world of labor.

This scene, though, undercuts her rather snobbish opinions about Robert Martin and his world. In this ideal landscape there is no harsh divide between Donwell Abbey, home of the gentlemanly Mr. Knightley, and Abbey-Mill Farm; they are instead two parts of one harmonious whole. In the same way, the educated gentry, to which Emma belongs, and the hardworking yeomanry—with which she claims to "have nothing to do" (I.4)—are parts of a communal whole, connected by bonds of mutual dependency.

Gilpin's ideal landscapes were often anti-communal; if they included people at all, they were generally ones thought to live outside society, in tune with nature: idle peasants, gypsy beggars, or romantic "banditti." Austen's ideal landscape, on the other hand, was not just communal in its own right, but in a larger, metaphorical sense as well. Emma, as she views the scene, has a vision of national harmony: "English verdure, English culture [meaning agriculture], English comfort" (III.6).

In *The Tour of Doctor Syntax*, Combe, too, offers an updated vision of the picturesque. That is a little surprising, considering that his views on the picturesque were very close to Gilpin's. Like Gilpin, he believed that nature "is [the picturesque's] fostering parent, and art its mortal foe." The defining elements of the picturesque, for Combe, were "[r]uggedness, roughness, and abruptness"—nothing new there, either ("Old Houses," *The Thames*, Vol. I, unpaginated). Combe did object to some of Gilpin's excesses, though. At times he uses Syntax to model those excesses in a ridiculous way, as in the guidepost scene. At others, he has Syntax directly criticize Gilpin: for instance, when the Doctor mocks those who "can a real beauty see / In a decay'd and rotten tree" (XIX.86-7). In neither case, though, is there a significant building on Gilpin's ideas.

Combe's fresh spin on the picturesque comes not in the form of any new theory, but in his relaxed attitude toward the old one. Doctor Syntax can enter the high picturesque mode when he wishes, pontificating and laying down aesthetic laws, but he can just as easily fall out of it and joke around with a farmer or a tavern maid instead. That is exactly what you would expect a picturesque dogmatist *not* to do. The "picturesque eye, in quest of scenes of grandeur," was blind, wilfully blind, to simple, everyday human life, but Syntax's eye is not. He'll chat about home-brewing with a blacksmith's wife; he'll belt out popular songs with the local squire; he'll play his fiddle for a group of peasants when their regular fiddler is too drunk to do it. There is a decidely non-dogmatic willingness on Syntax's part to find the good and the fun in just about anything that comes along, picturesque or otherwise. For a self-proclaimed picturesque tourist, this was something new.

Austen and Combe, then, challenged the anti-social strain in picturesque aesthetics in different ways. Austen did so in the form of carefully constructed dialogue and landscape description, developing a new ideal, as Edward Ferrars put it, that would unite beauty with utility. Nor was she content to stop there. Her best landscape descriptions are national in scope; they seek to define the spirit of England itself, and of the English people. Combe's challenge to picturesque orthodoxy in *The Tour of Doctor Syntax* is not as sophisticated as Austen's, but it has wisdom of his own. What if, instead of updating the picturesque rules, we simply relaxed them? The "picturesque eye" had acquired, over the course of Gilpin's writings, a certain judginess, always imposing abstract standards on what it beheld. Combe, in the character of Doctor Syntax, models a different kind of viewing, and a different kind of tourism—one that is receptive rather than critical, ready to embrace any source of delight, however unexpected. For Gilpin, the picturesque was all about the picture. Doctor Syntax cares about the picture too, but he is just as interested in what lies outside the frame.

A CHRONOLOGY OF WILLIAM COMBE

25 March 1742: William Combe born.

1748: Combe's mother dies.

c. 1752-6: Sent to Eton College.

1756: Robert Combes dies; Combe left in care of his godfather William Alexander.

1760-4: Takes up residence at the Inner Temple to study law.

c. 1764-9: Enters society and lives extravagantly before running out of money.

c. 1770-3: Obscurity and penury. Rumored to have joined the army, become a waiter at an inn, or served as a cook in a French monastery.

1775: Debut as a writer. Publishes two-part *Philosopher in Bristol* and *Clifton*; *The Flattering Milliner* performed in Bristol.

1776: Marries Maria Foster.

1777: Publishes the *Diaboliad*.

1785-7: First imprisonment in King's Bench Debtors' Prison.

1787-9: Revises Adam Anderson's *Origin of Commerce* and writes an additional fourth volume.

1788-1806: On-and-off work as a paid pamphleteer for the government.

1792: Embarks on a tour of the Thames to write the letterpress for the *History of the Thames*, illustrated by Joseph Farington.

1795: Combe and Charlotte Hadfield elope.

1799-c. 1800: Second imprisonment in King's Bench Debtors' Prison.

1803-8: Works as a newspaper editor for the *Pic Nic* and the *Times*.

1808-12: Third imprisonment in King's Bench Debtors' Prison.

1809-11: *The Schoolmaster's Tour* published in *The Poetical Magazine*.

1812-9: *The Tour of Doctor Syntax in Search of the Picturesque* published in book form. Nine editions and ~20,000 copies are released.

1812-23: Released from debtors' prison. Continues to publish various works with Rudolph Ackermann.

19 July 1823: Dies, aged 81.

A CHRONOLOGY OF JANE AUSTEN

1768: Austens move to Steventon.

16 Dec. 1775: Jane Austen born.

1783: Educated by Mrs. Cawley at Oxford and Southampton; contracts typhus and is sent home.

1785-6: Attends Abbey Girl's School, Reading.

1787: Begins writing her juvenilia, chiefly poems and satirical stories.

1795-9: First major creative period: completes early drafts of *Sense and Sensibility*, *Pride and Prejudice*, and *Northanger Abbey*.

1797: Early draft of *Pride and Prejudice* rejected by publisher Thomas Cadell.

1800: Father gives up his living as rector of Steventon; family moves to Bath.

1801-6: Lives in Bath.

1802: Receives a proposal of marriage from Harris Bigg-Wither, which she rejects.

1803: Sells the copyright of *Northanger Abbey* (then titled *Susan*) to publisher Benjamin Crosby, but he chooses not to print it.

21 Jan. 1805: Father dies; in the following years, Austen, her sister, and her mother change their lodgings several times.

1809: Settles at Chawton Cottage, Hampshire on the estate of her brother Edward Austen Knight.

1809-16: Second major creative period: revises early novels, writes *Emma*, *Mansfield Park*, and *Persuasion*.

1811: *Sense and Sensibility* published.

1813: *Pride and Prejudice* published.

1814: *Mansfield Park* published; Austen refers to *Doctor Syntax* in a letter.

1815: *Emma* published.

18 July 1817: Dies, aged 42.

1817: *Northanger Abbey* and *Persuasion* published posthumously.

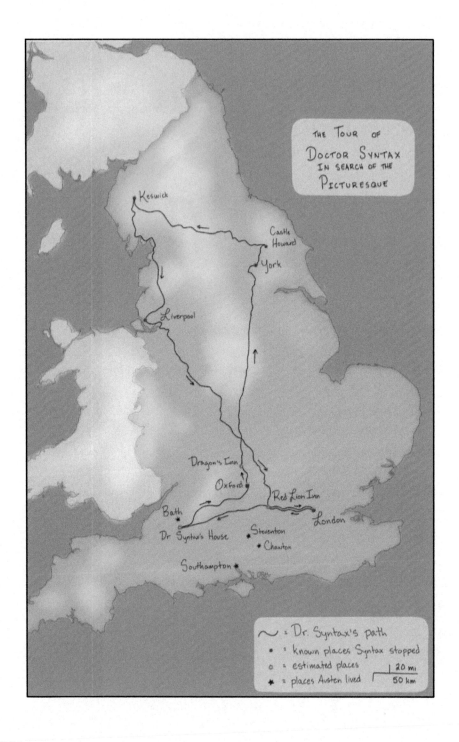

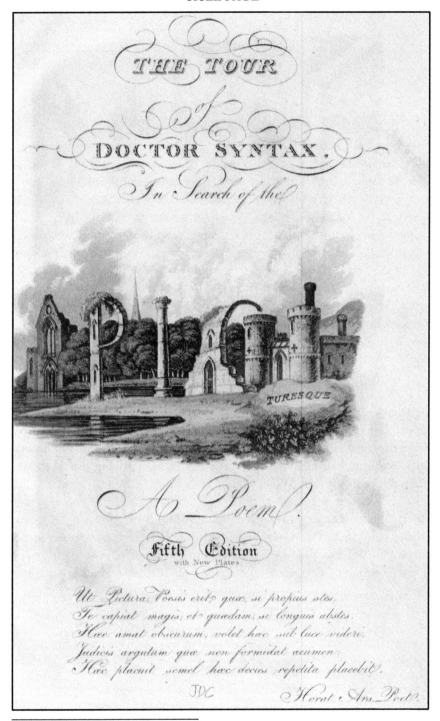

THE TOUR

of

DOCTOR SYNTAX,

In Search of the

TURESQUE

A Poem.

Fifth Edition
with New Plates.

Ut Pictura, Poesis erit; quæ, si propius stes,
Te capiat magis; et quædam, si longius abstes.
Hæc amat obscurum; volet hæc sub luce videri,
Judicis argutum quæ non formidat acumen.
Hæc placuit semel hæc decies repetita placebit.

JDC

Horat. Ars Poet.

† For a translation of the epigraph, see the first note on p. 2.

ADVERTISEMENT.

THE following Poem, if it may be allowed to deserve the name, was written under circumstances, whose peculiarity may be thought to justify a communication of them.—I undertook to give metrical Illustrations of the Prints with which Mr. ACKERMANN decorated the *Poetical Magazine*, a Work published by him in *Monthly Numbers*, for the reception of original compositions. Many of these Engravings were miscellaneous, and those, (which were, indeed, the far greater part of them,) whose description was submitted to such a Muse as mine, represented views of interesting objects, and beautiful Scenery, or were occasional decorations appropriate to the work.[1] Those designs alone to which this volume is so greatly indebted, I was informed would follow in a Series, and it was proposed to me to shape out a story from them.—An Etching or a Drawing was accordingly sent to me every month, and I composed a certain proportion of pages in verse, in which, of course, the subject of the design was included: the rest depended upon what my imagination could furnish.—When the first print was sent to me, I did not know what would be the subject of the second; and in this manner, in a great measure, the Artist continued designing, and I continued writing, every month for two years, 'till a work, containing near ten thousand Lines was produced: the Artist and the Writer having no personal communication with, or knowledge of each other. This vast collection of verses, however appeared to advance the purpose of the Magazine in which they grew into such an unexpected accumulation.—Mr. ACKERMANN was satisfied with my Service, and I was satisfied with the remuneration of it.—I felt no parental fondness for the work though it was written at that very advanced period of Life, when we are apt to attach Importance to any little

---

† In English, the epigraph on the title page reads: "Poetry is like painting: one picture attracts you more, the nearer you stand, another, the farther away. One favours shade, another will wish to be seen in the light, showing no fear of the critic's sharp insight; one gave you pleasure on a single occasion, another will continue doing so, though you turn back to it ten times." Horace, *Ars Poetica*, ln. 362-6.
[1] Most issues of *The Poetical Magazine* contained at least one such "miscellaneous" plate, usually with an accompanying lyric poem (this was in addition to the Doctor Syntax plates). Those poems are generally unsigned, but Combe implies here that most of them were by him.

unexpected exertion of decaying strength:—It would have been no more thought of by me:—But Mr. ACKERMANN has his reasons for risquing a republication of it, in its present form; and I now feel more than common solicitude that it should answer his expectations. My own vanity has a very small share in my wishes for its success; and in the indulgence of them I can truly declare, that I am principally actuated by the part I take in the interests of a man, who, in the course of my concerns with him, has grown in my esteem and regard—I have, therefore, given my best attention to the correction of the whole; and have endeavoured to lessen those defects which naturally arose from the irregular and undetermined mode of its composition.—*The Battle* of the *Books* was an after thought: and forms the *Novelty* of this volume.[2]

Liberius si
Dixero quid, si forte jocosius; hoc mihi juris,
Cum veniâ dabis.—Hor. s. Lib. i Sat. iv.[3]

I have only to add—that though on a first view of some of the prints, it may appear as if the Clerical Character was treated with Levity, I am confident in announcing a very opposite Impression from a perusal of the Work.

THE AUTHOR.

[2] Combe is referring to Canto XXV, which was added to the first book edition of *The Tour of Doctor Syntax*. The title "Battle of the Books" is a reference to an earlier satire of the same name by Jonathan Swift—a well-known work featuring a metaphorical battle between classical and modern literature. Combe tweaks the premise: his battle is between classical literature and modern *trade*, represented by various commercial documents.
[3] In English: "If something I say is too outspoken, perhaps too calculated to raise a laugh, you'll be forgiving and grant me this measure of justification." Horace, *Satires* 1.4.104-6.

A TOUR,

IN SEARCH OF THE PICTURESQUE,

BY THE REVEREND DOCTOR SYNTAX.[1]

CANTO I.

THE School was done, the bus'ness o'er,
When, tir'd of Greek and Latin lore,[2]
Good Syntax sought his easy chair,
And sat in calm composure there.
His wife was to a neighbour gone,   5
To hear the chit-chat of the town;
And left him the infrequent power
Of brooding thro' a quiet hour.
Thus, while he sat, a busy train
Of images besieged his brain.   10
Of Church-preferment[3] he had none,
Nay, all his hope of that was gone.
He felt that he content must be
With drudging in a Curacy.[4]
Indeed, on ev'ry Sabbath-day,[5]   15
Through eight long miles he took his way,
To preach, to grumble,[6] and to pray;
To cheer the good, to warn the sinner,
And, if he got it, eat a dinner.
To bury these, to christen[7] those,   20
And marry such fond folks as chose
To change the tenor of their life,
And risk the matrimonial strife.
Thus were his weekly journies made,
'Neath Summer suns and wintry shade;   25

¹ **DOCTOR SYNTAX:** The protagonist's unusual name alludes to his role as a schoolmaster and his enthusiasm for classical languages. In Latin, syntax is a wide branch of grammar that schoolboys would spend years studying.

² **THE School...Latin lore:** Clergymen often supplemented their income by teaching or tutoring boys. The curriculum focused on Greek and Latin authors.

³ **Church-preferment:** Promotion to higher or more lucrative positions in the Anglican Church. Most church positions or "livings" were in the gift of wealthy landlords or bishops; clergymen who lacked connections among these groups were unlikely to advance in their careers.

⁴ **Curacy:** The position held by a curate. When a clergyman was unable or unwilling to perform the duties of his living, he would hire a curate to do them on his behalf. The clergyman would continue to collect his usual income, out of which he would pay his curate a small stipend.

⁵ **Sabbath-day:** Sunday.

⁶ **grumble:** In other words, to read the service in a low, quick voice. With his heavy workload, Syntax has neither the time nor the energy for fine pulpit oratory.

⁷ **christen:** Christening is a religious ceremony during which infants are baptized and given their Christian names.

Jane's father, the Rev. George Austen, began taking boarding students in 1773 as a way of providing for his growing family.

Edward Ferrars (SS) plans to enter the church after being disinherited by his mother, but, like Syntax, he has little hope of preferment, expecting "nothing but a curacy" (III.2). When Col. Brandon, a stranger to Edward, offers him the living of Delaford, everyone is surprised, since church patrons usually reserved such positions for their own dependents and connections.

And all his gains, it did appear,
Were only thirty pounds[1] a year.
Besides, th' augmenting taxes[2] press
To aid expense and add distress.
Mutton and beef, and bread and beer,   30
And ev'ry thing was grown so dear;[3]
The boys[4] were always prone to eat,
Delighting less in books than meat;
That, when the time of Christmas came,
His earnings ceas'd to be the same;   35
And now, alas, could do no more,
Than keep the wolf without the door.[5]
E'en birch,[6] the pedant master's boast,
Was so increas'd in worth and cost,
That oft, prudentially beguil'd,   40
To save the rod, he spar'd the child.[7]
Thus, if the times refus'd to mend,
He to his school must put an end.
How hard his lot! how blind his fate!
What shall he do to mend his state?—   }   45
Thus did poor Syntax ruminate.

   When, as the vivid meteors fly,
And instant light the gloomy sky,
A sudden thought across him came,
That told the way to wealth and fame;   50
And, as th' expanding vision grew
Wider and wider to his view,
The painted fancy did beguile
His woe-worn phiz[8] into a smile:
But, while he pac'd the room around,   55
Or stood immers'd in thought profound,
The Doctor 'midst his rumination,
Was waken'd by a visitation
Which troubles many a poor man's life—
The visitation of his wife.   60
Good Mrs. Syntax was a lady
Ten years or more beyond her hey-day;
But tho' the blooming charms had flown
That grac'd her youth; it still was known

¹ **thirty pounds:** About $4,320 in 2024 money.

² **augmenting taxes:** Taxes were high during the Napoleonic Wars as the British government struggled to finance the war effort.

³ **dear**: Expensive.

⁴ **The boys:** The boarding students taught by Syntax.

⁵ **keep the wolf... door:** The idiom means "to barely ward off starvation or poverty." Its origins are uncertain.

⁶ **birch:** Rod made of bundled birch twigs used by schoolmasters to punish dull or unruly boys. Corporal punishment was so widespread in English schools that the birch rod was seen as something of a badge of office for teachers.

In her letters, Austen takes the beating of boys as a matter of course, placidly remarking in one that her two-year-old nephew, on the day he entered his boyhood by being put in breeches, "was whipped, into the Bargain" (5 Sept. 1796).

⁷ **save the rod... child:** Combe humorously reverses the maxim "spare the rod, spoil the child," derived from Proverbs 13:24. Syntax is forced to spare the child (by not beating him) lest he spoil his rod, which he cannot afford to replace.

⁸ **phiz:** Face.

A schoolmaster "birching" a schoolboy, John Augustus Atkinson, 1807. From *Sixteen Scenes taken from* The Miseries of Human Life, *By One of the Wretched* (William Miller, 1807), Plate 2nd.

The love of power she never lost,   65
As Syntax found it to his cost:
For as her words were us'd to flow,
He but replied or, YES, or NO.—
When e'er enrag'd by some disaster,
She'd shake the boys, and cuff the master: 70
Nay, to avenge the slightest wrong,
She could employ both arms and tongue;
And, if we list to country tales,[1]

[1] **list…tales:** Listen
to the village gossip.

She sometimes would enforce her nails.
Her face was red, her form was fat,   75
A round-about, and rather squat;
And, when in angry humour stalking,
Was like a dumpling set a-walking.
'Twas not the custom of this spouse
To suffer long a quiet house: 80
She was among those busy wives
Who hurry-scurry through their lives;
And make amends for fading beauty
By telling husbands of their duty.

'Twas at this moment, when, inspir'd,   85
And by his new ambition fir'd,
The pious man his hands uprear'd,
That Mrs. Syntax re-appear'd:
Amaz'd she look'd, and loud she shriek'd,
Or, rather like a pig she squeak'd,   90
To see her humble husband dare
Thus quit his sober ev'ning chair,
And pace, with varying steps, about,
Now in the room, and now without.
At first she did not find her tongue,   95
(A thing that seldom happen'd long,)
But soon that organ grew unquiet,
To ask the cause of all this riot.
The Doctor smil'd, and thus address'd
The secrets of his lab'ring breast—   100
"Sit down, my love, my dearest dear,

[2] **prithee:** "I pray
thee," or "please."

"Nay, prithee[2] do, and patient hear;

8

"Let me, for once, throughout my life,
"Receive this kindness from my wife:
"It will oblige me so:—in troth,
"It will, my dear, oblige us both;   105
"For such a plan has come athwart me,
"Which some kind sprite from heav'n has brought me;
"That, if you will your councils join,[1]   [1] **your councils**
"To aid this golden scheme of mine,   **join:** Contribute
"New days will come—new times appear,   110 your advice.
"And teeming plenty crown the year:
"We then on dainty bits will dine,
"And change our home-brew'd ale for wine:
"On summer days, to take the air,
"We'll put our Grizzle to a chair;[2]   115 [2] **Grizzle…chair:**
"While you, in silks, and muslins fine,   Grizzle is Syntax's
"The grocer's wife shall far outshine   horse, and a chair is
"And neighb'ring folks be forc'd to own,   a light carriage.
"In this fair town you give the ton."[3]   [3] **give the ton:** Set
"Oh! tell me," cried the smiling dame,   120 the fashion.
"Tell me this golden road to fame:

9

"You charm my heart, you quite delight it"—
"—*I'll make* a TOUR—*and then I'll* WRITE IT.¹
"You well know what my pen can do,
"And I'll employ my pencil too:—   125
"I'll ride and *write*, and *sketch* and *print*,
"And thus create a real mint;
"I'll *prose* it here, I'll *verse* it there,
"And *picturesque*² it ev'ry where.
"I'll do what all have done before;   130
"I think I shall—and somewhat more.
"At Doctor *Pompous*³ give a look;
"He made his fortune by a book:
"And if my volume does not beat it,
"When I return, I'll fry and eat it.   135
"Next week the boys will all go home,
"And I shall have a month to come.
"My clothes, my cash, my all prepare,
"Let Ralph look to the grizzle mare:
"Tho' wond'ring fools may laugh or scoff,   140
"By this day fortnight I'll be off;
"And when old Time a month has run,
"Our bus'ness, *Lovey*, will be done.
"I will in search of fortune roam,
"While you enjoy yourself at home."   145

    The story told, the Doctor eas'd
Of his grand plan, and Madam pleas'd,
No pains were spar'd by night or day
To set him forward on his way:
She trimm'd his coat—she mended all   150
His various clothing, great and small:
And better still, a purse was found
With twenty notes of each a pound.
Thus furnish'd, and in full condition
To prosper in his expedition,   155
At length the ling'ring moment came
That gave the dawn of wealth and fame.
Incurious Ralph, exact at four,
Led Grizzle saddled to the door;

¹ **TOUR...WRITE IT:** Specifically, a picturesque tour, one taken with the intention of admiring landscapes, ruins, and other scenic views. A book chronicling such a journey, usually accompanied by illustrations, was also called a tour.

² *picturesque:* "The picturesque" was an aesthetic theory popularized by William Gilpin which sought to define the types of beauty that made a scene (especially a landscape) suitable for drawing. Gilpin's tours of Great Britain, during which he sought out and sketched various picturesque sights, inspired generations of tourists and launched a new genre of travel literature: the "tour."

³ **Doctor *Pompous:*** Author of a picturesque tour. The name is probably a satire on picturesque writers generally, of whom there were many, rather than an allusion to any particular one.

Elizabeth Bennet (PP) is invited by her aunt and uncle to join them on a picturesque tour to the Lake District, a prospect which for a time serves as "the object of her happiest thoughts" (II.19). Eventually, though, the party has to settle for a shorter tour, which carries them, as luck would have it, into the neighborhood of Mr. Darcy.

Austen was a lifelong admirer of the picturesque. Her brother Henry, in his "Biographical Notice" of 1817, wrote that at "a very early age she was enamoured of Gilpin on the Picturesque; and she seldom changed her opinions either on books or men" (Pers. 330). When readers encounter satires of the picturesque in Austen's work, they should remember that Austen was fully capable of mocking what she loved.

And soon, with more than common state,[1]
The Doctor stood before the gate.
Behind him was his faithful wife;—
"One more embrace, my dearest life!"
Then his grey palfrey[2] he bestrode,
And gave a nod, and off he rode.
"Good luck! good luck!" she loudly cried,
"*Vale! O Vale!*"[3] he replied.

160

165

[1] **state:** An air of dignity, stateliness.
[2] **palfrey:** A gentle riding horse. The antiquated term contributes to the mock-epic tone of the passage.
[3] *Vale:* Latin for "farewell."

DOCTOR SYNTAX,
SETTING OUT ON HIS TOUR TO THE LAKES.

London, Pub.ᵈ May. 1ˢᵗ 1812, at R.Ackermann's Repository of Arts, 101 Strand.

CANTO II.

THE farewell ceremony o'er,
Madam went in, and bang'd the door:
No woeful tear bedew'd her eye,
Nor did she heave a single sigh;
But soon began her daily trade,   5
To chide the man and scold the maid;
While Syntax, with his scheme besotted,
Along the village gently trotted.
The folks, on daily labour bent,
Whistled and carrol'd as they went;   10
But, as the Doctor pass'd along,
Bow'd down their heads, and ceas'd their song;
He gravely nodded to the people;
Then, looking upwards to the steeple,
He thus, in mutt'ring tones express'd   15
The disappointments of his breast:—
"That thankless parent, Mother Church,[1]
"Has ever left me in the lurch;
"And, while so many fools are seen
"To strut a Rector or a Dean,[2]   20
"Who live in ease, and find good cheer
"On ev'ry day of ev'ry year;
"So small her share of true discerning,
"She turn'd her back on all my learning.
"I've in her vineyard labour'd hard,   25
"And what has been my lean reward?
"I've dug the ground, while some rich Vicar
"Press'd the ripe grape, and drank the liquor;
"I fed the flock, while others eat
"The mutton's nice delicious meat;[3]   30
"I've kept the hive, and made the honey,
"While the drones[4] pocketed the money.

14

Detail from "The Clerical Alphabet" showing a poor curate and a rich dean, Richard Newton, 1795. British Museum.

¹ **Mother Church:** The Anglican or Established Church.

² **Rector or a Dean:** A dean was the head of a cathedral. A rector was a parish clergyman, responsible for preaching, leading worship, and promoting the spiritual welfare of his parishioners. A vicar (ln. 27) was like a rector, except that he received only a part of the tithes of the parish; a rector received the full tithes.

³ **her vineyard...meat:** See 1 Cor. 9:7: "who planteth a vineyard, and eateth not of the fruit thereof? or who feedeth a flock, and eateth not of the milk of the flock?" Syntax complains that, as a curate, he does all the work of the parish while an absentee rector or vicar receives the tithes.

⁴ **drones:** People who do little work of their own, living off others (OED), derived from a comparison with drone (male) bees, who remain in the hive instead of gathering nectar.

Brooding on his own poverty, Syntax suggests that all clergy above the rank of curate were prosperous, which was not the case. Austen's novels tell a more nuanced story. While Mr. Collins (PP) enjoys a "very sufficient income" (I.15) as rector of Hunsford, Edward Ferrars (SS) earns just £200 ($28,800) a year from the small rectory of Delaford. Mr. Watson (Wat.), also a rector, is downright poor. Livings ranged in value depending on the population of the parish, the productivity of its farmland, and other factors.

Henry Tilney (NA) appears to fit Syntax's criticism, as he is often away from his parish at Woodston, leaving the bulk of the work, presumably, to his curate. In Henry's case, though, the arrangement is only temporary. He does intend to take up residence eventually, perhaps after fitting up his parsonage.

"But now, on better things intent,
"On far more grateful labours bent,
"New prospects open to my view: 35
"So, thankless Mother Church, adieu!"
Thus having said his angry say,
Syntax proceeded on his way.

  The morning lark ascends on high,
And with its music greets the sky: 40
The blackbird whistles, and the thrush
Warbles his wild notes in the bush;
While ev'ry hedge and ev'ry tree
Resounds with vocal minstrelsy:[1]   [1] **vocal minstrelsy:**
But Syntax, wrapt in thought profound, 45 Song.
Is deaf to each enliv'ning sound:——
Revolving many a golden scheme,
And yielding to the pleasing dream,
The reins hung loosely from his hand,
While Grizzle, senseless of command,   50
Unguided pac'd the road along,
Nor knew if it were right or wrong.
Through the deep vale,[2] and up the hill,   [2] **vale:** Valley.
By roaring stream and tinkling rill,[3]   [3] **rill:** Brook or
Grizzle her thoughtful master bore, 55 rivulet.
Who, counting future treasure o'er,
And, on his weighty projects bent,
Observ'd not whither Grizzle went.
Thus did fond Fancy's soothing power
Cheat him of many a fleeting hour;   60
Nor did he know the pacing Sun
Had half his daily circuit run.
Sweet, airy sprite,[4] that can bestow   [4] **sprite:** Spirit, in
A pleasing respite to our woe,   this case "Fancy" or
That can corroding care beguile, 65 imagination.
And make the woe-worn face to smile!
But ah! too soon the vision passes,
Confounded by a pack of asses!
The donkies bray'd; and lo! the sound
Awak'd him from his thought profound;   70
And, as he star'd, and look'd around,

He said—or else he seem'd to say—
"I find that I have lost my way.
"Oh! what a wide expanse I see,
"Without a wood, without a tree;   75
"No one's at hand, no house is near,
"To tell the way, or give good cheer:
"For now a sign would be a treat,
"To tell us we might drink and eat:
"But sure there is not in my sight   80
"The sign of any living wight;[1]
"And all around upon this common[2]
"I see not either man or woman;
"Nor dogs to bark, nor cocks to crow,
"Nor sheep to bleat, nor herds to low; 85
"And if these asses did not bray,
"And thus some signs of life betray,
"I well might think that I were hurl'd
"Into some sad, unpeopled world.
"How could I come, misguided wretch! 90
"To where I cannot make a sketch?"

Thus, as he ponder'd what to do,
A guide-post rose within his view;
And, when the pleasing shape he spied,
He prick'd his steed, and thither hied;[2] 95
But some unheeding, senseless wight,
Who to fair learning ow'd a spite,
Had ev'ry letter'd mark defac'd,
Which once its several pointers grac'd.
The mangled post thus long had stood, 100
An uninforming piece of wood;
Like other guides, as some folks say,
Who neither lead, nor point the way.[3]
The Sun, as hot as he was bright,
Had got to his meridian height; 105
'Twas sultry noon—for not a breath
Of cooling zephyr fann'd the heath—
When Syntax cried—" 'Tis all in vain
"To find my way across the plain;

[1] **wight:** Person.

[2] **common:** A piece of open land available to the community for foraging, grazing, and other purposes.

[2] **thither hied:** Hurried there.

[3] **Like other guides…way:** Possibly a reference to Matthew 23:13, in which Jesus condemns the Pharisees for neither entering the kingdom of heaven themselves, nor helping others to enter.

"So here my fortune I will try,   110
"And wait till some one passes by:
"Upon that bank awhile I'll sit,
"And let poor Grizzle graze a bit;
"But as my time shall not be lost,
"I'll make a drawing of the post;   115
"And, tho' your flimsy tastes may flout it,
"There's something *picturesque* about it:
" 'Tis rude and rough,[1] without a gloss,
"And is well cover'd o'er with moss;
"And I've a right—(who dares deny it?) 120
"To place yon group of asses[2] by it.
"Aye! this will do: and now I'm thinking,
"That self-same pond where Grizzle's drinking,
"If hither brought 'twould better seem,
"And faith I'll turn it to a stream;   125
"I'll make this flat a shaggy ridge,
"And o'er the water throw a bridge;
"I'll do as other sketchers do—
"Put any thing into the view;
"And any object recollect,   130
"To add a grace, and give effect.
"Thus, tho' from truth I haply[3] err,
"The scene preserves its character.[4]
"What man of taste my right will doubt,
"To put things in, or leave them out? 135
" 'Tis more than right, it is a duty,
"If we consider landscape beauty:—
"He ne'er will as an artist shine,
"Who copies nature line by line;
"Whoe'er from nature takes a view, 140
"Must copy and improve it too:[5]
"To heighten ev'ry work of art,
"Fancy should take an active part:
"Thus I (which few, I think, can boast)
"Have made a Landscape of a Post. 145

 "So far, so good—but no one passes,
"No living creature but these asses;

¹ **rude and rough:** For Gilpin, roughness was the defining quality of the picturesque. As he once put it, "make it *rough*; and you make it also *picturesque*" (TE 8). Throughout his writings, he applied this principle to everything from craggy mountains to ruined abbeys to the human face.
² **group of asses:** Small gatherings of livestock, including asses, were considered by Gilpin to greatly enhance a landscape.

Edward Ferrars (SS), less enchanted with picturesque "roughness" than the romantic Marianne, tells her that she must pardon him for calling "surfaces strange and uncouth, which ought to be," according to picturesque terminology, "irregular and rugged" (I.18).

³ **haply:** Perhaps.
⁴ *The scene preserves its character:* "Character" here refers to the artistic or thematic unity of a scene. According to Gilpin, "Seldom does [nature] produce a scene *perfect in character*." Thus, "the *imaginary* scene," in which the artist judiciously revises nature, "preserves more the *character* of landscape, than the *real* one" (TE 164).
⁵ **Must copy and improve it too:** Gilpin argued that essentially no landscape is perfectly picturesque on its own; thus, alterations to it in a picture are "a liberty, that must always be allowed" (OW 32). These alterations could be quite substantial: "This ill-shaped mountain may be pared [...]. Upon yon bald declivity [...] may be reared a forest of noble oak. [...] On a gentle rise, opening to the lake, and half incircled by woody hills, some mouldring abbey may be seated" (OCW Vol. I, 119-20). Next to flights of fancy such as these, Syntax's inventions seem less like an exaggerated parody of Gilpin than a spot-on impression.

Henry Tilney (NA), an amateur landscape artist, cannot resist an addition of his own while sizing up the picturesque qualities of Beechen Cliff. A "piece of rocky fragment" is incomplete without the "withered oak <u>which he had placed</u> near its summit" (I.14, our emphasis). Catherine, meanwhile, with a beginner's enthusiasm, strikes the "whole city of Bath" from the view as "unworthy to make part of a landscape"!

19

"And, should I sit and hear them bray,
"I were as great a beast as they:
"So I'll be off;—from yonder down[1]   150 [1] **down:** Hill.
"I may, perhaps, descry a town;
"Or some tall spire,[2] among the trees,   [2] **spire:** Church
"May give my way-worn spirit ease."   towers, visible for
    miles around,
    would often
  Grizzle again he soon bestrode,   155 provide the traveler
And wav'd his whip, and off he rode;   his first glimpse of a
But all around was dingy green,   village or town.
No spire arose, no town was seen.
At length he reach'd a beaten road;
How great a joy the sight bestow'd!
So on he went in pleasant mood,   160
And shortly gain'd a stately wood,
Where the refreshing zephyrs play'd,
And cool'd the air beneath the shade.
Oh! what a change, how great the treat,
To fanning breeze from sultry heat!   165
But ah! how false is human joy!
When least we think it, ills annoy:
For now, with loud impetuous rush,
Three ruffians issued from a bush;

One Grizzle stopp'd, and seiz'd the reins,   170
While they all threat the Doctor's brains.
Poor Syntax, trembling with affright,
Resists not such superior might,
But yields him to their savage pleasure,
And gives his purse, with all its treasure.   175
Fearing, howe'er, the Doctor's view
Might be to follow and pursue;
The cunning robbers[1] wisely counted
That he, of course, should be dismounted;
And still that it would safer be,   180
If he were fasten'd to a tree.
Thus to a tree they quickly bound him—
The cruel cords went round and round him;
And, having of all pow'r bereft him,
They tied him fast—and then they left him.   185

[1] **cunning robbers:** Highwaymen had long been a problem in England, though the danger had peaked in the early 18th century, well before Combe was writing. Some highwaymen, like Dick Turpin, became figures of popular legend, and highwaymen in general made frequent appearances in the literature of the time. This scene bears a particularly strong resemblance to the robbery of Joseph Andrews in Henry Fielding's 1742 novel of that name—one of the many lines of influence that can be traced from that work to this.

In Northanger Abbey, *Austen mocks the literary cliché of the highway robbery. She writes that* "[n]either robbers nor tempests befriended" *Catherine and the Allens on their way to Bath (1.2), implying—with the word* "befriended"—*that such disasters were less a realistic danger than a convenient way to spice up a story. Still, the roads were not an entirely safe and suitable place for unaccompanied young women; this is partly why General Tilney's decision to send Catherine away* "alone, unattended" *is so shocking (II.13).*

DOCTOR SYNTAX.
STOPT BY HIGHWAYMEN.

CANTO III.

BY the road side, within the wood,
In this sad state poor Syntax stood;
His bosom heav'd with many a sigh,
And the tears stood in either eye.
What could he do?—he durst[1] not bawl;   5   [1] **durst:** Dared.
The noise the robbers might recall:
The villains might again surround him,
And hang him up where they had bound him.
Sure never was an helpless wight*
In more uncomfortable plight,   10
Nor was this all; his pate[2] was bare,   [2] **pate:** Head.
Unshelter'd by one lock of hair:
For when the sturdy robbers took him,
His hat and peruke[3] both forsook him: [3] **peruke:** Wig.
The insect world were on the wing,   15
Whose talent is to buz and sting;
And soon his bare-worn head they sought,
By instinct led, by nature taught;
And dug their little forks within
The tender texture of his skin.   20
He rag'd and roar'd, but all in vain,
No means he found to ease his pain.
The cords, which to the tree had tied him,
All help from either hand denied him;
He shook his head, he writh'd his face   } 25
With painful look, with sad grimace,
And thus he spoke his hapless case:

"Ah! miserable man," he cried,
"What perils do my course betide!
"In this sad melancholy state,   30
"Must I, alas, impatient wait

25

"Till some kind soul shall haply find me,
"And with his friendly hands unbind me;
"Nay, I throughout the night may stay,
" 'Tis such an unfrequented way: 35
"Tho' what with hunger, thirst, and fright,
"I ne'er shall last throughout the night;
"And could I e'en these ills survive,
"The flies would eat me up alive!
"What mad ambition made me roam?   40
"Ah! wherefore did I quit my home?
"For there I liv'd remote from harm;
"My meals were good, my house was warm;
"And, though I was not free from strife,
"With other ills that trouble life,   45
"Yet I had learn'd full well to bear
"The nightly scold, the daily care;
"And, after many a season past,
"I should have found repose at last:
"Fate would have sign'd my long release,   50
"And Syntax would have died in peace;
"Nor thus been robb'd, and tied and beaten,
"And all alive by insects eaten."

But while he thus at fate was railing,
And Fortune's angry frowns bewailing,   55
A dog's approaching bark he hears;
'Twas sweet as music to his ears;
And soon a sure relief appears.
For, tho' it bore that gen'ral form,[1]
Which oft' at home, foretold a storm,   60
It now appear'd an angel's shape
That promis'd him a quick escape:
Nor did La Mancha's val'rous knight[2]
Feel greater pleasure at the sight,
When, overwhelm'd with love and awe,   65
His Dulcinea[3] first he saw:—
For, on two trotting palfreys came,
And each one bore a comely dame.
They started as his form they view;
The horses, also, started too: 70

26

Don Quixote and his squire Sancho Panza, Francis Hayman. One of the illustrations for the 1755 translation of *Don Quixote* by Tobias Smollett (A. Millar), p. 126.

[1] **that gen'ral form:** That is, the form of a woman.

[2] **La Mancha's val'rous knight:** Eponymous hero of Miguel de Cervantes' novel *Don Quixote* (1605). Don Quixote is a kind but foolish man who, obsessed with chivalric tales, sets out to restore knighthood to its former glory. There are many parallels between Don Quixote and Doctor Syntax, who also plays the role of a bookish and endearingly naive comic hero animated by his love of literature.

[3] **Dulcinea:** Don Quixote's beloved, a common working woman whom he imagines to be a beautiful and elegant lady. Quixote's idealized image of Dulcinea inspires many of his knightly deeds.

Cervantes' concept of the hero who sees the real world through the lens of romantic fiction received significant attention in the 18th c., most notably in Charlotte Lennox's 1752 novel The Female Quixote; or, the Adventures of Arabella, *which replaced the aged Spaniard with an English girl and the tales of chivalry with French romances. While we have no evidence that Austen read* Don Quixote *itself, she read Lennox's work at least twice, praising it effusively in a letter to Cassandra (7-8 Jan. 1807). Many of the themes of the Quixote tradition appear in* Northanger Abbey, *in which Catherine Morland is led astray by her affinity for Gothic novels.*

The dog with insult seem'd to treat him,
And look'd as if he long'd to eat him.
In piteous tones he humbly pray'd
They'd turn aside, and give him aid;
When each leap'd quickly from her steed,   75
To join in charitable deed.
They drew their knives to cut the noose,
And let the mournful pris'ner loose:
With kindest words his fate bewail,
While grateful Syntax tells his tale.   80
The rustic matrons sooth his grief,
Nor offer, but afford, relief;
And, turning from the beaten road,
Their well-lin'd panniers[1] they unload;
When soon upon the bank appear'd   85
A sight his fainting spirits cheer'd.
They spread the fare with cheerful grace,
And gave a banquet to the place:
Most haply, too, as they untied him,
He saw his hat and wig beside him: 90
So, thus bewigg'd and thus behatted,
Down on the grass the Doctor squatted:
He then uplifted either eye,
With grateful accents to the sky.
" 'Tis thus," he humbly said, "we read   95
"In sacred books of heav'nly deed;
"And thus I find, in my distress,
"The manna[2] of the wilderness.
" 'Tis hermit's fare; but thanks to heav'n,
"And those kind souls by whom 'tis given."   100
'Tis true that bread, and curds, and fruit,
Do with the pious hermits suit;
But Syntax surely was mistaken
To think their meals partake of bacon;
Or that those rev'rend men regale,   105
As our good Doctors do—with ale:
And these kind dames, in nothing loth,[3]
Took care that he partook of both.

[1] **panniers:** Baskets for food, typically carried by a horse or pack animal.

[2] **manna:** Food miraculously provided by God to the Israelites during their wandering in the desert (Exodus 16).

[3] **loth:** Reluctant, unwilling.

At length 'twas time to bid adieu,
And each their diff'rent way pursue: 110
A kind farewell, a kiss as kind,
He gave them both with heart and mind:
Then off he trudg'd, and, as he walk'd,
Thus to himself the Parson talk'd.
" 'Tis well, I think, it is no worse,   115
"For I have only lost my purse.
"With all their cruelty and pains,
"The rogues have got but trifling gains;
"Poor four[1] and four-pence is the measure
"Of all their mighty pilfer'd treasure;   120
"For haply there was no divining
"I'd a snug pocket in my lining;
"And, thanks to Spousy, ev'ry note
"Was well sew'd up within my coat.
"But where is Grizzle?—Never mind her;   125
"I'll have her cried,[2] and soon shall find her."
Thus he pursu'd the winding way,
Big with the evils of the day:
Though the good Doctor kept in view
The favour of its blessings too.   130
Nor had he pac'd it half an hour
Before he saw a parish tow'r,
And soon, with sore fatigue opprest,
An inn receiv'd him as its guest:
But still his mind, with anxious care,   135
Ponder'd upon his wand'ring mare:
He therefore sent the bellman[3] round,
To try if Grizzle might be found.

Grizzle, ungrateful to her master,
And careless of his foul disaster,   140
Left him tied up, and took her way,
In hopes to meet with corn or hay;
But, as that did not come to pass,
She sought a meadow full of grass:
The farmer in the meadow found her,   145
And order'd John, his man, to pound[4] her.

---

[1] **four:** Four shillings, about $30 in 2024.

[2] **have her cried:** Have the fact that she is missing publicly announced.

[3] **bellman:** A bellman's job was to walk the streets announcing matters of public importance—in this case, a missing horse—while ringing a bell to get people's attention.

[4] **pound:** Place in an enclosure for stray or trespassing livestock.

30

Now John was one of those droll folk,
Who oft take mischief for a joke;
And thought 'twould make the master stare,
When he again beheld his mare,
(Perhaps the g'emman[1] might be shockt)
To find her ready cropt and dockt:[2]
At all events, he play'd his fun:
No sooner was it said than done.
But Grizzle was a patient beast,
And minded nought, if she could feast:
Like many others, prone to think
The best of life was meat and drink;[3]
Who feel to-day nor care nor sorrow,
If they are sure to feast to-morrow.
Thus Grizzle, as she pac'd around
The purlieus[4] of the barren pound,
In hungry mood might seem to neigh—
"If I had water, corn, and hay,
"I should not thus my fate bewail,
"Nor mourn the loss of ears or tail."

[1] **g'emman:** Corruption of "gentleman"—an indicator of John's rusticity.

150

[2] **cropt and dockt:** To crop an animal is to cut its ears, and to dock it is to cut its tail. Neither practice was common with horses.

155

[3] **best of life...drink:** See Ecclesiastes 8:15: "a man hath no better thing under the sun, than to eat, and to drink, and to be merry."

160

[4] **purlieus:** Borders, confines.

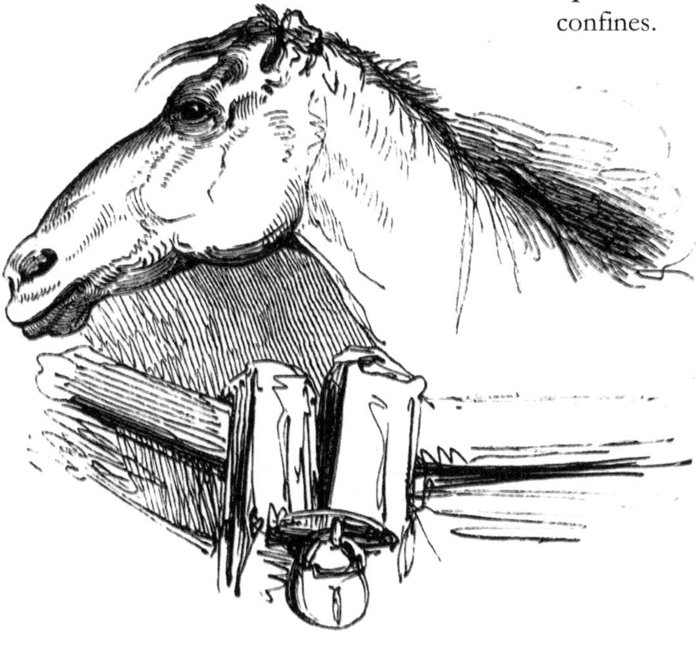

165

In the mean time, securely hous'd,
The Doctor boos'd it,[1] and carous'd,
The hostess spread her fairest cheer,
Her best beef-steak, her strongest beer;   170
And sooth'd him with her winning chat,
Of "Pray eat this—and now take that.
"Your Rev'rence, after all your fright,
"Wants meat and drink, to set you right."
His Rev'rence prais'd the golden rule,   180
Nor did he let his victuals cool:
And, having drank his liquor out,
He took a turn to look about;—
When to the folks about the door
He told the dismal story o'er.   185
The country-people on him gaz'd,
And heard his perils all amaz'd:
How the thieves twin'd the cords around him;
How to a tree the villains bound him:
What angels came to his relief,   190
To loose his bonds, and soothe his grief:
His loss of cash, and what was worse,
Of saddle, saddle-bags, and horse.
Thus as their rude attention hung
Upon the wonders of his tongue,   195
Lo! Grizzle's alter'd form appears,
With half its tail, and half its ears!
"Is there no law?" the Doctor cries:—
"Plenty," a Lawyer straight replies:
"Employ me, and those thieves shall swing   200
"On gallows-tree, in hempen string:
"And, for the rogue, the law shall flea[2] him,
"Who maim'd your horse, as now you see him."
"No," quoth the Don,[3] "your pardon pray,
"I've had enough of thieves to-day: 205
"I've lost four shillings and a groat.[4]
"But you would strip me of my coat:
"And ears and tails won't fatten you,
"You'll want the head and carcase too."
He chuckled as he made the stroke,   210
And all around enjoy'd the joke:

[1] **boos'd it:** Drank a lot of booze.

[2] **flea:** Flay, skin.

[3] **Don:** Scholar.

[4] **groat:** Coin worth four pence ($2.40).

32

But still it was a sorry sight
To see the beast in such a plight:
Yet what could angry Syntax do?
'Twas all in vain to fret and stew:—   215
His well-stuff'd bags, with all their hoard
Of sketching tools, were safe restor'd;
The saddle too, which he had sought
For small reward, was quickly brought;
He therefore thought it far more sage   220
To stop his threats and check his rage:
So to the ostler's[1] faithful care
He gave his mutilated mare;
And while poor Grizzle, free from danger,
Cropp'd the full rack and clean'd the manger,   225
Syntax, to ease his aching head,
Smok'd out his pipe, and went to bed.

[1] **ostler's:** An ostler is a stableman at an inn (OED).

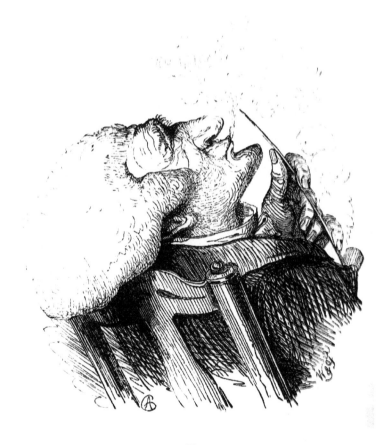

CANTO IV.

BLESS'D be the man, said he of yore,
Who Quixote's lance and target[1] bore!
Bless'd be the man who first taught sleep
Throughout our wearied frames to creep;[2]
And kindly gave to human woes   5
Th' oblivious mantle of repose!
Hail! balmy pow'r! that canst repair
The constant waste of human care;
To the sad heart afford relief,
And give a respite to its grief!   10
Canst calm, through night's composing hours,
The threat'ning storm that daily low'rs[3]:
On the rude flint[4] the wretched cheer
And to a smile transform the tear!

Thus wrapt in slumber, Syntax lay—   15
Forgot the troubles of the day:
So sound his sleep, so sweet his rest,
By no disturbing dreams distrest;
That, all at ease, he lay entranc'd,
Till the fair morn was far advanc'd.   20
At length, the hostess thought it wrong
He should be left to sleep so long:
So bid the maid to let him know
That breakfast was prepar'd below.
Betty then op'd the chamber door,   25
And, tripping onward 'cross the floor,
Undrew the curtains, one by one,
When, in a most ear-piercing tone,
Such as would grace the London cries,[5]
She told him it was time to rise.   30
The noise his peaceful slumbers broke;—
He gave a snort—or two, and woke.

[1] **target:** Shield.

[2] **BLESS'D… creep:** Alludes to a speech of Sancho Panza, squire of Don Quixote, which begins "praise be to him who invented sleep" (Part II, Ch. LXVIII).

[3] **low'rs:** Scowls or threatens.

[4] **rude flint:** A rough stone floor on which one is forced to sleep, a standard metaphor for poverty and its discomforts.

[5] **London cries:** The loud cries of street merchants in London.

Now, as the Doctor turn'd his head,
Betty was court'sying by the bed:—
"What brought you here, fair maid, I pray?"— 35
"To tell you, Sir, how wears the day;
"And that it is my special care
"To get your worship's morning fare.
"The kettle boils, and I can boast
"No small renown for making toast. 40
"There's coffee, Sir, and tea, and meat,
"And surely you must want to eat;
"For ten long hours have pass'd away
"Since down upon this bed you lay!"
The Doctor rubb'd his op'ning eyes, 45
Then stretch'd his arms, and 'gan to rise:
But Betty still demurely stands,
To hear him utter his commands.
"Begone," he cried, "get something nice,
"And I'll be with you in a trice." 50

Behold him then, renew'd by rest,
His chin well shav'd, his peruke[1] drest,
Conning[2] with solemn air the news,
His welcome breakfast to amuse;—
And when the well-fed meal was o'er, 55
Grizzle was order'd to the door:
Betty was also told to say,
The mighty sum there was to pay.

[1] **peruke:** Wig. To "dress" a wig is to comb or arrange it.
[2] **Conning:** Scanning.

Betty, obedient to his will,
Her court'sy makes, and gives the bill.   60
Down the long page he cast his eye,
Then shook his head, and heav'd a sigh,
"What! am I doom'd, where'er I go,
"In all I meet to find a foe?
"Where'er I wander to be cheated,   65
"To be bamboozled and ill-treated?"
Thus, as he read each item o'er,
The hostess op'd the parlour door;
When Syntax rose in solemn state,
And thus began the fierce debate:—   70

   SYNTAX.
 "Good woman; here, your bill retake,
"And, prithee, some abatement make:
"I could not such demands afford,
"Were I a Bishop or a Lord;
"And though I hold myself as good   75
"As any of my brotherhood,[1]
"Howe'er, by bounteous Fortune crown'd,
"In wealth and honours they abound,
"It is not in my pow'r to pay
"Such long-drawn bills as well as they.   80
"The paper fills me with affright;—
"I surely do not read it right;
"For, at the bottom here, I see
"Th' enormous total—one pound, three!"[2]

   HOSTESS.
 "The charges are all fairly made;   85
"If you will eat, I must be paid.
"My bills have never found reproaches
"From Lords and Ladies, in their coaches.
"This house, that's call'd the Royal Crown,
"Is the first inn throughout the town: 90
"And the best gentry, ev'ry day,
"Become my guests, and freely pay:
"Besides, I took you in at night,
"Half-dead, with hunger and affright,
"Just 'scap'd from robbers."   95

[1] **my brotherhood:** The clergy.

[2] **one pound, three:** One pound, three shillings ($165), a steep price for a single night at an inn.

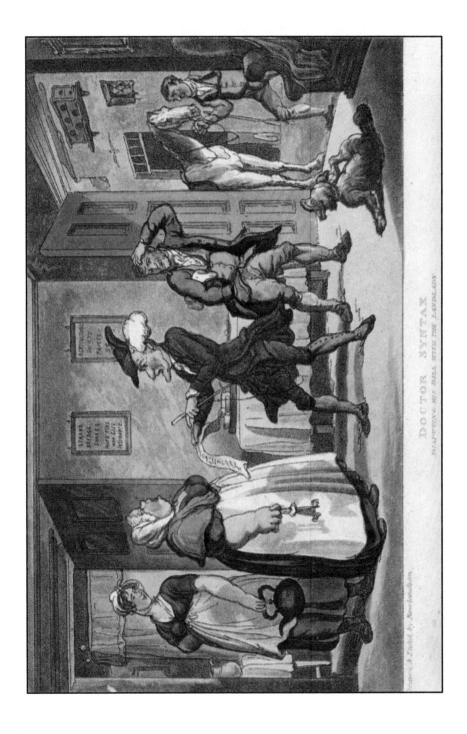

SYNTAX.

—————————————"That's most true,   *95*
And now I'm to be robb'd by you."

HOSTESS.

"Sir, you mistake; and did not I
"Disdain rude words, I'd say—you lie.
"I took you in last night, I say."—

SYNTAX.

" 'Tis true;—and, if this bill I pay,   100
"You'll *take me in*[1] again to-day."

HOSTESS.

"I gave you all my choicest cheer,
"The best of meat, the best of beer;
"And then you snor'd yourself to rest
"In the best bed—I say the best.   105
"You've had such tea as few can boast,
"With a whole loaf turn'd into toast."

SYNTAX.

"And for your beef and beer, and tea,
"You kindly charge me—one pound, three!"

HOSTESS

" 'Tis cheap as dirt—for well I know   110
"How things with country Curates go:[2]
"And I profess that I am loth
"To deal unkindly with the cloth:[3]
"Nay, oft and oft, as I'm a sinner,
"I've given hungry Clerks[4] a dinner."   115

SYNTAX.

"And there's a proverb, as they say,
"That for the Clerks the Parsons pay;
"Which you, I trow,[5] can well fulfil,
"Whene'er you make a Parson's bill.[6]
"Why, one pound three, the truth I speak,   120
"Would keep my household for a week.
"Dear Mrs. Syntax, how she'd vapour[7]
"Were she to read this curious paper!"

¹ *take me in:* Cheat or sucker me.

² **How things…go:** The hostess is referring to the notorious poverty of curates, particular those serving rural parishes. According to one historian, at the start of the nineteenth century the average curate's income was no more than £60 ($8,640), scarcely more than a farm laborer would make (Hart, 109).

³ **the cloth:** The clergy, so called on account of their distinctive black garb.

⁴ **Clerks:** Antiquated term for clergymen.

⁵ **trow:** Believe.

⁶ **a proverb…Parson's bill:** A complicated joke hinging on the dual meaning of "clerk" (a clergyman and a clergyman's lay assistant). The gist of it is that if the Hostess does give free dinners to some clergymen, then she makes other clergymen pay for them by marking up their bills.

⁷ **vapour:** Storm or fume.

Austen was well aware of the plight of country curates. Sir Walter Elliot (Pers.) speaks contemptuously of a man whose father was "a country curate, without bread to eat" (I.3). With more sympathy, Mrs. Jennings (SS) estimates that Edward Ferrars would earn only £50 ($7,200) a year as a curate: "Lord help 'em! how poor they will be!" (III.2).

HOSTESS.
"If that's your living, on my life,
"You starve your servants and your wife."   125

SYNTAX.
"I wish my wife were here to meet you,
"In your own fashion would she greet you:
"With looks as fierce, and voice as shrill,
"She'd make you, mistress, change your bill."

HOSTESS.
"Think you, besides, there's nought to pay   130
"For all your horse's corn and hay?
"And ointments too to cure the ail
"Of her cropp'd ears and mangled tail?"

SYNTAX.
"I wish the wight* would bring the shears
"Which dock'd that tail and cropp'd those ears,   135
"And just exert the self-same skill
"To crop and dock your monstrous bill.
"But, I'm in haste to get away,
"Tho' one pound, three, I will not pay:
"So, if you'll take one half th' amount,   140
"We'll quickly settle the account.
"There is the money, do you see?
"And let us part in charity."

HOSTESS.
"Well, as a charitable deed,
"I'll e'n consent—so, mount your steed,
"And on your journey straight proceed: } 145
"But well you know, where'er you roam,
"That charity begins at home."[1]

[1] **charity...home:**
The saying means a person should take care of their own family before helping others. The hostess may be saying that an innkeeper shouldn't be expected to help poor travelers at the expense of her establishment.

40

CANTO V.

THE Doctor smil'd—the bill was paid,
The hostess left him to the maid:
When Betty stood in humble guise,
With expectation in her eyes,
That he was, surely, so good-hearted,   5
He'd give her something ere they parted.
Now, Nature, in her wanton freaks,[1]
Had given Betty rosy cheeks;
And caus'd her raven locks to break
In native ringlets on her neck.   10
The roving bee might wish to sip
The sweetness of her pouting lip;
So red, so tempting to the view,
'Twas what the Doctor long'd to do.
"You're a nice girl," he smiling said,   15
"Am I?" replied the simp'ring[2] maid.
"I swear you are, and if you're willing
"To give a kiss, I'll give a shilling."
"—If 'tis the same thing, Sir, to you,
"Make the gift two-fold, and take two."   20
He grimly grinn'd with inward pleasure,
And soon he seiz'd the purchas'd treasure.
"Your lips, my dear, are sweet as honey:
"So one smack more—and there's your money."

This charming ceremony o'er,
The Parson strutted to the door;
Where his poor wounded mare appears
In cruel state of tail and ears.
The neighbours all impatient wait,
To see him issue from the gate;
For country-town, or village-green,
Has seldom such a figure seen.

[1] **wanton freaks:** Unaccountable whims.

[2] **simp'ring:** Smiling in a coy or mischievous way.

41

Labour stood still to see him pass,
While ev'ry lad and ev'ry lass
Ran forward to enjoy the feast,   35
To jeer the Don*, and mourn the beast,
But one and all aloud declare
'Twas a fit sight for country fair,
Far better than a dancing bear.[1]

  At length, escap'd from all the noise   40
Of women, men, and girls and boys,
In the recesses of a lane
He thus gave utt'rance to his pain.—
"It seems to be my luckless case,
"At ev'ry point, in ev'ry place,   45
"To meet with trouble and disgrace.
"But yesterday I left my home,
"In search of fancied wealth to roam:
"And nought, I think, but ills betide me;
"Sure some foul spirit runs beside me: 50
"Some blasting demon from the east,[2]
"A deadly foe to man and beast,
"That loves to riot in disaster,
"And plague alike both horse and master.
"Grizzle, who full five years, and more,   55
"A trumpeter[3] in triumph bore;
"Who had in many a battle been,
"And many a bloody conflict seen;
"Who, having 'scap'd with scarce a scar,
"From all the angry threats of war;   60
"When her best days are almost past,
"Feels these ignoble wounds at last.
"Ah! what can thy fond master do?
"He's cut and slash'd as well as you:
"But tho' no more with housing[4] gay,   65
"And prancing step, you take your way;
"Or, with your stately rider, lead
"The armed troop to warlike deed;
"While you've a leg, you ne'er shall cease
"To bear the minister of peace.[5]   70

[1] **dancing bear:** A bear trained to dance as part of a street or circus act.

[2] **blasting demon…east:** In the Bible, east winds often bring evil or disaster.

[3] **trumpeter:** A mounted soldier whose role is to give directions to a body of cavalry by means of trumpet signals.

[4] **housing:** Covering for a horse, in a military context often brightly colored and ornamental.

[5] **minister of peace:** Clergyman.

"Long have you borne him, nor e'er grumbled,
"Nor ever started, kick'd, or stumbled."
  But mildest natures sometimes err
From the strict rules of character:
The tim'rous bird defends its young,   75
And beasts will kick when they are stung.
'Twas burning hot, and hosts of flies,
With venom'd stings, around them rise:
They seiz'd on Grizzle's wounded part,
Who strait began to snort and start,   80
Kick'd up behind, rear'd up before,
And play'd a dozen antics more.
The Doctor coax'd, but all in vain,
She snorted, kick'd, and rear'd again:
"Alas!" said Syntax, "could I pop   85
"Just now upon a blacksmith's shop,
"Where cooling unguents would avail
"To save poor Grizzle's ears and tail!"
When scarce had he his wishes spoke,
Than he beheld a cloud of smoke,   90
That from a forge appear'd to rise,
And for a moment veil'd the skies;

While the rude hammers, to his ear,
Proclaim'd the aid he wish'd was near.
By the way-side the cottage rose,   95
Around it many a willow grows,
Where Syntax, in a tone of grief,
Shew'd Grizzle's wounds, and pray'd relief.
The sooty Galen[1] soon appear'd,
And with fair hopes the Doctor cheer'd.   100
"Trust me, good Sir, I've got a plaster,[2]
"Will cure the beast of her disaster;
"And while the dressing I prepare,
"With all becoming skill and care,
"You in that harbour may regale   105
"With a cool pipe and jug of ale:
"I've long a two-fold trade profess'd,
"And med'cine sell for man and beast."
Syntax now sought the cooling shade,
While Galen's dame the banquet made: 110
She well knew how her guests to please,
And added meat, and bread and cheese:
Besides, she told the village-tale—
Who came to drink their home-brew'd ale;[3]
How that the laughter-loving Vicar;   115
Would sometimes walk to taste their liquor;
That their gay landlord was renown'd,
For hunting fox,[4] with horn and hound;
That he'd a daughter passing fair,
Who was his Honour's only heir;   120
But she was proud, nor could a 'Squire
Approach to tell his am'rous fire;
A Lord alone, as it was said,
She would receive into her bed.
Throughout the village, ev'ry name   125
Became a subject for the dame;
And thus she play'd her chatt'ring part,
Till Syntax thought it time to part.
  And now poor Grizzle re-appears,
With plaster'd tail and plaster'd ears,   130
Which thus cas'd up, might well defy
The sharpest sting of gnat or fly.

¹ **Galen:** A celebrated physician of the second century, used satirically for the name of the blacksmith.

² **plaster:** Bandage spread with a medicinal substance.

³ **home-brew'd ale:** Ale or beer was generally safer to drink than water in the early nineteenth century and was thus consumed on a daily basis in most households. To save money, ale was often brewed at home—usually by the women of the family. Many women, like the blacksmith's wife, no doubt took pride in the quality of their ale as a testament to their superior housekeeping.

Austen herself was a home brewer. In her letters, one detects a subtle pride in her spruce beer specifically. (9 Dec. 1808; 7-9 Oct. 1808).

Bachelor's Hall: Breaking Cover, Francis Calcroft Turner, 1835-6. YCBA.

⁴ **hunting fox...hound:** Fox hunting was a popular recreation among the rural gentry and aristocracy. The actual hunting was done by a pack of hounds, guided by a master of hounds and his assistants; the gentlemen followed on horseback. For them, the fun and the challenge lay in riding fast over open country, leaping hedgerows and streams and hopefully sticking close enough to the hounds to be "in at the kill"—that is, present when the hounds finally cornered the fox and killed it. The best rider was often given the brush or tail of the fox as a trophy.

Fox hunting, which was really a form of pell-mell, cross-country riding, could be quite dangerous for an inexperienced or overly bold rider. This helps explain Fanny Price's (MP) concern when Edmund Bertram and Henry Crawford invite her brother William to join them in a fox hunt. As usual, though, the charmed William sails through the danger with his limbs and his boyish confidence intact.

The Doctor having had his fill,
Without a word discharg'd his bill:
But, as it was the close of day,   135
He trotted briskly on his way;
And, ere the Sun withdrew his light,
An inn received him for the night.
His frame fatigu'd, his mind oppress'd,
He tiff'd[1] his punch, and went to rest. 140 [1] **tiff'd:** Drank
The morning came, when he arose   slowly.
In spirits from his calm repose;
And, while the maid prepar'd the tea,
He look'd around the room, to see
What story did the walls disclose, 145
Of human joys, of human woes.
The window quickly caught his eye,   [2] **motley:** Various,
On whose clear panes he could descry   miscellaneous.
The motley[2] works of many a Muse: [3] **I'll strive...book:**
There was enough to pick and choose;   An early reviewer
And, "faith," said he, "I'll strive to hook 150 saw this moment as
"Some of these lines into my book;[3]   a spot-on satire of
"For here there are both grave and witty, the modern tour-
"And some, I see, are very pretty."   writer, who "put[s]
From a small pocket in his coat   down in his tablets
He drew his tablets,—and he wrote 155 every thing which
Whate'er the pregnant[4] panes possess'd; he thinks will add
And these choice Lays[5] among the rest.   to the size of his
               work" (*Critical
————   *Review* [May 1813],
              547).
 "If my breast were made of glass,
 "And you could see what here doth pass, 160 [4] **pregnant:** Full of
 "Kitty, my ever charming fair!   meaning.
 "You'd see your own sweet image there." [5] **Lays:** Poems or
              songs.
————   [6] **free-booting:**
 "I once came here a free-booting,[6]   Pursuing pleasure
 "And on this fine manor went shooting; or wealth without
 "And if the 'Squire this truth denies, 165 regard to law or
 "This glass shall tell the 'Squire—he lies." responsibility. This
              freebooter is a
————   poacher.
 "Dolly's as fat as any sow,
  "And, if I'm not mistaken,

"Dolly is well-dispos'd, I trow*,
  "To trim her husband's bacon."[1]

170 [1] **trim…bacon:** The line is somewhat unclear, but may mean that Dolly trims the fat from her husband's 175 bacon to have more for herself.

———

"Jenny, while now your name I hear,
  "No transient glow my bosom heats;
"And when I meet your eye, my dear,
  "My flutt'ring heart no longer beats.
"I dream, but I no longer find
  "Your form still present to my view;
"I wake, but now my vacant mind
  "No longer waking dreams of you.
"I can find maids, in ev'ry rout,[2]
  "With smiles as false and forms as fine;
"But you must hunt the world throughout,
  "To find a heart as true as mine."

[2] **rout:** A 180 fashionable evening party.

———

"I hither came down
  "From fair London town
    "With Lucy, so mild and so kind;
185
"But Lucy grew cool,
"And call'd me a fool,
  "So I started and left her behind."

———

But as he copied quite delighted,
All that the Muse had thus indited,
190
A hungry dog, and prone to steal,
Ran off with half his breakfast meal;
While Dolly, ent'ring with a kettle,
Was follow'd by a man of mettle,
Who swore he'd have the promis'd kiss;
195
And, as he seiz'd the melting bliss,
From the hot ill-pois'd kettle's spout,
The boiling stream came pouring out,
And drove the Doctor from the muse,
By quickly filling both his shoes.
200

DOCTOR SYNTAX.
COPYING THE BIT OF THE WINDOW.

CANTO VI.

WHAT various evils man await,
In this sad, sublunary[1] state!
No sooner is he cheer'd by joy,
Than sorrows come, and pains annoy;
And scarce his lips are op'd to bless   5
The transient gleam of happiness,
Than some dark cloud obscures the sky,
And grief's sad moisture fills his eye.

  Thus, while the Doctor smiling stole
From the clear glass each witty scroll,   10
He felt, to interrupt the treat,
The scalding torment in his feet;
And, thus awaken'd from his trance,
Began to skip, and jump, and dance.
"Take off my shoes," he raving cried,   15
"And let my gaiters[2] be untied."
When Dolly with her nimble hand,
Instant obey'd the loud command;
And, as he loll'd upon the chair,
His feet and ankles soon were bare.   20
Away th' impatient damsel run,
To cure the mischief she had done;
And quick return'd with liquid store,
To rub his feet and ankles o'er:
Nor was the tender office vain,   25
That soon assuag'd the burning pain.
A tear was seen on Dolly's cheek;—
She sigh'd as if her heart would break.
"Be not, my girl, with care opprest:
"I'm now," says Syntax, "quite at rest: 30
"My anger's vanish'd with the pain,
"No more, my dear, shall I complain,

[1] **sublunary:** Relating to the earthly, mortal realm (literally, under the moon).

[2] **gaiters:** Coverings for the lower legs.

49

"Since, to get rid of my disaster,
"So fair a maid presents the plaister*."
Thus did he Dolly's care beguile,   35
And turn'd her tears into a smile:
But, while she cool'd the raging part,
She somehow warm'd the Doctor's heart;
And, as she rubb'd the ointment in,
He pinch'd her cheeks, and chuck'd her chin;   40
And, when she had redress'd his shanks,
He with a kiss bestow'd his thanks:
While gentle Dolly, nothing loath,[1]
Consenting smil'd, and took them both.
"I think," said she, "you'd better stay,   45
"Nor travel further on, to-day."
And tho' she said it with a smile,
His steady purpose to beguile,
The Doctor clos'd the kind debate,
By ord'ring Grizzle to the gate.   50
   Now, undisturb'd, he took his way,
And travell'd till the close of day;
When, to delight his wearied eyes,
Before him Oxford's tow'rs[2] arise.
"O, Alma Mater!" Syntax cried,   55
"My present boast, my early pride;
"To whose protecting care I owe
"All I've forgot, and all I know:
"Deign from your nursling to receive
"The homage that his heart can give.   60
"Hail! sacred, ever-honour'd, shades[3]
"Where oft I woo'd th' immortal maids;[4]
"Where strolling oft, at break of day,
"My feet have brush'd the dews away!
"By Isis and by Cherwell's[5] stream,   65
"How oft I wove the classic[6] dream,
"Or sought the cloisters dim, to meet
"Pale Science[7] in her lone retreat!
"The sight of you, again inspires
"My bosom with its former fires: 70
"I feel again the genial glow
"That makes me half forget the woe,

¹ **loath:** Reluctant, unwilling. "Nothing loath," of course, would be the opposite.

² **Oxford's tow'rs:** Oxford was one of the two universities in England at this time, the other being Cambridge. Most young men from the nobility and gentry spent time at one of them, though only a minority graduated. Of those who did, the vast majority, like Syntax, became clergymen. The training of clergymen, in fact, was the primary educational purpose of the universities at this time. (Jacob, 43-5)

³ **shades:** Places shaded by trees.

⁴ **immortal maids:** The nine muses of Greek mythology, who lent inspiration to poets and artists. As a student, Syntax would wake up early to wander the university's shady paths, composing poetry as he went.

⁵ **Isis…Cherwell's:** The Isis Lock and the River Cherwell are both tributaries of the Thames River, passing by Oxford University.

⁶ **classic:** Relating to the literature of the Greeks and Romans.

⁷ **Pale Science:** Knowledge of any kind gained by scholarly study, and not, as now, the study of the material universe specifically. Science was often described in the poetry of the period as pale—apparently because one pursues it indoors ("cloisters dim") without the physical exertion or animating emotion that brings color into the face.

Austen's father George and two of her brothers, James and Henry, graduated from St. John's College, Oxford, and all went on to become clergymen. George and James became fellows of the college as well, responsible for tutoring undergraduates. Austen herself would have had memories of the city: she attended a boarding school there at the age of seven.

Jane Austen's brother James also courted the muses while at Oxford. Indeed, at that time poetry seems to have been part of his life's calling. In a poem written shortly after his matriculation, he imagined himself settling down as a homely sort of poet-parson, "woo[ing] in lowly strain / The nymphs of fountain, wood or plain / To bless my peaceful lays" (Complete Poems 2). With its beautiful walks, intelligent company, and leisurely academic schedule, Oxford had a way of stirring the poetic inclinations of young men.

51

"And all my aching heart could tell,
"Since last I bid these scenes farewell."
 Thus Syntax mov'd, in sober pace,   75
Beset with academic grace;
While Grizzle bore him up the town,
And at the *Mitre*[1] set him down.

[1] the *Mitre:* A famous inn in Oxford.

The night was pass'd in sound repose,
And as the clock struck nine he rose.   80
The barber now applies his art,
To shave him clean, and make him smart:
From him he learn'd that *Dickey Bend,*
His early academic friend,
As a reward for all his knowledge,   85
Was now the Provost[2] of his college;

[2] **Provost:** The head of a college, especially one within a larger university system.

And fame declar'd that he had clear
At least twelve hundred pounds a year.
"O ho!" says Syntax, if that's true,
"I cannot, surely better do   90
"Than further progress to delay,
"And with *Friend Dickey* pass a day."
Away he hied, and soon he found him,
With all his many comforts round him.
The Provost hail'd the happy meeting,   95
And, after kind and mutual greeting,
To make inquiries he began:
And thus the conversation ran.

PROVOST.

"Good Doctor Syntax, I rejoice
"Once more to hear your well-known voice;   100
"To dine with us I hope you'll stay,
"And share a college-feast to-day.
"Full many a year is gone and past
"Since we beheld each other last:
"Fortune has kindly dealt with me,   105
"As you, my friend, may clearly see;
"And pray how has she dealt with thee?"

[3] **I took a wife:** Fellowships (teaching positions) at Oxford were generally unavailable to married men. Syntax may be implying that by marrying he threw away his chance at the comfortable, academic life that the Provost enjoys.

SYNTAX.

"Alas! alas! I've play'd the fool;
"I took a wife,[3] and keep a school;

"And, while on dainties you are fed,   110
"I scarce get butter to my bread."

PROVOST.

"For my part, I have never married,
"And grieve to hear your plans miscarried:
"I hope then, my old worthy friend,
"Your visit here your fate will mend.   115
"My services you may command;—
"I offer them with heart and hand:
"And while you think it right to stay,
"You'll make this house your home, I pray."

SYNTAX.

"I'm going further, on a scheme,
"Which you may think an idle dream;   120
"At the famed Lakes[1] to take a look,
"And of my *Journey* make a *Book*."

[1] **famed Lakes:** The lakes of the Lake District in the north of England, a popular picturesque destination.

PROVOST.

"I know full well that you have store
"Of modern as of classic* lore;   125
"And, surely, with your weight of learning,
"And all your critical discerning,
"You might produce a work of name,
"To fill your purse and give you fame.
"How oft have we together sought   130
"Whate'er the ancient sages taught!"——

SYNTAX.

"I now perceive that all your knowledge
"Is pent, my friend, within your college:
"Learning's become a very bore—
"That fashion long since has been o'er.   135
"A Bookseller may keep his carriage,
"And ask ten thousand pounds in marriage;
"May have his mansion in a square,
"And build a house for country air;
"And yet 'tis odds the fellow knows   140
"If Horace wrote in verse or prose.[1]
"Could Doctor G——[2] in chariot ride,
"And take each day his wine, beside,
"If he did not contrive to cook,
"Each year, his Tour into a book;   145
"A flippant, flashy, flow'ry style,
"A lazy morning to beguile;
"With, ev'ry other leaf, a print
"Of some fine view in *aqua-tint?*[3]
"Such is the book I mean to make,   150
"And I've no doubt the work will take;
"For tho' your wisdom may decry it,
"The simple folk will surely buy it.
"I will allow it is but trash,
"But then it furnishes the cash."   155

PROVOST.

"Why things are not the same, I fear,
"As when we both were scholars here;
"But still, I doubt not your success,
"And wish you ev'ry happiness;

William Gilpin, George Clint after Henry Walton, 1805. National Portrait Gallery.

Austen, to her credit, seems to have been mostly free of the classist fear that tradespeople were rising too quickly. Upwardly mobile families like the Coles (Em.) sometimes elicit suspicion in her novels (in the case of the Coles, from Emma herself), but they usually turn out to be no better or worse than the established gentry. The snobbery of those who insist on class lines is always more ridiculous in Austen's work than the ambition of those who would cross them.

[1] **Bookseller...prose:** Syntax complains that a mere tradesman can now rise to wealth and status without any education at all (even a schoolboy would know Horace wrote in verse). He can afford a house in town and another in the country, and he can expect his bride to bring a considerable dowry to the marriage.

[2] **Doctor G——:** William Gilpin, the foremost popularizer and codifier of picturesque aesthetics. While he was not quite as prolific as Syntax implies, he did write ten books on the picturesque over forty years, most of them recounting various tours. Gilpin died in 1804, but he was still very much on the public mind: most of his picturesque writings were republished in 1808, just before Combe began work on *The Schoolmaster's Tour.* For more on Gilpin, see pp. xxxii-xxxvii in this book.

[3] *aqua-tint:* Aquatint is a method of etching copper plates that produces the effect of shade in a printed illustration. It is done by covering a portion of the plate with a powdered resin and then submerging the plate in acid. The acid will bite into the small gaps between the grains of resin, creating channels that can hold ink. When the ink is transferred to a sheet of paper, it resembles a diluted wash. All of Rowlandson's plates in this book were shaded with aquatint.

As a teenager, Austen was an ardent admirer of William Gilpin—in contemporary terms, we might say he was her "celebrity crush." In her History of England *she classes him as one of the "first of Men" (Juv. 182); and in* Sense and Sensibility, *written during her late teens, she has Marianne speak reverently of "the taste and elegance of him who first defined what picturesque beauty was" (I.18). It must be said, of course, that both passages are partly ironic. Like Marianne, Austen adored Gilpin, but unlike Marianne, she could laugh at her adoration, too.*

"Myself, and my whole college tribe,   160
"Depend upon it, will subscribe."[1]

  At length, the bell began to call
To dinner, in the college-hall;
Nor did the guests delay to meet,
Lur'd by the bounty of the treat.   165
The formal salutations over,
Each drew his chair and seiz'd his cover;[2]
The Provost, in collegiate pride,
Plac'd Doctor Syntax by his side;
And soon they heard the hurrying feet   170
Of those that bore the smoking meat.

  Behold the dishes due appear—
Fish in the van,[3] beef in the rear;
But he who the procession led,
By some false step or awkward tread,   175
Or curs'd by some malignant pow'r,
Fell headlong on the marble floor!
Ah, heedless wight*! ah, hapless dish!
Ah! all the luxury of fish
Thus in a moment spoil'd and wasted,   180
Ah! never, never to be tasted!
But one false step begets another,
So they all tumbled one o'er t'other:
And now the pavement was bestrew'd
With roast and boil'd, and fried and stew'd.   185
The waiters squall'd, their backs bespatter'd
With scalding sauce; the dishes clatter'd
In various discord; while the brawl
Re-echo'd thro' th' astonish'd hall.
"Well," said a Don*, "as I'm a sinner,   190
"We must go elsewhere for a dinner."
" 'Tis no such thing," the *Head* replied,
"You all shall soon be satisfied:
"We are but ten; I'm sure there's plenty;
"I order'd full enough for twenty.[4]   195
"I see, my friends, the haunch unspoil'd,
"With chickens roast, and turkey boil'd;

[1] **subscribe:** When a book was published by subscription, subscribers paid in advance and then received a copy of the book upon publication.

[2] **cover:** Table settings such as napkin, fork, knife, etc.

[3] **in the van:** The phrase refers to those leading a charge or advance, in this case a culinary one.

[4] **enough for twenty:** Oxford was, and still is, famous for its sumptuous college dinners.

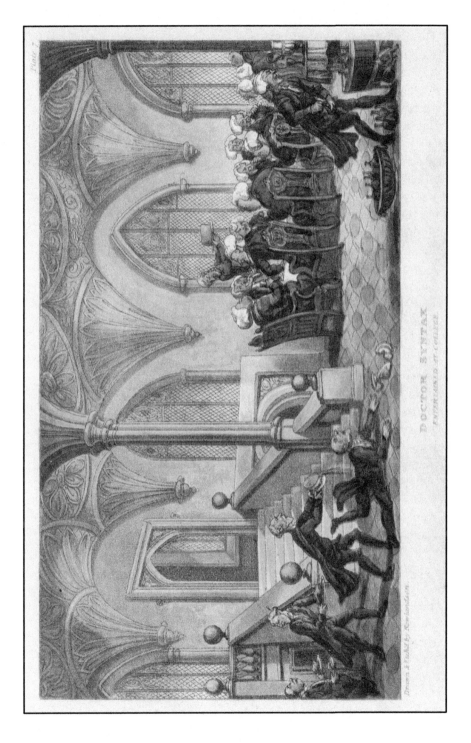

DOCTOR SYNTAX
ENTERTAINED AT COLLEGE

"The ven'son pasty is secure,
"The marrow pudding's safe and sure;
"With ham, and many good things more,   200
"And tarts, and custards, full a score.
"Sure, here's enough to cut and carve;
"To-day, I think, we shall not starve:
"But still I'll make the boobies[1] pay
"For the good things they've thrown away."   205
Thus ev'ry eye was quickly cheer'd
With all the plenty that appear'd;
They eat, they drank, they smok'd, they talk'd,
And round the college-garden walk'd:
But the time came (for time will fly)   210
When Syntax was to say—good-bye.
His tongue could scarce his feeling tell,
Could scarce pronounce the word, farewell!
The Provost too, whose gen'rous heart
In those same feelings bore a part,   215
Told him, when he should want a friend,
To write, or come, to *Dickey Bend*.
  Next morning at an early hour,
Syntax proceeded on his tour;
And, as he saunter'd on his way,   220
The scene of many a youthful day,
He thought 'twould give his book an air,
If *Oxford* were well painted there;
And, as he curious look'd around,
He saw a spot of rising ground,   225
From whence the turrets of the city
Would make a picture very pretty;
Where *Radcliffe's* dome[2] would intervene,
And *Magd'len* tower[3] crown the scene.
So Grizzle to an hedge he tied,   230
And to the spot impatient hied;
But, as he sought to choose a part
Where he might best display his art,
A wicked bull no sooner view'd him,
Than loud he roar'd, and straight pursu'd him.   235
The Doctor finding danger near,
Flew swiftly on the wings of Fear,

[1] **boobies:** Fools or blunderers.

[2] ***Radcliffe's* dome:** Radcliffe Camera, a library in Oxford famous for its cylindrical, domed design. An artist sketching the city from a distance would be sure to include it.

[3] ***Magd'len* tower:** The bell tower of Magdalen College and another Oxford landmark.

And nimbly clamber'd up a tree,
That gave him full security;
But as he ran to save his bacon,   240
By hat and wig he was forsaken;
His *sketch-book* too he left behind,
A prey to the unlucky wind;
While Grizzle, startled by the rout,[1]   [1] **rout:** Commotion.
Broke from the hedge, and pranc'd about.   245
Syntax, still trembling with affright,
Clung to the tree with all his might;
Then call'd for help—and help was near,
For dogs, and men, and boys appear;
So that his foe was forc'd to yield,   250
And leave him master of the field.
No more of roaring bulls afraid,
He left the tree's protecting shade;
And, as he pac'd the meadow round,
His hat, his wig, his book he found.   255
"Come, my old girl," the Doctor said;
The faithful steed the call obey'd;
So Grizzle once more he bestrode,
Nor look'd behind,—but off he rode.

CANTO VII.

FIX'D in cogitation deep,
Adown the hill and up the steep,
Along the moor and through the wood,
Syntax his pensive way pursued:
And now his thoughts began to roam   5
To the good woman left at home;
How she employ'd the passing day
When her fond mate was far away:
For they possess'd, with all their pother,[1]
A sneaking kindness for each other.   10
Proud of her husband's stock of learning,
His classic* skill and deep discerning,
No tongue she suffer'd to dethrone
His fond importance—but her own.
Besides, she was a very bee   15
In bustle and in industry;
And tho a pointed sting she bore,
That sometimes made the Doctor sore,
She help'd to make the household thrive,
And brought home honey to the hive.   20
He too had not forgot her charms,
When first he took her to his arms;
For, if Report relates the truth,
She was a beauty in her youth:—
The charming Dolly was well known   25
To be the toast of all the town;
And, tho' full many a year had flown
Since this good dame was twenty-one,
She still retain'd the same air and mien
Of the nice girl she has once been.   30
For these, and other charms beside,
She was indeed the Doctor's pride;

[1] **pother:** Fuss.

61

Nay, he would sometimes on her gaze
With the fond looks of former days;—
And, whatsoe'er she did or said,   35
He kept his silence, and obey'd.
Besides, he thus his mind consol'd:—
" 'Tis classical* to be a scold;
"For as the antient tomes record,
"Xantippe's tongue[1] was like a sword: 40
"She was about my Dolly's age,
"And was the wife too of a sage.
"Thus Socrates, in days of yore,
"The self-same persecution bore:
"Nor shall I blush to share the fate   45
"Of one so good,—of one so great."

   'Twas now five days since they had parted,
And he was ever tender-hearted:
Whene'er he heard the wretched sigh,
He felt a Christian sympathy;   50
For tho' he play'd the demi-god
Among his boys, with rule and rod;[2]
What, tho' he spoke in pompous phrase,
And kept the vulgar in amaze:
Tho' self-important he would stride   55
Along the street with priestly pride;
Tho' his strange figure would provoke
The passing smile, the passing joke;
Among the high, or with the low,
Syntax had never made a foe;   60
And, tho' the jest of all he knew,
Yet while they laugh'd they lov'd him too:[3]
No wonder then, so far from home,
His head would shake, the sigh would come.—
Thus he went gently on his way,   65
Till the sun mark'd declining day.

   But Thought as well as Grief is dry,
And, lo! a friendly cot[4] was nigh,
Whose sign, high dangling in the air,
Invites the trav'ller to repair,   70

"X: Xantippe," George Cruikshank, *The Comic Alphabet*, 1836.

^{1} **Xantippe's tongue:** Xantippe or Xanthippe, the wife of the philosopher Socrates, was famous for her bad temper and her sharp tongue.

^{2} **rule and rod:** Symbols of a schoolmaster's authority. The rule (ruler) and the birch rod were often used for spanking.

^{3} **Among the high...lov'd him too:** This passage marks a turning point in Combe's conception of Doctor Syntax. Until now, Syntax has been a hapless and even somewhat cynical character, fed up with his clerical work. Here, he emerges as a conscientious and kind-hearted (though still eccentric) clergyman, sympathizing with the cares of all his parishioners, whether rich or poor, and loved by them in return. He remains a laughing-stock, but a laughing-stock who also inspires affection and esteem.

^{4} **cot:** Cottage.

This new Syntax is much closer to Austen's ideal clergyman, one who doesn't merely preach on Sundays, but who "live[s] among his parishioners and prove[s] himself by constant attention their well-wisher and friend" (MP II.7).

Where he in comfort may regale
With cooling pipe and foaming ale.
The Doctor gave the loud command,
And sees the Host beside him stand;
Then quits his steed with usual state,   75
And passes thro' the wicket-gate:
The Hostess opes the willing door,
And then recounts the humble store
Which her poor cottage could afford,
To place upon the frugal board.   80
The home-spun napkin soon was laid,
The table all its ware display'd;
The well-broil'd rasher then appear'd,
And with fresh eggs his stomach cheer'd;
The crusty pie, with apples stor'd,   85
Was plac'd in order on the board;
And liquor, that was brew'd at home,
Among the rest was seen to foam.
The Doctor drank,—the Doctor eat,
Well-pleas'd to find so fair a treat;   90
Then to his pipe he kindly took,
And, with a condescending[1] look,
Call'd on the Hostess to relate
What was the village name, and state;
And to whose office it was given   95
To teach them all the way to Heav'n.[2]

HOSTESS.

  The land belongs to 'Squire Bounty,
No better man lives in the county:
I wish the Rector were the same,
One Doctor Squeeze'em[3] is his name;   100
But we ne'er see him—more's the shame!
And while in wealth he cuts and carves,[4]
The worthy Curate prays and starves.

SYNTAX.

  I truly wish that he were here,
To take a pipe, and share my beer;   105
I know what 'tis, as well as he,
To serve a man I never see.

"She had even vouchsafed to suggest some shelves in the closets upstairs," C.E. Brock, in *Pride and Prejudice* (J.M. Dent & Sons, 1907). British Library.

Today, we use this word to describe an insulting, arrogant generosity. Interestingly enough, one can see this modern sense emerging in Pride and Prejudice. *Austen uses the word no fewer than ten times with respect to the high-and-mighty Lady Catherine de Bourgh. It always seems to be a compliment (Mr. Collins, who venerates Lady Catherine, uses it six times), but as the reader sees more of her character, the word acquires a marked irony.*

[1] **condescending:** In Austen's time, condescension was actually a virtue—it meant a generous attention bestowed by a superior on an inferior. Syntax, who readily falls into conversation with common people and takes a friendly interest in their concerns, is "condescending" in this older, positive sense of the word.

[2] **whose office...Heav'n:** Syntax asks who is the local clergyman.

It was a clergyman's responsibility to collect his tithes. Some were lenient, perhaps waiving tithes for the poor, while others were more exacting. Lucy Steele (SS), after her fiancé is given the living of Delaford, is determined that the parish's "tythes should be raised to the utmost" (III.5). While this would likely raise her future husband's income, it might also poison relations between him and his parishioners.

[3] **Doctor Squeeze'em:** The satirical name may refer to the rector's rigorous collection of tithes, which (as seems likely) he "squeezes" out of his parishioners. He also "squeezes" his curate, demanding much work for little pay.

[4] **cuts and carves:** Refers to the carving of meat.

Just as he spoke, the Curate came:—
This, this is he! exclaim'd the dame.
Syntax his brother Parson greeted,   110
And begg'd him to be quickly seated.
"Come, take a pipe, and taste the liquor,
" 'Tis good enough for any Vicar."

CURATE.

Alas! Sir, I'm no Vicar;—I,
Bound to an humble Curacy,   115
With all my care can scarce contrive
To keep my family alive.
While the fat Rector can afford
To eat and drink like any Lord:[1]
But know, Sir, I'm a man of letters,[2]   120
And ne'er speak evil of my betters.

SYNTAX.

That's good;—but, when we suffer pain,
'Tis Nature's office to complain;
And when the strong oppress the weak,
Justice, tho' blind, will always speak.   125
Tell me, have you explain'd your case,
With due humility and grace?
The great and wealthy must be flatter'd,
They love with praise to be bespatter'd:
Indeed, I cannot see the harm,   130
If thus you can their favour charm:
If by fine phrases you can bend
The pride of Pow'r to be your friend.

CURATE.

I wrote, I'm sure, in humblest style,
And prais'd his goodness all the while: 135
I begg'd, as things were grown so dear,
He'd raise my pay ten pounds a year,
I urg'd that I had children five,[3]
The finest little bairns alive;
While their poor, fond, and faithful mother,   140
Would soon present me with another;

Mary Crawford (MP) *makes a similar critique of the clergy. A well-paid clergyman, she says, does nothing "but eat, drink, and grow fat. […] His curate does all the work, and the business of his own life is to dine" (I.11). Edmund takes issue with the caricature, but concedes that in the case of Dr. Grant, there is some truth to it.*

¹ **Bound…any Lord:** Clerical satires of the period often contrasted a feasting rector or vicar with a starving curate, as in the paired illustrations below.

² **man of letters:** A scholar and a gentleman.

"A Tuck Out" and "A Pic Nic," from the series *Feasting Scraps*, Charles Williams, 1824. Lewis Walpole Library. Two vicars and their families dine sumptuously in the first image, while a curate and his family gnaw bones in the second. A caption informs us that the curate earns just £30 ($4,320) a year, the same income as Doctor Syntax.

³ **children five:** In literature and art, poor curates were often depicted with large families.

Mrs. Jennings (SS), *who assumes Edward will become a curate, predicts an inconveniently large family: "they will have a child every year! […] how poor they will be!" (III.2)*

And, as the living brought him, clear,
At least a thousand pounds a year,[1]
He'd grant the favour I implore,
Nor let me starve upon threescore.

SYNTAX.

Now I should like, without delay,
To hear what this rich man could say;
For I can well perceive, my friend,
That you did not obtain your end.

CURATE.

The postman soon a letter brought,
Which cost me sixpence, and a groat;[2]
Nor can your friendly heart suggest
The rudeness which the page express'd.
"Such suits as your's may well miscarry,
"For beggars should not dare to marry;
"At least, for I will not deceive you,
"I never, never will relieve you;
"And, if you trouble me, be sure
"You shall be ousted from the Cure."[3]
But I shall now, good Sir, refrain,
Because I know 'twould give you pain,
From telling all that, in his spite,
The arch old scoundrel chose to write;
But know, Sir, I'm a man of letters,
And never will abuse my betters.

SYNTAX.

Zounds![4]—'tis enough to make one swear,
Nor can I such a monster bear:
But, think, my friend, on that great day
Of strict account, when he must pay
For all his cruelty and lies—
When he shall sink, and you will rise.

CURATE.

The terms, I own, are not quite civil,
But he's the offspring of the devil;
And, when the day of life is past,
He'll with his father dwell at last:

145

150

155

160

165

170

175

[1] **thousand pounds a year:** About $144,000 in 2024 money. Rectors' incomes varied greatly, but the average was closer to £300 ($43,200).

[2] **cost me…groat:** The recipient usually paid the postage. The high postage of this letter (ten pence or $6 today) suggests it has traveled about 200 miles. Doctor Squeeze'em lives nowhere near his parish.

[3] **ousted from the Cure:** Curates lacked security in their positions and could be dismissed at the discretion of the parish priest.

[4] **Zounds:** A mild oath, formed by contracting "God's wounds."

But know, Sir, I'm a man of letters,
And ne'er wish evil to my betters.

   'Twas thus they talk'd, and drank their ale,
Till the dim shades of eve prevail;

When Syntax settled each demand,[1]   180   **[1] settled each**
And while he held the Curate's hand,   **demand:** Paid the
Bid him be stout, and not despair—   bill.
"The poor are God's peculiar care:
"You're not the only one my friend,
"Who has with evil to contend:—   185
"Resign yourself to what is given:
"Be good, and leave the rest to Heaven."
Syntax, we've said, was tender hearted,—
He dropp'd a tear, and then departed.

   The ev'ning low'r'd*:—a drizzly rain   190
Had spread a mist o'er all the plain;

Besides, the home-brew'd beer began
To prey upon the inward man;
And Syntax, muddled, did not know
Or where he was, or where to go.   195
An active horseman by him trotted,
And Syntax was not so besotted
But he could hiccup out "My friend,
"Do tell me if this way will tend
"To bring me to some place of rest?"   200
"Yes," 'twas replied,—"the very best
"Of all our inns, within a mile,
"Will soon your weariness beguile."
Who should this be but 'Squire *Bounty*,
So much belov'd throughout the county;   205
And he resolv'd, by way of jest,
To have the Parson for his guest;
So on he gallop'd, to prepare
His people for the friendly snare.
The Doctor came in tipsy state,   } 210
The 'Squire receiv'd him at the gate,
And to a parlour led him straight;
Then plac'd him in an easy chair,
And ask'd to know his pleasure there.

SYNTAX.

  Landlord, I'm sadly splash'd with mire,   215
And chill'd with rain; so light a fire;
And tell the Ostler* to take care
Of that good beast, my Grizzle mare;
And what your larder can afford,
Pray place it quickly on the board.   220

'SQUIRE.

  We've butcher's meat, of ev'ry kind;
But if that is not to your mind,
There's poultry, Sir, and if you please,
Our cook excels in fricassees.[1]

SYNTAX.

  Tell me, my honest friend, I pray,   225
What kind of fowl or fish are they?

[1] **fricassees:** Dishes made from chopped meat cooked or dressed in a flavorful sauce.

70

Besides, my very civil Host,
I wish to know what they will cost;
For a poor Parson can't afford
To live on dainties like a Lord.   230

     'SQUIRE.
The clergy, Sir, when here they stay,
Are never, never ask'd to pay;
I love the Church, and, for its sake,
I ne'er make bills, or reck'nings take;
Proud if its ministers receive   235
The little that I have to give.

     SYNTAX.
Why then, my friend, you're never dull;
Your inn, I trow*, is always full:—
'Tis a good rule, must be confest,
But, tho' I blink, I see a jest.   240

     'SQUIRE.
No, Sir; you see the cloth is laid,
And not a farthing¹ to be paid.

     SYNTAX.
I find my head's not very clear;
My eyes see double too, I fear;
For all these things can never be   245
Prepared for such a guest as me:
A banquet, it must be allow'd,
Of which Olympus might be proud.

Thus Syntax eat and drank his fill,
Regardless of the morrow's bill;   250
He rang the bell, and call'd the waiters
To take his shoes off, and his gaiters.
"Go tell the maid to shew the bed,
"Where I may lay my aching head:
"Here, take my wig, and bring a cap,   255
"My eyelids languish for a nap:
"No court'sying, pray; I want no fawning,
"For I shall break my jaws with yawning."

¹ **farthing:** A quarter of a penny and the smallest unit of money at the time.

71

Now Kitty, to adorn his crown,
Brought him a night-cap of her own;   260
And, having put it on, she bound it
With a pink ribbon round and round it.
In this fine guise was Syntax led
Up the best stairs, and put to bed.
Tho' mirth prevail'd the house throughout,   265
Tho' it was all one revel rout,[1]
He heard it not, nor did he know
The merriment he caus'd below;
For, with fatigue and wine oppress'd,
He grunted, groan'd, and went to rest.   270
But when the sun in Thetis' lap,
Had taken out his usual nap,—[2]
When Syntax woke, and look'd around,
The sight his senses did confound.
He saw that he had laid his head   275
Within a fine-wrought silken bed:
A gaudy carpet grac'd the floor,
And gilded mouldings deck'd the door;
Nor did the mirror fail to shew
His own sweet form from top to toe.   280

[1] **revel rout:** Scene of uproarious laughter. Combe may have intended *level* instead of *revel.*

[2] **when the sun...nap:** That is, "when the sun rose." Thetis was a sea nymph and, as here, the sea itself personified.

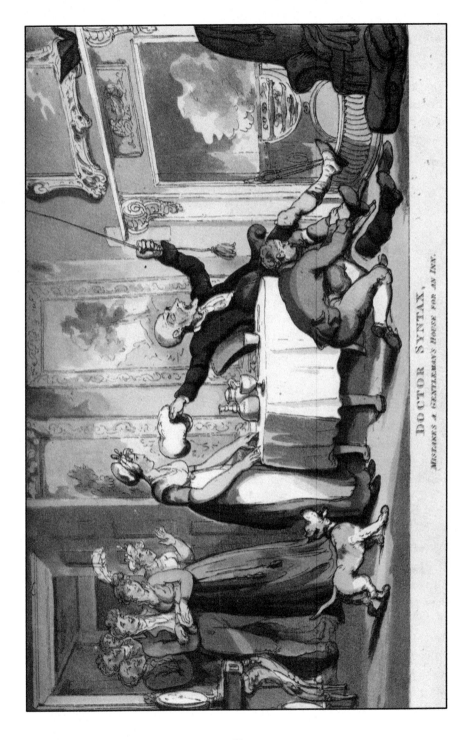

DOCTOR SYNTAX,

MISTAKES A GENTLEMAN'S HOUSE FOR AN INN.

"If I," said he, "remember right,
"I was most lordly drunk last night:
"And, as the Tinker in the play[1]
"Was taken, as dead-drunk he lay,
"And made a Lord for half a day ;   285
"I think that some one has made free
"To play the self-same trick with me;
"But I'll contrive to be possest
"Of this same secret when I'm drest:
"I'll find it out—I'll ring the bell;   290
"The chambermaid the truth may tell."
She soon appear'd, and court'sying low;
Requested his commands to know.—
"When and how did I come here?
"You'll be so good to say my dear."   295
"—You came last night, not very late,
"About the time the clock stuck eight;
"And I have heard the servants say,
"They thought that you had lost your way:"
"—Inform me, also, how you call   300
"This noble inn?"—" 'Tis *Welcome Hall.*"
"And pray, who have you in the house?"
"We've 'Squire Bounty and his spouse;
"With Lady and Sir William Hearty,
"And, if you choose, you'll join the party,   305
"Indeed I'm order'd to request
"That you will be their morning guest."

   To question more he did not stay,
But bid the damsel shew the way.
O! 'twas a very pleasant meeting;   310
The Landlord gave an hearty greeting,
And plac'd the Doctor in a chair,
Between two ladies, young and fair.
Syntax, well-pleas'd began to prate,
And all his history relate;   315
While mirth and laughter loud prevail,
As he let forth the curious tale.
At length the 'Squire explain'd the joke;
When thus the Doctor quaintly spoke:—

[1] **Tinker in the play:** A reference to Shakespeare's *Taming of the Shrew,* in which a lord tricks a drunken tinker into believing he is a nobleman.

"I beg, Sir, no excuse you'll make,   320
"Your merriment I kindly take;
"And only wish the gods would give
"Such jesting every day I live."

The ladies press'd his longer stay,
But Syntax said—he must away;   325
So Grizzle soon her master bore,
Some new adventure to explore.

CANTO VIII.

"IN ev'ry way, in ev'ry sense,
"Man is the care of Providence;[1]
"And, whensoe'er he goeth wrong,
"The errors to himself belong:
"Nor do we always judge aright   5
"Of Fortune's favours, or her spite.
"How oft with pleasure we pursue
"Some glitt'ring phantom in our view;
"Not rightly seen or understood,
"We chase it as a real good: 10
"At length the air-born vision flies,
"And each fond expectation dies!
"Sometimes the clouds appear to low'r*,
"And threat Misfortune's direful hour:
"We tremble at th' approaching blast;   15
"Each hope is fled—we look aghast;
"When lo! the darkness disappears,
"The glowing sun all Nature cheers:
"The drooping heart again acquires
"Its former joys, its former fires.   20
"Last night I wander'd o'er the plain,
"Thro' unknown ways and beating rain,
"Nor thought 'twould be my lot to fall
"On such an inn as *Welcome Hall;*
"Indeed with truth I cannot say   25
"When there I came I lost my way,
"Where all was good, and nought to pay."[2]

Thus Syntax, with reflection fraught,
Soliloquiz'd the moral thought;
While Grizzle, all alive and gay,   30
Ambled along the ready way.

[1] **care of Providence:** The protective care of God.

[2] **Indeed...to pay:** Syntax implies that Providence must have guided him to Welcome Hall, given the extraordinary comforts he found there, and that therefore he was never really lost.

Last night she found it no disaster
To share the fortune of her master;
She 'mong the finest hunters[1] stood,
And shared with them the choicest food;   35
In a fine roomy stable plac'd,
With ev'ry well-trimm'd clothing grac'd,
Poor Grizzle was as fair a joke
To all the merry stable-folk
As the good Doctor's self had been,   40
To the kind gentry of the inn.

Enrapt by Contemplation's pow'r,
Syntax forgot the fleeting hour;
Till, looking round, he saw the sun
Had past his bright meridian run.
A shepherd-boy he now espied,
Strolling along the highway side;
And, on his wand'ring flock intent,
The stripling[2] whistled as he went.
"My honest lad, perhaps you know   50
"What distance I shall have to go,
"Before my eager eyes may greet
"Some place where I may drink and eat."

"Continue, Master, o'er the down,
"And soon you'll reach the neighb'ring town; 55
"In less, I think, than half an hour,
"You'll pass by yonder lofty tow'r;
"Keep onward by the churchyard-wall,
"And soon you'll see an house of call:[3]
"The sign's a dragon,—there you'll find   60
"Eating and drinking to your mind."
Across the down the Doctor went,
And towards the church his way he bent.
"Thus," Syntax said, "when man is hurl'd
"Upwards and downwards in the world;   65
"When some strong impulse makes him stray
"From Virtue's path to Folly's way,
"The church, Religion's holy seat,
"Will guide to peace his wand'ring feet.

[1] **hunters:** Horses bred and trained for hunting, generally more expensive than riding or carriage horses.

[2] **stripling:** A youth.

[3] **house of call:** A place—often an inn—where tradesmen would assemble when out of work, ready to be called upon by employers.

"But, hark! the death-bell's solemn toll 70
"Tells the departure of a soul;
"The Sexton[1] too, I see prepares
"The place where end all human cares.
"Behold a crowd of tombs appear:
"I may find something curious here: 75
"Oft-times poetic flow'rs are found
"To flourish in sepulchral ground. [2]
"I'll just walk in and take a look,
"And pick up matter for my book.
"The living, some wise man has said, 80
"Delight in reading of the dead.
"What golden gains my book would boast,
"If I could meet a chatty ghost;
"Who would some news communicate
"Of its unknown and present state: 85
"Some pallid figure in a shroud,
"Or sitting on a murky cloud;
"Or kicking up a new-made grave,
"And screaming forth some horrid stave;
"Or bursting from the hollow tomb, 90
"To tell of bloody deeds to come:
"Or adverse skeletons embattling,
"With ghastly grins, and bones a rattling;
"Something to make the Misses stare,
"And force upright their curly hair; 95
"To cause their pretty forms to shake,
"And make them doubt if they're awake;
"And thus to tonish[3] folks present,
"*The Picturesque of Sentiment.*[4]
"But 'tis, I fear, some hours too soon— 100
"Ghosts slumber all the afternoon:
"I'll ask the Sexton if, at night,
"I may perchance pick up a spright."

  The Doctor in canonic state,[5]
Now op'd at once the churchyard-gate; 105
While Grizzle too thought fit to pass,
Who knew the taste of churchyard-grass.

¹ **Sexton:** Officer of the parish church whose duties included the maintenance of the church grounds and the digging of graves.

² **poetic flow'rs...sepulchral ground:** A reference to epitaphs, which were often in verse. Travel writers would often visit churchyards in the course of their tours to gaze on monuments and record curious or affecting epitaphs.

Even the retiring Fanny Price (MP) seems to have caught a bit of the epitaph-hunting bug: she is disappointed to find "no inscriptions" in the chapel at Sotherton (I.9). "This is not my idea of a chapel," she whispers to Edmund.

Illustration by Charles Landseer for an 1834 edition of Thomas Grey's "Elegy Written in a Country Churchyard" (1751). The poem inspired widespread interest in churchyard scenes, including epitaphs. This drawing shows the poet meditating on the "uncouth rhymes" inscribed on the tombstones.

³ **tonish:** Fashionable.

⁴ ***The Picturesque of Sentiment:*** Syntax appears to be saying that the frightened young women, with their hair standing on end, will themselves present a picturesque spectacle. Picturesque scenes were certainly thought to evoke strong emotions, but the idea that these emotions themselves might be picturesque is likely a comical extrapolation of Combe's.

⁵ **in canonic state:** Solemnly, in his character as a clergyman.

The image of a young lady wrought to a state of high terror by her reading recalls Catherine Morland (NA) in Bath, indulging in "the luxury of a raised, restless, and frightened imagination over the pages of Udolpho" (I.7). In the period, young unmarried women were thought to be especially susceptible to these sorts of intense reading experiences. Austen tweaks this gendered stereotype, however, by later having Henry Tilney admit to a very similar experience: "I remember finishing [Udolpho] in two days— my hair standing on end the whole time" (I.14).

"Sir," cried the Sexton, "let me say
"That you must take your mare away,
"Or else, believe me, I am bound   110
"To lead her quickly to the pound*."

　"You do mistake, my honest friend—
" 'Tis a foul wrong that you intend;
"A Parson's mare will claim a right
"In a churchyard to take a bite;   115
"And, as I'm come to meditate
"Among these signs of human fate,
"I beg you will not make a riot,
"But let the poor beast feed in quiet."
No more the conscious Sexton said,   120
But urg'd[1] his labours for the dead;
While Syntax cull'd, with critic care,
What the sad Muse had written there.

EPITAPHS.
　Here lies poor Thomas and his wife,
Who led a pretty jarring life;   125
But all is ended, do you see?
He holds his tongue, and so does she.

　If drugs and physic[2] could but save
Us mortals from the dreary grave,
'Tis known that I took full enough,   130
Of the Apothecary's stuff,[3]
To have prolong'd life's busy feast
To a full century at least;
But, spite of all the Doctor's skill,
Of daily draught[4] and nightly pill,   135
Reader, as sure as you're alive,
I was sent here at twenty-five.

　Within this tomb a lover lies,
Who fell an early sacrifice   ⎫
To Dolly's unrelenting eyes.   ⎬   140
For Dolly's charms poor Damon[5] burn'd— ⎭
Disdain the cruel maid return'd:

80

"The Quack Doctor," Thomas Rowlandson, 1814. For *The English Dance of Death*. British Museum. Behind the curtain, Death mixes a concoction in a mortar and pestle labelled "slow poison."

¹ **urg'd:** Vigorously performed.

² **physic:** Medicine.

³ **Apothecary's stuff:** Apothecaries were sellers of drugs and medicines. Medical satires of the time often mocked such treatments as ineffective or downright harmful, which, indeed, they often were.

⁴ **draught:** A dose of liquid medicine.

⁵ **Dolly's… Damon:** Dolly and Damon were common names in pastoral poetry for young lovers.

Austen does not appear to have placed much trust in "Apothecary's stuff" either. The Parker sisters (San.), not unlike the subject of this epitaph, have undermined their health by taking a great deal of "medicine, especially quack medicine" (LM 192). At one point the narrator, rather cheekily, attributes their worn appearance to "illness and medicine"— essentially drawing no distinction between the two (LM 193).

But, as she danc'd in May-day[1] pride,
Dolly fell down, and Dolly died,
And now she lays by Damon's side. } 145
Be not hard-hearted then, ye fair!
Of Dolly's hapless fate beware!
For sure you'd better go to bed
To one alive, than one who's dead.[2]

———

Beneath the sod the soldier sleeps, 150
  Whom cruel War refus'd to spare:—
Beside his grave the maiden weeps,
  And glory plants the laurel[3] there.
Honour is the warrior's meed,[4]
  Or spar'd to live or doom'd to die; 155
Whether 'tis his lot to bleed,
  Or join the shout of Victory;
Alike the laurel to the truly brave
That binds the brow or consecrates the grave.[5]

———

Beneath this stone her ashes rest, 160
Whose mem'ry fills my aching breast;
She sleeps unconscious of the tear
That tells the tale of sorrow here;
But still the hope allays my pain
That we may live and love again: 165
Love with pure seraphic[6] fire,
That never, never, shall expire.

———

Syntax the Sexton now address'd,
As on his spade he lean'd to rest.

SYNTAX.
"We both, my friend, pursue one trade; 170
"I for the living, you the dead.
"For whom that grave do you prepare,
"With such keen haste, and cheerful air?"

SEXTON.
"And please your Rev'rence, *Lawyer Thrust,*
"Thank Heav'n, will moulder here to dust: 175

[1] **May-day:** The first of May, traditionally an occasion for springtime festivities.

[2] **you'd better go to bed...dead:** This call on young women to enjoy love while they can recalls Andrew Marvell's *To His Coy Mistress* (1681).

[3] **laurel:** In ancient Rome, victorious generals were given laurel wreaths.

[4] **meed:** Reward.

[5] **Alike the laurel...grave:** In other words, the truly brave do not care whether they live or die, as long as they act with honor and courage in battle.

[6] **seraphic:** Angelic. The idea that true lovers will be reunited in heaven is a major theme in Combe's novel *Original Love Letters between a Lady of Quality and a Person of Inferior Station* (1784).

Drawn & Etch'd by Rowlandson

DOCTOR SYNTAX
AMONG THE TOMB STONES.

"Never before did I take measure
"Of any grave with half the pleasure:
"And, when within this hole he's laid,
"I'll ram the earth down with my spade:
"I'll take good care he shall not rise,   180
"Till summon'd to the last assize;[1]
"And, when he sues for Heaven's grace,
"I would not wish to take his place.
"Now that his foul misdoings cease,
"I hope we all shall live in peace.—   185
"He, once on cruel deed intent,
"Seiz'd on my goods for want of rent:
"Nay, I declare, as I'm a sinner,
"He took away the children's dinner;
"For, as they sat around the table,   190
"Eating as fast as they were able,
"He seiz'd the dishes, great and small,
"The children's bread, and milk, and all!
"The urchins cried, the mother pray'd,
"I beg'd his rigour might be stay'd   195
"Till I could on our Parson call,[2]
"Who would engage to pay it all;
"But he disdain'd a Parson's word,
"And mock'd the suit which I preferr'd.
"He knew a better way to thrive;   200
"To pay two pounds—by taking five.[3]
"Bursting with rage, I knock'd him down,
"And broke the cruel rascal's crown;
"For which in county-gaol I lay,
"Half-starving, many a bitter day.   205
"But our good Parson brought relief,
"And kindly sooth'd a mother's grief:
"He, while in prison I remain'd,
"My little family sustain'd;
"And, when I was from durance[4] free,   210
"Made me his Sexton, as you see.
"But Doctor Worthy, he is gone;—
"You'll read his virtues on the stone
"That's plac'd aloft upon the wall,
"Where you may see the ivy crawl: 215

[1] **last assize:** A reference to the Last Judgment, during which God will weigh the good and evil in each soul and determine rewards and punishments.

"Distraining for Rent," engraving by Abraham Raimbach, 1828, after a painting by Sir David Wilkie, 1815, YCBA.

[2] **Till I could on our Parson call:** Clergymen sometimes served as advocates for tenants who found themselves at odds with their landlords. They were well positioned for the role. Their pastoral work often gave them a nuanced and sympathetic understanding of the situations of their parishioners, while their education and status as gentlemen gave them standing among the gentry.

Mr. Collins (PP) falls short in this respect. Instead of advocating for his parishioners, he spies on them, reporting their "minutest concerns" to their overbearing landlady, Lady Catherine (II.7).

[3] **pay two pounds…five:** Lawyer Thrust may mean that he will seize five pounds' ($720) worth of goods, even though his tenant only owes two.

[4] **durance:** Imprisonment.

"The good man's ashes rest below;—
"He's gone where all the righteous go.
"I dug his grave with many a moan,
"And almost wish'd it were my own.
"I daily view the earthy bed,   220
"Where death has laid his rev'rend head;
"And, when I see a weed appear,
"I pluck it up, and shed a tear!
"The parish griev'd, for not an eye
"In all its large extent was dry,   225
"Save one:—but such a kindly grace
"Ne'er deck'd the *Lawyer's* iron face.
"The aged wept a friend long known,
"The young a parent's loss bemoan:
"While we, alas! shall long deplore   230
"The bounteous patron of the poor."

    The Doctor heard, with tearful eye,
The Sexton's grateful eulogy:
Then sought the stone with gentle tread,
As fearing to disturb the dead,   235
And thus, in measur'd tones, he read:—

    "For fifty years the Pastor trod
"The way commanded by his God;
"For fifty years his flock he fed
"With that divine celestial bread[1]   240
"Which nourishes the better part,
"And fortifies man's failing heart.
"His wide, his hospitable door,
"Was ever open to the poor;
"While he was sought, for counsel sage,[2]   245
"By ev'ry rank and ev'ry age.
"That counsel sage he always gave,
"To warn, to strengthen, and to save:
"He sought the sheep that went astray,[3]
"And pointed out the better way.   250
"But while he with his smiles approv'd
"The virtue he so dearly lov'd,

[1] **divine celestial bread:** A reference to Christ. "I am the living bread which came down from heaven: if any man eat of this bread, he shall live for ever" (John 6:51).

[2] **counsel sage:** Wise advice.

[3] **sought...astray:** A reference to the parable of the lost sheep (Mat. 18:10-14), which illustrates the love of Christ for sinners.

"He did not spare the harsher part,
"To probe the ulcer in the heart: 255
"He sternly gave the wholesome pain
"That brought it back to health again.
"Thus, the Commands of Heav'n his guide,
"He liv'd,—and then in peace he died."

SYNTAX.
  "Pray tell me, friend, who now succeeds   260
"This Pastor, fam'd for virtuous deeds?"

SEXTON.
  "A very worthy pious man,
"Who does us all the good he can;
"But he, good Sir, has got a wife,"

SYNTAX.
"Who may perhaps disturb his life;   265
"A tongue sometimes engenders strife."

SEXTON.
  "No:—she's a worthy woman too;—
"But then they've children not a few;
"I think it is the will of Heaven
"That they are bless'd with six or seven;   270
"And then you will agree with me,
"That home's the scene of charity."[1]

SYNTAX.
  " 'Tis true;—nor can your Parson preach
"A sounder doctrine than you teach.
"And now, good Sexton, let me ask,   275
"While you perform your mortal task,
"As day and night you frequent tread
"These dreary mansions of the dead,
"If you, in very truth, can boast
"That you have ever seen a ghost?"   280

SEXTON.
  "Your Rev'rence, no!—Though some folks say
"That such things have been seen as they.
"Old women talk, in idle chat,
"Of ghosts and goblins, and all that;

[1] **home's...charity:** A rephrasing of the proverb "charity begins at home."

87

"While, round the glimm'ring fire at night, 285
"They fill their hearers with affright.
" 'Tis said that Doctor Worthy walks,
"And up and down the church-yard stalks;
"That often, when the moon shines bright,
"His form appears all clad in white: 290
"But to his soul it is not given
"To walk on earth,—for that's in Heav'n.
"I, at all hours, have cross'd this place,
"And ne'er beheld a spirit's face.
"Once, I remember, late at night, 295
"I something saw, both large and white,
"Which made me stop, and made me stare,—
"But 'twas the Parson's grizzle mare.
"Such things as these, I do believe,
"The foolish people oft deceive; 300
"And then the parish-gossips talk,
"How witches dance, and spectres walk."

SYNTAX.
"Your reasoning I much commend;
"So fare you well, my honest friend.
"If we act right, we need not dread 305
"Either the living or the dead:
"The spirit that disturbs our rest
"Is a bad conscience in our breast;[1]
"With that a man is doubly curst:"—

SEXTON.
"That spirit haunted *Lawyer Thrust*." 310

SYNTAX.
"His race is run, his work is o'er—
"The wicked man can sin no more:
"He's gone where justice will be done
"To all who liv'd beneath the sun:
"And, tho' he wrong'd you when alive, 315
"Let not your vengeance thus survive:
"Forgive him, now he's laid so low,—
"Nor trample on a fallen foe.

[1] **The spirit
...breast:** Even though earlier he was excited to collect ghost stories for his book, it is clear that Syntax, an orthodox clergyman, never really believed in them.

"Once more farewell! but, ere we part,
"There's something that will cheer your heart."[1]   320

SEXTON.

"Your Rev'rence, 'twill be some time yet
"Ere I forgive;—but, to forget,—
"No, no, for tho' I may forgive,
"I can't forget him while I live.
"For your good gift, kind Heav'n I bless,   325
"And wish you health and happiness;
"I thank my God, each coming day,
"For what he gives and takes away:[2]
"And now I thank Him, good and just,
"That he has taken *Lawyer Thrust*."   330

Syntax along the village pass'd,
And to the Dragon came at last;
Where as the shepherd-boy had said,
There seem'd to be a busy trade:
And, seated in an easy chair,   335
He found that all he wish'd was there.

[1] **There's...heart:** Syntax gives the Sexton some money.

[2] **I thank...takes away:** A reference to Job 1:21: "The LORD gave, and the LORD hath taken away; blessed be the name of the LORD."

89

CANTO IX.

ALONG the varying road of Life,
In calm content, in toil or strife—,
At morn or noon, by night or day,
As time conducts him on his way,—
How oft doth man, by care oppress'd,   5
Find in an inn a place of rest?
Whether intent on worldly views,
He, in deep thought, his way pursues;
Whether, by airy Pleasure led,
Or by Hope's fond delusions fed,   10
He bids adieu to home, and strays
In unknown paths and distant ways;
Where'er his fancy bids him roam,
In ev'ry inn he finds a home.
Should Fortune change her fav'ring wind,   15
Tho' former friends should prove unkind,
Will not an inn his cares beguile,
Where on each face he sees a smile?
When colds winds blow, and tempests lour*,
And the rain pours in angry show'r,   20
The dripping trav'ller looks around,
To see what shelter may be found;
Then on he drives, thro' thick and thin,
To the warm shelter of an inn.
Whoe'er would turn their wand'ring feet,   25
Assur'd the kindest smiles to meet;
Whoe'er would go, and not depart
But with kind wishes from the heart;
O let them quit the world's loud din,
And seek the comforts of an inn: 30
And, as the Doric Shenstone sung,[1]
With plaintive music on his tongue—

[1] **Doric Shenstone:** William Shenstone, an eighteenth-century poet. "Doric" suggests an elegant or classical rusticity, a nod to Shenstone's extensive landscape gardening at his family estate, The Leasowes.

"Whoe'er has travell'd Life's dull round,
 "Where'er his changeful tour has been,
 "Will sigh to think how oft he found   35
 "His warmest welcome at an inn."[1]

'Twas at an inn, in calm repose,
Heedless of human joys or woes,
That Syntax pass'd the quiet night
In pleasing dreams, and slumbers light: 40
But in the morn the thunder roar'd,
The clouds their streaming torrents pour'd;
The angry winds impetuous blew,
The rattling casement open flew.
Scar'd at the noise, he rear'd his head,   45
Then, starting quickly from the bed,
"Is it," he cried, "the day of doom?"[2]
As he bestrode the trembling room.
The houses' tops with water stream'd,
The village-street a river seem'd: 50
While, at the tempest all amaz'd,
The rustics[3] from their windows gaz'd.
"I'm not," he said, "dispos'd to fear,
"But faith I will not loiter here;
"I'll change the scene, I'll soon retire,   55
"From flaming flash to kitchen fire:
"And, while rude Nature's threats prevail,
"I'll lose the storm in toast and ale."
Half-dress'd he made a quick retreat,
And in the kitchen took his seat,   60
Where an old woman told the Host
What by the lightning she had lost;
How a blue flash her sow had struck,
Had kill'd a cock, and lam'd a duck.
With open mouth another came,   65
To tell a rick[4] was in a flame;
And then declar'd that on the spire
He saw the weathercock on fire:
Nay, that so loud the winds were singing,
They'd set the peal of bells a-ringing.   70

[1] **Whoe'er...inn:** The last stanza of Shenstone's poem "Written at an Inn at Henley" (1758), which celebrates the joys of staying at an inn. The inn which is thought to have inspired the poem, the Red Lion in Henley-on-Thames, may be the one Syntax briefly visits in Canto XXII.

[2] **day of doom:** Judgment Day.

[3] **rustics:** People living in the countryside.

[4] **rick:** Stack of hay or corn.

A dripping taylor enter'd next,
And preach'd upon the self-same text:—[1]
He swore, that sitting on his board,
While the winds blew and thunder roar'd,
A kind of fiery flame came pop,   75
And bounc'd, and ran about his shop;
Now here, now there, so quick and nimble,
It sing'd his finger through his thimble:
That all about his needles ran,
If there was any truth in man;   80
While buttons, at least half a score,
Were driven thro' the kitchen-door.
The Sexton, with important mien,[2]
Gave his opinion on the scene:
And, to the Doctor drawing near,   85
Thus gently whisper'd in his ear:
"The Devil himself his cell has burst,
"To fly away with *Lawyer Thrust.*"

    Now, having with due patience heard
The story which each wight* preferr'd,   90
Syntax was to the parlour shown,
Where he might breakfast all alone.
"I see," said he, "I here must stay
"And at the Dragon pass the day:
"And this same Dragon,[3] on my life,   95
"Just hints that I have got a wife;
"Nor can I pass the morning better
"Than to indite this wife a letter."
He paus'd—and sigh'd ere he began,
When thus the fond epistle ran: 100

    "My dearest Doll,—Full many a day
"From you and home I've been away;
"But, tho' we thus are doom'd to part,
"You're ever present in my heart:
"Whene'er my pray'rs to Heav'n arise,   105
"At morn or ev'ning sacrifice,—
"Whene'er for Heaven's care they sue,
"I ask it for my Dolly too.

[1] **preach'd...text:**
Told a similar story.

[2] **important mien:**
The air of one with
something
important and
confidential to say.

[3] **Dragon:** A fierce
woman was
sometimes called a
dragon. Thus the
name of the inn
reminds Syntax of
his wife.

"My Journey, like Life's common road,
"Has had its evils and its good: 110
"But I've no reason to complain,
"When pleasure has outweigh'd the pain.
"With flatt'ring Fortune in my view,
"Glad I the toilsome way pursue;
"For I've no fear to make a book,   115
"In which the world will like to look:
"Nor do I doubt 'twill prove a mine
"For my own comfort, and for thine!
"But should all fail, I've found a friend
"In my old school-mate, *Dicky Bend;*   120
"Who, kind and wealthy, will repay,
"If Hope should cheat me on my way,
"My ev'ry loss I may sustain,
"And ease ill-fortune of its pain;
"He has engag'd to glad our home,   125
"With promise of much good to come.
"Particulars of what I've seen,
"What I have done—where I have been,
"I shall reserve for my return,
"When as the crackling faggots burn,   130
"I will in all domestic glory,
"Smoke my pipe, and tell my story:
"But, be assur'd, I'm free from danger;—
"To the world's tricks I'm not a stranger;
"Whatever risks I'm forc'd to run,   135
"I shall take care of number *one;* [1]
"While you, at home, will keep in view
"The self-same care of number *two.*
"To my kind neighbours I commend
"The wishes of their distant friend: 140
"Within ten days, perhaps a week,
"I shall York's famous city seek,
"Where at the post, I hope to find
"A line from Dolly, ever kind:
"And, if you will the pleasure crown,   145
"Tell me the prattle of our town;
"Of all that's passing, and has past,
"Since your dear Hub beheld it last:

[1] **take care...*one:*** Look out for myself.

"And know the truth which I impart
"The offspring of my honest heart,   150
"That, wheresoe'er I'm doom'd to roam,
"I still shall find that home is home:
"That, true to Love and nuptial vows,
"I shall remain your faithful spouse.
"Such are the tender truths I tell:—   155
"*Conjux carissima*[1]—farewell!"

   Thus he his kindest thoughts reveal'd—
But scarce had he his letter seal'd,
When straight appear'd the trembling Host,
Looking as pale as any ghost: 160
"A man's just come into the town,
"Who says the castle's tumbled down:
"And that, with one tremendous blow,
"The lightning's force has laid it low."
"What castle, friend?" the Doctor cry'd,   165
"The castle by the river side:
"A famous place, where as folks say,
"Some great King liv'd in former day:
"But this fine building long has been
"A sad and ruinated scene,   170
"Where owls, and bats, and starlings dwell,—
"And where, alas, as people tell,
"At the dark hour when midnight reigns,
"Ghosts walk, all arm'd, and rattle chains."
"Peace, peace," says Syntax, "peace, my friend,   175
"Nor to such tales attention lend.
"—But this new thought I must pursue:
"A castle, and a ruin too;[2]
"I'll hasten there, and take a view."

   The storm was past, and many a ray   180
Of Phœbus[3] now reviv'd the day,
When Grizzle to the door was brought,
And this fam'd spot the Doctor sought.
Upon a rock the castle stood,
Three sides environ'd by a flood,   185

[1] *Conjux carissima:* "Dearest spouse" in Latin.

"Landscape with a ruined castle,"
William Gilpin, c. 1745-8. YCBA.

[2] **A castle, and a ruin too:** Castles and other architectural ruins were common destinations in picturesque tours. As Gilpin puts it, "Is there a greater ornament of landscape, than the ruins of a castle?" (TE 27)

[3] **Phœbus:** Another name for Apollo, the sun god; here, a poetic reference to the sun.

The other type of ruin much favored by picturesque writers was the abbey, a relic of England's Catholic past. In her satirical History of England, *a teenage Austen joked that Henry VIII's decision to break with the Catholic Church, which resulted in the abandonment and ruination of many abbeys, "has been of infinite use to the landscape of England in general, which probably was a principle motive for his doing it"* (Juv. 181).

Where confluent streams uniting lave,
The craggy rift with foaming wave.
Around the moss-clad walls he walk'd,
Then thro' the inner chambers stalk'd;
And thus exclaim'd, with look profound,   190
The Echos giving back the sound.—
"Let me expatiate here awhile:—
"I think this antiquated pile[1]
"Is, doubtless, in the Saxon style.[2]
"This was a noble, spacious hall,   195
"But why the chapel made so small?[3]
"I fear our fathers took more care
"Of festive hall than house of pray'r.
"I find these Barons fierce and bold,[4]
"Who proudly liv'd in days of old,   200
"To pray'r preferr'd a sumptuous treat,
"Nor went to pray when they could eat.
"Here all along the banners hung,
"And here the welcome minstrels[5] sung:
"The walls, with glitt'ring arms bedight,[6]   205
"Display'd an animating sight.
"Beneath that arch-way, once a gate,
"With helmed crest, in warlike state,
"The bands march'd forth, nor fear'd the toil
"Of bloody war that gave the spoil.   210
"But now, alas! no more remains
"Than will reward the painter's pains:
"The palace of the feudal victor
"Now serves for nought but for a picture.
"Plenty of water here I see,   215
"But what's a view without a tree?[7]
"There's something grand in yonder tow'r,
"But not a shrub to make a bow'r;
"Howe'er, I'll try to take the view,
"As well as my best art can do."   220

 An heap of stones the Doctor found,
Which loosely lay upon the ground,
To form a seat, where he might trace
The antique beauty of the place:

[1] **pile:** A grand house or mansion.

[2] **the Saxon style:** Syntax makes a mistake here. The term "Saxon" was used to describe a certain kind of *church* architecture, heavier and less graceful than the Gothic style which succeeded it. The Anglo-Saxons, for whom the style was named, did not build castles.

[3] **why the chapel made so small?:** Great houses often had a chapel where the household would gather for prayer and worship. Syntax, a clergyman, notes with disapproval that the chapel of this castle is dwarfed by the great hall, where feasts would have been held.

[4] **these Barons fierce and bold:** A reference to the nobles of feudal England, who enjoyed a great deal of power and independence during the Middle Ages. Syntax's picture of the feudal barons as hot-tempered and lawless, but at the same time rather grand, was a familiar one in the period. It features prominently, for example, in Sir Walter Scott's novel *Ivanhoe* (1819).

[5] **minstrels:** Musicians or performers who entertained at medieval courts.

[6] **with glitt'ring arms bedight:** Decked with shining weapons. The antiquated term "bedight" savors of the Middle Ages.

[7] **what's a view without a tree?:** In his sketches, Gilpin would often place a single tree in the foreground to frame the main subject of the scene and create a sense of perspective. See the image on p. 95 for an example.

Like Syntax, Fanny Price (MP) sees the chapel of a great house as an expression of its moral character. "There is something in a chapel and chaplain so much in character with a great house, with one's ideas of what such a household should be! A whole family assembling regularly for the purpose of prayer, is fine!" (I.9). The unused chapel of Sotherton, on the other hand, is a picture to Fanny of a house that has lost something of its soul.

Henry Tilney (NA) would probably agree with Syntax. In explaining picturesque principles to Catherine, he draws her attention to a rocky outcropping and encourages her to imagine a single "withered oak" atop it (I.14).

But, while his eye observ'd the line   225
That was to limit the design,[1]
The stones gave way, and sad to tell,
Down from the bank he headlong fell.
The slush collected for an age
Receiv'd the venerable sage;   230

[1] **the line…design:**
The line that
separates the
foreground from
the distance, or the
distance from the
background (also
called the second
distance).

For, at the time, the ebbing flood
Was just retreating from the mud:
So, after floundering about,
Syntax contriv'd to waddle out,
Half stunn'd, amaz'd and cover'd o'er   235
As seldom wight* had been before.—
O'erwhelm'd with mud, and stink, and grief,
He saw no house to give relief;
So thus, amid the village din,
He ran the gauntlet to the inn.[2]   240
An angler[3] threw his hook so pat,
He caught at once the Doctor's hat;
A bathing boy, who naked stood,
Dash'd boldly in the eddying flood,
And, swimming onward like a grig,[4]   245
Soon overtook the Doctor's wig.
Grizzle had trac'd the barren spot,
Where not a blade of grass was got,

[2] **amid the village din…inn:** That is, Syntax had to run back to the inn through a crowd of laughing villagers.

[3] **angler:** Fisherman.

[4] **grig:** A small, darting fish.

98

And, finding nought to tempt her stay,
She to the Dragon took her way.   250
The ostler* cried, "here's some disaster—
"The mare's return'd without her master!"
But soon he came, amid the noise
Of men and women, girls and boys,
Glad in the inn to find retreat   255
From the rude insults of the street.

  Undress'd, well-wash'd, and put to bed,
With mind disturb'd, and aching head,
In vain poor Syntax sought repose,
But lay and counted all his woes.   260
The friendly Host, with anxious care,
Now hastes the posset[1] to prepare:—
The healing draught he kindly gives;
Syntax the cordial boon receives:—
Then seeks, in sleep, a pause from sorrow, 265
In hope of better fate to-morrow.

[1] **posset:** A drink made from hot milk curdled with liquor, often used as a remedy.

100

CANTO X.

POOR mortal man, in ev'ry state,
What troubles and what ills await![1]
His transient joy is chas'd by sorrow,—
To-day he's blest;—a wretch to-morrow:
When in this world he first appears,   5
He hails the light with cries and tears:
A school-boy next, he fears the nod
Of pedant pow'r, and feels the rod:
When to an active stripling grown,
The Passions seize him as their own;   10
Now lead him here, now drive him there,
Th' alternate sport of Joy and Care—
Allure him with the glitt'ring treasure,
Or give the brimming cup of pleasure;
While one eludes his eager haste,   15
The other palls upon the taste.
The pointed darts from Cupid's quiver
Wound his warm heart, and pierce his liver;
While charm'd by fair Belinda's[2] eyes,
He dines on groans, and sups on sighs.   20
If from this gay and giddy round
He should escape both safe and sound,
Perhaps, if all things else miscarry,
He takes it in his head to marry;
And in this lottery of life,   25
If he should draw a scolding wife,
With a few children, eight or ten
(For such things happen now and then),
Poor hapless man! he knows not where
To look around without a care.   30
Ambition, in its airy flight,
May tempt him to some giddy height;

[1] **POOR mortal… await:** A paraphrase of the line "Man's feeble race what ills await!" from Thomas Gray's 1757 poem "The Progress of Poesy."

[2] **Belinda's:** A generic name, often used in literature to denote a beautiful, elegant woman.

But, ere the point he can attain,
He tumbles ne'er to rise again.
Pale Av'rice may his heart possess,   35
The bane of human happiness,
Which never feels for other's woe,
Which never can a smile bestow;
A wretched, meagre, griping elf,
A foe to all, and to himself.   40
Then comes Disease, with baneful train,
And all the family of Pain,
Till Death appears in awful state,
And calls him to the realms of Fate.
How oft is Virtue seen to feel   45
The woeful turn of Fortune's wheel,
While she with golden stores awaits
The wicked in their very gates.
But Virtue still the value knows
Of honest deeds, and can repose   50
Upon the flint her naked head;
While Vice lies restless on the bed.
Of softest down, and courts in vain
The opiate to relieve its pain.

   It was not Vice that e'er could keep   55
Poor Syntax from refreshing sleep;
For no foul thought, no wicked art,
In his pure life e'er bore a part:
Some ailment dire his slumbers broke,
And, ere the sun arose, he woke: 60
When such a tremor o'er him pass'd;
He thought that hour would prove his last;
His limbs were all besieg'd by pain;
He now grew hot, then cold again:
His tongue was parch'd, his lips were dry;   65
And, heaving the unbidden sigh,
He rung the bell, and call'd for aid,
And groan'd so loud, th' affrighted maid
Spread the alarm throughout the house;
When straight the landlord and his spouse   70

Made all dispatch to do their best,
And ease the sufferings of their guest.
"Have you a Doctor?" Syntax said;
"If not, I shortly shall be dead."
"O yes; a very famous man;— 75
"He'll cure you, Sir, if physic[1] can.
"I'll fetch him quick—a man renown'd
"For his great skill the country round."

The Landlord soon the Doctor brought,
Whose words were grave, whose look was thought;
By the bed-side he took his stand,
And felt the patient's burning hand;
Then, with a scientific face,
He told the symptoms of the case:—
"His frame's assail'd with fev'rish heats; 85
"His pulse with rapid movement beats:
"And now, I think, 'twould do him good,
"Were he to lose a little blood.[2]
"Some other useful matters too,
"To ease his pain, I have in view. 90
"I'll just step home, and, in a trice,
"Will bring the fruits of my advice;
"In the mean time, his thirst assuage
"With tea that's made of balm, or sage."
He soon return'd,—his skill applied,— 95
From the vein flow'd the crimson tide:
And, as the folk behind him stand,
He thus declar'd his stern command:
"At nine, these powders let him take;
"At ten, this draft,—the phial shake; 100
"And you'll remember, at eleven,
"Three of these pills must then be given:
"This course you'll carefully pursue,
"And give, at twelve, the bolus[3] too:
"If he should wander, in a crack 105
"Clap this broad blister[4] on his back;
"And, after he has had the blister,
"Within an hour give the clyster.[5]

[1] **physic:** Medicine.

[2] **lose a little blood:** Bloodletting was a common medical practice in the early nineteenth century, intended to relieve the patient of an "excess" of one of the four bodily humours.

[3] **bolus:** A large pill.

[4] **blister:** A caustic substance applied to the skin to raise a blister, with the intent of draining unhealthy humours or interrupting the course of a disease.

[5] **clyster:** A medicine injected through the rectum.

103

"I must be gone; at three or four
"I shall return, with *something more.*" 110

   Now Syntax and his fev'rish state
Became the subject of debate.
The mistress said she was afraid
No medicine would give him aid;
For she had heard the screech-owl scream, 115
And had besides a horrid dream.
Last night the candle burn'd so blue;
While from the fire a coffin flew;
And, as she sleepless lay in bed,
She heard a death-watch at her head.[1] 120
The maid and ostler* too declar'd
That noises strange they both had heard.
"Ay," cried the Sexton, "these protend[2]
"To the sick man a speedy end;
"And, when that I have drank my liquor, 125
"I'll e'en go straight and fetch the Vicar."[3]

   The Vicar came, a worthy man,
And, like the good Samaritan,[4]
Approach'd in haste the stranger's bed,
Where Syntax lay with aching head; 130
And, without any fuss or pother*,
He offer'd to his rev'rend brother
His purse, his house, and all the care
Which a kind heart could give him there.

   Says Syntax, in a languid voice, 135
"You make my very soul rejoice;
"For, if within this house I stay,
"My flesh will soon be turn'd to clay;
"For the good Doctor means to pop
"Into my stomach all his shop. 140
"I think, dear Sir, that I could eat,
"And physic's but a nauseous treat:—
"If all that stuff's to be endur'd,
"I shall be kill'd in being cur'd."[5]

"Doctor Syntax cupped," Thomas Rowlandson, c. 1808. YCBA. This unpublished drawing shows Syntax being treated with cupping, a method of drawing blood with heated cups. The same procedure was used twice on Austen's father during his final illness.

[1] **screech-owl…head:** Combe refers to a number of superstitions involving "death omens." If a screech owl screeched at a person; or if the flame of a candle turned pale or bluish; or if a coal in the shape of a coffin flew out of the fire; or if the ticking of an invisible "death-watch" was heard—then death, it was thought, was not far off. Combe may have relied on Francis Grose's *Provincial Glossary* here (47-52), which lists all these omens in the same order and in relatively close proximity to each other.

[2] **protend:** Portend.

[3] **fetch the Vicar:** Probably to administer communion, which many people sought on their deathbeds.

[4] **good Samaritan:** A reference to a parable of Jesus in which a stranger helps a man who has been beaten and left for dead on the road.

[5] **I shall…cur'd:** This scene is a typical specimen of early 19th-c. medical satire. Such satire focused on the over-prescription of medicine and the miseries and indignities of medical procedures. A central figure was the "quack" doctor—the unregulated practitioner who concocted homemade remedies and feigned professionalism. This doctor, with his knowing air and his avalanche of prescriptions, savors strongly of quackery.

Although plenty of Austen's characters fall sick, few are cured by medical treatment. The most her doctors can do, usually, is to assess the progress of an illness. Mr. Harris (SS) is an example: he is able to say, with some accuracy, whether or not Marianne is improving, but his medicine is useless. In the end Marianne simply recovers: God, nature, and kind nursing may all play a role; the only thing certain is that the doctor does not.

"O," said the Vicar, "never fear;   145
"We'll leave this apparatus here.
"Come, quit your bed—I pray you, come,—
"My arm shall bear you to my home,
"Where I, and my dear mate will find
"Med'cine more suited to your mind."   150

   Syntax now rose, but feeble stood,
From want of meat and loss of blood;
But still he ventur'd to repair
To the good Vicar's house and care;
And found at dinner pretty picking,   155
In pudding boil'd and roasted chicken.
Again 'twas honest Grizzle's fate
To take her way thro' churchyard-gate;
And, undisturb'd, once more to riot
In the green feast of churchyard diet.   160
The Vicar was at Oxford bred,
And had much learning in his head;
But, what was far the better part,
He had much goodness in his heart.
The Vicar also had a wife,   165
The pride and pleasure of his life;
A loving, kind, and friendly creature,
As blest in virtue as in feature,
Who, without blisters, drugs, or pills,
Her patient cur'd of all his ills.   170
Three days he stay'd, a welcome guest,
And eat and drank of what was best:
When, on the fourth, in health renew'd,
His anxious journey he pursued.

   In two days more, before his eyes   175
The stately tow'rs of York arise.
"But what," said he, "can all this mean?
"What is yon crowded busy scene?
"Ten Thousand souls, I do maintain,
"Are scatter'd over yonder plain."   180

"Ay, more than that," a man replied,—
Who trotted briskly by his side,
"And, if you choose, I'll be your guide:
"For sure you will not pass this way,
"And miss the pleasures of the day.
"These are the races, to whose sport
"Nobles and gentry all resort."[1]
Thought Syntax, I'll just take a look;
'Twill give a subject to my book.
So on they went;—the highway friend
His services did oft commend.
"I will attend you to the course,
"And tell the name of ev'ry horse;
"But first we'll go and take a whet,
"And then I'll teach you how to bet:
"I'll name the horse that's doom'd to win—
"The knowing ones we'll soon take in."
Just as he spoke, the sport began;
The jockies whipp'd, the horses ran,—
And, when the coursers reach'd the post;
The man scream'd out—"Your horse has lost;
"I've had the luck,—I've won the day,
"And you have twenty pounds to pay."

[1] **the races...**
185 **resort:** York was
one of the major
centers of English
horse racing in the
early 19th c. Its
190 grandstand,
according to two
historians of racing
architecture, was
"the first
195 grandstand of any
sporting venue
anywhere in the
world" (Roberts
and Taylor, inside-
200 left dust jacket). See
p. 110 below for
Rowlandson's
depiction of it.

Syntax look'd wild—the man said "Zounds*!
"You know you betted twenty pounds;   205
"So pay them down, or you'll fare worse,
"For I will flog you off the course."[1]
The Doctor rav'd, and disavow'd
The bold assertion to the crowd.
What would have been his hapless fate,   210
In this most unexpected state,
May well be guess'd. But, lo! a friend
Fortune was kind enough to send.
An honest 'Squire, who smok'd the trick,[2]
Appear'd well arm'd with oaken stick,   215
And, placing many a sturdy blow
Upon the shoulders of the foe,
"It is with all my soul I beat
"This vile, this most notorious, cheat,"
The 'Squire exclaim'd; "and you, good folk,   220
"Who sometimes love a pleasant joke,
"As I am partly tir'd with thumping,
"Should treat the scoundrel with a pumping."[3]
The crowd, with their commission pleas'd
Rudely the trembling black-leg[4] seiz'd,   225
Who, to their justice forc'd to yield,
Soon ran off dripping from the field.

   Syntax his simple story told,—
The 'Squire, as kind as he was bold,
His full protection now affords,   230
And cheer'd him both with wine and words:—
"I love the clergy from my heart,
"And always take a Parson's part.
"My father, Doctor, wore the gown—
"A better man was never known: 235
"But an old uncle, a poor elf,
"Who, to save riches, starv'd himself,
"By his last will bequeath'd me clear
"At least two thousand pounds a year,
"And sav'd me all the pains, at college,   240
"To pour o'er books, and aim at knowledge.

¹ **You know…course:** Syntax's new "friend" falsely claims that Syntax had bet £20 ($2,880, essentially his life savings) on a race, and now demands that he pay up. He hopes that Syntax will be intimidated into doing so by the crowd, which would likely have little mercy on a defaulting bettor. Rowlandson's illustration on the next page, by contrast, suggests that Syntax really did lose a bet: the race is still in progress as Syntax storms and rages, likely because his horse is trailing. This is one of many moments in the poem when image and text tell different stories, a result of the unique collaboration between Rowlandson and Combe (see pp. xxv-xxvii for more on this collaboration).

² **smok'd the trick:** Discovered the fraud.

³ **a pumping:** A rough, extrajudicial punishment during which a person is held under under a pump and soaked.

⁴ **black-leg:** A swindling bookmaker (OED).

A gentleman who did not pay his gambling debts was disgraced, whether or not those debts were legally enforceable. This is probably why Sir Thomas (MP) goes to such lengths to pay his son's debts (which, given Tom's love of horse racing, may have been run up at the race track). If Sir Thomas had not, the honor of his son and of the entire house of Bertram would have been sunk. Syntax, of course, is not the heir of a great house, but the fraudster in this passage is still hoping to marshal society's contempt for non-paying bettors to extort money from him.

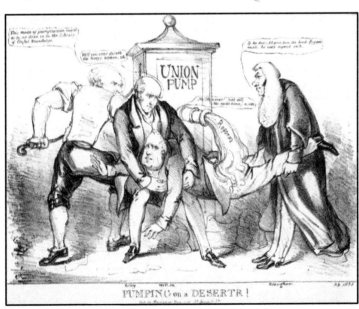

"Pumping on a Desertr [sic]," Anon., 1835. British Museum. While the print is allegorical, relating to political reform in the 1830s, it still gives a picture of the punishment meted out to the black-leg.

Designd & Etchd by Rowlandson.

DOCTOR SYNTAX

LOSES HIS MONEY ON THE RACE GROUND AT YORK.

London, Published 1 May 1812, at R.Ackermann's Repository of Arts 101, Strand.

"Thus free from care, I live at ease—
"Go where I will, do what I please—
"Pursue my sports, enjoy my pleasure,
"Nor envy Lords their splendid treasure.   245
"I have an house at York beside,
"Where you shall go and straight reside;
"And ev'ry kindness shall be shown,
"Both for my dad's sake, and your own:
"For know, good Sir, I'm never loth   250
"To mark my friendship for the cloth*.
"*Hearty*'s my name, and you shall find
"A hearty welcome too, and kind:
"I have a wife, so free and gay,
"She ne'er say *yes* when I say *nay*."   255
Syntax observ'd, that was a blessing
A man might boast of in possessing.

   At length arriv'd, a Lady fair
Receiv'd them with a winning air.
"Ah," said the 'Squire, "I always come,   260
"My dearest girl, with pleasure home:
"You see a rev'rend Doctor here,
"So give him of your choicest cheer:"
"*Yes*," she replied, "O *yes* my dear."
"Nor fail all kindness to bestow:"   265
"O *no*, my dear," she said, "O *no*."
Thus happy Syntax join'd the party
Of Madam and of 'Squire *Hearty*.

"York Minster, Moonlight View," William Miller after Clarkson Frederick
Stanfield, 1844. From Vol. IV of the Abbotsford edition of Sir Walter Scott's
Waverley Novels (Edinburgh: Cadell, Houlston and Stoneman, 1844).

CANTO XI.

IN this sad variegated life,
Evil and good, in daily strife,
Contend, we find, which shall be master:—
Now Fortune smiles—then sad Disaster
Assumes, in turn, its frowning pow'r,   5
And gives to man his checquer'd hour.
With checquer'd hours, good Syntax thought,
And well he might, his journey fraught:
But still he hop'd, when all was past,
That he should comfort find at last.   10
Thus, with the 'Squire's kindness blest,
No fears alarm his tranquil breast;
He eats, and drinks, and goes to rest:
And, when the welcome morrow came,
The 'Squire and Madam were the same.   15
Just as the Minster-clock[1] struck nine,
Coffee and tea, and fowl and chine,[2]
Appear'd in all their due array,
To give the breakfast of the day.
The 'Squire then the talk began,   20
And thus the conversation ran.

'SQUIRE HEARTY.
"Doctor, you truely may believe
"The pleasure which I now receive,
"In seeing you as you sit there,
"On what was once my father's chair.   25
"I pray you think this house your home,—
"Aye, tho' it were three months to come.
"Here you will find yourself at ease—
"May read or write—just as you please.
"At nine we breakfast, as you see,—   30
"Dinner is alway here at three;
"At six my wife will give you tea."

[1] **Minster-clock:** York Minster is a cathedral in York. The Minster-clock is the church's clock.

[2] **chine:** A cut of meat containing the backbone and surrounding flesh of a pig.

113

MRS. HEARTY.
"And should you find the evening long,
"I'll play a tune or sing a song."

'SQUIRE HEARTY.
"Besides, you'll range the country round,—   35
"Some curious things may there be found:
"Your genius too may chance to trace,
"Within this celebrated place,
"Some ancient building worth a look,
"That may, perhaps, enrich your book.   40
"I'm a true Briton, as you'll see:
"I love good cheer, and liberty;
"And what I love myself I'll give
"To others, while I'm doom'd to live.
"This morning I intend to go   45
"To see the military show:
"The light dragoons,¹ now quarter'd here,
"Will all in grand review² appear.
"They are a regiment of renown,
"And some great Gen'ral is come down   50
"To see them all, in bright array,
"Act the fierce battle of the day.
"If you should like such sights as these,
"If warlike feats your fancy please,
"We'll to the Common* take a ride,   55
"And I myself will be your guide:
"So, if you please, within an hour
"Our nags³ shall be before the door."

SYNTAX.
"I will be ready to attend
"The summons of my worthy friend.   60
"The laurell'd Hero's⁴ my delight,
"With plumed crest and helmet bright;
"E'en when a boy, at early age,
"I read in Homer's lofty page
"How the stout Greeks, in times of yore   65
"Brought havoc to the Phrygian⁵ shore:
"I revell'd in that ancient story,
"And burn'd with ardent love of glory.

"Private, 12ᵗʰ Light Dragoons," Denis Dighton, c. 1812. Royal Collection Trust. Captain Tilney (NA) belongs to the 12ᵗʰ Light Dragoons.

¹ **light dragoons:** A type of light cavalry and a mainstay of the British army during the Napoleonic Wars.

² **grand review:** A review was a military inspection conducted by a high-ranking commander during which a body of soldiers would demonstrate their discipline, skill, and overall readiness for battle. The impressive spectacle of thousands of blue- or scarlet-clad soldiers maneuvering in unison often drew civilian onlookers as well.

³ **nags:** Small riding horses.

⁴ **laurell'd Hero's:** In antiquity, a laurel wreath symbolized military conquest and glory.

⁵ **Phrygian shore:** The region of Troy, site of the Trojan War recounted in Homer's *Iliad*.

The light dragoons were primarily a combat force, but the speed with which they could be mobilized and deployed also made them useful in responding to civil unrest. Henry Tilney (NA) alludes to this secondary role when he teases his sister with the prospect of their brother, a captain in the 12ᵗʰ Light Dragoons, being called from Northampton to quell a London riot.

After Lydia runs away with an officer, Mr. Bennet (PP) tells Kitty that he will be taking a stricter line as a father, and that therefore her own days of flirting with officers are over. When she begins to cry, he jokes that if she is "a good girl for the next ten years," he will take her to a review as a reward (III.6). To the officer-crazed Kitty, attending a review would indeed have been a treat, though probably not worth the ten-year probation.

"Whene'er I trac'd the field of Troy
"My heart beat high with martial joy.   70
" 'Tis true, I pray that war may cease,
"And Europe hail returning Peace;[1]
"Yet still I feel my bosom glow
"When British heroes meet the foe:
"When our arm'd legions make him fly,   75
"And yield the palm of victory;
"Or when our naval thunders roar,
"And terrify the Gallic shore.[2]
"This grand review will give me pleasure,
"And I shall wait upon your leisure."   80

  But, as no time was to be lost,
Syntax now hasten'd to the post:
The post obey'd his loud command,
And gave a letter to his hand.
With eager haste the seal he broke,   85
And thus the fond epistle spoke:

———————

  "My dearest husband,—on my life
"I thought you had forgot your wife:
"While she, to her affection true,
"Was always thinking, Love, on you.   90
"By this time, I presume, you've made
"No small advancement in your trade:
"I mean, my dear, that this same book,
"To which I with impatience look,
"Is full of promise; and I'm bold   95
"To hope for a return in gold.
"I have no doubt that ample gains
"Will well reward your learned pains,
"And will, with bounteous store, repay
"Your anxious toil of many a day;   100
"For well, my dearest friend, I know,
"Where'er you are compell'd to go,
"You still must sigh that you should be
"So long away from Love and me.
"I truly say my heart doth burn   105
"With ardent wish for your return;

[1] **And Europe...Peace:** When this canto was published in 1809, France had been at war with various coalitions of European states for seventeen years, with only a single short interval of peace (1802-3).

[2] **When British heroes...Gallic shore:** Syntax's boast about British naval supremacy was well founded: Britain had defeated France in a series of naval battles in the West Indies, the Mediterranean, and the English Channel (Gallic shore) in the late 1790s and early 1800s. The record of the British army during that time, however, was more checkered. On land, Napoleon and the French rarely "yield[ed] the palm of victory" to the British.

In her novels, Austen betrays a preference for the navy over the army. Naval characters like William Price (MP), Captain Wentworth (Pers.), and Admiral Croft are unpretentious and forthright, while those in the army and militia include dishonest smooth-talkers such as Mr. Wickham (PP) and Captain Tilney (NA). Austen may have felt that naval service, with its long and perilous sea voyages, required greater sacrifice, and therefore attracted or forged men of higher character. Family pride may have shaped her views as well: two of her brothers were sailors.

The Battle of Trafalgar, 21 October 1805, JMW Turner, 1824. National Maritime Museum.

"And, that I may my Syntax greet
"With all due honour when we meet,
"The milliner is now preparing
"A dress that will be worth the wearing;   110
"Just such an one as I have seen
"In ACKERMANN'S LAST MAGAZINE,[1]
"Where, by the skilful painter's aid,
"Each fashion is so well display'd.
"A robe of crape, with satin boddice,   115
"Will make me look like any goddess:
"A mantle too is all the ton,
"And therefore I have order'd one:
"I've also got a lilac bonnet,
"And plac'd a yellow feather on it: 120
"Thus I shall be so very smart,
" 'Twill vex Miss Raisin to the heart;
"Oh! it will make me burst with laughter,
"To plague the purse-proud[2] grocer's daughter;
"While, thro' the town, as you shall see   125
"No one will be so fine as me.
"Oh! with what pleasure and delight
"I shall present me to your sight;
"How shall I hug you, dearest honey,
"When you return brimful of money."   130

    Syntax exclaim'd, in accents sad,
"The woman's surely gone stark mad!
"To ruin, all her airs will tend;
"But I'll read on, and see the end."

    "As to the news, why you must know,   135
"Things in their usual order go:
"Jobson the Tanner's run away,
"And has not left a doit[3] to pay:
"Bet Bumpkin was last Thursday marry'd
"And Mrs. Stillborn has miscarry'd.   140
"In the High-street, the other day,
"Good Mrs. Squeamish swoon'd away,
"And was so ill, as it is said,
"That she was borne away for dead;

[1] **ACKERMANN'S LAST MAGAZINE:** Combe provides a playful bit of marketing here: Rudolph Ackermann, Combe's employer and the publisher of *Doctor Syntax*, had launched a monthly magazine earlier in the year called *The Repository of Arts, Literature, Commerce, Manufactures, Fashions and Politics*. Each issue contained, among other features, colored plates showing the latest in women's fashion.

[2] **purse-proud:** Vulgarly arrogant on account of one's money, despite lacking other claims to status such as birth and education.

[3] **doit:** A tiny sum of money, literally a small coin.

A ball dress and a walking dress with mantle, *RA* (May 1809), opp. 329. These appear to be the garments Mrs. Syntax has ordered. The former is described as a "[w]hite satin slip, under a crape dress, made to fit the figure very exactly" (328).

For readers living in the country, publications like The Repository *were a convenient way to find out what was being worn in the metropolis. Otherwise, one waited for news from friends and relatives. When Mrs. Gardiner (PP) visits Longbourn, the "first part of [her] business" is to "describe the newest fashions" (II.2). Austen was a conscientious purveyor of fashion news herself: her letters from London often make note of new styles in hats, bonnets, and dresses.*

BALL DRESS.   WALKING DRESS.

"But Mother Gossip, who knows all   145
"The neighbours round, both great and small,
"Has hinted to me, as she thinks,
"That pious Mrs. Squeamish drinks.
"There is a Lady just come down,
"A dashing, frisky dame from Town,   150
"To visit Madam Stapleton:
"She's said to be a London toast,
"But has no mighty charms to boast;
"For it is clear to my keen sight,
"That she lays on both red and white.[1]   155
"She drives about in chaise and pair,[2]
"And I have heard can curse and swear:
"But I mind not these things, not I,
"I never deal in calumny.
"So fare you well, my dearest life,—   160
"And I remain—your loving wife."

[1] **red and white:** Cosmetics. The ideal complexion was fair with rosy cheeks.

[2] **chaise and pair:** Carriage drawn by two horses.

POSTSCRIPT.
   "But if you fear that you shall come
"Without a bag of money home,
" 'Twere better far that you should take
"A leap, at once, into the lake:—   165
"I'd rather hear that you were drown'd,
"Than that you should my hopes confound."

—————

   These tender lines did not impart
Much comfort to the Doctor's heart;
He therefore thought it would be better   170
To lay aside this pretty letter;
Nor suffer its contents to sour
The pleasure of the present hour.

   The 'Squire now became his guide,
So off they trotted, side by side;   175
And, ere they'd pass'd a mile or two,
Beheld the scene of the review.
The troops drawn up in proud array,
An animating sight display;

The well-form'd squadrons wheel'd around—   180
The standards wave, the trumpets sound;
When Grizzle, long matur'd to war,
And not without an honour'd scar,
Found all her former spirits glow
As when she us'd to meet the foe: 185
No ears she prick'd, for she had none:
Nor cock'd her tail, for that was gone;
But still she snorted, foam'd, and flounc'd,
Then up she rear'd, and off she bounc'd;
And, having play'd these pretty pranks,   190
Dash'd, all at once, into the ranks;
While Syntax, tho' unus'd to fear,
Suspected that his end was near:
But, tho' his courage 'gan to addle,
He still stuck close upon his saddle;   195
While, to the trumpets on the hill,
Grizzle sped fast, and then stood still:
With them she clos'd her warlike race,
And took with pride her ancient place;
For Grizzle, as we've told before,   200
Once to the wars a trumpet bore.[1]

  At length, recover'd from his fright,
The Doctor stay'd and view'd the sight;
And then, with heart as light as cork,
He with his friend jogg'd back to York,   205
Where was renew'd the friendly fare,
And ev'ry comfort promis'd there.
The time in chit-chat pass'd away,
Till the chimes told the closing day;
And now, says pleasant Madam Hearty,   210
What think you if our little party
Should each to sing a song agree?
'Twill give a sweet variety.
Thus, let the passing moments roll—
Till Thomas brings the ev'ning bowl: 215
The Doctor, sure, will do his best
And kindly grant my poor request.
The Doctor, tho' by nature grave,
And rather form'd to tune a stave,[2]

[1] **a trumpet bore:** When Grizzle was a warhorse, her rider was a trumpeter, responsible for giving directions to the rest of the company, such as charge, retreat, etc.

[2] **stave:** A section of written music. Combe draws a contrast between formal, dignified written music and livelier, more spontaneous folk tunes.

Whene'er he got a little mellow,[1]
Was a most merry, pleasant fellow;
Would sing a song, or tell a riddle,
Or play a hornpipe[2] on the fiddle;
And, being now a little gay,
Declar'd his wishes to obey.
Then I'll begin, 'Squire Hearty said,
But tho' by land my tours are made,
Whene'er I tune a song, or glee,[3]
I quit the land, and go to sea.

THE 'SQUIRE'S SONG.
The signal giv'n, we seek the main,[4]
    Where tempests rage, and billows roar;
Nor know we if we e'er again
    Shall anchor on our native shore.

But, as thro' surging waves we sail,
    And distant seas and isles explore,
Hope whispers that some future gale
    Will waft us to our native shore.

When battle rages all amain,[5]
    And hostile arms their vengeance pour,
We British sailors will maintain
    The honour of our native shore.

But, should we find a wat'ry grave,
    A nation will our loss deplore;
And tears will mingle with the wave
    That breaks upon our native shore.

And after many a battle won,
    When ev'ry toil and danger's o'er,
How great the joy, each duty done,
    To anchor on our native shore.

MRS. HEARTY'S SONG.
CUPID, away! thy work is o'er,—
    Go seek Idalia's flow'ry grove;[6]
Your pointed darts will pain no more,—
    HYMEN[7] has heal'd the wounds of Love.

220

225

230

235

240

245

250

[1] **mellow:** Tipsy.

[2] **hornpipe:** An energetic type of dance music, associated with common folk.

[3] **glee:** A type of song meant for several voices.

[4] **main:** Ocean.

[5] **all amain:** Violently.

[6] **Idalia's flow'ry grove:** Idalia, located on the island of Cyprus, was one of the dwelling places of Venus, goddess of love and mother of Cupid.

[7] **HYMEN:** Greek god of weddings. Mrs. Hearty contrasts Cupid, who creates amorous desire (and the pains attending it), with Hymen, who fulfills that desire.

HYMEN is here, and all is rest;
   To distant flight thy pinions move: 255
No anxious doubts, no fears molest;—
   HYMEN has sooth'd the pangs of Love.

CUPID, away!—the deed is done;—
   Away, 'mid other scenes to rove:
For *Ralph* and *Isabel* are one,   260
   And HYMEN guards the home of Love.

The Doctor now his rev'rence made,
And Madam's smiling nod obey'd.
"Your songs," he said, "have giv'n me pleasure,
"As well in subject as in measure;   265
"But, in some modern songs, the taste
"Is far, I'm sure, from being chaste.
"They do not make the least pretence
"To poetry or common sense.
"Some gaudy nonsense, a brisk air,   270
"With a *da capo*[1] here and there,
"Of uncouth words, which ne'er were found
"In any language above ground;
"And these, set off with some strange phrase,
"Compose our sing-song now-a-days: 275
"The dancing-master[2] of my school
"In this way oft will play the fool;
"And makes one laugh—one knows not why,—
"But we had better laugh than cry.
"The song, which you're about to hear   280
"Will of this character appear;
"From London it was sent him down,
"As a great fav'rite thro' the town."

DOCTOR SYNTAX'S SONG.
I've got a scold of a wife,
The plague and storm of my life;   285
O! were she in coal-pit bottom,
And all such jades,[3] 'od rot 'em![4]
My cares would then be over,
And I should live in clover.[5]
With harum scarum,[6] horum scorum,—   290
    Stew'd prunes for ever!
    Stew'd prunes for ever!

Brother Tom's in the codlin-tree,[7]
As blithe as blithe can be:
While Dorothy sits below,   295
Where the daffodillies grow;

[1] *da capo:* A musical term instructing a player or singer to repeat a previous section of music.

[2] **dancing-master:** A man employed to teach dancing.

[3] **jades:** General term of reprobation for women.

[4] **'od rot 'em:** God rot them.

[5] **live in clover:** Enjoy comfort and plenty.

[6] **harum scarum:** Recklessly. Also a nonsense phrase that appears in songs from the period.

[7] **codlin-tree:** A tree producing hard, sour apples.

And many a slender rush,
And the blackberries all on the bush.
With harum scarum, &c. &c.

We'll to the castle go   300
Like grenadiers[1] all of a row,
While the horn and trump shall sound
As we pace the ramparts round;
Where many a lady fair
Comes forth to take the air.   305
With harum scarum, &c. &c.

The vessel spreads her sails
To catch the willing gales,
And dances o'er the waves;
While many a love-lorn slave   310
To his mistress tells his tale,
Far off in the distant vale*.
With harum scarum, &c. &c.

[1] **grenadiers:** The company in a regiment with the tallest and finest men was given the name of grenadiers (OED).

When the dew is on the rose,
And the wanton zephyr[1] blows;
When lillies raise their head,
And harebells fragrance shed;
Then I to the rocks will hie,
And sing a lullaby.
With harum scarum, &c. &c.

315 [1] **zephyr:** Breeze.

320

By fam'd Ilyssus' stream[2]
How oft I fondly dream,
When I read in classic* pages
Of all the ancient sages;
But they were born to die,
And so were you and I.
With harum scarum, horum scorum,—
Stew'd prunes for ever!
Stew'd prunes for ever!

[2] **Ilyssus' stream:**
A river in Athens
that is now largely
underground. In
325 ancient days, when
it was above
ground, Plato,
Aristotle, Epicurus,
and other famous
philosophers
330 studied on the
river's banks.

———————

Thus, with many a pleasant lay,
The party clos'd th' exhausted day.

CANTO XII.

LIFE is a journey:——on we go
Thro' many a scene of joy and woe,
Time flits along, and will not stay,
Nor let us linger on the way:——
Like as a stream, whose varying course   5
Now rushes with impetuous force;
Now in successive eddies plays,
Or in meanders gently strays;——
Still it moves on, till spreading wide,
It mingles with the briny tide;   10
And, when it meets the ocean's roar,
The limpid waves are seen no more.
Such, such is Life's uncertain way;——
Now the sun wakes th' enliv'ning day:——
The scene around enchants the sight;   15
To cool retreat the shades invite:
The blossoms balmy fragrance shed,
The meads a verdant carpet spread;
While the clear rill* reflects below
The flow'rs that on its margin grow;   20
And the sweet songsters of the grove
Attune to harmony and love.
But, lo! the clouds obscure the sky,
And tell the blust'ring tempest nigh:
The livid flash, the pelting storm,   25
Fair Nature's ev'ry grace deform;
While their assailing powers annoy
The pensive pilgrim's tranquil joy:
But, tho' no tempest should molest
The Bower where he stops to rest,   30
Care will not let him long remain,
But sets him on his way again.

Thus Syntax, whom the 'Squire had press'd
For a whole month to take his rest,
Sigh'd when he found he could not stay   35
To loiter thro' another day:
"No," he exclaim'd, "I must away.—
"I have a splendid book to make,
"To form a tour, to paint a lake;
"And by that well-projected *tome*,   40
"To carry fame and money home:
"And, should I fail, my loving wife
"Would lead me such a precious life,
"That I had better never more
"Approach my then forbidden door."   45
'Twas thus he ponder'd as he lay,
When the sun told another day:
Nor long the downy couch he press'd,
Where busy Thought disturb'd his rest;
But quick prepar'd, with grateful heart,   50
From this warm mansion to depart.
The 'Squire, to his professions true,
Thus spoke at once his kind adieu.

     'SQUIRE.
  "I'm sorry, Sir, with all my heart,
"That you and I so soon must part: 55
"Your virtues my regard engage,
"I venerate the rev'rend sage:
"And, tho' I've not the mind to toil
"In Learning's way, by midnight oil,
"Yet still I feel the rev'rence due   60
"To Science*, and such men as you:
"Nor can I urge your longer stay,
"When science calls you far away.
"But still I hope you'll not refuse
"My friendly tribute to the Muse;   65
"And, when again you this way come,
"Again you'll find this house a home.
"Besides, I mean to recommend
"Your labours to a noble friend,

"Who well is known to rank as high   70
"In learning as in quality;[1]
"Who can your merits well review,
"A statesman, and a poet too:
"He will your genius truly scan,[2]
"And, tho' a lord, a learned man.   75
"For C*******[3] is an honour'd name,
"Whose virtue and unsully'd fame
"Will decorate th' historic page,
"And live thro' ev'ry future age.
"That noble Lord doth condescend   80
"To know me for a faithful friend;
"And, when you to his Lordship give
"The letter which you now receive,
"You'll find, on his right noble part,
"A welcome that will cheer your heart. 85
"To ——— ———[4] then repair,
"And Honour will attend you there.
"Nor fear, my friend, that gilded state
"Will frown upon your humble fate;
"My Lord is good as he is great."   90

SYNTAX.
 "Your kindness, surely, knows no end;—
"You are in truth a real friend;
"Nor can my feeble tongue express
"This unexpected happiness:
"For, if this noble Lord should deign 95
"My feeble labours to sustain
"With the all-cheering, splendid rays
"Of his benign, protecting praise,
"My fortune will at once be made,
"And I shall bless the author's trade." 100

 Thus, as he spoke, the 'Squire gave
The letter Syntax long'd to have;
And with it a soft silky note,
On which two coal-black words were wrote;
The sight of which his sense confounds, 105
For these said words were—**TWENTY POUNDS**.

130

[1] **quality:** Social station.

[2] **truly scan:** Properly recognize.

[3] **C******:** Frederick Howard, 5th Earl of Carlisle (1748-1825), politician, occasional poet, and patron of the arts. He is best remembered as the guardian of Lord Byron, with whom he had a rocky relationship. Carlisle and Combe were contemporaries at Eton but it is unknown whether they had any relationship as adults that might explain Carlisle's glowing treatment in *Syntax*. In any case, Combe's flattery was well-timed. In 1810, when Canto XII was published, Carlisle was probably still smarting from his ward Byron's savage attack the year before in *English Bards and Scotch Reviewers:* "No Muse will cheer with renovating smile, / The paralytic puling of CARLISLE" (56). His favorable portrayal in *Syntax* may have helped to salve the wound, especially since Combe's lines would go on to reach many more readers in the 1810s than Byron's.

Frederick Howard's son, the 6ᵗʰ Earl of Carlisle, praised Austen in an 1835 poem called "The Lady and the Novel," possibly the first published tribute to her in verse. He hails her as "all-perfect Austin [sic]" and admires the "unstrain'd purity, and unmatch'd sense" of her style (Howard, 28).

[4] The elision refers to Castle Howard, the seat of the Earl of Carlisle since the early eighteenth century.

Engraving of Castle Howard, 1787, after a watercolor by William Marlow. Royal Collection Trust.

"Check," said the 'Squire, "your wond'ring look;
" 'Tis my subscription[1] to your book;
"And, when 'tis printed, you will send
"A copy to your Yorkshire friend;   110
"Besides, I'll try to sell a score
"Among my neighbours here, or more."

  The Doctor's tongue made no reply,
But his heart heav'd a grateful sigh.
Thus, as he sits, we can't do better   115
Than to repeat the promis'd letter:—

  "MY LORD,   *117*
            "THIS liberty I take,
"For Laughter and for Merit's sake;
"And, when the bearer shall appear
"In ——— ———'s atmosphere,   } 120
"His figure will your spirits cheer.
"You need no other topic seek;
"He'll furnish laughter for a week:
"But still I say, and tell you true,
"You'll love him for his merit too.   125
"You'll see, at once, in this Divine,
"Quixote and Parson Adams[2] shine:
"An hero well combin'd you'll view
"For *Fielding* and *Cervantes* too:
"Besides, my Lord, if I can judge,   130
"In classic* lore he's us'd to drudge.
"O do but hear his simple story,
"Let him but lay it all before you:
"And you will thank me for my letter,
"And say that you are *Hearty's* debtor;   135
"Nay, when your sides are tir'd with mirth,
"Your heart will feel his real worth.
"I know full well how you'll receive him,
"And to your favour thus I leave him.
"So I remain with zeal most fervent,   140
"Your Lordship's true and *hearty* servant.

"York, Thursday."   "J.H."

¹ **subscription:** Twenty pounds ($2,880) is many times what a subscription would have cost for a book like Syntax's. The banknote is in fact a generous gift.

² **Parson Adams:** Parson Adams is a major character in Henry Fielding's novel *Joseph Andrews* (1742) and an important literary precedent for Doctor Syntax. Like Syntax, he is a highly educated but impoverished curate, hoping to make his fortune with a book—in his case, a book of sermons. The characters are also both idealists living in a pragmatic, disenchanted world—a situation first explored in fiction by Miguel Cervantes in his novel *Don Quixote*, mentioned earlier in the line.

The conventional wisdom is that Austen disapproved of Fielding's novels on account of their raciness. Her brother Henry wrote that she did not rank them "quite so high" as Richardson's (Pers. 330), and Austen herself made Tom Jones *(1749), another of Fielding's novels, a favorite of the eminently thick-headed John Thorpe (NA). But this evidence is far from conclusive. "Not quite so high" is hardly the same as "low," and another author Thorpe admires, Ann Radcliffe, is also enjoyed by the discerning Henry and Eleanor Tilney. Regardless of Austen's feelings toward Fielding, early readers found in their work a similar realism and humor. As one put it, Austen is "a Fielding without his grossness"* (The Standard *[9 May 1833], 4).*

"Parson Adams," EJ Wheeler, 1899. From *Joseph Andrews* (J.M. Dent, 1899), p. 104.

The Doctor now prepar'd to go,
With heart of joy and look of woe;
He silent squeez'd the 'Squire's hands,   145
And ask'd of Madam her commands.
The 'Squire exclaim'd, "why so remiss?
"She bids you take an *hearty* kiss;
"And, if you think that one won't do,
"I beg, dear Sir, you'll give her *two:*"   150
"Nay then," says Syntax, "you shall see:"
And straight he gave the Lady *three;*
Nor did he linger to exclaim
He ne'er had kiss'd a fairer dame.
The Lady blush'd, and thank'd him too;   155
And, in soft accents, said, Adieu!

   Syntax, since first he left his home,
Had no such view of good to come
As now before his fancy rose,
To bid him laugh at future woes.   160
"Fortune," he cried, "is kind at last,
"And I forgive her malice past,
"Clad in C——'s benignant form,
"Her pow'r no more will wake the storm,
"Nor e'er again her anger shed   165
"In frequent show'rs upon my head."

   Now, after a short morning's ride,
In eager Hope and Fancy's pride,
The Doctor views, with conscious smile,
Fair ——— ———'s splendid pile.   170
Not Versailles[1] makes a finer show,
As, passing o'er the lofty brow,
The stately scene is view'd below.
My Lord receiv'd him with a grace
Which marks the sov'reign of the place;   175
Nor was poor Syntax made to feel
The pride which fools so oft reveal;
Who think it a fine state decorum,
When humble merit stands before 'em:

[1] **Versailles:** Palace built by Louis XIV of France, famous for its grandeur and opulence.

But here was birth from folly free,— 180
Here was the true nobility,
Where human kindness gilds the crest;[1]
The first of virtues, and the best.

An hour in pleasant chit-chat past,
The welcome dinner came at last; 185
And now the hungry Syntax eats
Of high ragouts[2] and dainty meats:
Nor was the good man found to shrink
Whenever he was ask'd to drink.

MY LORD.
"What think you, Doctor, of the show 190
"Of pictures that around you glow?"

SYNTAX.
"I'll by-and-by enjoy the treat:
"But now, my Lord, I'd rather eat."

MY LORD.
"What say you to this statue here?
"Does it not flesh and blood appear?" 195

SYNTAX.
"I'm sure, my Lord, 'tis very fine;
"But I, just now, prefer your wine."

SIR JOHN.
"I wonder you can keep your eye
"From forms that do with Nature vie;
"Nay, in my mind, my rev'rend friend, 200
"Nature's best works they far transcend.
"Look at that picture of the Graces,[3]
"What lovely forms!—what charming faces!"

SYNTAX.
"Their charms, Sir John, I shall discover,
"I have no doubt, when dinner's over: 205
"At present, if to judge I'm able,
"The finest works are on the table.
"I should prefer the cook just now,
"To *Rubens* or to *Gerrard Dow*."[4]

[1] **crest:** Part of a coat of arms, used here as a symbol of nobility.

[2] **ragouts:** Highly seasoned dishes associated with fine dining.

[3] **Graces:** Three daughters of Zeus representing the higher pleasures of life.

[4] *Rubens... Gerrard Dow:* Peter Paul Rubens and Gerrit Dou were Flemish and Dutch painters, respectively, of the 17th century.

MY LORD.
"I wish to judge, by certain rules,   210
"The Flemish and Italian schools;[1]
"And nicely to describe the merits
"Or beauties which each school inherits."

SYNTAX.
"Tho', in their way, they're both bewitching,
"I now prefer your Lordship's kitchen."   215

The dinner done, the punch appears,
And many a glass the spirits cheers.
The festive hours thus pass'd away,
Till Time brought on the closing day:
The Doctor talk'd, nor ceas'd his quaffing,   220
While all around were sick with laughing.

MY LORD.
"Again the subject I renew,
"And wish you would the pictures view."

SYNTAX.
"To view them now would be a trouble,
"For faith, my Lord, my eyes see double."   225

MY LORD.
"To bed then we had best repair,—
"I give you to the Butler's care;
"A sage grave man, who will obey
"Whate'er your Rev'rence has to say."

The sage grave man appear'd, and bow'd:—   230
"I am of this good office[2] proud;
"But 'tis the custom of this place,
"From country yeoman to his Grace,[3]
"Whene'er a stranger-guest we see,
"To make him of the cellar free.   235
"To you the same respect we bear,
"And, therefore, beg to lead you there;
"Where ev'ry noble butt[4] doth claim
"The honour of some titled name."

[1] **Flemish and Italian schools:** Two schools of painting. Painters of the Italian Renaissance tended to offer idealized depictions of classical and religious subjects. The Dutch and Flemish painters who came a century or so later focused on scenes of middle-class domestic and commercial life, which they treated in a minutely detailed, realistic style. The real Lord Carlisle preferred the Flemish school, though he collected many specimens of both (Duncan, 265).

In the first major review of Austen's novels, the novelist Sir Walter Scott compared her work to the Flemish school: "The author's knowledge of the world, and the peculiar tact with which she presents characters that the reader cannot fail to recognize, reminds us something of the merits of the Flemish school of painting. The subjects are not often elegant, and certainly never grand; but they are finished up to nature, and with a precision which delights the reader" (Quarterly Review [Oct. 1815], 197).

Girl Chopping Onions, Gerrit Dou, 1646. Royal Collection Trust.

[2] **this good office:** That is, the office of attending to Syntax's wishes. Rather than hear them, though, the Butler steers a tipsy Syntax to the cellar for more drinking, which makes one suspect that his "sage grave" air is a front for a mischievous sense of humor.

[3] **From country yeoman to his Grace:** From a respectable commoner to a duke.

[4] **butt:** A large barrel.

DOCTOR SYNTAX MADE FREE OF THE CELLAR.

The servants waited on the stairs,   240
With cautious form and humble airs.
"Lead on," says Syntax, "I'll not stay,
"But follow where you lead the way."

The Butler cried, "You'll understand
"It is our noble Lord's command   245
"To give this rev'rend Doctor here
"A sample of our strongest beer;—
"So tap her Grace of *Devonshire*."[1]
At length the potent liquor flows,
Which makes poor man forget his woes.   250
Syntax exclaim'd, "Here's Honour's boast:—
"The health of our most noble Host;—
"And let fair Devon crown the toast."
    The cups were cheer'd with loyal song;
But cups like these ne'er lasted long: 255
And Syntax stammered, "Do you see?
"Now I'm of this fam'd cellar free,
"I wish I might be quickly led
"'T' enjoy my freedom in a bed."
He wish'd but once, and was obey'd   260
And soon within a bed was laid,
Where, all the day's strange business o'er,
He now was left to sleep and snore.

[1] **her Grace of *Devonshire*:** Probably Georgiana Cavendish, Duchess of Devonshire, a famous society belle and political organizer who died in 1806. Why there is a vintage in the cellar named after her is unclear.

CANTO XIII.

HOW oft, as thro' Life's vale* we stray,
Doth Fancy light us on our way!
How oft, with many a vision bright,
Doth she the wayward heart delight;
And, with her fond enliv'ning smile,   5
The heavy hour of care beguile!
But tho' so oft she scatters flowers,
To make more gay our waking hours,
Night is the time when o'er the soul
She exercises full control.   10
While Life's more active functions pause,
And Sleep its sable[1] curtain draws,
'Tis then she waves her fairy wand:
And strange scenes rise at her command:—
She then assumes her motley[2] reign,   15
And man lives o'er his life again;
While many an airy dream invites
Her wizard masks, her wanton sprites:
Thro' the warm brain the phantoms play,
And form a visionary day.   20

   Thus Syntax, while the bed he prest,
And pass'd the night in balmy rest,
Was lead in those unconscious hours,
By Fancy, to her fairy bow'rs,
Where the light spirits wander free   25
In whimsical variety.

   No more an humble Curate, now
He feels a mitre[3] on his brow;
The mildew'd surplice,[4] now withdrawn,
Yields to the fine, transparent lawn;[5]   30

[1] **sable:** Dark.

[2] **motley:** Various, multi-colored (because of the many forms dreams take).

[3] **mitre:** Headdress worn by bishops during official ceremonies.
[4] **surplice:** Loose white robe worn by clergymen in church.
[5] **lawn:** Fine material from which bishops' sleeves were made.

And peruke, that defied all weather,
Is nicely dress'd to ape a feather.[1]
Grizzle no more is seen to 'wail,
Her mangled ears and butcher'd tail;—
Six Grizzles now, with ev'ry ear,   35
And all their flowing tails appear;
When, harness'd to a light barouche,[2]
The ground they do not seem to touch.
Whirl'd onward in a wild surprise,
The air-blown prelate[3] thinks he flies.   40
Now thro' the long cathedral aisle,
Where vergers[4] bow and virgins smile,
With measur'd step and solemn air,
He gains at length the sacred chair;[5]
And to the crowd, with look profound,   45
Bestows his holy blessings round.
Above the pealing organs blow
To the respondent choir below;
When, bending to Religion's shrine,
He feels an energy divine.   50
Now, 'scap'd from Dolly's angry clutches,
He thinks he's marry'd to a Duchess;
And that her rank and glowing beauty
Enlivens his prelatic duty.

   Thus Fancy, with her antic train,   55
Pass'd nimbly thro' the Doctor's brain;
But, while she told her varying story
Of short-liv'd pomp and fading glory,
A voice upon the vision broke,—
When Syntax gave a grunt—and woke: 60
"And may it please you, I've a word
"To tell your Rev'rence from my Lord."
"A Lord," he cried, "why, to be free,
"I've been as good a Lord as he:
"Throughout the night, I've been as great   65
"As any Lord, with all his state:
"But now that fine-drawn scene is o'er,
"And I'm poor Syntax as before.

[1] **peruke...feather:** Syntax imagines his wig, which has suffered wear and tear from the elements, tranformed into a feathered hat.

[2] **barouche:** A fashionable, open-air, four-wheeled carriage usually drawn by two horses (Ewing). Syntax's dream, in which he rides a barouche drawn by *six* horses, is extravagant indeed.

[3] **prelate:** Bishop.

[4] **vergers:** Attendants of a church.

[5] **sacred chair:** The cathedra, a raised chair where the bishop would sit during divine service. A cathedral, literally speaking, is a church with a cathedra.

In Austen's novels, as here, the barouche is usually a form of conspicuous consumption. Fanny Dashwood (SS) wants her brother Edward Ferrars "to make a fine figure in the world" by going into politics or some other lofty profession. Until then, though, "it would have quieted her ambition to see him driving a barouche" (I.3). Lady Catherine de Bourgh (PP), Henry Crawford (MP), and Lady Dalrymple (Pers.), who share Fanny's focus on appearances, all project their prestige by driving or being driven in barouches.

"A Barouche with Ackermann's Patent Moveable Axles," C. Blunt. *RA* (Jan. 1820), opp. 43.

"You spoil'd my fortune, 'tis most certain,
"The moment you withdrew the curtain: 70
"So, if you please, my pretty maid,
"You'll tell me what my Lord has said."
"—My Lord has sent to let you know
"That breakfast is prepar'd below."
"—Let my respects upon him wait,   75
"And say that I'll be with him straight."
Out then he bounc'd upon the floor:
The maid ran shouting thro' the door,—
So much the figure of the Doctor,
In his unrob'd condition, shock'd her.   80

   Syntax now hasten'd to obey
The early summons of the day.
He humbly bow'd and took his seat;
Nor did his Lordship fail to greet
With kindest words his rev'rend guest—   85
As how he had enjoy'd his rest;
Hop'd every comfort he had found,
That his night's slumbers had been sound;
And that he was prepar'd to share
With keen regard the morning's fare.   90
The Doctor smil'd, and soon made free
With my Lord's hospitality;
Then told aloud his golden dream,
Which prov'd of mirth a fruitful theme.
" 'Tis true," he said, "when I awoke,   95
"The charm dissolv'd, the spell was broke;
"The mitre* and its grand display,
"With my fine wife all pass'd away.
"Th' awak'ning voice my fortune cross'd,
"I op'd my eyes, and all was lost;   100
"But still I find, to my delight,
"I have not lost my appetite."

    SIR JOHN.
  "As for the mitre* and the gold,
"Which Fancy gave you to behold,

144

"They, to a mind with learning fraught,   105
"Do not deserve a passing thought:
"But I lament that such a bride
"Should thus be stolen from your side."

SYNTAX.

  "For that choice good I need not roam;
"I've got, Sir John, a wife at home,   110
"Who can from morn to night contrive
"To keep her family alive;
"Such sprightly measures she doth take,
"That no one sleeps when she's awake.
"For me, if Fortune would but show'r   115
"Some portion of her wealth and pow'r,
"I would forgive her, on my life,
"Tho' she forgot to add a wife.
"Indeed, Sir John, we don't agree,
"Nor join in our philosophy;   120
"For did you know what that man knows,
"Had you e'er felt his cutting woes,
"Who has of taunts a daily plenty,
"Whose head is comb'd,[1] whose pocket's empty;
"You ne'er would call those shiners[2] trash,   125
"Whose touch is life—whose name is cash."

    MY LORD.
  "A truce, I pray, to your debate;
"The hunters[3] all impatient wait;
"And much I hope our learned Clerk*
"Will take a gallop in the park."   130

    SYNTAX.
  "Your sport, my Lord, I cannot take,
"For I must go and hunt a lake;
"And while you chase the flying deer,
"I must fly off to *Windermere*.[4]
"Instead of hallowing to a fox,   135
"I must catch echoes from the rocks.
"With curious eye and active scent,
"I on the *picturesque* am bent.

[1] **comb'd:** Beaten, drubbed (by his wife).

[2] **shiners:** Coins.

[3] **hunters:** Horses bred and trained for hunting.

[4] ***Windermere:*** The largest lake in England and an immensely popular picturesque destination.

"This is my game; I must pursue it,
"And make it where I cannot view it.   140
"Though in good truth, but do not flout me,
"I bear that self-same thing about me.
"If in man's form you wish to see
"The *picturesque*—pray look at me.
"I am myself, without a flaw,   145
"The very *picturesque* I draw.
"A Rector, on whose face so sleek
"In vain you for a wrinkle seek;
"In whose fair form, so fat and round,
"No obtuse angle's to be found;   150
"On such a shape no man of taste
"Would his fine tints or canvas waste:
"But take a Curate who's so thin,
"His bones seem peeping thro his skin;
"Make him to stand, or walk or sit,   155
"In any posture you think fit;
"And with all these fine points about him,
"No well-taught painter e'er would scout him:[1]
"For with his air, and look, and mien,
"He'd give effect to any scene.   160
"In my poor beast, as well as me,
"A fine example you may see:
"She's so abrupt in all her parts:
"O what fine subjects for the arts![2]
"Thus we travel on together,   165
"With gentle gale or stormy weather;
"And, tho' we trot along the plains,
"Where one dead level ever reigns;
"Or pace where rocks and mountains rise,
"Who lift their heads, and brave the skies;   170
"I Doctor Syntax, and my horse,
"Give to the landscape double force.[3]
"—I have no doubt I shall produce
"A volume of uncommon use,
"That will be worthy to be plac'd   175
"Beneath the eye of men of taste;
"And I should hope, my Lord, that you
"Will praise it, and protect it too;

Bandits on a Rocky Coast, Salvator Rosa, 1655-60. The Met. Rosa was a major influence on Gilpin, who praised his use of figures in landscape.

¹ **A Rector...scout him:** Combe likely has in mind a comparison in Gilpin's *Three Essays* between the face of a beautiful girl and that of an old man. The former, Gilpin says, certainly has its charms, but the latter, with its craggy features, its "forehead furrowed with wrinkles," represents the "human face in it's [sic] highest form of *picturesque beauty*" (TE 10). In the human body as in landscape, roughness is king.
² **In my poor beast...the arts:** Gilpin again: "as an object of picturesque beauty, we admire more the worn-out cart-horse, the cow, the goat, or the ass; whose harder lines, and rougher coats, exhibit more the graces of the pencil" (TE 14).
³ **Give to...double force:** Syntax is referring to a running theme in Gilpin's work: the inclusion of human or animal figures in a landscape. In general Gilpin cautioned against overpopulating a view, but he allowed that a few well-chosen figures could "add a deeper tinge to the character of a scene" (OCW Vol. II, 46). Bandits were a natural fit for a scene of wild grandeur (see image above), while a fisherman might be added to a tamer, bucolic scene. Syntax jokes that he and Grizzle, as perfect embodiments of the picturesque, are an enhancement to any landscape.

This passage in Doctor Syntax *may have inspired a famous quip by the wit and clergyman Sydney Smith, whom Austen met in Bath and possibly used as a model for Henry Tilney (NA): "The rector's horse is beautiful—the curate's is picturesque" (Lockhart, 99).*

Gilpin was especially drawn to figures who partook of the same "wildness" as his ideal landscapes, such as bandits or Gypsy beggars. Regular working folk, he thought, would spoil the view. Edward Ferrars (SS), by contrast, prefers the sight of "tidy, happy villagers" to "the finest banditti in the world" (I.18). In his view, beauty and wholesomeness go hand in hand.

"Will let your all-sufficient name
"The noble patronage proclaim; 180
"That time may know, till time doth end,
"That C******* was my honour'd friend."

SIR JOHN.
"And can you, learned Doctor, see
" When that important time[1] will be?"

SYNTAX.
"Sir Knight, that was not wisely spoke; 185
"The point's too serious for a joke:
"And you must know, by Heav'n's decree,
"That time will come to you and me,
"And then succeeds—Eternity."

MY LORD.
"Peace, peace, Sir John, and let me tell 190
"The Doctor that I wish him well.
"I doubt not but his work will prove,
"Most useful to the arts I love.
"But pray, good Sir, come up to town,[2]
"That seat of wealth and of renown: 195
"Come up to town nor fear the cost,
"Nor time nor labour shall be lost.
"I'll ope my door and take you in—
"You've made me laugh, and you shall win:
"We'll then consult how I can best 200
"Advance your real interest:
"And here this piece of writing[3] take;—
"You'll use it for the donor's sake:
"I mean, you see, that it shall crown
"Your wishes while you stay in town: 205
"But you may, as it suits you, use it,—
"No one, I fancy, will refuse it."
The Doctor, when he view'd the paper,
Instead of bowing—cut a caper.[4]

My Lord now sought th' expecting chase, 210
And Syntax, in his usual pace,

[1] **that important time:** The divinely appointed end of the world. Sir John forgets that "of that day and hour knoweth no *man*" (Matthew 24:36).

[2] **town:** London.

[3] **piece of writing:** A check.

[4] **cut a caper:** Danced and frolicked.

When four long tedious days had pass'd,
The town of Keswick[1] reach'd at last,
Where he his famous work prepar'd,
Of all his toil the hop'd reward.   215

[1] **Keswick:** A town
in the Lake District.

p. 149

    Soon as the morn began to break,
Old Grizzle bore him to the lake;[2]
Along its banks he gravely pac'd,
And all its various beauties trac'd;
When, lo, a threat'ning storm appear'd: 220
Phœbus the scene no longer cheer'd:
The dark clouds sink on ev'ry hill:
The floating mists the valleys fill:
Nature, transform'd, began to lour*,
And threaten'd a tremendous show'r.   225
"I love," he cry'd, "to hear the rattle,
"When elements contend in battle;
"For I insist, tho' some may flout it,
"Who write about it and about it,
"That we the *picturesque* may find   230
"In thunder loud, or whistling wind;
"And often, as I fully ween,
"It may be heard as well as seen;
"For, tho' a pencil cannot trace
"A sound as it can paint a place,   235
"The pen, in its poetic rage,
"Can make it figure on the page."

[2] **the lake:**
Presumably
Derwentwater, the
lake on whose
banks Keswick lies.
Syntax had spoken
of visiting lake
Windermere, but
apparently his plans
changed.

A fisherman, who pass'd that way,
Thought it civility to say—
"An' please you, Sir, 'tis all in vain   240
"To take your prospects in the rain;
"On horseback too you'll ne'er be able—
" 'Twere better, sure, to get a table."
"Thanks," Syntax said, "for your advice,
"And faith I'll take it in a trice;   245
"For, as I'm moisten'd to the skin,
"I'll seek a table at the inn:"—
But Grizzle, in her haste to pass,
Lur'd by a tempting tuft of grass,
A luckless step now chanc'd to take,   250
And sous'd[1] the Doctor in the lake;   [1] **sous'd:**
But, as it prov'd no worse disaster   Drenched.
Befell poor Grizzle or her master,
Than both of them could well endure,
And a warm inn would shortly cure;   255
To that warm inn they quickly hied,
Where Syntax, by the fire-side,
Sat, in his landlord's garments clad,
But neither sorrowful nor sad;
Nor did he waste his hours away,   260
But gave his pencil all its play,
And trac'd the landscapes of the day.

CANTO XIV.

"NATURE, dear Nature, is my goddess,[1]
"Whether array'd in rustic boddice,
"Or when the nicest touch of Art
"Doth to her charms new charms impart:
"But still I, somehow, love her best,   5
"When she's in ruder mantle drest:
"I do not mean in shape grotesque,
"But when she's truly *picturesque*."[2]

   Thus the next morning, as he stray'd,
And the surrounding scene survey'd,   10
Syntax exclaim'd.—A party stood
Just on the margin of the flood;[3]
Who were, *in statu quo*,[4] to make
A little voyage on the Lake.
The Doctor forward stepp'd to shew   15
The wealth of his port-folio.
The ladies were quite pleas'd to view
Such pretty pictures as he drew;
While a young man, a neighb'ring 'Squire,
Express'd a very warm desire,   20
Which seem'd to come from honest heart,
That of the boat he'd take a part.

   Now from the shore they quickly sail'd;
And soon the Doctor's voice prevail'd.
"This is a lovely scene of Nature;   25
"But I've enough of land and water:
"I want some living things to show
"How far the *picturesque* will go."

LADY.
   "See, Sir, how swift the swallows fly:
"And see the lark ascends on high;   30
"We scarce can view him in the sky.

152

¹ **NATURE...goddess:** An allusion to Edmund's famous soliloquy in *King Lear*, which begins, "Thou, nature, art my goddess" (1.2.1).

² **truly *picturesque:*** Syntax invokes a variety of scenic views in this opening passage—the open countryside cultivated by peasant farmers (nature in "rustic boddice"); the elegant grounds of an estate (improved by the "nicest touch of art"); and nature pure and simple, unaltered by humans ("in ruder mantle drest"). The lines closely mirror a passage in Gilpin's *Three Essays*, in which Gilpin praises the beauty of landscapes shaped by humans, "whether in a grand, or in a humble stile," before declaring his preference for untouched nature: "From scenes indeed of the *picturesque kind* we exclude the appendages of tillage, and in general the works of men; which too often introduce preciseness, and formality" (TE 9-10.)

³ **margin of the flood:** Bank of the lake.

⁴ *in statu quo:* In that state.

Austen's ideal landscapes, unlike Gilpin's, almost always include instances of "the works of men." The view from Donwell Abbey (Em.) is picturesque in Gilpin's sense at first—woods and a river of "considerable abruptness and grandeur"—but it culminates in a well-ordered, productive farm (III.6). The union of the natural and the human is what perfects the scene: "English verdure, English culture, English comfort." Nature provides the verdure, people provide the culture (agriculture), and the result of the two together is "comfort"—well-being and plenty.

"Vale of Keswick and Derwentwater," Joseph Farington, c. 1780. YCBA.
This is the lake Syntax is viewing at the beginning of this canto.

"Behold the wild-fowl, how they spread
"Upon the lake's expansive bed:
"The kite sails through the airy way,
"Prepared to pounce upon its prey: 35
"The rooks too from their morning food
"Pass cawing to the distant wood."

SYNTAX.
  "When with a philosophic eye
"The realms of Nature I descry,
"And view the grace that she can give   40
"To all the varying forms that live,
"I feel with awe the plastic art[1]
"That doth such wond'rous pow'rs impart
"To all that wing the air, or creep
"Along the earth, or swim the deep.   45
"I love the winged world that flies
"Thro' the thin azure of skies;
"Or, not ordain'd those heights to scan,
"Live the familiar friends of man,
"And in his yard, or round his cot*,   50
"Enjoy, poor things! their destin'd lot:
"But tho' their plumes are gay with dies,[2]
"In endless, bright diversities—
"What tho' such glowing tints prevail,
"When the proud peacock spreads his tail—   55
"What tho' the nightingales prolong
"Thro' the charm'd night th' enchanting song—
"What tho' the blackbird and the thrush
"Make vocal ev'ry verdant bush—
"Not one among the winged kind   60
"Presents an object to my mind;
"Their grace and beauty's nought to me;
"In all their vast variety
"The *picturesque* I cannot see.
"A carrion fowl ty'd to a stake   65
"Will a far better picture make,[3]
"When as a scare-crow 'tis display'd,
"For thievish birds to be afraid,

154

"Study of Birds," Unknown, c. 1840. YCBA.

[1] **plastic art:** The power (divine or natural) that causes the growth or formation of living things. Syntax's use of the term, along with his wonder in the face of nature's diversity, recalls a famous passage from Coleridge's "Eolian Harp": "And what if all of animated nature / Be but organic Harps diversely fram'd, / That tremble into thought, as o'er them sweeps / Plastic and vast, one intellectual breeze, / At once the Soul of each, and God of all?" (*Works*, Vol. 1, 102)

[2] **gay with dies:** Bright with many colors (dyes).

[3] **A carrion fowl...make:** In this satirical passage, the smoothness, grace, and beauty of birds (dead vultures excepted) exclude them from the picturesque, which prioritizes roughness above all else. Gilpin himself never denounced birds; in fact he encouraged sketchers of landscapes to embrace "that ornamental aid / The feathered race afford" (TE 120). However, he did express a general preference for animals whose "harder lines, and rougher coats, exhibit more the graces of the pencil" (TE 14). See note 2 on p. 147 for more on animals and the picturesque.

In the Romantic period, an ability to feel awe in the presence of nature was seen as an indicator of virtue and even piety. Fanny Price (MP) channels something of this natural piety while "rhapsodising" over the variety of trees near Mansfield Parsonage: "When one thinks of it, how astonishing a variety of nature! [...] that the same soil and the same sun should nurture plants differing in the first rule and law of their existence" (II.4). Worldly and narcissistic Mary Crawford jokingly replies that, for her, the most wonderful thing in the scene is her own self. Mary's indifference to nature is of a piece with her indifference to religion, morality, and serious subjects generally.

"Than the white swan, in all its pride,
"Sailing upon the crystal tide.   70
"As a philosopher I scan
"Whate'er kind Heav'n has made for man;
"I feel it a religious duty
"To bless its use and praise its beauty:
"I care not whatsoe'er the creature,   75
"Whate'er its name, its form and feature,
"So that fond Nature will aver
"The creature doth belong to her:—[1]
"But tho', indeed, I may admire
"The greyhound's form, and snake's attire,   80
"They neither will my object suit
"Like a good shaggy, ragged brute.
"I will acknowledge that a goose
"Is a fine fowl, of sov'reign use:
"But for a picture she's not fitted—   85
"The bird was made but to be spitted.
"The pigeon, I'll be bound to shew it,
"Is a fine subject for a poet;
"In the soft verse his mate he'll woo,
"Turn his gay neck, and bill, and coo;   90
"And, as in am'rous strut he moves,
"Soothes the fond heart of him who loves;
"But I'll not paint him, no, not I—
"I like him better in a pye,
"Well rubb'd with salt and spicy dust,   95
"And thus embody'd in a crust.[2]
"How many a bird that haunts the wood,
"How many a fowl that cleaves the flood,
"With their sweet songs enchant my ear,
"Or please my eye as they appear,   100
"When in their flight, or as they row
"Delighted on the lake below!
"But still, whate'er their form or feather,
"You cannot make them group together:[3]
"For, let them swim or let them fly,   105
"The *picturesque* they all defy.
"The bird that's sitting quite alone
"Is fit but to be carv'd in stone;

¹ **I feel it...to her:** The moral logic of this passage recalls Coleridge's *Rime of the Ancient Mariner*, in which a seaman suffers a curse for arbitrarily killing an albatross. The curse is lifted, and the mariner is able to pray to God, only when he learns to bless and see the beauty in all living things, including those he used to find hideous.

"Beyond the shadow of the ship I watched the water-snakes," Gustave Doré, 1884. *The Rime of the Ancient Mariner* (Boston: Estes and Lauriat, 1884), p. 27.

For Edward Ferrars (SS), this is the problem at the heart of the picturesque system: its indifference and, at times, direct hostility to "matters of utility"—and by extension human comfort and thriving. He considers a "fine country" to be one that "unites beauty with utility," and he goes on to name a "snug farm-house" and "tidy, happy villagers" among the things he likes to see in a view (I.18). Edward's pragmatism puts him at odds with Marianne, who relishes natural grandeur but cares little for the common concerns of common people.

² **I will acknowledge...crust:** Gilpin insisted that the picturesque was purely an aesthetic category, utterly indifferent, as he rather loftily put it, to "matters of utility" (FS 298)—such as whether a piece of land was suitable for cultivation. Syntax is making a similar point: just because an animal is useful for food doesn't mean it is a suitable subject for painting. At the same time, his eager descriptions of roasted geese and well-flavored pigeon pies make one wonder if the pragmatic stomach is getting the better of the picturesque eye in this scene.

³ **cannot make them group together:** Gilpin preferred small groups of animals in a landscape. Syntax may be saying that birds, which tend to gather in large flocks, resist such grouping.

"And any man of taste 'twould shock
"To paint those wild geese in a flock.   110
"Though I like not a single figure,
"Whether 'tis lesser or 'tis bigger.
"That fisherman, so lean and lank,
"Who sits alone upon the bank,
"Tempts not the eye; but, doff his coat,   115
"And quickly group him with a boat,
"You then will see the fellow make
"A pretty object on the lake.[1]
"If a boy's playing with a hoop,
" 'Tis something, for it forms a group,   120
"In painter's eyes—O! what a joke
"To place a bird upon an oak:
"At the same time, 'twould help the jest,
"Upon a branch to fix a nest.
"A trout, with all its pretty dies   125
"Of various hues, delights the eyes;
"But still it is a silly whim
"To make him on a canvas swim:
"Yet, I must own, that dainty fish
"Looks very handsome in a dish;   130
"And he must be a thankless sinner
"Who thinks a trout a paltry dinner.

   "The first, the middle, and the last,
"In *picturesque* is *bold contrast;* [2]
"And painting has no nobler use   135
"Than this grand object to produce.
"Such is my thought, and I'll pursue it;
"There's an example—you shall view it:
"Look at that tree—then take a glance—
"At its fine, bold protuberance;   140
"Behold those branches—how their shade
"Is by the mass of light display'd;
"Look at that light, and see how fine
"The backward shadows make it shine:
"The sombre clouds that spot the sky   145
"Make the blue vaulting twice as high;

¹ **That fisherman...lake:** Another allusion to Gilpin. In one of his tours, Gilpin argued that a fisherman in a boat on a lake is picturesque, but one on the bank, as a "single figure," is not (OCW Vol. II, 45). Combe interprets the moment as part of Gilpin's theory of grouping, and proceeds to mock such hair-splitting with a series of arbitrary and ridiculous "groups": a boy becomes picturesque when you add a hoop; a bird when you add a nest; a fish when you add a plate. Combe actually misreads Gilpin's fisherman passage, which isn't about grouping at all, but the joke still lands. Gilpin often opined on the proper grouping of objects and figures, and his "rules" on the subject sometimes were absurdly fastidious.

² ***bold contrast:*** Another picturesque law, though not one that Combe seems to be mocking. Gilpin hailed contrast as "Beauty's surest source" (TE 108). In the lines that follow, Syntax gives a largely accurate survey of the kinds of contrast that, according to Gilpin, enrich a picturesque scene.

One of Gilpin's rules on grouping concerned cattle. Three, he thought, were ideal: if you wished to add a fourth, then the fourth should be "detached" from the other three (OCW Vol. II, 258). Elizabeth Bennet (PP) alludes to this rather arbitrary rule when she tells Darcy, Mrs. Hurst, and Miss Bingley that they are "charmingly group'd [...]. The picturesque would be spoilt by admitting a fourth" (I.10). One wonders if any of the party realized they had just been compared to cattle!

A group of cattle, William Gilpin, 1786. *The Mountains, and Lakes of Cumberland and Westmorland*, opp. p. 259. Gilpin used this image to illustrate his claim that a group of three cattle is ideal, with an optional detached fourth. Austen likely had it in mind when she devised the scene discussed in the above-right note.

"And where the sunbeams warmly glow,
"They make the hollow twice as low.
"The Flemish painters all surpass
"In making pictures smooth as glass: 150
"In Cuyp's[1] best works there's pretty painting:
"But, the bold *picturesque* is wanting.

  "Thus, tho' I leave the birds to sing,
"Or cleave the air with rapid wing—
"Thus, tho' I leave the fish to play   155
"Till the net drags them into day—
"Kind Nature, ever-bounteous mother!
"Contrives it in some way or other,
"Our proper wishes to supply
"In infinite variety.   160
"The world of quadrupeds displays
"The painter's arts in various ways;
"But, 'tis some shaggy, ragged brute
"That will my busy purpose suit;
"Or such as, from their shape and make,   165
"No fine-wrought high-bred semblance take.
"A well-fed horse, with shining skin,
"Form'd for the course, and plates to win,
"May have his beauties, but not those
"That will my graphic art disclose: 170
"My raw-bon'd mare is worth a score
"Of these fine pamper'd beasts, and more,
"To give effect to bold design,
"And decorate such views as mine.
"To the fine steed you sportsmen bow,   175
"But *picturesque* prefers a cow:
"On her high hips and horned head
"How true the light and shade are shed.
"Indeed I should prefer by half,
"To a fine colt, a common calf,   180
"The unshorn sheep, the shaggy goat,
"The ass[2] with rugged, ragged coat,
"Would, to a taste-inspir'd mind,
"Leave the far-fam'd *Eclipse*[3] behind:

[1] **Cuyp's:** Aelbert Cuyp was a 17th-c. Dutch painter known for his bucolic paintings of animals and landscapes. Syntax implies that his peaceful scenes lack the grandeur and roughness of the picturesque.

[2] **cow...goat...ass:** This scene mirrors a passage in *Three Essays* where Gilpin declares rough-coated livestock to be more picturesque than glossy racehorses (14-16).

[3] ***Eclipse:*** A famous, undefeated 18th-c. racehorse.

"In a grand stable he might please,   185
"But ne'er should graze beneath my trees."

Caught by his words, the northern 'Squire
Fail'd not his learning to admire;
But yet he had a wish to quiz[1]   [1] **quiz:** Tease or
The Doctor's humour, and his phiz.[2]   190 mock.
"I have a house," he said, "at hand,   [2] **The Doctor's**
"Where you my service may command;   **humour, and his**
"There I have cows, and asses too,   **phiz:** His
"And pigs, and sheep, Sir, not a few,   enthusiasm for
"Where you, at your untroubled leisure,   195 picturesque animals
"May draw them as it suits your pleasure.   and his unusual face
"You shall be welcome, and your mare;   (phiz).
"And find a country 'Squire's fare:
"With us a day or two you'll pass,—
"We'll give you meat—and give her grass."   200
Thus 'twas agreed;—they came on shore;—
The party saunter'd on before;
But, ere they reach'd their mansion fair,
Grizzle had borne her master there.
It was, indeed, a pleasant spot   205
That this same country 'Squire had got:
And Syntax now the party join'd
With salutation free and kind.

    'SQUIRE.
  "This, Doctor Syntax, is my sister:
"Why, my good Sir, you have not kiss'd her."   210

    SYNTAX.
  "Do not suppose I'm such a brute
"As to disdain the sweet salute."

    'SQUIRE.
  "And this, Sir, is my loving wife,
"The joy and honour of my life."

    SYNTAX.
  "A lovely Lady to the view!   215
"And, with your leave I'll kiss her too."

161

Thus pleasant words the converse cheer'd
Till dinner on the board appear'd.
Where a warm welcome gave a zest
To the fair plenty of the feast.   220
The Doctor eat, and talk'd and quaff'd;
The good Host smil'd, the Ladies laugh'd.

      'SQUIRE.
"As you disdain both fowl and fish,
"Think you your art could paint that dish?"

      SYNTAX.
"Tho' 'twill to hunger give relief,—   225
"There's nothing *picturesque* in Beef:
"But there are artists—if you'll treat 'em—
"Will paint your dinners; that is—eat 'em."

      'SQUIRE.
"But, sure, your pencil might command
"Whate'er is noble, vast and grand,—
"The beasts, forsooth, of Indian land;   230
"Where the fierce, savage tyger scowls,
"And the fell, hungry lion growls."

162

SYNTAX.
"These beasts may all be subjects fit;
"But, for their likeness, will they sit?   235
"I'd only take a view askaunt,
"From the tall back of elephant:
"With half an hundred Indians round me,
"That such sharp claws might not confound me:
"But now, as we have ceas'd to dine,   240
"And I have had my share of wine,
"I should be glad to close the feast
"But drawing some more harmless beast."
The Doctor found a quick consent,
And to the farm their way they bent.   245
A tub inverted form'd his seat;
The animals their painter meet:
Cows, asses, sheep, and ducks and geese,
Present themselves, to grace the piece:
Poor Grizzle, too, among the rest,   250
Of the true *picturesque* possest,
Quitted the meadow to appear,
And took her station in the rear:
The sheep all baa'd, the asses bray'd
The moo-cows low'd, and Grizzle neigh'd: 255
"Stop, brutes," he cry'd, "your noisy glee;
"I do not want to hear—but see;
"Tho' by the *picturesquish* laws,
"You're better too with open jaws."[1]

The Doctor now, with genius big,   260
First drew a cow, and next a pig:
A sheep now on the paper passes,
And then he sketch'd a group of asses;
Nor did he fail to do his duty
In giving Grizzle all her beauty.   265
"And now," says Miss, (a laughing elf)
"I wish, Sir, you wou'd draw yourself."
"With all my heart," the Doctor said,
"But not with horns[2] upon my head."

[1] *picturesquish* **laws...jaws:** Gilpin advanced no opinion on open jaws, but he did suggest that the human body, at least, was more picturesque when "agitated" than when "quiescent" (TE 12). Combe may be extrapolating from that passage.

[2] **not with horns:** Horns denoted a cuckold, a man whose wife had been unfaithful to him.

DOCTOR SYNTAX DRAWING AFTER NATURE.

"—And then I hope you'll draw my face!" 270
"In vain, fair maid, my art would trace
"Those winning smiles, that native grace.
"The beams of beauty I disclaim;—
"The *picturesque's* my only aim:
"My pencil's skill is mostly shown 275
"In drawing faces like my own,
"Where Time, alas, and anxious Care,
"Have plac'd so many wrinkles there."[1]

   Now all beneath a spreading tree
They chat, and sip their evening tea,
Where Syntax told his various fate, 280
His studious life and married state;
And that he hop'd his Tour would tend
His comforts and his purse to mend.
At length they to the house retreated, 285
And round the supper soon were seated;
When the time quickly pass'd away,
And gay good-humour clos'd the day.

[1] **The beams of beauty…wrinkles there:** For more on the mock-picturesque qualities of Syntax's face, see note 1 on p. 147.

CANTO XV.

"VIRTUE embraces ev'ry state;
"And, while it gilds the rich and great,
"It cheers their hearts who humbly stray
"Along Life's more sequester'd way.
"While, from beneath the portals proud,   5
"Wealth oft relieves the suppliant crowd;
"The wayworn pilgrim smiles to share,
"In lowly homes, the welcome fare.
"In splendid halls and painted bow'rs
"Plenty may crown the festive hours;   10
"Yet still within the secret dell
"The hospitable Virtues dwell;
"And in this isle,[1] so brave and fair,
"Kind Charity is ev'rywhere.
"Within the city's ample bound   15
"Her stately piles[2] are seen around;
"Where ev'ry want and ev'ry pain,
"That in man's feeble nature reign—
"Where the sad heir of pining grief
"May, bless'd be Heav'n! obtain relief: 20
"While, on the humble village-green,
"How oft the low-roof'd pile[3] is seen,
"Where poverty forgets its woes,
"And wearied age may find repose.

"Thrice happy Britons! while the car[4]   25
"Of furious, unrelenting War
"Leaves the dire tracks of streaming gore
"On many a hapless, distant shore,—
"While a remorseless tyrant's hand[5]
"Deals mis'ry thro' each foreign land,   30
"And fell destruction, from the throne
"To him who doth the cottage own,—

166

A Lady and Children Relieving a Cottager, William Redmore Bigg, 1781. Philadelphia Museum of Art.

¹ **this isle:** Great Britain.

² **Her stately piles:** Syntax is referring to large charitable institutions such as the London "voluntary hospitals" for the poor. He also alludes to madhouses like Bethlem Hospital ("Bedlam") which offered a refuge to those suffering from the "sad heir of pining grief"— that is, insanity.

³ **low-roof'd pile:** An almshouse. Almshouses provided free or subsidized housing to the poor and elderly of a particular locale.

⁴ **car:** A chariot such as would be used in battle in the ancient world. Here a symbol of war.

⁵ **tyrant's hand:** Syntax refers to Napoleon Bonaparte, whose military campaigns did indeed topple thrones while also wreaking terrible devastation on common folk.

Austen's view of the extent of charity in Great Britain was not as sunny as Syntax's. In the rural communities of her novels, the people best positioned to help the poor are wealthy landlords, and they are a mixed bag. Darcy (PP) is "a liberal man" and does "much good among the poor" (III.2). His aunt Lady Catherine, however, prefers to "scold [her tenants] into harmony and plenty," substituting dictatorial advice for real help (II.7).

As the party from Mansfield Park approaches Sotherton, Maria Bertram points out some almshouses built by the Rushworth family. It is one of several signs that the house of Rushworth, in former generations, took their moral and social responsibilities seriously, even if the current master of Sotherton does not.

"Peace beams upon your sea-girt isle,
"Where the bright virtues ever smile;
"Where hostile shoutings ne'er molest   35
"The happy inmate's[1] genial rest.
"Where'er it is his lot to go,
"He will not meet an armed foe;
"Nay, wheresoe'er his way doth tend,
"He sure may chance to find a friend."   40

  Thus, having rose at early day,
As thro' the fields he took his way,
The Doctor did his thoughts rehearse,
And, as the Muse inspir'd, in verse;
For, while with skill each form he drew,   45
His Rev'rence was a poet too.

  But soon a bell's shrill, tinkling sound
Re-echo'd all the meads around,
And said, as plain as bell could say—
"Breakfast is ready—come away."   50
The welcome summons he obey'd,
And found an arbour's pleasing shade,
Where, while the plenteous meal was spread,
The woodbine[2] flaunted o'er his head.

  "Ah! little do the proud and great,   55
"Amid the pomp and toil of state,
"Know of those simple, real joys,
"With which the bosom never cloys!
"O! what a heart-reviving treat
"I find within this rural seat!   60
"All that can please the quicken'd taste,
"Is offer'd in this fair repast.[3]
"The flowers, on their native bed,
"Around delicious odours shed;
"A bloom that with the flow'ret vies   65
"On those fair cheeks, attracts my eyes;
"And what sweet music greets my ear,
"When that voice bids me welcome here!

[1] **inmate's:** An inmate is a person dwelling where he does not usually live, like Syntax.

[2] **woodbine:** A climbing plant such as honeysuckle.

[3] **repast:** Meal.

"Indeed, each sense combines to bless
"The present hour with happiness."   70

   Thus Syntax spoke, nor spoke in vain;
The Ladies felt the flatt'ring strain;[1]
Nor could they do enough to please
The Doctor for his courtesies:—
"All that you see, if that's a charm,   75
"Is, Sir, the produce of our farm:
"The rolls are nice, our oven bakes 'em;
"Those oat-cakes too, my sister makes 'em.
"The cream is rich, pray do not save[2] it;
"The brindled cow[3] you drew, Sir, gave it: 80
"And here is some fresh-gather'd fruit—
"I hope it will your palate suit:
" 'Tis country fare which you receive,
"But 'tis the best we have to give."

   "O!" said the 'Squire, "the Doctor jokes   85
"With us poor harmless country folks:
"I wonder that with all his sense,
"And such a tickling eloquence,
"He has not turn'd an humble priest
"Into a good fat dean,[4] at least.   90
"We know how soon a Lady's ear
"Will list, the honey'd sound to hear:
"At the same time, I'm free to say
"I think the men as vain as they.
"How happens it, my learned friend,   95
"That you have not attain'd your end;
"That all your figures and your tropes
"Have not fulfill'd your rightful hopes?
"I should suppose your shining parts,
"And, above all, your flatt'ring arts,   100
"Would soon have turn'd your grizly mare
"Into a handsome chaise and pair*.
"I live amidst my native groves,
"And the calm scene my nature loves:
"But still I know, and often see,   105
"What gains are made by flattery."

[1] **strain:** A stream of impassioned language (OED).

[2] **save:** Conserve.

[3] **brindled cow:** One whose coat is streaked.

[4] **I wonder… dean:** Squire Worthy expresses surprise that Syntax, with his gift for flattery, has not risen in the church.

"That may be true," the Doctor said;
"But flattery is not my trade.
"Indeed, dear Sir, you do me wrong—
"No sordid int'rest[1] guides my tongue.
"Honour and Virtue I admire,   110
"Or in a Bishop, or a 'Squire;[2]
"But falsehood I most keenly hate,
"Tho' gilt with wealth, or crown'd with state.[3]
"For *TRUTH* I'm like a lion bold;
"And a base lie I never told: 115
"Indeed, I know, too many a sinner
"Will lie by dozens for a dinner;
"But, from the days of earliest youth
"I've worshipp'd, as I practis'd, truth;
"Nay, many a stormy, bitter strife   120
"I've had with my dear loving wife,
"Who often says she might have seen
"Her husband a fine pompous dean:
"Indeed, she sometimes thinks her spouse
"Might have a mitre* on his brows,   125
"If, putting scruples out of view,
"He'd do as other people do.[4]
"No—I will never lie nor fawn,
"Nor flatter, to be rob'd in lawn.[5]
"I too, can boast a certain rule   130
"Within the precincts of my school:
"Whatever faults I may pass by,
"I never can forgive a lie.
"I hate to use the birchin rod;
"But, when a boy forswears his God,   135
"When he in purpos'd falsehood deals,
"My heavy strokes the culprit feels.
"Vice I detest, whoever shews it,
"And, when I see it, I'll expose it:
"But, to kind hearts my homage due   140
"I willing pay, and pay to you;
"Nor will you, Sir, deny the share
"That's due to these two Ladies fair."

¹ **int'rest:** Ulterior motive.

² **Bishop...'Squire:** Bishops and wealthy landowners controlled the majority of church livings; Syntax says that, while he will praise virtue wherever he finds it, he will not flatter the powerful with an eye to career advancement.
³ **state:** High status.

⁴ **Indeed...people do:** Syntax's wife thinks he might have become a bishop if he had been willing to flatter. As there were only around twenty bishops in the entire Anglican church, Dolly's confidence in her husband's abilities, and in the power of flattery, must have been great indeed.
⁵ **lawn:** Fine material from which bishops' sleeves were made.

Detail from "The Clerical Exercise," George Woodward, 1791. Lewis Walpole Library. The captions read, "Approach your patron / Ask for a living / Take leave of your Patron."

Austen does not say what led Lady Catherine (PP) to offer Mr. Collins, a stranger and a fool, the living of Hunsford. This conversation, though, may point to the answer: his talent, as Mr. Bennet puts it, of "flattering with delicacy" (1.14).

In Austen's novels, too, clergymen's wives (and fiancées) tend to be eager for their husbands' advancement. The ever-active Lucy Steele (SS) is not above soliciting her rival Elinor's help in finding her fiancé a living. Charlotte Collins (PP), meanwhile, is willing to endure frequent visits to Rosings Park in the hope that Lady Catherine will bestow further preferment on her husband. Even her wishes for Elizabeth's marriage hinge on Mr. Collins' advancement: she thinks her friend would be happier with Col. Fitzwilliam, but hopes she will instead marry Darcy, who has "considerable patronage in the church" (II.9).

The 'Squire replied, "I e'en must yield,
"And leave you master of the field: 145
"These Ladies will, I'm sure, agree
"That you have fairly conquer'd me;
"But, be assur'd, all joke apart,
"I feel your doctrine from my heart.
"Your free-born conduct I commend,   150
"And shall rejoice to call you friend;
"O! how it would my spirits cheer
"If you were but the Vicar here.
"Our Parson, I'm concern'd to say,
"Had rather drink and game¹ than pray.   155
"He makes no bones² to curse and swear,
"In any rout³ to take a share,   }
"And, what's still worse, he'll springe a hare.⁴
"I wish his neck he would but break,
"Or tumble drunk into the lake!   160
"For, know the living's mine to give,
"And you should soon the Cure receive:
"The benefice,⁵ I'm sure, is clear,
"At least three hundred pounds a year."

    "I thank you, Sir, with all my heart,"   165
Said Syntax, "but we now must part."
The fair-ones cry'd—"We beg you'll stay,
"And pass with us another day."
"—Ladies, I would 'twere in my pow'r,
"But I can't stay another hour: 170
"I feel your kindness to my soul,
"And wish I could my fate control.
"Within ten days the time will come
"When I shall be expected home;
"Nor is this all—for, strange to say,   175
"I must take London in my way."
Thus converse kind the moments cheer'd,
Till Grizzle at the gate appear'd.
"Well," said the 'Squire, "since you must go,
"Our hearty wishes we bestow: 180
"And if your genius bids you take
"Another journey to the Lake,

"Parsonic Piety (do as I say not as I do)," Isaac Cruikshank, 1794. YCBA.

[1] **game:** Gamble.

[2] **makes no bones:** Does not hesitate.

[3] **rout:** Disturbance or riot.

[4] **springe a hare:** Trap a hare—a form of poaching. It is revealing that Squire Worthy considers this the worst of his vicar's offenses. English landowners tended to take their hunting rights very seriously, and could be harsh indeed against those who caught game animals like hares for food.

[5] **Cure…benefice:** Both these words refer to a clerical living; the cure is the responsibility to care for the souls of a given parish; the benefice is the right to the clerical income of that parish. Except in the case of curates, who had the cure but not the benefice, the two would go together.

Despite the vicar's shocking behavior, Squire Worthy would have had almost no way to get rid of him, since rectors and vicars held their positions for life. Mr. Darcy (PP) no doubt has this fact in mind when he readily agrees to Mr. Wickham's proposal to accept cash in lieu of a living. Had Wickham become a clergyman, Squire Worthy's plight might very well have become Darcy's.

Like Squire Worthy, Mr. Rushworth (MP) is full of "zeal after poachers" (I.12). For Austen, this is evidence of a distinctly masculine small-mindedness. Poaching did little harm besides interfering with the amusement of rich men, and thus hardly justified the outrage it often excited.

"The Poacher," Thomas Rowlandson, 1806. The Met.

"Remember *Worthy-Hall*, we pray,
"And come, and make a longer stay:
"Write too, and tell your distant friends   185
"With what success your journey ends.
"We do not mean it as a bribe,
"But to your work we must subscribe."
The Ladies too exclaim'd—"repeat
"Your visit to our northern seat."   190

  Poor Syntax knew not how to tell
The gratitude he felt so well;
And, when at length he said, "Good bye."
A tear was bright in either eye.

  The Doctor pac'd along the way   195
Till it grew nigh the close of day,
When the fair town appear'd in sight,
Where he propos'd to pass the night:
But when he reach'd the destin'd inn,
The landlord, with officious grin,   200
At once declar'd he had no bed
Where Syntax could repose his head:
At least where such a rev'rend guest
Would think it fit to take his rest.
There was a main of cocks[1] that day,   205
And all the gentry chose to stay.
"Observe, my friend, I mind not cost,"
Says Syntax to his cringing host;
"But still, at least, I may be able
"To sleep with Grizzle in the stable;   210
"And many a Doctor after all,
"Is proud to *slumber in a stall*: [2]
"In short, I only want to sleep
"Where neither rogue nor knave[3] can creep:
"I travel not with change of coats,   215
"But in these bags are all my notes;
"Which, should I lose, would prove ruin,
"And be for ever my undoing."
Thus as he spoke, a lively blade,[4]
With dangling queue[5] and smart cockade,[6]   220

"Royal Cock Pit," Thomas Rowlandson, 1808.
The Lewis Walpole Library.

[1] **main of cocks:** A large event featuring a number of cock fights. Cock fighting was a popular, if somewhat disreputable, entertainment up and down the social ladder.

[2] *slumber in a stall:* A joke on prebendaries, high-ranking cathedral dignitaries. During divine service, prebendaries sat in special seats called "stalls." The position was known to provide a comfortable income in exchange for very little work.

[3] **knave:** Scoundrel.

Dr. Grant (MP) is elevated to a prebendal stall at Westminster Cathedral, which enhances his income while allowing him to retire, more or less, from his parish duties. It is not hard to imagine the indolent and well-fed Dr. Grant "slumbering in a stall."

[4] **blade:** A dashing, jaunty fellow.

[5] **queue:** The long pigtail of certain wigs worn by men.

[6] **cockade:** A bunch of ribbons pinned to a hat, here as a military insignia.

Reply'd at once, "I have a room:
"The friend I look'd for is not come;
"And of two beds where we may rest,
"You, my good Sir, shall have the best;
"So you may sleep without alarm,   225
"No living wight* shall do you harm;
"You may depend upon my word;—
"I serve the King, and wear a sword."
"Your offer, Sir, I kindly greet,"
Says Syntax, "but you'll let me treat   } 230
"With what is best to drink and eat;
"And I request you will prepare
"To your own taste, the bill of fare."[2]

[2] **bill of fare:** Menu.

  The Doctor and the Captain sat,
Till tired of each other's chat,   235
They both agreed it would be best
To seek the balmy sweets of rest.

Syntax soon clos'd each weary eye,
Nor thought of any danger nigh;
While, like the ever-watchful snake,   240
His sharp companion lay awake,
Impatient to assail his prey:
When, soon as it was dawn of day,
He gently seiz'd the fancied store;[1]
But, as he pass'd the creaking door,   245
Syntax awoke, and saw the thief:
When, loudly bawling for relief,
He forward rush'd in naked state,
And caught the culprit at the gate:
Against that gate his head he beat,   250
Then kick'd him headlong to the street.

  The ostler* from his bed arose,
In time to hear and see the blows.
Says Syntax, "I'll not make a riot;
"I've saved my notes, and I'll be quiet.   255
"The rascal, if I'm not mistaken,
"Will ask his legs to save his bacon:
"But, what a figure I appear!
"I must not stand and shiver here;
"So take me back into the room,   260
"From whence in this strange way I'm come."
The ostler then the Doctor led,
To the warm comforts of his bed.
Into that bed he quickly crept,
Beneath his head his bags he kept,   } 265
And on that pillow safely slept.

[1] **fancied store:**
When the captain
hears Syntax speak
of notes, he
assumes he means
banknotes. In fact
he means the notes
for his book.

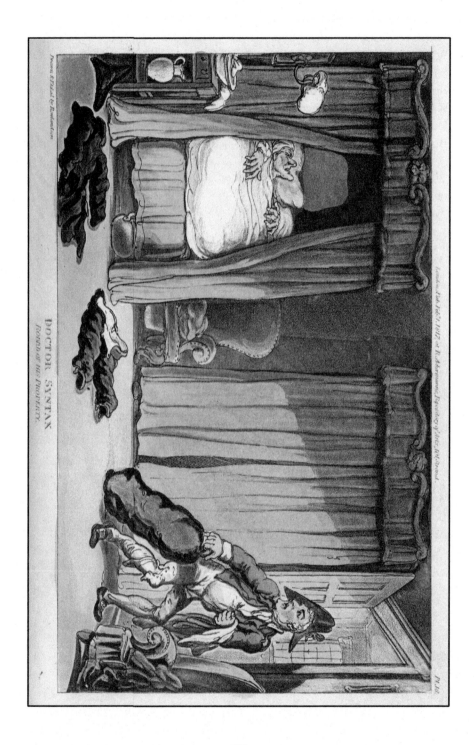

CANTO XVI.

FAIR Virtue is its own reward,
For Heav'n remains its constant guard;
And it becomes us all to rest
In this grand truth—that Heav'n is just.
Whatever forms the human lot,   5
Whether in palace or in cot*,
In the calm track or frequent strife,
Man leads his variegated life;
Whether he feasts his smiling hours
In stately halls or painted bow'rs[1];   10
Whether he labour thro' the day
In Winter cold or Summer's ray;
Or, in long nights of tort'ring pain,
He strives to close his eyes in vain;
Comfort will on his lot attend   15
If Virtue be his bosom friend.
In youth, when Love's creative pow'r
Forms the young passion's roseate bow'r;[2]
When, life matur'd, the eager game
That hunts for wealth, or seeks for fame,   20
So oft is play'd with various art,
To seize the mind and fill the heart:
When pleasure doth its charms display,
And Syrens[3] sing but to betray;
Virtue stands forth, and dares defy   25
Th' attack of ev'ry enemy.
When age comes on, with stealing pace,
And the crutch marks the closing race,
Virtue supports her champion's cause,
And cheers him with her fond applause: 30
Nay, e'en at Death's resistless hour,
She still displays her conscious pow'r;

[1] **painted bow'rs:** Lavishly decorated homes or rooms.

[2] **In youth... bow'r:** In other words, "When young Love conjures up visions of happiness..."

[3] **Syrens:** Mythical creatures who lure sailors to their ruin with their enchanting song, used here to symbolize deceptive pleasures.

Nor fails to make the flow'rets bloom
Round the dark confines of the tomb.

   Thus Syntax ponder'd—when around 35
His head he turn'd, and grateful found
His bags and notes all safe and sound:
Pleas'd with the prospect, he was fain
To yawn, and go to sleep again.

   But, while he still enjoy'd his dream, 40
His story was the gen'ral theme
Of ev'ry tongue, and made a din
Thro' all the purlieus* of the inn.
The ostler* told it to the maid,
And she the whole, and more, betray'd; 45
Nay, in her idle eager prate,[1]   [1] **prate**: Prattle,
Mistook the window for the gate: loose talk.
For, tho' she lay all snug and quiet,
And slept, unconscious of the riot,
She swore that, all within her view, 50
The Parson from the window threw
A full-grown man into the street,
Who haply lighted on his feet,
And then ran off, all thro' the dirt,
With night-cap on, and half a shirt. 55

   The barber caught the story next,
Who stuck no closer to the text;
But left a man half-shav'd, and ran
To tell it to the clergyman.
"O! bless me, Sir," he cry'd, "I fear 60
"To utter, what you now must hear:
"At the *Blue Bell* there's been such doing—
"The house, I'm certain, it must ruin;
"Nay, as I live, I'll tell no further,—
"A bishop has committed murther! 65
"He seiz'd a Captain by the pate,
"And dash'd it so against the gate,
"That all the planks are cover'd o'er
"With scatter'd brains and human gore.

"His lordship gave him such a banging,   70
"That he will scarce escape with hanging.
"They quarrell'd, Sir, as it was said,
"About the colours, black and red,[1]
"The Captain manfully profess'd
"That the bright scarlet was the best;   75
"And they, who that fine colour wore,
"The first of all professions bore;—
"While black (it was not very civil)
"Was the known liv'ry[2] of the devil.
"Thus soon a loud dispute arose,   80
"Which from hard words went on to blows:
"And ended in this bloody strife,
"Which robb'd the Captain of his life;
"And, if fair Justice does not faulter,
"Will deck the Bishop with a halter."[3]   85
The Parson smil'd, and bid the calf[4]
Go home, and shave the other half:
But, when he came, th' impatient elf
Had shav'd the other half himself.
   The Tailor laid aside his needle   90
To hear the story from the Beadle,[5]
Who swore he had strange news to tell
Of what had happen'd at the *Bell*:—

[1] **black and red:** Indicative of the clergy and the army, respectively.

[2] **liv'ry:** Livery, distinctive clothing worn by servants indicating which master they serve.

[3] **halter:** Noose, for hanging.

[4] **calf:** A bit of a fool. The term is mildly affectionate.

[5] **Beadle:** Officer charged with keeping the peace and carrying out various matters of parish business.

"Would you believe it, that, last night,
"A highwayman, a man of might,   95
"Down in his bed a lawyer bound,
"And robb'd him of a thousand pound;
"Then gagg'd him, that he might not rouse
"The people sleeping in the house."
"No, no," says Snip, "however strong,   100
"No gag will stop a Lawyer's tongue;
"And, after all, the stolen pelf,[1]   [1] **pelf:** Worldly
"Is what, I'm sure, he stole himself;   goods or ill-gotten
"For, if the real truth we knew,   gain.
"He's the worst villain of the two!
"They're thieves in grain—they never alter—   105
"Attorneys all deserve a halter.
"If that is all, I'll mind my stitches,
"Nor lay aside John Bumpkin's breeches."

    The Blacksmith, while a trav'ller stay'd
That a new horse-shoe might be made,   110
Inform'd him that a rev'rend Clerk*
Last night was strangled in the dark:
No one knew how—'twas at the *Bell*,—
The murd'rer—not a soul could tell.
The Justice tho' would make a rout,[2]   115 [2] **make a rout:**
And try to find the fellow out.—   Cause a
Thus Rumour spread the simple case,   commotion, sound
In ev'ry form, throughout the place.   the alarm.

    The Doctor now unclos'd his eyes,
And thought that it was time to rise: 120
So up he got, and down he went,
To scold the Landlord fully bent;
Who, pale, and trembling with affright
At what had happen'd in the night,
Approach'd with such an humble look,   125
The Doctor's rage at once forsook
His Christian breast: and, with a voice
That did the poor man's heart rejoice,
He bid him, soon as he was able,
To let the coffee grace the table.   130

"I do aver," the Landlord said,
"That since I've carried on my trade,
"Since I've been master of the *Bell*,
"As all throughout the town can tell,
"(And that is now ten years, and more,)   135
"I ne'er knew such mishap before.
"The fellow, Sir, upon my word,
"Let loose his money like a Lord.
"I receive all who come this way,
"And care not, Sir, how long they stay,   140
"So they but eat and drink—and pay.
"I ask not from whence people come,
"What is their name, or where their home.—
"That he's a rogue, I think, is clear,
"Nor e'er again shall enter here.   145
"He is some sharper,[1] I suppose,
"Who round about the country goes;
"While, to assist his lawless game,
"He takes the soldier's noble name.
"I understand the rogue you bang'd,   150
"And in good time, Sir, he'll be hang'd:
"I hope that all your notes you've found,—
"I'm told they're worth a thousand pound."
"Prove that," says Syntax, "my dear honey,
"And I will give you half the money.   155
"Think not, my friend, I'm such a fool,
"That I have been so late at school,[2]
"To put my bank-notes in a bag
"That hangs across my Grizzle nag*.
"No, they were notes to make a book,   160
"The Thief my meaning, friend, mistook;
"For know, the man would not have found
"Them worth—to him—a single pound;
"Tho' much I hope that they will be
"The source of many a pound to me."   165
Thus Syntax cheer'd the Landlord's heart
Till the time warn'd him to depart;
When soon, along the beaten road,
Poor Grizzle bore her rev'rend load.

[1] **sharper:** Swindler.

[2] **Think not...
school:** "Don't
suppose that I am
so unfamiliar with
the world."

The Doctor's pleasant thoughts beguile 170
The journey onward many a mile:
For many a mile he had not seen
But one unvarying, level green;[1]
Nor had the way one object brought
That wak'd a *picturesquish* thought. 175
A spire, indeed, across the down,
Seem'd to denote a neighb'ring town;
And that he view'd with some delight—
For there he hop'd to pass the night.

  A farmer now, so blithe and gay, 180
Came trotting briskly on his way.
"I pray," says Syntax, "tell me, friend,
"If to yon town this way doth tend!"—
"This road, good Sir, will take you there:
"You're surely going to the fair; 185
" 'Tis the first mart both far and near,
"For horses, cows, and such-like geer;[2]
"And, from the beast I've in my eye,
"You're going, Sir, a nag to buy:
"I think, if I the truth may tell, 190
"You have not got a nag to sell;
"For not a person in the fair
"Will give ten shillings for your mare."[3]
Syntax, who dearly lov'd a joke,
And long had liv'd 'mong country folk: 195
Thought he could work a little mirth
Out of this rustic son of earth:
So thus the conversation flow'd,
As they jogg'd on the beaten road.

     SYNTAX.
  "I'll tell you, Farmer; long together, 200
"In sunshine, and in stormy weather,
"My mare and I have trotted on,
"Nor is, as yet, our labour done;
"And, tho' her figure you despise,
"Did you but know her qualities 205

¹ **unvarying, level green:** A plain. In Gilpin's view, a plain cannot be picturesque unless it is broken up by other objects or features: "the mere *simplicity* of a plain produces no beauty. Break the surface of it, […] add trees, rocks, and declivities; that is, give it *roughness*, and you give it also *variety* […]; from whence results the picturesque" (TE 28).

Countryside between Cambridge and Ely, the rare picture by Gilpin of entirely flat terrain: "the only ornaments of this dreary surface are windmills" (ONSE 15; image opp. 16).

² **geer:** Stuff.

³ **ten shillings…mare:** An insultingly cheap price ($72), about what a knacker, or horse-slaughterer, would pay for a worn-out horse. An ordinary, functional riding horse might cost £25-40 (Pool, 143), which is 50-80 times the farmer's appraisal of Grizzle.

Austen may have Gilpin's strictures against "level greens" in mind when she writes that the view from the drawing room of Henry Tilney's (NA) parsonage is "pleasant, though only over green meadows" (II.11). Catherine's joy in this "unpicturesque" view suggests that, for all her romantic excesses, she appreciates steadiness and practicality as well (along with anything relating to Henry). Gilpin's broken, rugged terrain might be more striking, but a green meadow is better for grazing cattle, and thus supporting a community.

A knowledge of horse prices brings the humor of a scene in Northanger Abbey *into sharper focus. John Thorpe brags that he bought a gig for £50 ($7,200) that a friend offered to buy for £60 shortly after. James Morland, however, reminds him that his horse was included in the latter offer. Assuming the friend's offer was fair, this means either that Thorpe overpaid for his gig, or that his horse, of which he is so proud, is worth only £10, a very small sum.*

"You would not rate her quite so low
"As now you seem dispos'd to do."

FARMER.
"I'll lay a pound, if you are willing,
"She does not fetch you twenty shilling."

SYNTAX.
"First, my good friend, one truth I'll tell;—   210
"I do not want my mare to sell:
"While to lay wagers I am loth,—[1]
"The practice would disgrace my cloth*:
"Nor ever, while Life's path I trace,
"Will I my sacred rank disgrace: 215
"But yet I think you under-rate
"Poor Grizzle's qualities and state:
" 'Tis true, she's past the age of beauty,
"Yet still the old girl does her duty;
"And some one surely will be found   220
"To think, at least, she's worth a pound:
"Nay, to amuse the country-folk,
"We'll put her up, by way of joke,
"But no one must the wager smoke:[2]
"And I propose that, if you lose,   225
"(No Christian will the bet refuse)
"The money to the poor you'll give,—
" 'Twill be a Christian donative:
"And if my old and faithful mare
"Should be so treated in the fair,   230
"That not a person would be willing
"To offer for her twenty shilling,
"On honour I will do the same,
"As sure as Syntax is my name.
"Such are the terms that I propose,   235
"So let us now the bargain close."
"Give me your hand," the Farmer said,
"The terms I'll keep;—the bargain's made."
Thus they rode on and reach'd the town:—
The pipe and bowl the ev'ning crown.   240

[1] **to lay…loth:** "I am unwilling to bet."

[2] **smoke:** Find out.

The morrow came, and thro' the fair
The Farmer led the Grizzle mare.
Says one, "I would not bid a pound;
"She's only fit to feed a hound;[1]
"But would a hound the gift receive,   245
"For she has nought but bones to give?
"Where must we look her ears to find?
"And faith she's left her tail behind."
"Why," says another, "view her scars;
"She must have left them in the wars."   250

[1] **feed a hound:** Horses that had reached the end of their useful lives were sometimes slaughtered and their meat used as dog food.

As a warm Yeoman[2] pass'd along,
He heard the jeerings of the throng,
And felt a strong desire to know
What pleas'd the laughing people so.
"A parson, Sir," says one, "distress'd,   255
"Wants to sell that poor wretched beast;
"And asks, I hear, a pound, or two:
"I think he'll ne'er get that from you."
"If that's the case," the Yeoman said,—
"I'll ease his heart, and buy the jade.[3]   260
"I'll bid two pounds, my friend, that's plain,
"And give him back his beast again."

The Farmer own'd the wager lost,
And op'd his bag to pay the cost.
"No, Sir," says Syntax, " 'tis to you   265
"To pay where'er you think it due:

[2] **Yeoman:** A small farmer who owns some or all of the land he farms, above the rank of a typical tenant farmer but below that of a gentleman.

[3] **jade:** Worn-out horse.

"But, as we pass'd the Common* o'er,
"I saw, beside a cottage door,
"A woman, with a spinning-wheel,
"Who turn'd her thread around the reel,   270
"While joyful frolick'd by her side
"Three children, all in Nature's pride;
"And I resign it to your care
"To leave the welcome bounty there."

The Yeoman, when he heard the joke,   275
In friendly words to Syntax spoke:
"I, Sir, an humble mansion own,
"About five furlongs¹ from the town;   ¹ **five furlongs:**
"And there your Rev'rence I invite   About one
"To go and dine, and pass the night,   280 kilometer.
"To-day I give an annual feast,
"Where you will be the honour'd guest.
"I love the cloth*;—and humbly crave
"That we may there your blessing have.
"Come then, and bring your mare along;   285
"Come, share the feast, and hear the song;
"And in the ev'ning will be seen
"The merry dancers on the green."
"With joy," said Syntax, "I receive
"The invitation which you give;   290
"In your kind feast I'll bear a part,
"And bring with me a grateful heart."
"I," said the Yeoman, "must be gone;
"But shall expect you, Sir, at one."
Nor did the Doctor long delay: 295
To the farm-house he took his way;
And chang'd the bustle of the fair,
For a kind, noiseless welcome there.

CANTO XVII.

YE courtesies of life, all hail!
Whether along the peaceful vale*,
Where the thatch'd cot* alone is seen,
The humble mansion of the green,
Or in the city's crowded way,   5
Man—mortal man, is doom'd to stray;
You give to joy an added charm,
And woe of half its pangs disarm.
How much in ev'ry state he owes
To what kind courtesy bestows—   10
To that benign engaging art
Which decorates the human heart—
And, free from jealousy and strife,
Gilds all the charities of life.
To ev'ry act it gives a grace;   15
It adds a smile to ev'ry face:
And Goodness' self we better see
When dress'd by gentle Courtesy.

Thus Syntax, as the house he sought,
Indulg'd the grateful, pleasing thought;   20
And soon he stepp'd the threshold o'er,
Where the good Farmer went before.
Plenty appear'd, and many a guest
Attended on the welcome feast.
The Doctor then, with solemn face,   } 25
Proceeded to th' appointed place,
And, in due form, pronounc'd the grace.
That thankful ceremony done,
The fierce attack was soon begun;
While meat and pudding, fowl and fish,   30
All vanish'd from each ample dish.

The dinner o'er, the bowl¹ appear'd;
Th' enliv'ning draughts the spirits cheer'd;
Nor did the pleasant Doctor fail,
Between the cups of foaming ale,
To gain the laugh by many a tale. } 35
But so it hap'd—among the rest—
The Farmer's landlord was a guest;
A buckish blade,² who kept a horse,
To try his fortune on the course; 40
Was famous for his fighting cocks,
And his staunch pack to chase the fox:
Indeed, could he a booby* bite,
He'd play at cards throughout the night;³
Nor was he without hopes to get 45
Syntax to make some silly bet.
"I never bet," the Doctor said,
While a deep frown his thoughts betray'd:
"Your gold I do not wish to gain,
"And mine shall in my purse remain: 50
"No tempting card, no gambling art,
"Shall make it from my pocket start.
"Gaming, my worthy Sir, I hate:
"It neither suits my means nor state;
" 'Tis the worst passion, I protest, 55
"That's known to haunt the human breast;
"Of all vile habitudes the worst—
"The most delusive and accurst:
"And, if you please, I'll lay before you
"A very melancholy story; 60
"Such as, I think, will wring your heart,
"And wound you in the tend'rest part;
"That will in striking colours shew
"The biting pangs, the bitter woe, }
"That do, too oft, from gaming flow." 65
    "Nay," said the 'Squire, "I don't deny
"I often like my luck to try;
"And no one here, I'm sure will say,
"That when I lose I do not pay;
"But, as you think it such a sin, 70
"Pray try to cure me—and begin."

¹ **bowl:** Of alcoholic punch.

² **buckish blade:** A dashing, jaunty fellow; a high-spirited man of fashion.

³ **Indeed…night:** If he could lure a fool to the gambling table, he would spend the whole night fleecing him at cards.

SYNTAX.

How many of the human kind,
Who, to their common honour blind,
Look not in any path to stray
But where fell Passion leads the way;   75
Who, born with ev'ry real claim
To wear the fairest wreath of Fame,
Reject the good by Nature given:
And scoff at ev'ry gift of Heav'n?
Yes; such there are, and such we find   80
At ev'ry point that gives the wind:[1]
But, when among the crowd we see
One whom, in prodigality,
Fortune and Nature had combin'd
To fill his purse and form his mind;   85
Whose manly strength is grac'd with ease,
And has the happy pow'r to please;
Whose cooler moments never heard
The frantic vow to Heav'n preferr'd;
And near whose steps Repentance bears   90
The vase of purifying tears;—[2]
When such a victim we behold,
Urg'd by the rampant lust of gold,
Yielding his health, his life, his fame,
As off'rings to the god of Game;   95
The tear grows big in Virtue's eye,
Pale Reason heaves the poignant sigh;
The guardian spirit turns away,
And hell enjoys a holiday.[3]

Is there on earth a hellish vice?   100
There is, my friend—'tis avarice.
Has avarice a more hellish name?
It has my friend—the lust of game.
All this, perhaps, you'll thus deny:—
"There's no one with more grace than I   } 105
"Let shillings drop and guineas[4] fly.
"To the dejected hapless friend
"My doors I ope, my purse I lend;

"The Hazard Table," Thomas Rowlandson, 1792.
The Victoria and Albert Museum.

[1] **At ev'ry point...wind:** Wherever the wind blows.

[2] **Whose cooler...tears:** These difficult lines may be paraphrased thus: "In his more rational moments, the young man does not make desperate, hollow promises of reform, as he does while gambling. Instead he has opportunities to repent soberly and sincerely, if he would only take them."

[3] **hell enjoys a holiday:** While Combe was not an especially moralistic writer, he loathed gambling, which he often (as here) suggested was hell's favorite vice. Hell, he writes in an earlier piece, "is more indebted to the passion for play, than to the whole consolidated calendar of human vices" (*Devil upon Two Sticks*, Vol. I, 43).

[4] **guineas:** A guinea was a gold coin worth twenty-one shillings ($151).

In Austen's novels, there is a distinction between low-stakes genteel betting, which we see at many a dinner-party card table, and the reckless, high-stakes gambling that could ruin fortunes and run up crushing debts. Even Austen's most principled heroines, such as Fanny Price (MP), take part in the former, whereas only her most hardened villains sink to the latter. Indeed, Jane Bennet (PP) seems to regard Wickham's gambling as the worst of his sins, hearing of it "with horror. 'A gamester!' she cried. 'This is wholly unexpected. I had not an idea of it' " (III.6).

"To purchase joy my wealth I give,
"And like a man of fashion live."   110
This may be true—but still your breast
Is with the love of gold possest.
Why watch whole nights the fatal card,
Or look to dice for your reward?
Why risk your real wealth with those   115
Whom you know not, and no one knows;[1]
With maggots whom foul Fortune's ray
Has rais'd from dunghills into day;
Who would in your misfortune riot,
And seek your ruin for their diet?   120
Pleasure it cannot be, for pains
Will mingle with your very gains—
Will hover round the golden store,
Which, ere the passing moment's o'er,
May, horrid chance! be your's no more.   125

As yet you cannot use the plea
Of beggar'd men—necessity.
Plenty as yet adorns your board,[2]
And num'rous vassals[3] own you Lord.
Your woods look fair—their trunks increase— 130
The Hamadryads[4] live in peace:
But cards and dice, more pow'rful far
Than e'en the sharpest axes are,
At one dire stroke have oft been found
To level forests with the ground;[5]   135
Have seiz'd the mansion's lofty state,
And turn'd its master from the gate.

A youth in wealth and fashion bred,
But by the love of gaming led,
Soon found that ample wealth decay;   140
Farm after farm was play'd away,
Till, the sad hist'ry to complete,
His park, his lawns, his ancient seat,[6]
Were all in haste and hurry sold,
To raise the heaps of ready gold.   145

[1] **those…no one knows:** Sharpers and other seedy types.

[2] **board:** Table.
[3] **vassals:** Here, servants and tenants.
[4] **Hamadryads:** Tree spirits.

[5] **level forests with the ground:** In other words, gentlemen have sometimes been forced to sell their forests for timber to pay off gambling debts.
[6] **ancient seat:** Ancestral manor.

They, like the rest, soon pass'd away,
The villain's gain, the sharper's prey;
While he, alas! resolv'd to shun
The arts by which he was undone.
Sought, by hard labour, to sustain   150
His weary life of woe and pain;
But nature soon refus'd to give
The strength by which he strove to live;
And nought was left him but to try
What casual pity would supply: 155
To stray where chance or hunger led,
And humbly ask for scanty bread.
One day to his despairing eyes
He saw a stately mansion rise;
Nor long he look'd before he knew   160
Each wood and copse that round it grew;
For all the scene that seem'd so fair
Once knew in his a master's care.
Struck with the sight, and sore oppress'd,
He sought a bank wheron to rest: 165
There long he lay, and sigh'd his grief;—
Tears came—but did not bring relief.
At last he took his tott'ring way
Where once he lov'd so well to stray,
And, press'd by hunger, sought the gate   170
Where suppliant Want[1] was us'd to wait—
Where suppliant Want was ne'er deny'd
The morsel left by glutted Pride.
But, ah! these gen'rous times were o'er,
And suppliant Want reliev'd no more.   175
The mastiff growl'd—the liv'ried thief[2]
With insolence deny'd relief.
The wretch, dissolving in a groan,
Turn'd from the portal once his own;
But ere he turn'd, he told his name,   180
And curs'd once more the love of game:
Then sought the lawn, for Nature fail'd,
And sorrow o'er his strength prevail'd.
Beneath an oak's wide-spreading shade
His weary limbs he careless laid;   185

[1] **suppliant Want:** The poor.

[2] **liv'ried thief:** A servant of the new master of the house. From the perspective of the young man or the community, the new master might seem like a thief, even if he did buy the estate.

Then call'd on Heav'n:—(the bitter pray'r
Of Mis'ry finds admittance there!)
And ere the sun, with parting ray,
Had heighten'd the last blush of day,
Sunk and worn out with want and grief,   190
He found in death a kind relief.

The oak records the doleful tale,
Which makes the conscious reader pale;
And tells—"In this man's fate behold
"The love of play—the lust of gold."   195
No moral, Sir, shall I impart;
I trust you'll find it in your heart.

You're young, you'll say, and must engage
In the amusements of the age.
Go then, and let your mountain bare   200
The forest's verdant liv'ry wear;
Let Parian marble grace your hall,
And Titian glow upon your wall;
Its narrow channels boldly break,
And swell your riv'let to a lake:[1]   205
To richer harvests bend your soil,
While labour fattens in the toil:[2]
Encourage Nature, and impart
The half-transparent veil of Art.[3]

The landscape gardener Humphry Repton often made twinned drawings of estate grounds for clients—the first showing the status quo, and the second showing his proposed alterations. The second image is revealed by lifting a flap of paper. This pair shows a view of Sheringham Hall in Norfolk, England. From Repton's "Red Book" for Sheringham, 1812. Felbrigg Hall.

Elizabeth Bennet (PP) notices with approbation such a feature on the grounds of Pemberley: "a stream of some natural importance was swelled into greater, but without any artificial appearance" (III.1).

¹ **Its narrow channel…lake:** Landscape gardeners sometimes sought to lend grandeur to the grounds of an estate by enlarging natural bodies of water.

² **To richer harvests…toil:** In other words, seek to improve your farmlands, an endeavor that will enrich both you and your tenants.

³ **Encourage Nature…Art:** Landscape gardeners of the time, influenced by ideas of the picturesque, saw themselves not as ordering nature according to a fixed plan, but encouraging it by subtle and judicious interventions. Ideally, many of the improver's touches would seem, in the final product, like the work of nature herself. Thus, the improver's "art" should be, to use Combe's term, "half-transparent"—partly seen and partly unseen, adding some new beauties to the scene, without obscuring the ones nature had already given it.

Austen, too, believed that, in landscape gardening, art should follow nature's lead. This is the secret of Pemberley's (PP) beauty. The natural advantages of the place have been subtly enhanced, not "counteracted by an awkward taste" (III.1). By contrast, Mr. Rushworth (MP), who plans to radically remake the grounds of Sotherton, is forcing rather than encouraging nature.

Let music charm your melting breast,   210
And soothe each passion into rest;
Let Genius from your hand receive
The bounty that can make it live;
And call the Muses from on high,
To give you immortality.[1]   215 [1] **Let Genius…**
To these the hardy pleasures join,   **immortality:**
Where exercise and health combine: Syntax urges the
At the first op'ning of the morn,   young gentleman to
O'er hill and dale, with hound and horn,   patronize artists and
Boldly pursue the subtle prey,   220   writers, and ensure
And share the triumphs of the day;   a lasting name for
Nor let the evening hours roll   himself by writing
Unaided by the social bowl;   works of his own.
Nor should fair Friendship be away
But crown with smiles the festive day.   225
Nor need I add the joys they prove
Who live in bonds of virtuous love.
Where fond affection fills the heart,
The baser passions all depart.
While the babe hangs on Beauty's breast,   230
While in a parent's arms caress'd,
Each low-bred thought, all vicious aims
The pure, domestic mind disclaims.
Virtue inspires his ev'ry sense,
Who looks on cherub innocence:—   235
Then seek a shield 'gainst passion's strife
In the calm joys of wedded Life.

    This is to live, and to enjoy
Those pleasures which our pains destroy:
This is to live, and to receive   240
The praises which the good will give:
This is to make that use of wealth
Which heightens e'en the flush of health;
Improves the heart, and gives a claim
To a fair, fragrant wreath of Fame.   245

    "I thank you, Sir," the Farmer said;—
" 'Tis a sad tale you have display'd.

"How I the poor man's lot deplore!
"The more I think, I feel the more;
"And much I wish my Landlord too   250
"Would keep his wretched fate in view;
"But, while my poor good woman weeps,
"Behold how very sound he sleeps.
"I beg that we may change the scene,
"And join the dancers on the green."   255
Sal now exclaim'd, "The people say
"*Ralph* is so drunk he cannot play:"
"Then I'll be fiddler," Syntax cry'd;
"By me his place shall be supply'd.
"Ne'er fear, my lasses, you shall soon   260
"Be ambling to some pretty tune,
"And in a measur'd time shall beat
"The green sod with your nimble feet.
"While Virtue o'er your pleasure reigns,
"You're welcome to my merry strains;[1]   265
"While Virtue smiles upon your joy,
"I'll gladly my best skill employ;
"For, sure, 'twill give me great delight
"To be your fiddler thro' the night.
"I know full well I do not err   270
"From any point of character:
"To Heaven I ne'er can give offence
"While I enliven Innocence:
"For thus to virtuous man 'tis given
"To dance, and sing, and go to Heaven.   275
"Your merry minstrelsy[2] prolong,
"And to your dances add the song:
"E'en while you caper, loudly sing
"In honour of your noble King."[3]

CHORUS OF PEASANTS.

"Strike, strike the lyre! awake the sounding shell![4]
How happy we who in these vallies dwell!
How blest we live beneath his gentle sway,
Whom mighty realms and distant seas obey!

[1] **strains:** Passages of music.

[2] **minstrelsy:** Music.

[3] **your noble King:** George III, who reigned from 1760-1820.

[4] **shell:** Another word for lyre, typically used in poetry.

Make him, propitious Heav'n! your choicest care!
O make him happy as his people are!"　　　　285

'Twas thus they fiddled, danc'd, and sung:
With harmless glee the village rung.
At length dull Midnight bid them close
A day of joy with calm repose.

CANTO XVIII.

LET Grandeur blush, and think how few
Of all the many-colour'd crew,
The motley[1] groupe of fools and knaves,
Who hourly prove themselves its slaves,
However Fashion gilds the dress,   5
Attain th' expected happiness!
Let Grandeur blush, and blushing own
How seldom is to greatness known
That pure and unimbitter'd lot
Which often cheers the peasant's cot*;   10
The hallow'd bliss, the nameless charm,
That decorates the fertile farm.

    Thus Syntax ponder'd as his eye
Survey'd the cheerful family;
Who 'round the breakfast-table seated,   15
With one accord his entrance greeted:
At the same time, they all express'd
Much sorrow that their rev'rend guest
Had order'd Grizzle to the door,
In order to pursue his tour.   20
"Doctor, I'm griev'd so soon to part,"
Burst from the Yeoman's friendly heart;
"Yet hope, whene'er you this way come,
"You'll not forget you have a home:—
"You see how we poor farmers live,—   25
"A welcome's all we have to give;
"But that's sincere—so come and try."
A few kind words were the reply.
    Syntax once more his beast bestrode;
He bade farewell, and off he rode.   30

[1] **motley:** A reference to the garb traditionally worn by jesters or fools, which was made of patches of different colors.

Now Nature's beauties caught his eye,
Array'd in gay simplicity;
And as he pass'd the road along,
The blackbird's note, the thrush's song,
With musical and native mirth,   35
Seem'd to do homage to his worth.
The vary'd landscape here combin'd
To fascinate the eye and mind,
To charm the gazer's ev'ry sense
From the commanding eminence.   40
Th' expanding plain, with plenty crown'd,
Diffuses health and fragrance round;
While, on a lofty, craggy height,
A castle rises to the sight,
Which, in its day of strength and pride,   45
The arms of threat'ning foes defy'd.
Beneath the mouldering abode
In mazy course a riv'let flow'd,
And, free from the tempestuous gale,
Its silent stream refresh'd the vale*.   50
The vale the scatter'd hamlet cheer'd,
And many a straw-roof'd cot* appear'd;

While smiling groups at ev'ry door
Spoke grief a stranger to the poor.[1]
With pious thought, and eye serene,   55
Syntax survey'd th' enchanting scene,
And thus in grateful mood began:—
"So deals th' Omnipotent with man.
"Such are thy gifts, all-gracious Pow'r!
"To us, the creatures of an hour: 60
"And yet how oft we barter these;
"How oft we risk our health and ease,
"Thy best bequests, thy choicest treasure,
"For follies which we mis-name pleasure;
"And slaves to vanity and art,[2]   65
"Check the best feelings of the heart.
"How the scene charms my ravish'd eye!
"I cannot, will not, pass it by,"
He said,—and from his pocket took
The pencil, and the sketching-book;   70
While Grizzle, in contented mood,
Close by her busy master stood:
When, clouds of dust proclaim'd th' approach
Of something Syntax deem'd a coach.
Four wheels in truth it had to boast,   75
Altho' what it resembled most
Were hard to say:—suffice, this *tub*
Was built in London, where a club,
Yclept[3] *Four-horse*, is now the rage,
And fam'd for whims in equipage.   80
Dashers! who once a month assemble;
Make creditors and coachmen tremble;
And, dress'd in colours vastly fine,
Drive to some public-house to dine;
There game, and drink, and swear, and then—   85
Drive in disorder back again.[4]

  Now Syntax, with some kind of fear,
Beheld the vehicle draw near;
And, like her master, Grizzle too
Was far from happy at the view;   90

[1] **Spoke…poor:** Syntax fondly imagines that the villagers, with their simple lives, have never known grief.

[2] **art:** Artificial pleasures or modes of life, as contrasted with rural wholesomeness and simplicity.

"A Landaulet," C. Blunt. *RA* (March 1819), opp. 125. This was the type of carriage favored by the Four-Horse Club.

[3] **Yclept:** Called.

[4] **this *tub*…back again:** The Four-Horse Club, founded in 1808, was composed of gentlemen who enjoyed driving their own carriages at a time when most drivers were hired coachmen. Members had to follow precise rules about the design, color, and trappings of their carriages ("whims in equipage"), and they adhered to a strict dress code as well ("dress'd in colours vastly fine"), which included, among other eccentricities, mother-of-pearl buttons the size of five-shilling pieces. Early on, some of its members were known for wild driving: one contemporary wrote that 'an "ungovernable phrenzy" would possess "those youths, who fancied, no doubt, they were in the act of directing the Roman chariots in the field of Mars, by their declared hostility to every thing which came in their way" (*Morning Post* [11 Jan. 1809], 3).

In Northanger Abbey, the driving habits of young men are an important marker of character. John Thorpe drives his gig "with all the vehemence that could most fitly endanger the lives of himself, his companion, and his horse" (I.7). By contrast, Henry Tilney drives "so well,—so quietly—without making any disturbance, without parading to [Catherine], or swearing at" his horses (II.5). Two pictures of coachmanship, two pictures of masculinity: the first based on loudness and aggression, the second on gentleness and courtesy.

For a long whip had caught her eye,
Moving about most rapidly;
Tho' little thought the helpless nag
The joke which the exalted wag,[1]
Who held the reins with skilful hand,   95
Against both mare and master plann'd.
But now the curious Doctor spy'd
The emblem of Patrician pride;[2]
Which on the pannels of the coach
Prolaim'd a noble Lord's approach: 100
Nay (for facts will plainly prove it)
It was a noble Lord who drove it;
For 'tis well known to men of rank
That Lords will sometimes play a prank;
And thus indulge themselves in jokes   105
As low as those of vulgar folks.
But 'tis not easy to express
The wild surprize, the deep distress
Which Syntax felt when this same Lord
Aim'd at his back the flaunting cord;   110
And when the whip, with skilful turn,
Was well applied to Grizzle's stern;—
That stern,—enough to make one shudder,—
Which we all know had lost its rudder;
Her rage appear'd in either eye,   115
And then she neigh'd indignantly.
Such seem'd she as when erst she bore
A trumpeter to fields of gore;
When, in the battle's heat, at large,
She led whole squadrons to the charge;   120
While Syntax, as she scour'd the plain,
Indulg'd the moralizing strain,
"Can I in this foul conduct scan[3]
"The Peer, or well-bred Gentleman?
"Or rather must not Virtue frown   125
"On such a high-born, titled clown?
"Thus, then, do Nobles play the fool?
"A conduct, which in my poor school,
"If 'mong my boys it dare appear;
"If they should ape that monkey there;   130

[1] **wag:** A mischievous jokester.

[2] **The emblem… pride:** A coat of arms. Nobles and other wealthy people often had their family crests emblazoned on their carriages.

[3] **scan:** Perceive, discern (OED).

206

"They for their fun should pay full dearly;—
"I'd whip the blackguards[1] most severely.

[1] **blackguards:**
Villains.

"But I'll not waste another word
"Upon this vulgar, booby* Lord;
"For I have something else to do,—   135
"And, Grizzle, what's become of you?"
A farmer's well stor'd barn, hard by,
Attracted her observing eye,
Where many a truss of fragrant hay
Induc'd the prudent beast to stay.   140
Meanwhile her discontented master,
Reflecting on the late disaster,
Pac'd slowly on, brimful of care,
And wonder'd who had got his mare.
Indeed he fear'd she might be found   145
Within the precincts of a pound*;
But soon his quadruped he saw:
Up to her girths[2] in hay and straw,

[2] **girths:** Straps
belted around a

While he, who own'd the neighb'ring farm,
Prepar'd to raise his weighty arm;   150

horse's body to

And, having just observ'd the theft,

hold in place a

Brandish'd a horsewhip right and left,

saddle.

(Alas! it cannot be deny'd,)
To lay about on Grizzle's hide.
Syntax beheld the harsh intent: 155
"Forbear," he cried, "the punishment!
"Why make her feel the chast'ning thong?
"She knows not she is doing wrong.
"Forgive my warmth, but truly, Sir,
"This suits not with the character   160
"Of one who treads on British ground,—
"A land for justice so renown'd:
"I'll pay for all the straw that's wasted,
"And all the hay that she has tasted,
"Your courtesy I now invoke,   165
"So name the cost, and spare the stroke."

    The farmer paus'd—as by a charm—
And dropp'd at once th' uplifted arm:—

"Forgive me, Sir, for what," he cried,
"Cannot, indeed, be justified: 170
"But for my haste I'll make amends;
"And let us, now, good Sir, be friends.
"That is my house: you'll enter there,
"And, Thomas, take the Doctor's mare;
"Come, rev'rend Sir, I'll lead the way:"
The Doctor did not disobey,
And soon was met with welcome glee,
By all the farmer's family.
At length some bus'ness of the day
Summon'd the honest host away;
So Syntax thought he'd look about
To find some curious object out;
When, lo! a dairy met his view,
Where, full of cream, in order due,

The pans, the bowls, the jugs were plac'd,   185
Which tempted the Divine to taste;
But he found something better there;
A village damsel young and fair
Attracted his admiring eye;
Who, as he enter'd heav'd a sigh.
Now, Syntax, as we all must know,
Ne'er heard a sigh or tale of woe,
But instant wish'd to bring relief—
To dry the tear and soothe the grief.
"Come here, sweet girl," he softly said;
"Tell me your grief—nor be afraid:
"Come here, and seat you by my side;
"You'll find in me a friendly guide.
"Relate your sorrows—tell the truth;
"What is it? does some perjured youth   200
"Unfaithful to his promise prove,
"Nor make the fond return of love?
" 'Tis so, I see; but raise your eye;
"On me, my pretty girl, rely:
"You have my tend'rest sympathy.   205
"Again, I say, your grief impart;—
"You've gain'd an int'rest in my heart:

DOCTOR SYNTAX & DAIRY MAID.

Designd & Etchd by Rowlandson

"For well I know the pangs they prove
"Who grieve for unrequited love."

   The list'ning mother, who had heard   210
Love talk'd of, kindled at the word;
And, rushing in, express'd her rage:—
"For shame! for shame! while hoary age
"Whitens your head, I see your eye
"Is beaming with iniquity.   215
"Begone, you old, you wanton goat!
"Your heart is black as is your coat.
"A Parson too! may Heav'n forgive
"The wicked age in which we live!
"I'll go and tell my honest spouse   220
"The snake he harbours in his house:
"He'll give such hypocrites their due,
"I'll warrant it;" and off she flew.
The Host arriv'd, but by that time
The false alarm, th' imputed crime,   225
Nancy had ventur'd to unfold,
And mother now had ceas'd to scold;
While, the rude anger turn'd to mirth,
They all confess the Doctor's worth.[1]

   Dinner was soon upon the table,   230
And Grizzle feeding in the stable;
While joyful Syntax once again
Forgot past accidents and pain;
And, when night came, repos'd his head
In peace upon the welcome bed: 235
But ne'er did he to sleep consign
His weary'd limbs till to the shrine
Of Heaven he had address'd the pray'r
Which ever finds admittance there.

"Kitty Overcome," Thomas Rowlandson, c. 1808. YCBA. The
drawing, which was never published, gives a clue as to Rowlandson's
original vision for the character of Syntax.

¹ When Rowlandson first drew Doctor Syntax
with the Dairymaid, he had in mind a very
different tale than the one Combe eventually
wrote. His original caption read, "The Doctor
makes strong Love to Kitty over a Bowl of
Cream, and endeavours to enforce his old friend
Madam's Doctrine on Plurality of Wives—"
The next image (see above), which was rejected
by either Ackermann or Combe, shows Syntax
clasping the dairymaid in his arms as she shrieks
and flails, her bodice pulled down. No doubt
this was one of the scenes Combe had in mind
when he told a friend years later that he
suspected Rowlandson of intending "a satire
upon the national clergy" with the character of
Doctor Syntax. Combe had other plans: "I
respect the clergy; and I determined to turn the
edge of the weapon which I thought was
levelled against them" (*Letters to Marianne*, vi).
He certainly did so here, transforming an
episode of flagrant, unbridled lust into, at most,
a mildly suggestive picture of Syntax's
sentimental fondness for pretty young women.

*Austen's clerical characters
never commit outrages like
the one depicted above, but
some readers still objected to
her treatment of the clergy.
One Mrs. Wroughten
thought Austen "wrong, in
such times as these, to draw
such Clergymen as Mr
Collins [PP] & Mr Elton
[Em.]" (LM 238).
Readers like her felt the
Church was under duress
and worried that any
mockery of clergymen might
contribute to its decline.
Austen and Combe,
however, believed it was
possible to maintain respect
for the clergy as a whole
even while laughing at the
follies (though not the vices)
of some its members.*

CANTO XIX.

THE Sun arose in all his pride!
"Hail the bright orb," the Doctor cried,
"That makes the distant mountains glow,
"And clears the misty vales* below!
"O! let me bless the Pow'r divine[1]   5
"That bade its splendid fires to shine;
"Invigorating warmth to give
"To all that grow, and all that live:
"Which, in the bowels of the earth,
"Brings the rich metal into birth;   10
"Or, piercing through the secret mine,
"Makes rubies blush, and di'monds shine:
"While man, the first, the head of all
"That breathes upon this earthly ball,
"As freely feels its force as they   15
"Of insect tribe, who, in its ray,
"Pass their short hour, and pass away.
"O, what a picture greets my sight!
"How my heart revels in the sight;
"While I behold th' advancing day   20
"O'er the wide scene its pow'r display!
"While, as I gaze, th' enchanted eye
"Drinks in the rich variety![2]
"How the gleam brightens yonder tower!
"How deep the shade within the bower!   25
"The spreading oak and elm between,
"How fine those blushes intervene!
"Those brilliant lights!—they would demand
"Claude's pencil,[3] or a Titian's hand![4]
"E'en while the distant hills I view,   30
"Their orient colours change to blue.
"The stream, within whose silver wave,
"Poets might see the Naiads[5] lave,

¹ **let me…Pow'r divine:** Syntax's praise of nature leads to praise of God. Gilpin would have applauded this reaction. He thought it a very good thing if a person's admiration of picturesque beauty led him to contemplate "the great origin of all beauty"; or if it inspired him "with that complacency of mind, which is so nearly allied to benevolence." At the same time, he seemed to think such responses somewhat rare, and "dare[d] not *promise* […] more from picturesque travel, than a rational, and agreeable amusement" (TE 46-7).

² **rich variety:** According to Gilpin, "One uniform light, or one uniform shade produces no effect" (TE 20). Instead, the picturesque artist sought out scenes with a variety of hues and strong contrasts between light and dark.

³ **Claude's pencil:** The 17ᵗʰ-c. landscape artist Claude Lorrain was a major influence on the English picturesque movement. He was especially admired for his mastery of tints; Gilpin once declared that his merit "all lay in colouring" (OWP 75).

⁴ **Titian's hand:** Famous Italian painter of the 16ᵗʰ c. and another master of color.

⁵ **Naiads lave:** Water nymphs bathe.

While many of Austen's characters admire nature, perhaps the only one to respond to its beauties with deep religious feeling is Fanny Price (MP): "Here's harmony!" she cries in response to a lovely moonlit night. "Here's what may tranquillize every care, and lift the heart to rapture! When I look out on such a night as this, I feel as if there could be neither wickedness nor sorrow in the world; and there certainly would be less of both if the sublimity of Nature were more attended to" (I.11). Austen's own love of nature was intertwined with her faith: her grandnephew wrote that she felt such delight in a scenic view that she believed the beauty of nature "must form one of the joys of heaven" (William Austen-Leigh, 176).

Henry Tilney (NA) touches on "lights and shades," among many other subjects, during the long "lecture on the picturesque" to which he treats Catherine during their walk at Beechen Cliff (I.14). Side-screens, another of his topics, is mentioned by Syntax on line 63 of this canto.

"Now, lost in shade, no more is seen
"To flow among the alders green;   35
"But, let the eye its course pursue,
"Again it brightens in the view,
"Reflecting as its current flows,
"Each flower that on the margin blows.
    "Hail, favour'd casement!—where the sight   40
"Is courted to enjoy delight!
"T' ascend the hill, and trace the plain,
"Where lavish Nature's proud to reign;
"Unlike those pictures that impart
"The windows of Palladian art,   45
"From whence no other object's seen
"But gravel-walk, or shaven green;[1]
"Plann'd by the artist on his desk;—
"Pictures that are not *picturesque.*
"But I should not perform my duty   50
"Did I relinquish all this beauty;
"Nor snatch, from this expansive view,
"Some pretty little scene or two.
    "The cot* that's all bewhiten'd o'er,
"With children playing at the door;   55
"A peasant hanging o'er the hatch,
"And the vine mantling on the thatch,
"While the thick coppice,[2] down the hill
"Throws its green umbrage o'er the rill*,
"Whose stream drives on the busy mill;   60
"In pleasing group their forms combine,
"And suit a pencil such as mine.[3]
"Nor shall I miss the branchy screen[4]
"Of those fine elms, that hide the green,
"O'er which the tap'ring spire[5] is seen.   65
"I'll add no more—for, to my mind,
"The scene's complete—and well design'd.
"There are, indeed, who would insert
"Those pigs, which wallow in the dirt;
"And, tho' I hold a pig is good   70
"Upon a dish, prepar'd for food,
"I do not fear to say the brute
"Does not my taste in painting suit;

"The Cottage Door," Thomas Gainsborough, c. 1778. Cincinnati Art Museum.

[1] **Palladian…shaven green:** The Palladian style emphasized symmetry and smoothness, which were antithetical to the picturesque. The "shaven green" is a mowed lawn.

[2] **coppice:** A stretch of woods that has been cut back to encourage new growth.

[3] **The cot…mine:** Syntax parts ways with Gilpin here. To Gilpin, cottages and most human dwellings (unless handsomely ruined) belong to a class of objects "unconnected with picturesque beauty" (TE viii). Syntax, by contrast, is invoking a "cottage door scene"—a picture of idyllic peasant life popularized by the 18th-c. painter Thomas Gainsborough.

[4] **branchy screen:** Also called a side-screen, a tree or trees in the foreground that partially cover the middle- and backgrounds, lending perspective and variety to the scene.

[5] **tap'ring spire:** Syntax sees a church tower rising above the trees.

Picturesque cottage scenes inspired some rich folk to seek out snug rustic retreats of their own. Austen, though, doubted just how much rural solitude the wealthy were ready to bear. In one of her early sketches, a man finds an ideally situated cottage. The scene is hyper-quaint, with no fewer than "ten Rivulets meander[ing]" down a hill nearby (Juv. 225). But no sooner has he moved in than he invites a large party to share the two-room abode, housing the overflow under blankets held up with sticks! Austen returns to the joke with Robert Ferrars (SS), who imagines that a dance for eighteen couples could be held in a cottage with ease.

"For I most solemnly aver,
"That he from genuine taste must err,   } 75
"Who flouts at grace or character;
"And there's as much in my old wig
"As can be found about a pig;
"For, to say truth, I don't inherit
"This self-same *picturesquish* spirit   80
"That looks to nought but what is rough,
"And ne'er thinks Nature coarse enough.
"Their system does my genius shock,
"Who see such graces in a dock;
"Whose eye the *picturesque* admires   85
"In straggling brambles, and in briers;
"Nay, can a real beauty see
"In a decay'd and rotten tree.[1]
"I hate with them the trim of Art;
"But from this rule I'll ne'er depart.—   90
"In grandame Nature's vast collection,
"To make a fair and fit selection,
"Which, when in happy contrast join'd,
"Delights th' inform'd, well-judging mind."[2]

  But lo! the Farmer, at the gate,   95
Aloud proclaim'd the hour of eight;
And Syntax now in haste descends,
To join his kind expecting friends.
"Well," said his host, "another day
"I trust your Reverence will stay."   100
"I thank you for the offer made,
"But that can't be," the Doctor said:
"I have a weary way to go,
"And much to see, and more to know:
"Indeed so far I've got to roam,   105
"A fortnight scarce will take me home;
"And, thanking you for all your care,
"I must beg leave to seek my mare."
Grizzle was quickly to be found;
And, as the good folks stood around,   110
Syntax thought proper to discourse
Upon the virtues of his horse;

¹ **Their system...rotten tree:** Gilpin adored stricken or withered trees, part of his larger interest in roughness and ruination: "What is more beautiful [...], on a rugged foreground, than an old tree with a *hollow trunk?* or with a *dead arm*, a *drooping bough*, or a *dying branch?*" (FS 8). Syntax, for his part, sees this fascination with decay as proceeding from a distorted taste, one that, perversely, puts life and beauty at odds.

Edward Ferrars (SS) also objects to the picturesque tendency to aestheticize decay: "I do not like crooked, twisted, blasted trees. I admire them much more if they are tall, straight and flourishing" (I.18).

"Landscape with castle," William Gilpin, 1763. YCBA. Note the two dead trees in the left foreground.

² **But from this rule...well-judging mind:** This canto contains the poem's most earnest statement on the picturesque. Elsewhere, Syntax either directly mocks picturesque "rules" or embraces them with a pompous scrupulousness that is, perhaps, even funnier. Here, though, he carves out a serious middle-ground, rejecting both Palladian symmetry and the more extreme forms of Gilpin-esque roughness. In the middle ground between the two, life thrives. A field is neither reduced to an unvaried lawn ("shaven green"), nor overgrown with "brambles" and "briers." People, too, are neither artificial nor wild, but exist in harmony with nature even while enjoying the comforts of home and community.

Austen's taste in scenery also shunned extremes. There is something stifling about the enclosed and overly curated grounds of Northanger Abbey (NA), which seem, at times, scarcely more hospitable than the wild and remote manor-estates of Catherine's Gothic novels. The surroundings of Pemberley (PP) and Donwell Abbey (Em.), on the other hand, harmonize nature and culture. The balance is more in the direction of nature in the first, and of culture (especially agriculture) in the second, but this is no contradiction. It only shows that like Syntax, Austen embraced an expansive middle ground of picturesque beauty—one that was never at odds with human thriving.

Nor did he fail at large to tell
That she had serv'd him passing well:
While he forgot not to bewail   115
Her loss of ears, and loss of tail:
But tho' among the passing folk,
His beast created many a joke;
And tho' the foul and sad disaster
Oft forc'd a laugh against her master: 120
They should not part while he was able
To keep himself and keep a stable;
Nay, to the last he'd cut and carve,[1]
That his poor Grizzle might not starve.
Thus, as her hist'ry he recounted,   125
Into the saddle up he mounted;
And there for some time having sat,
He clos'd at length, his farewell chat.
He thought it best t' avoid caressing;
So gave no kiss, but gave his blessing.   130

   On home, on books, on fame, intent,
The Doctor ponder'd as he went:
At night he look'd his papers o'er,
And added to the learned store.
But, the next morn, another scene,   135
The vast expanse of liquid green—
The ocean's self—broke on his eye,
In inexpressive[2] majesty.
There, as he look'd, full many a sail
Gave its white canvas to the gale;   140
And many a freighted vessel bore
Its treasure to the British shore:
When, as he trac'd the winding coast,
In praise and admiration lost,
Up-rising in the distant view,   145
Half-seen thro' the ethereal blue,
A city's stately form appear'd;
Upon the shore the mass was rear'd,
With glist'ning spires: while below
Masts like a forest seem'd to grow.   150

[1] **cut and carve:** To dine well. The usage here is odd, as one expects Syntax to say that he denies himself in order to afford to maintain Grizzle.

[2] **inexpressive:** Impossible to express in words.

218

'Twas Liverpool, that splendid mart,[1]
Imperial London's counterpart,
Where wand'ring Mersey's rapid streams[2]
Rival the honours of the Thames;
And bear on each returning tide,   155
Whate'er by commerce is supply'd:
Whate'er the winds can hurry o'er
From ev'ry clime and distant shore.
Thus Syntax pac'd along the strand,
Through this fine scene of sea and land.   160

[1] **mart:** Market.

[2] **Mersey's rapid streams:** Liverpool is located at the mouth of the River Mersey. The narrow channel of the river as it empties into the Atlantic causes it to flow swiftly.

P. 214.

  But nearer now the town appears;
The hum of men salutes his ears;
And soon amid the noisy din
He found the comforts of an inn.
He eat, he drank, his pipe he smok'd,   165
And with the Landlord quaintly jok'd;
But, ere he slept, he pass'd an hour
In adding something to his Tour;
Then sought his couch, in hopes the morn
Would with new thoughts the page adorn.   170

The morning came—he sally'd out
To breath the air, and look about.
Where'er he turn'd, his ev'ry sense
Grasp'd one vast scene of opulence:
In all he saw there was display'd   175
The proud magnificence of trade.

   Syntax, an humble scholar bred,
With nought but learning in his head;
Profound, indeed, in classic* art,
And goodness reigning in his heart;   180
Yet forty pounds a year[1] was all
He could his fix'd revenue call;
For which, on ev'ry Sabbath-day,
He went eight miles to preach and pray.
His school too brought but little gains,   185
And scarce repaid him for his pains:
It gave, 'tis true, to drink and eat;
It furnish'd him with bread and meat,
And kept the wolf without the door;
But Syntax still was very poor.   190
His wife, indeed, had got the art
To keep herself a little smart;
Yet he, good man, was always seen
With scanty coat, and figure mean.
But still he never threw aside   195
The pedant's air—the pedant's pride.
Thus, thro' the streets of this rich place,
He strutted with his usual grace;
And thus he walk'd about the town,
As if its wealth had been his own: 200
But of his wealth he could not vapour—[2]
Twelve guineas, and a piece of paper
(The present of a noble Lord),
Was all his pockets did afford:
Though still the lining of his coat   205
Secreted 'Squire Hearty's note.
And now he thought 'twould not be rash
To turn the paper into cash.

[1] **forty pounds a year:** Possibly an error. Elsewhere in the poem, Combe gives Syntax's income as thirty pounds ($4,320).

[2] **vapour:** Boast.

Thus, at his breakfast, while he sat,
And social join'd the common chat,   210
He took occasion to enquire
Who would comply with his desire:
Who would his anxious wish fulfil,
And give him money for his bill.
An arch young sprig,[1] a banker's clerk,   215
Resolv'd to hoax the rev'rend spark,[2]
And counsell'd him to take a range
Among the merchants on the 'Change.[3]
"Some one, perhaps, may want to send
"A payment to a London friend;   220
"He'll in your wishes gladly join,
"And take the draft and pay the coin."

   The Barber now the Doctor shear'd,
And soon whipp'd off his three-days' beard,
His wig, which had not felt a comb,   225
Not once since he had quitted home,
Was destin'd now with friz and twirl
To be tormented into curl:
His coat, which long had ta'en the rust,
Was soon depriv'd of all the dust: 230
His gaiters too were fresh japann'd;[4]
Such were the Doctor's stern command:
And now, with spirits fresh and gay,
To the Exchange he took his way,
To try in this commercial town   235
A little commerce of his own.
Th' Exchange soon met his wond'ring sight;
The structure fill'd him with delight.
"Such are the fruits of trading knowledge!
"Learning," he cried, "builds no such college;   240
"Indeed, I entertain a notion
"(I speak the thought with true devotion),
"Tho' we in holy Scripture read
"That Tyre and Sidon[5] did exceed
"In wealth the cities of the world,   245
"Where ships their wand'ring sails unfurl'd;

[1] **sprig:** Slightly derogatory term for a youth.

[2] **spark:** The sense is unclear: possibly a pretentious fellow or would-be wit.

[3] **'Change:** Exchange, a building in which merchants gather to do business.

[4] **japann'd:** Varnished, made glossy.

[5] **Tyre and Sidon:** Key cities of the ancient mercantile empire of Phoenicia. In Isaiah 23:8, the prophet calls Tyre "the crowning city, whose merchants are princes, whose traffickers are the honourable of the earth."

"That e'en her merchants bore the bell[1]
"In eating and in drinking well;
"Were richer than the lordly great,
"And vy'd with princes in their state;
"Yet, with all their power and rule,
"I think that they ne'er went to school
"In such a 'Change as Liverpool."

He enter'd now—and heard within
The crowded mart—a buzzing din—
A sound confus'd—the serenade
Of ardent gain, and busy trade:
At length his penetrating eye
Was thrown around him, to descry
Some one in whose sleek smiling face
He could the lines of kindness trace:
And soon a person he address'd,
Whose paunch projected from his breast;
Who, looking with good humour fraught,
Appear'd the very man he sought:
When, with an unassuming grace,
To him he thus disclos'd the case:—
"I beg this paper you'll peruse;
"And then, perhaps, you'll not refuse
"The favour which I ask to grant,
"And give the money that I want;
"The draft[2] is good—and, on my word,
"It was a present from a Lord."

MERCHANT.
"That may be true: but Lords, I fear,
"Will meet but little credit here:
" 'Tis a fair draft upon the view—[3]
"Yes; he's a Lord—but who are you?"

SYNTAX.
"Look, and an honest man you'll see—
"A Doctor in Divinity,
"Whose word's his bond; nor e'er was known
"To do a deed he would not own."

250

255

260

265

270

275

280

[1] **bore the bell:** Led the way (derived from the practice of hanging a bell around the neck of one sheep so the others will follow it).

[2] **draft:** Check.

[3] **upon the view:** At first glance.

Dr SYNTAX AT LIVERPOOL.

MERCHANT.
"I've nought to say—all this may be—
"But have you no security?
"Pray, Doctor, can't you find a friend
"To answer for what you pretend?"   285

SYNTAX.
"That I have none:—I am not known
"Within the precincts of this town."

MERCHANT.
"And do you come to Liverpool
"To find a poor good-natur'd fool?
"With all your learning and your worth,   290
"Pray have you travell'd so far north,
"To think we have so little wit,
"As by such biters to be bit?[1]
"To learning we make no pretence:
"But, Doctor, we have common sense.   295
"For learned men we do not seek:
"And if I may with freedom speak,
"I take you for a very *Greek*."[2]

SYNTAX.
"To know the Greek I do profess—
" 'Tis my delight and happiness;
"And Homer's page I oft have read,   300
"Thro' the long night, with aching head,
"When my wife wanted me in bed."

MERCHANT.
"Then go to Homer, if you will,
"And see if he'll discount[3] your bill.
"But the clock strikes.—Good bye, old sinner!   305
" 'Tis time for me to go to dinner."

"You want the monies?" said another,
A bearded, Israelitish[4] brother.
" 'Tis a suspected bill, I find;
"But you look poor, and I am kind.   310
"Well, we must take the chance of trade;
"For twenty pounds the draft is made,

[1] **biters to be bit:** Cheaters to be cheated.

[2] **a very *Greek*:** A deceptive, conniving person, with a pun on Syntax's classical learning.

[3] **discount:** To pay part of. It would be fair for a merchant to pay Syntax a little less than the full amount of Lord Carlisle's draft in exchange for his services and for taking on himself the risk of the draft being fraudulent.

[4] **Israelitish:** Jewish. The miserly or usurious Jew is, of course, an age-old anti-semitic stereotype.

"It is too much, as I'm alive!
"But give it me—and, here—take five."   315
   "Patience, good Heav'n!" the Doctor said;
"Is this the boast and pride of trade—
"Each man they do not know to treat
"As an incorrigible cheat;
"And when he does his want prefer[1]   320
"To play the base extortioner?
"Commerce, I envy not thy gains,
"Thy hard-earn'd wealth, thy golden pains!
"(For, that's hard-earn'd, tho' gain'd with ease,
"Where Honour's sacred functions cease.)[2]   325
"The dangers which thy vot'ries[3] run,
"Or to undo, or be undone;
"Whose hungry maws are daily bent
"On the fine feast of *cent. per cent.;*[4]
"Whose virtue, talents, knowledge, health,   330
"Are all combin'd in that word—*wealth.*
" 'Tis a proud scene of money'd strife
"Forms this magnificence of life:
"But poor and rich, with all they have,
"Will find at length a common grave.
"Continue, bounteous Heav'n! to me,
"A feeling heart, and poverty.
"These wights despise me, 'cause I'm poor!
"But yet the wretched seek my door.
"I fear no Duns,[5] I'm not in debt,   340
"I tremble not at the *Gazette:*[6]
" 'Twould to my profit be, and fame,
"Did but its page display my name,
"Can these proud merchants say the same?"
   More had he said—but now his bell   345
The Beadle[7] rang aloud, to tell
That the good folks should vanish straight,
As he must shut the pond'rous gate.
But Syntax did not seem to hear—
So the man rang it in his ear.   350

[1] **prefer:** Put forward.

[2] **For, that's... cease:** In other words, those who sacrifice honor for wealth have paid a high price, even if little labor was required.

[3] **vot'ries:** Worshippers.

[4] ***cent. per cent.:*** One hundred percent, or a doubling of one's investment.

[5] **Duns:** Debt collectors.

[6] ***Gazette*:** The *London Gazette*, which published bankruptcies. It also published various honors, and Syntax says if his name ever appeared, it would be for that reason.

[7] **Beadle:** Officer charged with keeping the peace and carrying out various pieces of parish business.

SYNTAX.
"I pray, my friend, what's all this rout
"With your fierce bell?"

BEADLE.
            "To ring you out."   352

SYNTAX.
"I've been us'd to hear the din
"Of bells that always rang me in."[1]

BEADLE.
"All I've to say, for you to know,   355
"I'll shut the gate if you don't go.
"I sure shall leave you in the lurch,
"For now, good Sir, you're not at church."

SYNTAX.
"Indeed, my friend, you speak most true:
"I know all that as well as you.   360
"This is no temple; for, 'tis clear
"I find no *money-changers* here;
"Nor will I say my mind conceives
"It may be call'd—*a den of thieves*.[2]
"Howe'er, I'll quit these sons of pelf*,   365
"And keep my paper to myself:
"They shall no more at Syntax scoff;—
"Grizzle and I will soon be off.
"Thanks to my stars, I've got enough
"Of that same yellow, useful stuff,   370
"As will my ev'ry want befriend,
"And bear me to my journey's end.
"Arriv'd in town, I'll see my Lord,
"Who'll welcome me to bed and board;
"'Twill make that witty noble sport,   375
"When I these trading tricks report—
"How near I was of being cheated:
"And how his Lordship's name was treated."

[1] **rang me in:** Church bells rang on Sunday morning to summon people to worship.

[2] **no temple... *thieves:*** A reference to Jesus' expulsion of the money-changers from the temple, which, he claimed, they had made a "den of thieves" (Matthew 21:13).

CANTO XX.

THUS as he spoke, there pass'd along,
Among the crowding, grinning throng,
One who was in full fashion drest,
In coat of blue and corded vest,
And seem'd superior to the rest.   5
His small-clothes[1] sat so close and tight;

His boots, like jet, were black and bright;
While the gilt spur, well-arm'd with steel,
Was seen to shine on either heel.
Loaded with seals, and all bespangled,   10
A watch-chain from his pocket dangled;[2]

[2] **Loaded with
seals...dangled:**
The man has a
fancy chain on
which he carries his
seals for authorizing
letters and
documents.

His hat a smiling face o'erspread,
And almost hid his well-cropp'd head.
He swung his whip about to greet
The friends he met with in the street.   15
When as he pass'd, all big with rage,
Syntax appear'd upon the stage,
And still continued talking loud
For the amusement of the crowd.

The well-dress'd man now stopp'd, to know   20
What work'd the angry Doctor so:
And, in a pleasant friendly way,
Demanded where his grievance lay;
When Syntax bowing, on they walk'd,
And thus the social strangers talk'd:—   25

SYNTAX.
"These traders, Sir, I can't admire:
"You, I presume, Sir, are a 'Squire."

MR. ———.
"I have (and here there pass'd an oath),
"To say the truth a spice of both:

"For now you have within your view   30
"A Trader and a 'Squire too.
"Here I can some importance claim,
"And —— —— is my well-known name:[1]
"Nay, there are few within this town
"Of more substantial renown.   35
"My house of trade is in this street;
"A few miles off my country-seat:
"Where I most frequently reside
" 'Mid all the charms of rural pride;—
"And I'll be ————[2] if e'er you see   40
"A Lord who better lives than me."

              SYNTAX.

  "Fie, fie, good Sir! I cannot bear
"To hear a fellow-Christian swear.
"You must well know such profanation
"Is a foul trick in ev'ry station;   45
"And will draw down celestial ire,
"Or on a Trader, or a 'Squire;
"And, 'tis the duty of my cloth*,
"Whene'er I hear, to check an oath.
"I'm a poor Parson—very poor—   50
"I keep a school, and hold a cure;[3]
"But when I'm in the parish church,
"Or when at home I wield the birch:
"I know the dignities that wait
"Upon the pow'r of either state:—   55
"I keep them always in my view—
"Aye, Sir, and I maintain them too;
"Nay, in your 'Change, where riches reign,
"I did that dignity maintain;—
"In that proud place, where, I am told,   60
"There sometimes pour down show'rs of gold;
"But not like that we read of Jove;
"For that, you know, was pour'd for love:[4]
"And nothing like it did I see;
"No love, nor e'en civility: 65
"I only ask'd a common grace,
"When the man mock'd me to my face.

[1] **well-known name:** The elision suggests that Combe is referring to a real person, but if so we have not been able to trace the reference.

[2] **I'll be ————:** Combe modestly elides the word "damned."

[3] **a cure:** The right to preach and minister in a particular parish.

[4] **pour'd for love:** Jove, or Jupiter, after falling in love with the beautiful Danaë, descended on her in a shower of gold.

"Had I an arrant swindler been,
"He could not with more scornful mien
"Have my polite proposal greeted: 70
"Indeed, I was most foully treated;
"And by this dolt was made a joke
"Among the rude, surrounding folk.
"Thus was I work'd into a stew,[1]
"By Turk, by Gentile, and by Jew:[2]   75
"How bless'd am I to meet with you!
"For, know, Sir, I've the art to scan
"The well-bred, finish'd gentleman;
"And, therefore, I shall lay before you
"Some items of my honest story.   80
"The object of the Tour I make
"Is chiefly for the profit's sake;
"At the same time, I trust, my name
"May find some literary fame.
"You, if you please, may take a look   85
"At what I've finish'd of my book.
"A noble Peer doth condescend
"To be my patron, and my friend:
"I saw him late in York's fair county,
"And was the object of his bounty.   90
"This draft,[3] with most becoming grace,
"The smile of goodness on his face,
"He soft convey'd unto my touch;—
"He said, indeed, it was not much;
"But, could I visit him in town,   95
"He'd make his further friendship known:
"And, here, alas! I was so rash
"To try to get it chang'd for cash;
"For which myself and this great Peer
"Of these rude raffs[4] became the jeer.   100
"Permit me, Sir, to shew the paper
"That made these purse-proud* tradesmen vapour:[5]
"To its full value you'll accord;—
"Perhaps, Sir, you may know my Lord."

[1] **stew:** Angry mood.

[2] **By Turk...Jew:** Three words that, in different contexts, denote an infidel. Syntax is implying that he has been treated in an unchristian manner.

[3] **draft:** Check.

[4] **raffs:** Low, contemptible people.

[5] **vapour:** Speak foolishly.

MR. ———.
"I know him well—'tis his hand-writing—   105
"It is his Lordship's own inditing.
"I'll give the coin—Why, blood and 'ounds![1]
"I wish 'twere for five hundred pounds!
"He is a Lord of great discerning;
"His friendship proves your store of learning: 110
"He's not more known for ancient birth
"Than for the charm of private worth;
"For all that elegance and grace
"Which decorate a noble race.
"Come here with me, and you shall find   115
"At least one trader to your mind."

  Syntax now smooth'd his angry look,
And straight prepar'd to shew his book.
In a fine room he soon was seated;
With all attention he was treated;   120
And, while they at their luncheon sat,
Ten minutes pass'd in friendly chat.
At length the bus'ness was arrang'd;
The deed was done, the draft was chang'd;
And, as the Doctor plac'd his note   125
In a small pouch within his coat,
"There," said the 'Squire, "there's another;
"I've match'd it with its very brother:
"The Bank of England is their mother:
"And, when they're offer'd to her eye,   130
"She'll own them as her progeny.
"So tell my Lord that I, for one,
"Am proud to do as he has done:
"Nor is this all, my learned friend;
"Here our acquaintance must not end: 135
"My carriage and my servants wait,
"All in due order at the gate:
"So you shall go along and see
"My rural hospitality.
"For a few days we will contrive   140
"To keep our spirits all alive,

[1] **'ounds:** An oath referring to the wounds of Christ. Mr. ——— has not heeded Syntax's warning against swearing.

"I'll send a groom to fetch your mare,
"So laugh at thought, and banish care."
Thus off they went, and, four-in-hand,[1]
Dash'd briskly tow'rds the promis'd land.   145
Syntax first told his simple story,
And then the 'Squire detail'd his glory.

       MR. ———.

  "Now we're away in chaise and four*,
"I am a Merchant, Sir, no more;
"At least whene'er I thus retire,   150
"To flourish as a country 'Squire:
"When you will see how I prepare
"An opiate for mercantile care.
"In learned labours some proceed,
"But I prefer the racing steed: 155
"Some to Ambition's heights ascend;
"I to the Racing-Course attend.
"In study I ne'er wander far;—
"Mine is the Racing Calendar.[2]
"While with keen eye the Heralds[3] see   160
"The long-trac'd line of ancestry,
"Give me a horse's pedigree.
"Others some powerful station boast;
"But let me gain the winning-post.[4]
"It may be sweet with babes to play,   165
"But I prefer the filly's neigh.
"You talk of men of wit and parts,
"Of the deep sciences, and arts;
"Give me the science that will teach
"The knowing one[5] to over-reach: 170
"And, as for pictures and such things,
"Which Taste from foreign countries brings;
"A brood-mare, in maternal pride,
"With a colt trotting by her side,
"Is to my eye more pleasing far   175
"Than hero in triumphant car,[6]
"Or sea-born Venus weeping o'er
"Adonis,[7] wounded by a boar."

[1] **four-in-hand:** Holding the reins of four horses.

[2] **Racing Calendar:** An annual publication listing recent and upcoming horse races.

[3] **Heralds:** Officers who study and record titles and pedigrees.

[4] **winning-post:** Finish line.

[5] **knowing one:** A person who claims to know a great deal about horse racing. Mr. ——— amuses himself with the idea of inducing such people to make unwise bets (over-reach).

[6] **car:** Chariot.

[7] **Adonis:** Youth loved by Venus who was slain by a boar. A common subject in painting.

SYNTAX.
"These points, good Sir, I can't discuss:
"I know no steed but Pegasus."[1]   180

MR. ——.
"Cut off his wings—I've got a horse
"Shall run him o'er the Beacon Course;[2]
"And, tho' Apollo should bestride him,
"I'd back my horse—for I would ride him."

Thus as he spoke, a row of trees,   185
Which a full age had felt the breeze,
And half that time, at least, had made
A long cathedral aisle of shade,[3]
Appear'd in view, and mark'd the road
Which led to this brave 'Squire's abode;   190
Whose stately chambers soon possest
The Doctor as a welcome guest.
The dinner came—a sumptuous treat—
Nor did the Parson fail to eat
In the same way he used to do—   195
As much as any other two.
The cakes he munch'd—the wine he quaff'd;—
His tale he told—the Ladies laugh'd;
And thus the merry moments past,
Till cap and slippers came at last.   200
At length his balmy slumbers o'er,
Morn smil'd, as it had smil'd before,
And as, without our care or pain,
It will not cease to smile again;
When Syntax, having prov'd as able   205
At breakfast as at dinner table,
Begg'd leave, with due respect, to say
He must pursue his anxious way,
"No," said the 'Squire, "before you go,
"I shall my stud of racers show."   210
So off they went;—from stall to stall
He shew'd the steeds, and nam'd them all;
Describ'd their beauty and their birth,
Their well-earn'd fame and golden worth;

[1] **Pegasus:** The winged horse of Greek mythology. Syntax is saying the only horses he knows are those he encounters in classical literature.

[2] **Beacon Course:** Famous racecourse at Newmarket (in southeast England), the center of English horse racing.

[3] **long cathedral aisle of shade:** An avenue, two rows of trees that form an approach to a country house. Combe's lovely description of the avenue as a "cathedral aisle of shade" recalls several lines in praise of avenues from William Cowper's poem *The Task:*

> How airy and how light the graceful arch,
> Yet awful as the consecrated roof
> Re-echoing pious anthems! (19)

Combe's avenue moment is brief, but it establishes Mr. ———— as a pillar of the old country gentry. In Combe's time, fashionable "improvers" were beginning to cut down avenues, some of which had stood for centuries, to open up more striking views. The avenue thus became a symbol of tradition and generational continuity, threatened by the impatient, irreverent forces of "improvement" or "reform."

Austen uses the avenue as a symbol of tradition in two novels. In Emma, *Donwell Abbey is full of "rows and avenues, which neither fashion nor extravagance had rooted up"—an indication of Mr. Knightley's wholesome, old-fashioned Englishness (III.6). In* Mansfield Park, *we meet a country squire with no such regard for the past: Mr. Rushworth wants the avenue at Sotherton cut down to improve the "prospect," or view, from the house. Fanny Price, with her love of trees and of tradition, is dismayed, and quotes from the same stretch of Cowper's* The Task *that Combe is likely alluding to: "Ye fallen avenues, once more I mourn your fate unmerited" (I.6).*

"A View down the Avenue at Strawberry Hill, Twickenham," Unknown, c. 1770-1800. Lewis Walpole Library.

The various feats they all had done,   215
The plates which they had lost and won.
At length th' astonish'd 'Squire saw
Poor Grizzle to her girths in straw.
"That, Sir," said Syntax, "is my steed;
"But tho' I can't detail her breed,   220
"I sure can tell what she has won—
"Those scars by Frenchman's sabre done.
"I cannot brag what she has cost;
"But you may see what she has lost."
"Where," said the 'Squire, "are her ears!"   225
Quoth Syntax, "you must ask the shears;
"And now, perhaps, her switchy tail
"Hangs on a barn-door from a nail!"
The Doctor then began to state
Poor Grizzle's character and fate.   230
"Who was her dam, or who her sire,
"I care not," says the merry 'Squire:
"But well I know, and you shall see,
"Who will her noble husband be;—
"Yon fam'd grey horse, of Arab birth—[1]   235
"A princely steed, of nameless worth."
"The match is very grand indeed,"
Said Syntax, "but it won't succeed;
"Our household is not form'd to breed.
"My dearest Dorothy and I   240
"Have never had a progeny.
"Our fortune has most wisely carv'd;
"Had she borne babes, they must have starv'd.
"What should we do with such dear elves,
"Who scarce know how to keep ourselves?"   245
"I'll hear no more," the 'Squire replied;
"The scheme shall be this instant try'd;
"*Grizzle* shall be young *Match'em's*[2] bride.
"You are a very worthy man,
"And may the depths of learning scan: 250
"But in these things you're quite a dolt;
"You'll get a hundred for the colt.
"I'll have my whim—it shall be carry'd:—"
So Grizzle was that morning marry'd.

[1] **of Arab birth:** Derived from a line of Arabian horses noted for their beauty and speed.

[2] *Match'em's:* Matchem, a famous 18th-c. racehorse and stud to whom Mr. ——— compares his prized Arabian. As it happens, the 19th-c. racehorse Doctor Syntax, named after the hero of this poem, descended from Matchem.

And now the 'Squire invites the stay
Of Syntax for another day.
"Your mare," he said, "we'll onward send,
"Ty'd to the London waggon's end:
"When she's got forty miles, or more,
"We'll follow in a chaise and four:[1]
"At the *Dun Cow*,[2] upon the road,
"Grizzle shall safely be bestow'd;
"And there, my friend, or soon or late,
"Her master's coming may await:
"You'll neither lose nor time nor space—
"Your way I'm going to a race,
"Where I've a famous horse to run;
"And if you do not like the fun,
"Why you may then proceed to town
"With my best wishes that renown
"And profit may your labours crown.
"To-morrow, by the close of day,
"We shall find Grizzle on the way."
"Just as you please," the Doctor said;
"Your kind commands shall be obey'd:
"I think myself supremely bless'd
"By noble minds to be caress'd:
"The kind protection you impart
"Pours oil of gladness on my heart."

The Ladies now desir'd to see
His Journey's pictur'd history:
The Book he shew'd, which prov'd a bribe
For those kind fair-ones to subscribe;
And, while they felt the gen'rous pleasure
Of adding to his growing treasure,
The 'Squire to keep the joke alive,
Had bid his stable-folk contrive,
Ere the good Doctor's Grizzle mare
Was given to the carrier's[3] care—
Ere on her voyage she set sail,
To furnish her with ears and tail.
Grizzle was soon a crop no more,
As she had been some weeks before;

255
260
265
270
275
280
285
290

[1] **forty miles... chaise and four:** Mr. ———— is offering Syntax a way to travel further and more comfortably. Syntax's daily mileage is limited by the endurance of his horse. Tied to a cart with no rider, Grizzle can travel about twice as far in a day as she otherwise could.
[2] ***Dun Cow:*** A common name for inns in the Midland Counties of England.
[3] **carrier's:** A carrier is a person transporting goods or people by carriage.

Nor was it long before her stump
Felt all the honours of the rump: 295
And thus equipp'd with specious art,
She pac'd behind the carrier's cart.
Their breakfast done, the following day,
The 'Squire and Syntax bounc'd away;
And, ere the sun had set at eve,   300
The *Dun Cow* did the sage receive;
Where Grizzle, her day's journey o'er,
Had a short time arriv'd before.

  Syntax now felt a strong desire,
To smoke his pipe by kitchen fire,   305
Where many a country neighbour sat;
Nor did he fail to join the chat:

[1] **Exciseman:**
Official responsible
for collecting the

When, having supp'd and drank his ale,
And silence seeming to prevail,
He slowly from his pocket took   310
His trav'lling memorandum-book;
And, as he turn'd the pages o'er,
Revolving on their curious lore,
Th' Exciseman,[1] a right village sage,
(For he could cast accounts and gage,[2])   315
Spoke for the rest—who would be proud
To hear his Rev'rence read aloud.

excise tax.
[2] **gage:** To measure
or calculate the
capacity of
something (for
instance, a cask)—
an essential skill for
a tax collector.

He bow'd assent, and straight began
To state what beauty is in man:
Or on the surface of the earth,   320
Or what finds, in its entrails—birth;[1]
With all things, in their due degrees,
That are on earth, in air, or seas;—
In all the trees and plants that grow,
In all the various flow'rs that blow;[2]—   325
Of all things in the realms of nature,
Or senseless forms, or living creature:
In short, he thus profess'd to show,
Through all the vast expanse below,
From what combined state of things   330
The varying form of beauty springs.
But, as he read, tho' full of grace,
Tho' strong expression mark'd his face—
Tho' his feet struck the sounding floor,
And his voice thunder'd thro' the door—   335
Each hearer as th' infection crept
O'er the numb'd sense, unconscious slept!
One dropp'd his pipe—another snor'd—
His bed of down an oaken board;—
The cobler yawn'd, then sunk to rest,   340
His chin reclining on his breast.
All slept at length but *Tom* and *Sue*,
For they had something else to do.
Syntax heard nought; th' enraptur'd elf
Saw and heard nothing but himself: 345
But, when a swineherd's bugle sounded,
The Doctor then, amaz'd—confounded—
Beheld the death-like scene about him;
And, thinking it was form'd to flout him,
He frown'd disdain—then struck his head—
Caught up a light, and rush'd to bed.

[1] **what finds… birth:** Such as precious metals and gems.

325 [2] **blow:** Bloom.

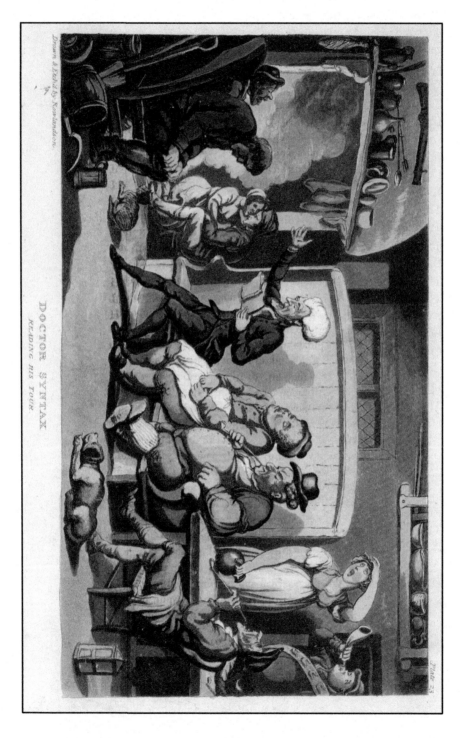

Drawn & Etched by Rowlandson.

DOCTOR SYNTAX
READING HIS TOUR.

Plate 23

CANTO XXI.

SLEEP, to the virtuous ever kind,
Soon hush'd the Doctor's turbid mind,
And, when the morning shed its dew,
He 'rose his journey to pursue.
Of tea and toast he took his fill,   5
Then told the Host to bring the bill:
But when it came, it made him stare
To see some curious items there.
"Go tell your Ostler* to appear;
"I wish to see the fellow here."   10
The Ostler now before him stands,
And bows his head, and rubs his hands.—
"In this same bill, my friend, I see
"You're witty on my mare and me:
"For all your corn, and beans, and hay,   15
" 'Tis a fair charge which I shall pay;
"But here a strange demand appears—
"*For cleaning of her tail and ears!*
"Now know, my lad, if this is done
"On me to play your vulgar fun,   20
"(For ears and tail my mare has none,)
"I'll make this angry horsewhip crack
"In all directions on your back."
The man deny'd all ill intent;
He knew not what his Rev'rence meant;   25
So thought it best to say no more,
But bring up Grizzle to the door.
Of painted canvas were her ears;
Upon her stump a tail appears:
So chang'd she was, so gay, so smart,   30
Deck'd out with so much curious art,
That even Syntax hardly dare
To claim his metamorphos'd mare.

He said no more—he knew the joke
Was not the sport of vulgar folk;   35
So trotted off—and kindly lent
His smile to aid the merriment.

   Now, as his journey he pursu'd,
He thus broke forth in solemn mood:—
"Tho' time draws on when those at home   40
"Expect that I should cease to roam
"(Tho' I have objects in my view
"Which are of great importance too);
"Yet, as this is the day of rest
"Appointed both for man and beast,[1]   45
"To the first church I will repair,
"And pay my solemn duties there."
Thus as he spoke, a village chime
Denoted it was service time:
And soon a ruddy Curate came,   50
To whom he gravely told his name,
His rank, and literary fame;
And said, as he'd been us'd to teaching,
He'd give him half an hour's preaching.[2]
This was accepted with a smile,   55
When they both strutted up the aisle;
And in due time, and with due grace,
Syntax display'd his preaching face.
When in bold tones, tho' somewhat hoarse,
He gave the following discourse:—   60

   "The subject I shall now rehearse,
"Is JOB the *fifth*,—the *seventh* verse:—

   " '*As sparks rise upards to the sky,*
  " '*So man is born to misery.*'

"This is a truth we all can tell;   65
"In ev'ry state we know it well.
"The infant in his cradle lies,
"And marks his trouble as he cries:

[1] **day of rest… beast:** The Sabbath, which falls on Sunday for Christians. Deut. 5:14 declares the Sabbath to be a day of rest for the whole community, including animals.

[2] **He'd give… preaching:** Traveling clergy often carried a sermon with them in case they were invited (or, as here, invited themselves) to preach (Cox, 80).

"From his young eyes the waters flow,
"The emblems of his future woe: 70
"His cheeks the varying signs display
"That mark a changeful April day;
"Symbols of joy and hope appear,
"And now a smile, and then a tear.
"The years of puling[1] childhood o'er,   75
"The Nurse's care he knows no more:
"To Learning's discipline resign'd,
"The Tutor forms his early mind.
"Now hopes and fears alternate rise
"In all their strange varieties.   80
"How oft, disdainful of restraint,
"His voice lifts up the loud complaint.
"While stern correction's[2] pow'rful law
"Keeps the fond urchin-mind in awe;
"And some dark cloud for ever low'rs*,   85
"To shade his bright and playful hours.
"Nor, when fair Reason's steady ray
"Begins to light Life's early day;
"Tho' the thick mist it instant clears,
"It dries not up the source of tears;   90
"Nay, 'tis its office, as we know,
"Sometimes to make those tears to flow:
"For now the Passions will impart
"Their impulse to th' unconscious heart;
"Will mingle in Youth's ardent hours,   95
"And plant the thorns amid the flow'rs;
"While Fancy, in its various guise,
"With plumage of a thousand dies,[3]
"Flits round the mind in wanton play,
"To bear each serious thought away: 100
"Nor Pleasure seldom tempts in vain
"To join her gay deluding train;[4]
"Courting the easy hearts to stray
"From Reason's path, and Wisdom's way;
"And oh! how oft the senses cloy   105
"With what is call'd the height of joy!
"While pale Repentance comes at last,
"To execrate the pleasure past!

[1] **puling:** Whining or crying querulously or weakly (OED).

[2] **stern correction's:** Likely a reference to corporal punishment.

[3] **dies:** Dyes, colors.

[4] **Nor Pleasure… train:** This couplet technically says that the temptations of Pleasure often fail, the opposite of Combe's intent. It was amended in the 9th ed. thus: "The Pleasures seldom tempt in vain / To join their gay, deluding train."

"At length, to finish'd manhood grown,
"The world receives him as its own.   110
"Life's active busy scenes engage
"Each moment of maturer age.
"Here Pleasure courts him to her bow'rs,
"Where serpents lurk beneath the flow'rs;
"Ambition tempts him to explore   115
"The height where daring spirits soar—
"While Wealth presents the glitt'ring ore,
"Which mingles with each mortal plan,
"And is the great concern of man.
"Thus pleasure, wealth, or love of pow'r,   120
"Employ man's short or lengthen'd hour.

  "In youth or manhood's early day,
"Pleasure first meets him on the way.
"The Syren[1] sings;—his eager ear
"Drinks in the sounds so sweet to hear.   125
"To the delicious song a slave,
"He leaves the vessel to the wave:
"The helm forsaken, on it goes;
"The light'nings flash, the whirlwind blows;
"When, by the furious tempest toss'd,   130
"The gay, the gilded bark,[2] is lost!
"But should he, 'mid the ocean's roar,
"Be cast upon some welcome shore;
"Then, wand'ring on the lonely coast,
"He'll sigh to think what he has lost;   135
"Health, ease, and ev'ry joy that Heav'n
"Had to his early wishes given.
"Life still is his—but life alone
"Cannot for follies past atone,
"When pain assails, and hope is flown.   140
"He feels no more the sunny rays
"Of smiling hours and prosp'rous days;
"The world turns from him, nor will know
"The man of sorrow and of woe;[3]
"But bids him to some cell[4] repair,   145
"In hope to find Contrition there.

[1] **Syren:** The sirens were mythical creatures who lured sailors to their ruin with their seductive song.
[2] **bark:** Small ship; here, a metaphor for a young man's fortunes or prospects.
[3] **The man of sorrow and of woe:** A botched application of Is. 53:3: "He is despised and rejected of men; a man of sorrows, and acquainted with grief." In the Christian tradition, the prophet is understood to be referring to the future Christ, not, as here, a washed-up pleasure-seeker.
[4] **cell:** A small room in a monastery; metaphorically, a place of withdrawal from the rigors or cruelties of the world.

"Nor is Ambition more secure,
"Nor less the ills which they endure
"Within whose bosom there doth dwell
"The vice by which the Angels fell.⁵   150
"The love of rule, the thirst of pow'r,
"Ne'er give a peaceful, tranquil hour;
" 'Tis the fierce fever of the soul
"That maddens for supreme control;
"Whose burning thirst continual glows,   155
"Whose pride no lasting pleasure knows;
"While Hatred, Envy, jealous Fear,
"Wait on the proud and bold career.
"Contention ev'ry act attends;
"Now friends are foes—now foes are friends: 160
"Enjoyment quickens new desire,
"And Hope for ever fans the fire.
"Whene'er the nearer height is gain'd,
"A loftier still must be attain'd;
"And then the eye looks keenly round   165
"In hope another's to be found;
"One—such is the aspiring soul—
"Whose tow'ring height shall crown the whole.
"But oft, as the aspirant gains
"The object of his toil and pains,   170
"The giddy view each sense appals—
"In vain for some kind aid he calls;—
"The faithless friend, th' insulting foe,
"Rejoice as to the gulf below
"He headlong falls—the prey to lie   175
"Of grinning Scorn and Infamy.

   "Now riches next demand our thought;
"E'en gold may be too dearly bought:
"Tho' in each clime, and ev'ry soil,
"It wakes the universal toil.   180
"For this, defying health and ease,
"The Sailor ploughs the distant seas:
"This shares the Soldier's daring aim,
"Who fights for wealth as well as fame:

⁵ **The vice...fell:** In Christian lore, Satan and his angels were cast out of heaven for their pride and ambition.

"But, tho' all wish its pow'r to wear,   185
"It is the source of many a care.
"Of all the vices that infest
"The purlieus* of the human breast,
"The love of mammon¹ is the worst,
"The most detested and accurst.   190
"Pleasure's gay moments may impart
"Some gladness to the human heart;
"Ambition, too, we often find
"The inmate of a noble mind;
"But love of riches ever bears   205
"The tokens of the lowest cares:
"We see one base unvarying vice
"In the pale form of Avarice;
"It only lifts its pray'r to Heav'n
"T' increase the store already given: 210
"Nor does it e'er the gift repay,
"By shedding one kind cheering ray
"Upon the weather-beaten shed,
"Where Want scarce finds the scanty bread;—
"By wiping from the widow's eye   215
"The flowing tears of misery;
"Or giving to the naked form
"The vestment that will keep it warm.
"For gold it courts the sleepless night,
"And toils thro' day's returning light.   220
"Nor these alone; the cool deceit—
"The treach'rous heart—the hidden cheat—
"The ready lie—the hard demand—
"And Law's oppressing griping³ hand;
"These demons never fail to wait   225
"At Mammon's dark and dreary gate.
"What does he love!—can that be told?—
"Yes, I can tell:—He loves his gold.
"In that one term he comprehends
"His kindred, neighborhood, and friends.   230
"But e'en should fortune daily pour
"Her treasures to increase his store,
"Say is he happy?—Does he feel
"A pleasure which he dare reveal?

¹ **mammon:**
Wealth as an object
of sinful worship.

³ **griping:**
Grasping.

"Ah, no!—His throbbing anxious breast   235
"Continu'd doubts and fears molest.
"See how he trembles with affright,
"When Justice claims the widow's right,
"And bids him at the bar[1] appear,
"To answer to the orphan's tear—   240
"By restoration to atone
"For many a wrong that he has done.
"Nay, a still far severer doom
"May aggravate the time to come:
"The scourge without—the scourge within—[2]   245
"May lash the unavailing sin;
"And, after all his toil and care,
" 'Tis well if he escape despair.[3]

"But e'en when Pleasure is not cross'd
"With ruin'd health and fortune lost,   250
"Yet still it leaves a void behind—
"No vigour to impel the mind.
"The season of enjoyment o'er,
"The phantom then can please no more;
"Brief is its time, it soon is past—   255
"A vernal bloom not made to last.
"Say, what presents its longest doom?
"A flow'r, a fever, and a tomb!

"What tho' Ambition holds its pow'r
"To life's extreme, but certain hour—   260
"Is not its most exalted joy
"Encumber'd with some base alloy?
"And, on its proudest, loftiest height,
"Say, does it alway find delight?
"Say, could it ever guard its heart   265
"From Fear's assault, and Envy's dart?
"Nor can it shut th' averted eye
"From passing life's mortality.
"Even from its most lofty brow,
"It must behold a grave below.   270

[1] **bar:** Court of law.

[2] **scourge without…within:** Possibly the scorn of society and one's own conscience, respectively. Alternatively, a reference to Is. 66:24, which prefigures the torments of hell.

[3] **despair:** The word carries a religious sense here: a loss of all hope for salvation, a conviction that one is doomed to hell.

"Tho' wealth should haply be attain'd
"By fair pursuits, with honour gain'd,
"Yet in its train, how oft we see
"The pallid forms of misery.
"Intemp'rance yields its foul delight,   275
"And feeds the obnoxious appetite;
"While Luxury in a thousand ways,
"To sensual carelessness betrays,
"And lights up in the mortal frame
"Disease's slow-corroding flame.   280
"Fortune, in fickle mood, may frown;
"The firmest base may tumble down:
"While it appears in strength secure,
"It falls, and leaves its owner poor.
"The largest heaps of treasur'd wealth   285
"Cannot restore declining health;
"They cannot bribe the Sun to stay,
"And mitigate his burning ray;
"Nor will the North's imperious cold
"Dissolve to genial warmth for gold.   290
"Time will not one short moment stay,
"Tho' millions lay athwart his way;
"Nor all the wealth that Crœsus[1] bore
"Can add to life one moment more.
"The regal palace and the cot*   295
"Are subject to one common lot:
"The rich and poor, the small and great,
"Alike must feel the stroke of fate:
"Virtue alone, we ought to know,
"Is real happiness below;   300
"And yet how oft her kindness proves,
"By toil and pain, the child she loves.[2]
"Honour, of noble minds the flow'r,
"Too oft's betray'd by Treachery's pow'r:
"And Charity we often see   305
"The dupe of base Hypocrisy.

   "Who then will venture to declare
"That man's mistitled Sorrow's Heir?

[1] **Crœsus:** An ancient king legendary for his wealth.

[2] **Virtue alone... child she loves:** An apparent reference to Heb. 12:6: "For whom the Lord loveth he chasteneth, and scourgeth every son whom he receiveth." Syntax is saying that suffering is not reserved for the wicked alone, but may actually be proof that one is loved by God (or Virtue)—another illustration of his theme that man is born to misery.

"But, Brethren, let us not complain
"That Heav'n's unjust when we sustain   310
"Th' allotted term of care and pain.
"Our life in such a mould is cast,
" 'Tis plain it is not made to last;
" 'Tis but a state of trial here,
"To fit us for a purer sphere;   315
"A scene of contest for a prize
"That in another region lies,
"In better worlds and brighter skies:
"Here doom'd a painful lot to bear,
"Our happiness is treasur'd there.   320
"To struggle with the woes of life,
"To wage with evil constant strife;
"T' oppose the Passions as they rise,
"And check our wild propensities;
"T' improve our nature, and to bear   325
"With patience the allotted share
"Of human woes—and thus fulfil
"The wise and the Eternal will—
"That forms the grand mysterious plan
"For Mortal and Immortal man.   330

    "Man is, indeed, by Heav'n's decree,
"As happy as he ought to be;
"As suited to his state and nature,
"A restless, frail, and finite creature,
"His work well done—his labour o'er—   335
"Evil and sorrow are no more;
"And, having pass'd the vale of death,[1]
"He claims the never-fading wreath;
"Glory's eternal crown to share,
"Which cherubs sing, and angels wear.   340
"Then is complete th' amazing plan,
"And Mortal is Immortal man."[2]

    Here Syntax thought it fit to close;—
Th' admiring congregation 'rose;
And, after certain hems and ha's,   345
The 'Squire nodded his applause:

[1] **vale of death:**
The valley of death.
The image is from
Psalm 23.

[2] **Then is
complete…man:**
The message of
Syntax's sermon is
familiar enough: the
miseries of this life,
if endured patiently,
are more than
repaid by the joys
of the next.
Elsewhere, though,
he suggests that
virtue ensures
happiness both here
and hereafter: "For
thus to virtuous
man 'tis given / To
dance, and sing, and
go to Heaven."
(XVII.274-5).

Nay, such attention he had given
To the sage Minister of Heaven,
That neither did he sleep nor snore—
A wonder never known before.   350
Then quickly issuing from the pew,
He came to thank the Doctor too:—
"Sir, your discourse, so good and fine,
"Proves you to be a great Divine;
"While I, alas! am but a sinner,   355
"So you'll go home with me to dinner;
"And, shortly after ev'ning pray'r,[1]
"The Curate too will meet you there."
The Doctor found the house well stor'd;
A chatt'ring wife, a plenteous board.[2]   360
The dinner was a pleasant sight,
For preaching gets an appetite;
And Syntax could perform them both
As well as any of the cloth*.
At length, the eatables remov'd,   365
The 'Squire began the talk he lov'd.

       'SQUIRE.
  "Have you much game, Sir, where you live?"

       SYNTAX.
  "An answer, Sir, I scarce can give:
"I never hunt, nor bear a gun;[3]
"I have no time, nor like the fun: 370
"Learning's the game which I pursue:
"I have no other sport in view:
"But I have heard the country round
"With hares and partridge does abound:
"Tho' on my table it is rare   375
"To see or one or t'other there.
"Oft when I rise at early morn,
"And hear the cheerful, echoing horn,
"I'm forc'd, from the inspiring noise,
"To hunt a pack of idle boys;   380
"And when they babble in their din,
"I am a special whipper-in;[4]

Jane Austen was an exception. Throughout life, she usually attended both morning and evening prayer. When she could not, she substituted family devotions—which usually involved reading a passage from the Book of Common Prayer *and perhaps a published sermon (Collins, 192).*

[1] **ev'ning pray'r:** Anglican priests typically held two services on Sunday, though most parishioners (like the Squire in this canto) only attended one.

[2] **board:** Table.

[3] **I never hunt…gun:** While Syntax has no interest in hunting, plenty of other clergyman did. This was accepted on the whole: a clergyman was a gentleman, and should be able to enjoy gentlemanly pastimes. A clergyman could, however, be criticized for living too much like the gentry and ignoring his humbler parishioners. In that case, a passion for hunting could be a sign of worldliness and pastoral neglect.

[4] **whipper-in:** An assistant to the master of hounds in a hunt, responsible for whipping straying dogs back to the pack.

At least two of Austen's clerical characters hunt: Henry Tilney and Edmund Bertram. Both men belong to wealthy, landed families, so it makes sense that they would have acquired a taste for hunting. Austen gives no indication that their hunting is at odds with their clerical duties. Instead, she may have used this character detail to show that one did not need to be somber in order to be a conscientious clergyman. There was room in the profession for spirited young men with a zest for life.

Detail from "The Clerical Exercise" showing a hunting parson, George Woodward, 1791. Lewis Walpole Library. The captions read, "Follow the hounds / Poise your Gun."

"Nay, if they should be found at fault,
"I crack my whip, Sir, as I ought."

   Syntax now told his story o'er—   385
A story told so oft before;
When soon the 'Squire began to feel
A slumber o'er his senses steal.
The Curate, too, bemus'd in beer,
Was more dispos'd to sleep than hear.   390
Said Syntax, "See th' effect of drink!
"Heav'n spare the souls that cannot think!
"But I will not their sleep molest;
"The Sabbath is a day of rest."
In short his words no more prevail;   395
There now was none to hear his tale:
He strove another pipe to smoke;
But there were none to hear his joke:
So on his elbow he reclin'd,
And thus the sleeping party join'd.   400
The clock struck ten ere they awoke,
When a shrill voice their slumbers broke:
In such a tone it seem'd to come,
That Syntax thought himself at home.
So having yawn'd, and shook their heads,   405
They wish'd good night, and sought their beds.

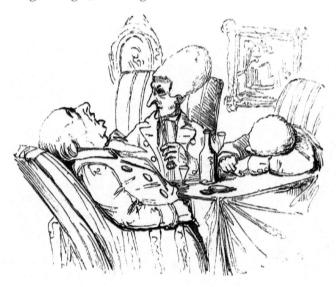

CANTO XXII.

THE clock struck five when Syntax woke—
The sounding door his slumbers broke—
When a soft female voice related
That breakfast and her master waited.
Up rose the Doctor; down he went,   5
With joyful look, and heart content.
"Well," said the 'Squire, "I hope you'll stay,
"And pass with me another day;
"The sporting season's coming on,
"And something now is to be done;   10
"For I must breathe my dogs a bit,
"And try my gun at some tom-tit.[1]
"You'll take a stroll around the fields,
"And see what game my manor yields."
Says Syntax, " 'Tis not in my pow'r   15
"To pass with you another hour:
"While you perform your sporting feats,
"I must be tramping London streets:
"You, therefore, will my thanks receive;
"For now, Sir, I must take my leave."   20
The 'Squire replied—"All I can say—
"Another time a longer stay."
He then walk'd off with dog and gun,
While Syntax travell'd slowly on;
And, o'er the hill or on the plain,   25
Indulg'd the contemplative strain:—
"I cannot, while I nature view,
"Cloth'd in her robe of verdant hue—
"Or when the changeful veil is thrown
"Of Summer's gold or Autumn's brown—   30
"Or midst the scenes of snow and frost,
"When her gay colouring is lost—

[1] **some tom-tit:** "Some bird or other."

"I cannot but the Pow'r admire
"That gives such charms to her attire:—
"Nor do her wond'rous shapes, that rise   35
"In countless forms to meet the eyes,
"Mark with less force th' unerring soul,
"Which gives such beauty to the whole:
"The mountain's top, that seems to meet
"The height of Heav'n's imperial seat;   40
"The rocks, the valley's guardian pride,
"Or bound'ries of the ocean's tide,
"That oft, in grand confusion hurl'd,
"Seem like the fragments of a world;—
"While the low hill and vale* between,   45
"Appear to variegate the scene.
"But lesser forms invite to trace
"Fair Nature's ever-varying face:—
"The humble shrub, the spreading tree,
"In this same principle agree.   50
"Along the ground the brambles crawl,
"And the low hyssop[1] tops the wall;
"The bullrush rises from the sedge,[2]
"The wild rose blossoms in the hedge;
"While flow'rs of ev'ry colour shed   55
"A fragrance from their native bed:
"The streamlet, winding thro' the glade,
"The hanging wood, the forest shade;
"The river's bold and flowing wave
"Doth many a peopled margin lave,[3]   60
"Till, with increasing course, 'tis seen
"To blend its white waves with the green.
"Nor these alone;—how various they
"Who cleave the air, or skim the sea;
"Or range the plains; or, from the brow,[4]   65
"Look down upon the vale below;
"The cygnet's snow, the peacock's dies;[5]
"The pigeon's neck, the eagle's eyes!—
"Nor in less beauty do they rove,
"Who form the beauty of the grove.   70
"The elephant's resistless force;
"The strength and spirit of the horse;

[1] **hyssop:** Syntax has in mind 1 Kings 4:33, which speaks of "the hyssop that springeth out of the wall."

[2] **sedge:** Coarse, grassy plants that grow in wet places (OED).

[3] **The streamlet… lave:** Syntax is contrasting small streams with mighty rivers that flow by towns and cities. Nature's diversity is his theme.

[4] **brow:** Clifftop.

[5] **dies:** Dyes, colors.

"The ermine's softness; and the boar,
"With rising bristles cover'd o'er.
"Thus, throughout Nature's various state, 75
"Of living, or inanimate,
"In ev'ry diff'rent class we see
"How boundless the variety!
"What playful change in all we know
"Of this mysterious world below; 80
"In all where instinct motion gives,
"In what by vegetation lives![1]
"But these are trivial when we look,
"By Reason's light in Nature's book;[2]
"When, half-inspir'd, we're taught to scan 85
"The vast varieties of man."

Thus, in deep metaphysic mood,
Syntax his shorten'd way pursu'd;
And many a system had been brought
To ripen in his learned thought: 90
But none arose which did not tend
Poor human nature to befriend;
None but were aptly form'd to prove
The firm support of social love,
Thus, all be-mus'd, he took his way, 95
Unconscious of the passing day!
And, thus employ'd in cogitating,
No wonder he ne'er thought of baiting;[3]
No wonder that it came to pass
When Grizzle saw a little grass, 100
That he, contemplating the view
Of knotty questions, never knew
She stopp'd to take a bite or two:
Or, when they pass'd a limpid brook,
That she a plenteous beverage took; 105
Or if, by chance, upon the road,
They found a cart with hay well stow'd,
She lagg'd behind to crop the fare,
And levy contributions[4] there.

[1] **What playful change...lives:** In other words, what delightful diversity we find in living things, whether animals or plants. "Vegitation" is the ability to live without sensation, as plants do.

[2] **By Reason's... book:** Syntax may be an example of what Patrick Armstrong calls the "parson-naturalist": a clergyman who studies not only Scripture but the natural world as well. The pursuits are complementary, both revealing the power and goodness of God.

[3] **baiting:** Pausing during a journey to let a horse feed.

[4] **levy contributions:** To impose a tax in order to support an army. Combe is referring playfully to Grizzle's former service as a warhorse.

But now a trumpet's warlike sound   110
'Woke Syntax from his dream profound;
While Grizzle frisk'd, and mov'd on straight,
With many a prancing, to the gate,
Where, in a gorgeous cap of fur,
Stood the proclaiming trumpeter,[1]   115
With face as the old *Lion* red[2]
Which dangling hung above his head.
"Oh!" he exclaim'd, "I now could swear
"I see again the Grizzle mare;
"I know her well by that same scar   120
"Which she got with me in the war:
"For she receiv'd that angry hack
"While I was sounding[3] on her back:
"A furious hussar[4] onward came,
"And struck at me, but miss'd his aim;   125
"When my poor mare receiv'd the blow,
"And straight the blood began to flow;—
"Nay, the same sword had crack'd my crown,
"But my brave comrade, *Stephen Brown*,
"Came up, and cut the Frenchman down.   130
"I have been borne by that same gray
"Thro' many a rough and bloody day:

[1] **cap of fur… trumpeter:** A trumpeter is a mounted soldier who gives directions to a body of cavalry by means of trumpet signals. In Combe's day, some cavalry regiments wore a cylindrical fur cap called a busby.
[2] **the old *Lion* red:** The sign for the Red Lion inn.
[3] **sounding:** Blowing the trumpet.
[4] **hussar:** A type of light cavalryman.

256

"Her ears well know the martial strain;[1]
"I'm glad to see her once again."

  "That well may be;—but for her ears—
"A wicked clown's[2] infernal shears
"Have robb'd her," Syntax smiling said,
"Of the fair honours of her head:
"Nor did one tender thought prevail,
"From the same fate to save her tail."
He then proceeded to relate
Her past mishap and present state;
And ask'd the trumpeter to share
A flowing bowl[3] and ev'ning fare.

  Now Syntax sat and heard the story
The soldier told of England's glory;
How British columns fought their way,
And drove the foe, and won the day;
How oft he did his breath enlarge,
To call to arms and sound the charge:
Tho' oft he rous'd to many a feat,
He never sounded a retreat:
But still he spoke in modest tone,
For England's glory was his own:—

  "Oft have I seen in bright array
"(Sure promise of a glorious day),
"The martial bands alive to meet
"Their foes, and lay them at their feet;
"And, when my breathing trumpet told 'em
"To go and conquer—to behold 'em
"At once their beaming blades display,
"And rush on their victorious way—
"I felt the inexpressive[4] joy
"Which grim-fac'd danger could not cloy.[5]
"If that same grizzle steed you rode
"Could speak, she'd tell the ground she trod
"Was oft, alas! all cover'd o'er
"With soldiers slain, and clotted gore.

[1] **martial strain:**
The military tune
the trumpeter has
135 just been playing.
[2] **clown's:** A clown
is a rude,
unsophisticated
person from the
140 country.

[3] **flowing bowl:**
Bowl of punch, an
145 alcoholic drink
usually consumed in
company.

150

155

160

[4] **inexpressive:**
Impossible to
165 express in words.
[5] **cloy:** Spoil.

"Full many a hair-breadth 'scape I've seen;
"In many a peril I have been: 170
"And soon again the time may come
"When, order'd from our native home,
"We shall seek foreign climes,[1] to share
"The dangers and the din of war.
"So be it, I'm prepar'd to go,   175
"Wherever I can meet the foe;
"And, should it be my lot to die,
"I have no wife or babes to cry;
"And, wheresoever I may fall,
"There'll be an end of *Thomas Hall.*"   180
   Said Syntax, "It is well my friend,
"To be prepared to meet our end:
"To do that well, I'm call'd to preach—
" 'Tis a prime duty which I teach:
"But thoughts of a far diff'rent kind   185
"Just now employ my anxious mind:
"The present busy hours must claim
"Attention to my purse and fame;
"And, as I think 'twould prove a joke
"To show my mare to London folk,   190
"It has just come into my mind
"To leave poor Grizzle here behind,
"And let some stage or mail[2] convey
"My bags and me my onward way.
"Perhaps, for old-acquaintance sake,   195
"Of my poor beast the care you'll take.
"If so"————The Trumpeter reply'd—
" 'Twill be my honour and my pride.
"God bless your Rev'rence;—never fear—
"Your mare shall have protection here: 200
"When you return her Looks will tell,
"That her Old Friend has us'd her well."

   A horn[3] now told the near approach
Of some convenient rapid coach;
And soon a vehicle and four[4]   205
Appear'd at the *Red Lion* door.

¹ **foreign climes:** During the Napoleonic Wars, the British army fought the French all over the world, from continental Europe to India to the Caribbean.

"The Miseries of Travelling: the Overloaded Coach," Thomas Rowlandson, 1807. The Met.

² **stage or mail:** A stagecoach or mail coach. A stagecoach was a public conveyance that stopped at predetermined stages, often inns, to change horses and allow passengers to refresh themselves. Mail coaches operated on the same principle, but because their primary purpose was to transport the mail, they usually carried fewer passengers and traveled faster. Most long-distance travel in the early nineteenth century was undertaken by these means, since passenger rail did not yet exist.

³ **horn:** A postillion perched atop the coach would blow a horn when approaching or departing a stop.

⁴ **vehicle and four:** A carriage pulled by four horses.

Most of Austen's characters, who are in easier circumstances than Syntax, rented a carriage when traveling (called traveling "post") or used their own private carriages. Austen herself, though, did travel by stagecoach at least once. Luckily, her fellow passengers were "very quiet & civil," and, just as important, "of a reasonable size" (23-4 Aug. 1814). The interior of a stagecoach was a tight space, and passengers no doubt felt some dismay when the coach stopped to pick up a particularly large traveler.

Into his place the Doctor pounc'd;
The coachman smack'd, and off they bounc'd:
The scene around was quite composing,
For his companions all were dozing;   210
So he, forsooth, conceiv'd it best
To close his lids, and try to rest.
When the morn dawn'd, he turn'd an eye
Upon his slumb'ring company:
A red-fac'd man, who snor'd and snorted— 215
A Lady, with both eyes distorted—
And a young Miss of pleasing mien,[1]
With all the life of gay sixteen.
A sudden jolt their slumbers broke;
They started all, and all awoke,   220
When Surly-boots yawn'd wide, and spoke:—
"We move," said he, "confounded slow:"
"La, Sir!" cried Miss, "how fast we go!"
While Madam with a smirking face,
Declar'd it was a middling pace.   225
"Pray what think you, Sir?"—"I agree,"
Said simp'ring* Syntax, "with all three:
"Up hill, our course is rather slow;
"Down hill, how merrily we go!
"But, when 'tis neither up nor down,   230
"It is a middling pace, I own."
"O la!" cried Miss, "the thought's so pretty!"
"O yes!" growl'd Red-face, "very witty!"
The Lady said, "If I can scan
"The temper of the Gentleman,   235
"He's one of those, I have no doubt,
"Who loves to let his humour out;
"Nor fails his threadbare wit to play
"On all who come within his way:
"But we who in these stages roam,   240
"And leave our coach-and-four at home,
"Deserve our lot when thus we talk
"With those who were ordain'd to walk!
"And now, my niece, you see how wrong
"It is to use your flippant tongue,   245

[1] **mien:** Face or expression.

"And chatter, as you're apt to do,
"With any one—the Lord knows who."
Surly turn'd round, and friendly Sleep
Soon o'er his senses 'gan to creep;
So Syntax thought he'd overlook   250
The embryo of his future book.
Thus all was silence till they came
To that great town we London name.

Our Sage thought wisely that the din
Which he should hear about an inn   255
Would not assist his studious hours,
Nor aid his intellectual pow'rs
To make his volume fit to show
The Dons of *Paternoster-row*;[1]
And as his patron of the North,   260
That Lord renown'd for sense and worth,
Had bid him make his house his home
Whenever he to town should come,
He was resolv'd to try his fate
In knocking at his Lordship's gate.[2]   265
At that same gate he soon appear'd;
My Lord with smiles the Doctor cheer'd:—
"You have done well, my learned friend,
"Hither your ready steps to bend;
"Bus'ness has brought me up to town,   270
"And thus you find me all alone.
"Here pitch your tent, and pass your hour
"In working up your pleasant Tour;
"And, when 'tis done, I'll aid your scheme—
"It shall not prove an idle dream."   275
Syntax receiv'd his Lordship's grace
With moisten'd eye, but smiling face,
And for ten days, at morn and night,
He toil'd to bring his book to light;

[1] **Dons of *Paternoster Row:*** Booksellers. Paternoster Row was a street in London primarily occupied by printers and publishers.

[2] **his Lordship's gate:** The London home of the Earl of Carlisle was at 12 Grosvenor Place, a fashionable spot bordering a park which is now Buckingham Palace Garden.

While the few intervening hours   280
Were render'd gay with wine and flow'rs†.

   My Lord, by gen'rous friendship mov'd,
Now read his volume, and approv'd:
"Think not," he said "I idly give
"Opinions tending to deceive: 285
"That I'm sincere, my friend, you'll see,
"When I declare that you are free
"To dedicate your book to me:[1]
"Nor is this all—I'll recommend
"My very pleasant, learned friend   290
"To one who has as lib'ral feeling
"As any in this kind of dealing:[2]
"And, when this letter you present,
"He'll take the work, and give content.
"Thus, my good Sir, I've done my best: 295
"You'll see him, and explain the rest."

   The Doctor now receiv'd his papers
In spirits almost to cut capers;
Nor did he then delay to go,
Not to the realms of sight and show,[3]   300
But those of *Paternoster-row.*
The shop he enter'd; all around
He saw the shelves with volumes crown'd,
In Russia and Morocco[4] bound;
And, when he had with fond delight   305
Glanc'd o'er the literary sight,
"Go, call your master," Syntax said,
To an attendant on the trade;
"Tell him that a D. D.[5] is here:"
The lad then answer'd, with a sneer,   310
"To no D. D. will he appear;

† Huc vina et unguenta et nimium breves,
Flores amœnæ ferre jube rosæ.

                    HOR.

[Combe's note. In English, "Tell them to bring the wines and the perfumes and sweet rose blossoms that live such a little while." Horace, *Odes* 2.3.]

¹ **dedicate your book to me:** Lord Carlisle's offer might seem a little self-serving to modern readers, but it was in fact an act of generosity—something like a free celebrity endorsement today. Since dedications were understood to be made with the consent of the dedicatee, readers would conclude from it that Carlisle approved of the book and had extended his patronage to its author. This was excellent publicity for an unknown, aspiring writer like Syntax.

² **one who has...dealing:** A bookseller, whom we meet on the next page.

³ **realms of sight and show:** Perhaps referring to the theater and other places of spectacle and amusement. In other words, Syntax didn't waste time but got straight to business.

⁴ **Russia and Morocco:** Types of leather used in bookbinding.

The ruler of England, the Prince Regent himself, loved Austen's novels and invited her to dedicate Emma *to him through his librarian, James Stanier Clarke. Some modern critics have suggested that Austen did so grudgingly, given her strong dislike of the Prince's character—in particular his treatment of his wife. On the other hand, she must have known that a dedication to the Prince Regent "by His Royal Highness's Permission," was a major publicity coup. In the end she avoided flattery and wrote a simple and respectful (some might say terse) dedication—doing her duty as a subject, and promoting her interests as an author, without compromising her principles as a woman and a Christian.*

"The Voluptuary under the horrors of Digestion," James Gillray, 1792. A caricature of the Prince of Wales, later Prince Regent.

⁵ **D.D.:** A doctor of divinity, a graduate of Oxford or Cambridge holding an advanced degree in theology.

In Austen's novels, the title "Dr." almost always indicates a doctor of divinity. The only definite exception is a reference in Mansfield Park *to the real-life Dr. Johnson, who held an honorary degree.*

"He would not come for all the knowledge
"Of Oxford or of Cambridge College:
"I cannot go, as I'm a sinner;[1]
"I dare not interrupt his dinner:
"You know not how I should be blam'd"——
Stamping his foot, Syntax exclaim'd—
"Apollo and the Muses nine!
"Must learning wait while tradesmen dine!"
"They're common hacks," reply'd the boy;
"We never such as those employ:
"I've heard their names, but this I know,
"They seldom come into the *Row.*"
The master, who had fill'd his crop[2]
In a smart room behind the shop,
On hearing a loud angry voice,
Came forth to know what caus'd the noise;
And left his wife and bottle too,
To see about this strange to-do.
He was a man whose ample paunch
Was made of beef, and ham, and haunch;
And, when he saw the shrivell'd form
Of Syntax, he began to storm.

[1] **as I'm a sinner:**
315 The phrase should
be read, "just as
surely as I am a
sinner," and not
"because I am a
320 sinner."

[2] **crop:** Gullet.

325

330

BOOKSELLER.

"I wish to know, Sir, what you mean,
"By kicking up, Sir, such a scene?   335
"And who you are, Sir, and your name,
"And on what errand here you came?"

SYNTAX.

"My errand was to bid you look
"With care and candour on this book;
"And tell me whether you think fit   340
"To buy, or print, or publish it?
"The subject which the work contains
"Is Art and Nature's fair domains;
" 'Tis form'd the curious to allure;—
"In short, good man, it is a Tour;   345
"With drawings all from Nature made,
"And with no common skill display'd:
"Each house, each place, each lake, each tree,
"These fingers drew—these eyes did see."

BOOKSELLER.

"A Tour, indeed!—I've had enough   350
"Of Tours, and such-like flimsy stuff.
"What a fool's errand you have made
"(I speak the language of the trade),
"To travel all the country o'er,
"And write what has been writ before!   355
"We can get Tours—don't make wry faces,
"From those who never saw the places.
"I know a man who has the skill
"To make your books of Tours at will;
"And from his garret in Moorfields[1]   360
"Can see what ev'ry country yields;
"So, if you please, you may retire,
"And throw your book into the fire:
"You need not grin,[2] my friend, nor vapour;[3]
"I would not buy it for waste paper!"   365

SYNTAX.

"Blockhead! and is it thus you treat
"The men by whom you drink and eat?

[1] **garret in Moorfields:** Moorfields was a seedy part of London. A garret is a small room in an attic, often associated with starving writers.
[2] **grin:** Bare your teeth [in anger].
[3] **vapour:** Fume or storm.

"Do you not know, and must I tell ye,
" 'Tis they fill out your monstrous belly?
"Yes, booby*! from such sculls as mine   370
"You lap your soup, and drink your wine,
"Without one single ray of sense
"But what relates to pounds and pence.
"Thus good and evil form the whole—
"Heav'n gave you wealth, and me a soul;   375
"And I would never be an ass
"For all your gold, with all your brass.[1]
"When humble Authors come to sue,
"(Those very men that pamper you),
"You feel like Jove in all his pride,   380
"With Juno squatting by his side."

BOOKSELLER.

"How dare you, villain, to defame
"My dearest wife's unsully'd name?
"Yes, she's my wife;—ten years ago,
"The parson join'd our hands at Bow,[2]   385
"And she's the flow'r of our *Row*.
"As for *Miss Juno*,[3] she's a harlot,
"You foul-mouth'd, and malicious varlet![4]
"A prostitute, who is well known
"To all the rakes about the town;   390
"First with a footman[5] off she ran,
"And now lives with an *Alderman*."[6]

SYNTAX.

"Have done—have done! pray read that letter;
"And then I think you'll treat me better."

BOOKSELLER.

"Sir, had you shewn the letter first,   395
"My very belly would have burst
"Before I would have said a word
"Your learned ears should not have heard;
"But, in this world wherein we live,
"We must forget, Sir, and forgive.   400
"These little heats will sometimes start
"From the most friendly, gen'rous heart.

[1] **brass:** Insolent pride.

[2] **Bow:** Saint Mary-le-Bow is a church in Cheapside, a neighborhood in London associated with trade.

[3] *Miss Juno:* In other words, the bookseller does not know that Juno was a Roman goddess. Combe often juxtaposes the hyper-educated Syntax with earthy people who know nothing whatsoever about the classics.

[4] **varlet:** Rascal.

[5] **footman:** A servant who attended a carriage, usually dressed in fancy livery.

[6] *Alderman:* A high-ranking officer in a borough or city (OED).

267

"My Lord speaks highly of your merit,
"As of the talents you inherit:
"He writes himself supremely well;
"His works are charming[1]—for they sell. 405
"I pray you take a glass of wine;
"Perhaps, Sir, you have yet to dine:
"We now, I fear, have nothing hot;
"My dear, put something in the pot;
" 'Twill soon be done; or tell our Nan[2] 410
"To toss a cutlet in the pan.
"His Lordship here expressly says
"Your work transcends his utmost praise;
"Desires the printing may commence, 415
"And he'll be bound for the expense.[3]
"The book will sell, I have no doubt;
"I'll spare no pains to bring it out:
"A work like this must not be stinted,
"Two thousand copies shall be printed. 420
"And if you please"

SYNTAX.
                    "I cannot stay;
"We'll talk of this another day:
"When I came out, I gave my word 421
"To take my dinner with my Lord.

BOOKSELLER.
  "Perhaps some other time you'll come, 425
"When my good Lord may dine from home;
"It will be kind, indeed, to share,
"Quite as a friend, our humble fare;
"In the mean time you may command,
"In ev'ry sense, my heart and hand." 430

  Thus (such are this world's odds and ends)
Tho' foes they met—they parted friends.

[1] **His works are charming:** Lord Carlisle wrote several books of poetry and two tragedies, as well as political pamphlets.

[2] **Nan:** Short for Anne or Nancy, presumably the cook.

[3] **he'll be bound... expense:** In other words, if the work does not sell well enough to cover the cost of publication, Lord Carlisle will make up the difference.

CANTO XXIII.

"WHATE'ER of genius or of merit
"The child of labour may inherit,
"They will not, in this mortal state,
"Or give him wealth, or make him great:
"Unless that strange capricious dame,   5
"Whom Pagan poets Fortune name,
"That unseen, ever-active pow'r,
"Propitious aids his toilsome hour.
"Throughout my life I've struggled hard;
"And what has been my lean reward?   10
"What have I gain'd by learned lore,
"By deeply reading o'er and o'er,
"What ev'ry ancient Sage has writ,
"Renown'd for pure and Attic¹ wit;
"Or those rich volumes which dispense   15
"The strains of Roman eloquence?
"No fav'ring patrons² have I got,
"But just enough to boil the pot.
"What tho', by toil and pain, I know
"Where ev'ry Hebrew root³ doth grow,   20
"And can each hidden truth descry
"From *Genesis* to *Malachi:*⁴
"Yet I have never been decreed
"To shear the fleeces⁵ that I feed:
"No, they enrich the idle dunce⁶   25
"Who never saw his flock but once,
"And meanly grudges e'en to spare
"My pittance for their weekly fare.
"Have I made any real friends
"By wasting eyes and candles' ends?   30
"And tho' a good musician too,
"What did my fiddle ever do?

¹ **Attic:** Greek or Athenian.

² **patrons:** People with the right to appoint clergymen to church livings.

³ **Hebrew root:** While most clergymen knew Latin and some Greek, knowledge of Hebrew, the language of the Old Testament, was very rare.

⁴ *Genesis* to *Malachi:* The first and last books of the Old Testament.

⁵ **shear the fleeces:** As a curate, Syntax has never had the right to collect tithes (fleeces) from his spiritual flock.

⁶ **idle dunce:** The absentee clergyman who holds the living Syntax serves. He collects the tithes, out of which he pays Syntax a small stipend.

"I sometimes might employ its pow'r
"To sooth an over-anxious hour:
"But, tho' it with my temper suits,   35
"It never yet could soften brutes.
"My sketching pencil, too, is known
"In every house in our town;
"For, to replace some horrid scrawl,
"My drawings hang on ev'ry wall: 40
"And yet, 'tis true, as I'm a sinner,
"They seldom paid me with a dinner.
"What do I get poor boys to teach,
"And drive in learning at the breech?[1]
"A task, which, Lucian says, is given   45
"As the worst punishment from Heaven.[2]
"While Fortune's boobies* cut and carve,
"I may be said to teach and starve:
"Too happy, if, on Christmas-day,
"I've just enough the duns[3] to pay.   50
"Tho' sometimes I have almost swore,
"When from the threshold of the door   }
"My poverty repell'd the poor;—[4]
"When the cask empty'd of its ale,
"No more the thirsty could regale.   55

    "At length the lucky moment came
"To fill my purse and give me fame;
"And, after all my labours past,
"Hope bids me look for rest at last.
"For scarce had I one prosp'rous hour   60
"Till Fortune bid me *write a Tour*.
"Oft have I said in words unkind,
"That strumpet Fortune's[5] very blind:
"But now I think the wench can see,
"Since she's become so kind to me.   65
"To say the truth, I scarce believe
"The favours which I now receive:
"In a Lord's house I take my rest,
"A welcome and an honour'd guest:
"The favours on my Tour I found   70
"Are by his present kindness crown'd.

[1] **breech:** Hindquarters. In other words, teaching boys requires frequent spanking.

[2] **Lucian says...Heaven:** The 2nd c. satirist Lucian once joked that in the afterlife, "kings and satraps" are reduced to "teaching the alphabet," in which role they are abused and scoffed at like "the meanest slaves" (Lucian, Vol. IV, 13).

[3] **duns:** Debt collectors.

[4] **My poverty repell'd the poor:** Clergymen were expected to set an example of Christian generosity in their parishes by giving alms (Cox, 74). Syntax, though, is only able to afford the necessities for himself and his wife. His inability to help the poor is clearly a source of shame and frustration to him—almost leading him to swear, a vice he deplores.

Austen's short sketch "The Generous Curate" describes a similar situation. A poor curate takes upon himself the education of the son of another poor clergyman, but he is unable to send the boy to anything better than a "twopenny Dame's School in the village" (Juv. 95). The curate's tiny income prevents him from being the ideal clergyman that he wishes to be— pitying and relieving those in distress. Instead he is the one in need of pity and relief, though his pride as an educated gentleman probably makes this a difficult fact to accept.

Frontispiece of Ackermann's 1817 edition of Oliver Goldsmith's *The Vicar of Wakefield* (first pub. 1766), illustrated by Thomas Rowlandson. The titular character, Dr. Primrose (seen here relieving a poor family), gives his entire clerical income to charity, living only on his inherited money. When he himself is ruined, though, his generosity becomes untenable. The kindly and naïve Primrose was a partial model for Dr. Syntax and may also have inspired Austen's "The Generous Curate."

[5] **strumpet Fortune's:** A reference to Hamlet, who declares that Fortune "is a strumpet," meaning that she is unfaithful and indiscriminate with her favors (2.2.238).

"I'd always heard that these same Lords
"Were only friendly in their words;
"Truth can alone my patron move,
"Whose gen'rous deeds his promise prove.   75

Thus Syntax did his feelings broach,
As he reclin'd within a coach;
For, pond'ring, as he pass'd along,
He was sore pummell'd by the throng:
Now by a porter's package greeted,   80
Now on the pavement he was seated;
While, deafen'd by a news-boy's din,
A fruit-girl's barrow strikes his shin;
And, as his cautious course he guides,
The passing elbows punch his sides;   85
While a cart-wheel, with luckless spirt,
Gives him a taste of London dirt.
At length, to get in safety back,
He sought the comforts of a hack.[1]

[1] **hack:** A hack-chaise or hired carriage.

His little journey at an end,   90
The Doctor join'd his noble friend:
Together they in comfort dine,
Then munch'd their cakes, and sipp'd their wine;
When Syntax, briefly, thus display'd
His parly[2] with the man of trade.   95

[2] **parly:** Parley, conversation.

"I owe unto your Lordship's name
"My future gains in gold or fame.
"My uncomb'd wig—my suit of black,
"Which had grown rusty on my back—
"My grisly visage, pale and thin—   100
"My carcase nought but bones and skin—
"Presented to the tradesman's eye
"The ghastly form of Poverty:
"Nor would he deign to cast a look
"Upon the pages of my book;   105
"But, with the fierceness of a Turk,[3]
"In sorry terms revil'd my work;

[3] **Turk:** The savage or cruel Turk was a common racial stereotype.

272

"And let loose all his purse-proud* spleen
"Against a thing he ne'er had seen.
"But your kind note, where it was said   110
"That all expenses should be paid,
"New-dy'd my coat, new-cock'd my hat,
"Powder'd my wig, and made me fat.
"His eye now saw me plump and sleek,
"With not a wrinkle in my cheek;   115
"And strength, and stateliness, and vigour,
"Completed my important figure.
"While in my pocket his keen look
"Glanc'd at your Lordship's pocket-book.
" 'Twas now—'I'm sure the work will sell,   120
"And pay the learned author well:'
"Then grac'd his shrill and sputt'ring speeches
"With pulling up his monstrous breeches:
"And made me all the humblest bows
"His vast protuberance allows: 125
"For, had he come with purse in hand,
"E'en Satan might his press command;
"So that the book had not a flaw
"To risk the dangers of the law.[1]
"Prove but his gains—and he'd be civil,   130
"Or to the Doctor—or the devil."

    Thus Syntax, and his patron sat,
And thus prolong'd the ev'ning chat.

                MY LORD.
    "Your rapid pencil fairly traces
"Men's characters as well as faces.
"Your latter sketch is true to Nature,   135
"And gives me *Vellum's*[2] ev'ry feature.
"With all your various talents fraught,
"So deeply read, so ably taught,
"I feel a curious wish to know
"From whence your high endowments flow: 140
"And how it happens that a man,
"Whose worth I scarce know how to scan,

[1] **dangers of the law:** Publishers could be fined and even jailed for printing material deemed libelous, obscene, or seditious by the government.

[2] *Vellum's:* The bookseller's name refers to a high-quality type of parchment. Combe may be implying that Vellum has found his niche in the upper echelons of the book market.

"Should ne'er have reach'd a better state
"Than seems to be your present fate."   145

    SYNTAX.
  "My Lord, a very scanty page
"Will tell my birth and parentage:
"A mod'rate circle will contain
"My round of pleasure and of pain,
"Till you, my ever-honour'd friend,   150
"Bade my horizon wide extend,
"And lighted up a brighter ray,
"To beam upon my clouded day.

  "My father was a noble creature
"As e'er was form'd by pregnant Nature: 155
"A learned Clerk*, a sound Divine,
"A fav'rite of the Virgins nine,
"Who dwell upon Parnassian hill,
"Or bathe in Heliconian rill*.[1]
"In the sequester'd vale* of life,   160
"An equal foe to pride and strife,
"He pass'd his inoffensive day
"In teaching Virtue's peaceful way:
"A shepherd, form'd his flock to bless
"In this world's thorny wilderness,   165
"And lead them, when their time is o'er,
"To where, good man, he's gone before.
"Ambition ne'er disturb'd his rest,
"Nor bred a serpent in his breast
"To sting his peace: no sordid care   170
"Corroded the contentment there:
"While he possess'd an income clear
"Of full five hundred pounds a year.

  "My mother, first of womankind,
"In figure, feature, and in mind,   175
"In her calm sphere contented mov'd,
"The counterpart of him she lov'd.
"Form'd to adorn the highest lot,
"She grac'd the Vicar's rural cot*.[2]

[1] **Virgins…rill:** The nine Muses of Greek mythology, goddesses who provide creative inspiration to poets and artists. Mount Parnassus and the springs of Mount Helicon were sites sacred to the Muses. In other words, Syntax's father was a writer and a learned man.

[2] **Form'd to adorn…cot:** Though Syntax's mother could have shone in high society, she instead chose to become a country clergyman's wife, a role she happily embraced.

"With all those manners that became
"The Parson's wife, the village dame.
"They liv'd and lov'd—and might have wore
"The *Flitch*[1] when twenty years were o'er. 180

"An only child appear'd, to prove
"The pledge of fond, connubial love.—
"I was that child—a darling boy; 185
"Their daily hope—their daily joy.
"My anxious father did not spare
"The urchin[2] to another's care;
"He taught the little forward elf 190
"To be the image of himself;
"And from the cradle he began
"To form and shape the future man.
"When fifteen summer suns had shed
"Their lustre on my curly head, 195
"To *Alma Mater*[3] he consign'd,
"With pious hope, my rip'ning mind.

"There, sev'n short years, (for short they were,)
"Fair Science* was my only care;
"I gave my nights, I gave my days, 200
"To Tully's[4] page and Homer's lays.
"Whate'er is known of ancient lore
"I fondly study'd o'er and o'er.
"I follow'd each appointed course,
"And trac'd up learning to its source; 205
"But in my way I gather'd flow'rs;
"I sought the muses in their bow'rs;
"And did their fav'ring smiles repay
"With many a lyric roundelay.[5]
"Nor did I fail the arts to woo 210
"Of Music and of Painting too.
"Thus was my early manhood pass'd
"In happiness too great to last.
"My father dy'd—and, ere his urn
"Had fill'd my arms, I had to mourn 215
"A mother, who refus'd to stay,
"When her lov'd mate was ta'en away.

[1] ***Flitch:*** It was a long-standing English tradition to award a flitch, or side, of bacon to a married couple who could claim, after a year and a day, never to have regretted their marriage. Syntax's parents had such a harmonious marriage that they could have made that claim after twenty years.

[2] **urchin:** A slightly wry term of endearment for a child, especially a mischievous one.

[3] ***Alma Mater:*** Oxford.

[4] **Tully's:** Marcus Tullius Cicero, Roman statesman and orator.

[5] **roundelay:** A quaint song, usually with pastoral associations.

"What follow'd?—I was left alone,
"And the world seiz'd me as its own.
"I sought gay Fashion's motley[1] throng,   220
"On Pleasure's tide I sail'd along;
"Till, by rude storms and tempests toss'd,
"My shatter'd bark at length was lost;
"While I stood naked on the shore—
"My treasure gone, my pleasures o'er.[2]   225

    "Now chang'd by Fortune's fickle wind,
"The friends I cherish'd prov'd unkind:
"All those who shar'd my prosp'rous day,
"Whene'er they saw me, turn'd away;
"And, as I almost wanted bread,   230
"I undertook a bear to lead;[3]
"To see the brute perform his dance,
"Thro' Holland, Italy, and France:
"But he was such a very Bruin,
"To be with him was worse than ruin;   235
"So, having pac'd o'er classic* ground,
"And sail'd the Grecian Isles around,
"(A pleasure, sure, beyond compare,
"Tho' link'd in couples with a bear),
"I took my leave, and left the cub   240
"Some humble Swiss[4] to pay and drub.
"Yet, when I reach'd my native shore,
"Determin'd to lead bears no more,
"No better prospect did I see
"Than a free-school[5] and curacy;   245
"The country tradesmen's sons to teach;
"In lonely village church to preach:
"With the proud sneer and vulgar taunt
"That's thrown at Learning when in want:
"All which you'll think, my noble friend,   250
"Did not to ease or comfort tend.
"But now another act displays
"The folly of my former days:—
"A new scene opens of my life;
"For faith, my Lord, I took a wife."[5]   255

¹ **motley:** Many-colored, a reference to the garb worn by fools or jesters.

² **My treasure…o'er:** Combe may be thinking of his own mis-spent youth. After his parents's and guardian's deaths, he inherited a substantial sum which he squandered in a few years of lavish living.

³ **a bear to lead:** Syntax did not actually lead a trained bear through Europe. "Bear-leading" was a metaphor for attending a rich young man on the so-called Grand Tour. It was common for privileged English men, after a brief period at Oxford or Cambridge, to travel around Europe acquiring polish and making connections, often with a tutor such as Syntax to guide and instruct them. Syntax's young charge, though, is so unmanageable that Syntax parts ways with him midway through the tour. In doing so, he probably threw away a golden career opportunity. If Syntax had toughed it out, he would have been near the front of the line for any livings (church jobs) that the "bear" or his father might have had at their disposal. In another of Combe's works, *Love Letters between a Lady of Quality and a Person of Inferior Station*, a poor scholar quits his job as a tutor half-way through the Grand Tour, only to find out later that the young man improved over time and presented his next tutor to a valuable living.

⁴ **Some humble Swiss:** The tutor who replaced Syntax.

⁵ **The folly…wife:** It was indeed reckless of Syntax to marry on his tiny £30 ($4,320) income with no expectation of anything better. A married couple without children would have needed an income of £100 at least to support a basic, lower-middle-class lifestyle.

Jane's older brother Edward, who was adopted by the wealthy but childless Knights, was sent on a four-year Grand Tour of Europe to prepare him for the life of a landed gentleman.

After Edward Ferrars is disowned by his mother, he and his fiancée Lucy Steele decide to wait to marry until he is able to obtain a living—a more prudent course than the one Syntax took. Even after he receives the living of Delaford, however, there is some disagreement about whether he is in a position to marry. The high-born Col. Brandon thinks the living is too small, but Mrs. Jennings, who rose from the trading classes, is unconcerned. As Austen shows, the exact income a young man needed in order to marry was a matter of perspective, but everyone in the novel agrees that a curate's income is too small.

My Lord.

"I should have thought a married mate
"Must have improv'd your lonely state;
"That a kind look and winning smile
"Would serve your labours to beguile."

Syntax.

"Love, in itself is very good,   260
"But, 'tis by no means solid food;
"And, ere our honeymoon was o'er,
"I found we wanted something more.
"This was the cause of all our trouble;
"My income would not carry double;—   265
"But, led away from Reason's plan
"By Love, that torturer of man,
"In our delirium we forgot
"What is life's unremitted lot;
"That man, and woman too, are born   270
"Beneath each rose to find a thorn.
"We thought, as other fools have done,
"That Hymen's laws[1] had made us one;
"But had forgot that Nature, true
"To her own purpose, made us two.   275
"There were two mouths that daily cry'd,
"At morn and eve, to be supply'd:
"Tho' by one vow we were betroth'd,
"There were two bodies to be cloth'd:
"And, to improve my happiness,   280
"Dolly is very fond of dress.
"My head's content with one hat on it,
"While Dorothy's has hat and bonnet:—
"In short there's no day passes through
"But I and my dear Doll are two.   285
"One good has my kind fortune sped;
"Dolly, my Lord, has never bred.
"Thus, tho' we're always *TWO*, you see
"We happ'ly yet have ne'er been *THREE*.
"She came a beauty to my arms;   290
"Her only dower was her charms:

[1] **Hymen's laws:**
Hymen was the
Greek god of
weddings.

"But much she sav'd me, I must own,
"By never bringing brats to town."

MY LORD.

"Another time my rev'rend guest,
"I hope you will relate the rest.   295
"I truly wish the whole to know,
"But bus'ness calls, and I must go.
"I need not, sure, repeat my words:—
"Command whate'er the house affords."

The Peer thus with the Doctor parted,   300
And left him gay and easy-hearted;
While many a pipe his thoughts digest,
Till his eyes told the hour of rest.

When the next morn and breakfast came,
Said Syntax, "I should be to blame,   305
"If I delay'd to tell my mind
"To one so gen'rous and so kind,
"In hopes such counsel to receive
"As he will condescend to give.
"For as I on my bed reclin'd   310
"A sudden thought possess'd my mind,
"Which may produce, as I've a notion
"A *North-West passage*[1] to PROMOTION.

"Loyal and true I've ever been
"And much of this same world I've seen: 315
"Well vers'd in the historic page
"Of this and ev'ry other age,
"I could employ my studious hour
"For those who hold the reins of power;
"And sure a well-turn'd pamphlet might   320
"Attention from the court invite;
"By which I could, in nervous[2] prose,
"Unveil the ministerial foes;[3]
"And with no common skill and care,
"Praise and support the powers that are.   325

[1] ***North-West passage:*** A hypothetical shipping route over the top of North America. European explorers sought such a passage as a shortcut to the lucrative markets of East Asia. Syntax is hoping to find his own shortcut by becoming a propagandist for the government—in his case, to a church living.

[2] **nervous:** Strong, vigorous.

[3] **ministerial foes:** The opposition party in Parliament.

279

"I then might be preferr'd[1] at once,
"No more the prey of any dunce,
"Who views poor authors as mere drudges,
"And ev'ry doit* he pays them grudges;
"Nor cares how much he makes them feel,   330
"Just as a cook-maid skins an eel.
"It would be better far I trow*
"Than this same *Paternoster Row*,
"Where the poor bees in Learning's hive
"Toil but to makes the tradesman thrive—   335
"And for their intellectual honey,
"Get but a poor return in money.
"It would be cutting matters short,
"Could I but get a friend at court,
" 'Twould be, and I repeat the notion,   340
"A North-West passage to Promotion."

MY LORD.

"Patient, my learned Doctor, hear;
"And to my counsels give an ear.
"I long have known, and known too well
"The country where you wish to dwell.   345
"Corruption, fraud, and envy wait
"At the proud Statesman's crouded gate,
"There fawning flatt'ry wins its way;
"There the base passions join the fray,
"Like beasts that on each other prey.   350
"While the smile hides the trait'rous heart—
"And interest plays a *Proteus*[2] part†.

[1] **preferr'd:** Helped along in one's career or appointed to a desirable position, especially one in the church.

[2] **interest...** ***Proteus:*** In other words, government pamphleteers write from self-interest alone, not conviction, changing their views to please those in power. Proteus was a Greek god who could take on a vast number of forms.

---

† L'Ingannare, il mentir, la fraude, il furto,
  Et la rapina di pieta vestita;
  Crescer col danno, e precipzio altrui,
  E far a se de l'altrui biasmo more,
  Son le virtu di quella gente infida.   PASTOR FIDO.

[Combe's note. The lines are from the 1590 Italian play *Il Pastor Fido*, by Giovanni Battista Guarini. An English translation from 1809 reads: "Cheats, lies, and frauds, and thefts, and cruelty / Beneath the cloak of pity; growing great / By rising on the ruins of the fall'n; / And seeking vilest praise from others' blame, / Are all the virtues of that treacherous race." (184)]

"You've too much virtue, my good friend, ⎫
"Your talents and your time to lend,   ⎬
"To such a pow'r—for such an end.   ⎭   355
"Can you work up the specious lie
"That does not quite the Truth deny?
"Can you that kind of Truth relate,
"On which you may prevaricate?
"Will you from others bear to seek   360
"What you must think and write and speak?
"Will you to-day their systems borrow,
"And calmly shake them off to-morrow?
"Will you, Camelion-like, receive
"The Hue a Patron wants to give?   365
"—You've too much honest pride to be
"A Scribbler to the *Treasury*, [1]
"Where you must wait the lagging hour,
"And cringe to *images of power;*
"To men in office, upstart elves,   370
"Who think of little but themselves.

  "When long an hacknied[2] slave you've been
"And dash'd and div'd through thick and thin;
"When you have chang'd each purer thought
"For morals which in courts are taught;   375
"When all distinctions that belong
"To what is right, and what is wrong,
"Have of your reason lost their hold,
"For driblets of a patron's gold;
"When the bold Logic, fram'd by Truth,   380
"Your filial boast in early youth,
"Yields to the vacilating rule
"Of policy's complying school:
"When guile and cunning, from your breast,
"Have driven that once honour'd guest: 385
"You may, perhaps, or you may not
"Be set aside, unheard, forgot.
"Or haply find, when virtue's lost,
"Repentance and some petty Post.
"This will not do, my learned friend,   390
"You must to better things attend,

[1] *Treasury:* The official title of the Prime Minister is First Lord of the Treasury. The treasury, then, is synonymous with the ministry or government.

[2] **hacknied:** Hired, usually with dishonorable connotations. Here, it has the more specific meaning of a hired writer, producing unoriginal work for someone else instead of writing what he actually thinks.

"All thoughts of *Downing-street* ¹ forego,
"And stick to *Paternoster-row*.²

   "The man of trade you cannot blame,
"For money is his native aim.   395
"It is the object of all trade
"To make as much as can be made;
"Bankers and Booksellers alike
"At ev'ry point of profit strike:
"And the same spirit you will meet   400
"In *Mincing-lane* or *Lombard-street*.³
" 'Tis not confin'd we all must know,
"To vulgar tradesmen in the *ROW*.
"Success depends on writing well—
"Booksellers bow, when Volumes sell.   405
"On the Exchange⁴ each day at three,
"This self-same principle you'll see
"Lead thither the vast, pressing throng;
"And know, dear Sir, or right or wrong,
" 'Tis that which makes Old England strong. 410
"Though Roguery in *Vellum's* shop,
"It is, my friend, the Nation's prop:
"And though you please, good Sir, to flout it,
"Old England could not do without it.
"Without it she might be as good,   415
"But half as great she never wou'd.
"I look with pleasure to the fame
"That now awaits your learned name,
"And when your labours are well paid,
"You'll be the Eulogist of Trade.⁵   420

   "*Vellum* may be a purse-proud* Cit,⁶
"With more of Money than of wit,
"But *Vellum*, my good Sir, can tell
"The kind of Book that's made to sell.
"Indeed, the man whose pocket's full,   425
"However empty be his scull,
"Although immeasurably dull,
"Will find, 'midst the misjudging crowd
"Far greater reason to be proud,

¹ *Downing-street:* The location of the Prime Minister's residence.

² **All thoughts...row:** Combe is writing from experience. He was hired by the government to write pro-ministerial pamphlets during the Regency Crisis of 1788-9 and continued to do so on and off until 1801, when a new ministry decided it no longer needed his services. The abrupt dismissal left a sour taste in his mouth.

³ *Mincing-lane* or *Lombard -street:* Streets in the mercantile part of London associated with the tea trade and banking, respectively.

⁴ **Exchange:** The Royal Exchange, a major commercial hub in the City of London.

⁵ **Eulogist of Trade:** Another semi-autobiographical moment. Combe himself eulogized trade on multiple occasions, including in the fourth volume of *The History of Commerce* (1787-9), a continuation of a work by Adam Anderson, and "A Word in Season to the Traders and Manufacturers of Great Britain" (1792), a political pamphlet.

⁶ **Cit:** A derogatory term for an urban tradesperson, implying a lack of cultivation or breeding.

Austen did not share the common attitude of her class toward people in trade: that they were uncultivated, vulgar, and therefore beneath the notice of gentlefolk. Mr. Gardiner (PP), in business in London, is most certainly a gentleman, despite what the snobbish Bingley sisters might say. The ending of the novel, which emphasizes the close friendship of the Gardiners and the Darcys, further suggests that Austen put little stock in the great divide between the rural landed gentry and the urban trading classes. Even when there were sharp differences in manners and social norms, she felt that friendship and respect were possible. The refined Elinor Dashwood (SS) is at first put off by the unfiltered gregariousness of Mrs. Jennings, who comes from trade, but she ultimately comes to "really love her" for her kind heart (III.7).

"Than he whose head contains a store 430
"Of Critic skill and learned lore,
"If to his wit he does not join,
"The blest command of ready coin.
"Write and get rich, nor fear the taunts
"Of Booksellers and such gallants;[1] 435 [1] **gallants:**
"*Vellum* has no more sordid tricks Swaggerers.
"Than those who deal in Politics.
"But till your various Learning's known,
"And your works sell throughout the Town;
"Till, having settled Fortune's spite, 440
"Your name shall sanction what you write,
"Let *Vellum* his rewards bestow,
"Nor scoff at *PATERNOSTER-ROW*."

     SYNTAX.
  "To your kind words, I've nought to say,
"But thank your Lordship and obey. 445
"And now, as twenty years have past
"Since I beheld fair London last,
"I shall employ the present day
"In strolling calmly to survey
"What changes time and chance have made, 450
"What Wealth has done and Art essay'd—
"What Taste has, in its fancies, shown,
"To give new splendour to the Town.
"That being done, I'll take my way
"To Covent-Garden[2]—to the play." 455 [2] **Covent-Garden:**
     The Theatre Royal
     at Covent Garden
  "Then," said his Lordship, "when we meet,   was one of the two
"I shall expect a special treat,   theaters in London
"To hear my learned friend impart   that were allowed to
"His notions of dramatic art."   put on plays. After
The Doctor bow'd, and off he went, 460 a fire destroyed it in
Upon his curious progress bent: 1808, it was rebuilt
He pac'd the Parks—he view'd each square—   in 1809, just before
And, staring, he made others stare.   Combe wrote this
At length, at the appointed hour,   canto.
He hasten'd to the Playhouse door, 465

And took his place within the pit,
Beside a critic and a wit;

As wits and critics now are known
To hash up nonsense for the Town:
And in the daily columns show
How small the sum of all they know.

"I think," said Syntax, looking round,
"It is not good, this vast profound:—
"I see no well-wrought columns here;
"No Attic Ornaments appear;
"Nought but a washy, wanton waste
"Of gaudy tints and puny taste:[1]
"Too large to hear—too long to see—[2]
"Full of unmeaning symmetry.
"The parts all answer one another;
"Each pigeon-hole reflects its brother;
"And all, alas! too plainly show
"How easy 'tis to form a Row:
"But where's the grand, the striking, whole?—
"A Theatre should have a soul."

[1] **I think…taste:** Combe is airing his own views here. He used one of his few day-passes while in debtor's prison to visit the new theater, finding in it "not a trace of Taste or science" (Hamilton, 238). But he sang a different tune in *The Microcosm of London,* when puffery was required. There, the new theatre had "rise[n], like the phoenix, from its own ashes, with 470 additional splendour" (Vol. III, 259).

[2] **Too large…to see:** This was a criticism Combe 475 had levelled years earlier in the *Pic Nic:* his chief complaint about the modern stage was that 480 theaters were too large, which forced actors to perform in an over-the-top manner in order to 485 be seen and heard.

Drawn & Etched by Rowlandson.

DOCTOR SYNTAX
AT COVENT GARDEN THEATRE.

Plate 26

"Excuse me, Sir," the Critic said—
"These Theatres are all a trade:
"Their owners laugh at scrolls and friezes;[1]
" 'Tis a full house alone that pleases:
"And, you must know, it is their plan 490
"To stick and stuff it as they can.
"Your noble, architect'ral graces
"Would take up room, and fill up places."

"This may be true, Sir, to the letter;
"But genius would have manag'd better," 495
Syntax reply'd.—"Nay, I am willing
"To let them gain the utmost shilling;
"But surely talents might be found,
"(The natives, too, of British ground,)
"Who could have blended Attic merit 500
"With this proprietory spirit."

[1] **scrolls and friezes:** Ornaments associated with ancient Greek architecture. The critic says that the theater was built to hold as many seats as possible, not to please the eye. It is another instance of the profit motive gaining the ascendancy over the higher aims of art.

Thus as he spoke the curtain rose,
And forc'd his harangue to a close:
But still, as they the drama view'd
The conversation was renew'd; 505

And lasted till the whole was o'er,
When, as they pass'd the Playhouse door,
The Critic said, " 'Twill wound my heart,
"If you and I so soon must part.
"O, how I long to crack a bottle   510
"With such a friend of Aristotle!
"Now, as you seem to know him well,
"Perhaps his residence you'll tell."[1]
"Where it is now I do not know,"
Syntax reply'd;—"and I must go;   515
"But this I can most boldly say,
"You'll never meet him at the play."[2]

  When fairly got into the street,
"Oh," thought the Doctor, "what a treat
"For my good Lord, when next we meet!"   520

[1] **his residence you'll tell:** The ignorant critic thinks Aristotle is still alive.

[2] **You'll never...the play:** In Combe's day, Aristotle's *Poetics* formed the basis of theater criticism. Combe takes a jab at modern plays by implying that Aristotle would not have been caught dead at one.

CANTO XXIV.

NOW Syntax, as he travell'd back
Lolling and stretching in a hack,[1]
Could not but ponder in his mind
On what he had just left behind.
"I've seen a play,"[2] he mutt'ring said;—   5
" 'Twas Shakespeare's—but in masquerade.
"I've seen a farce, I scarce know what;
" 'Twas only fit to be forgot.
"I've seen a Critic, and have heard
"The string of nonsense he preferr'd.[3]   10
"Heav'n bless me! where has learning fled?
"Where has she hid her sacred head?
"O how degraded is she grown,
"To spawn such boobies* on the town.
"The sterling gold is seen no more;   15
"In vain we seek the genuine ore:
"Some mixture doth its worth debase;
"Some wire-drawn[4] nonsense takes its place.
"How few consume the midnight oil!
"How few in Learning's labour toil!   20
"Content, as they incurious stray
"Thro' life's unprofitable day,
"With straws that on the surface flow,
"Nor look for pearls that live below:
"They ne'er the hidden depths explore;   25
"But gather sea-weed on the shore!

    "There was a period when the stage
"Was thought to dignify the age,
"When learned men were seen to sit
"Upon the benches of the Pit;   30

[1] **hack:** Hired carriage.

[2] **a play:** Based on Rowlandson's illustration (p. 286), *Henry IV, Part One*.

[3] **preferr'd:** Put forth.

[4] **wire-drawn:** Strained or forced.

"When, to his art and Nature true,
"GARRICK[1] his various pictures drew;
"While ev'ry passion, ev'ry thought,
"He to perfection fully wrought,
"By Nature's self supremely taught: 35
"He did her very semblance bear,
"And look'd as she herself were there:—
"Whether old *Lear's* form he wore,
"With age and sorrow cover'd o'er;
"Or *Romeo's* am'rous flame possess'd,   40
"That torture of the human breast;
"Or gay *Lothario's* glowing pride,
"In conquest o'er his rival's bride;
"Or when, with fell ambition warm,
"In *Macbeth's* or in *Glo'ster's*[2] form—   45
"He gave each passion to the eye
"In all its fine variety:
"The words he did not loudly quote:
"But acted e'en as Shakespeare wrote.

   "Nor was he less (for he could range   50
"In ev'ry wayward, busy change
"Known in the field of scenic art—
"The true cameleon of the heart)[3]
"When he assum'd the merry glee
"Of laughter-loving Comedy.   55

   "In *Ranger's* tricks, or when he strove
"In *Benedict* to hide his love;
"When he in *Drugger's* doublet shone,
"Or *Brute's* rude ribaldry put on;
"When he the jealous *Kitely* play'd;   60
"When the same passion he essay'd
"In *Felix;*[4]—with what truth and force
"He urg'd that passion's diff'rent course;
"Work'd up its features all anew—
"But still he was to Nature true!   65
"Nay, e'en in *Farce* he could awake
"The fun that made the Gall'ries shake.

¹ **GARRICK:** David Garrick, the greatest actor of the eighteenth century. Garrick was praised for his extraordinary versatility and for his naturalistic style of acting, which was considered revolutionary at the time.

Austen never saw Garrick act (she was three when he died), but she did experience him as a playwright. The Austen family put on two of his plays in their barn when Jane was a child, and as an adult she saw another, The Clandestine Marriage, *at Covent Garden, the same theater Syntax visits.*

Garrick between Comedy and Tragedy, Edward Fisher after Sir Joshua Reynolds, 1760-61. National Portrait Gallery.

² *Lear's...Glo'ster's:* Syntax lists some of Garrick's best-known tragic roles. All but Lothario, the seductive villain of Nicholas Rowe's *The Fair Penitent*, are from Shakespeare.
³ **The true cameleon of the heart:** In other words, Garrick was an actor of unlimited range, capable of representing any emotion.

One wonders if Austen, who would have read descriptions of Garrick's legendary acting, used him as a partial model for Henry Crawford (MP). Crawford is another "cameleon of the heart," a trait that makes him a dangerous suitor, but an excellent actor: "whether it were dignity or pride, or tenderness or remorse, or whatever were to be expressed, he could do it with equal beauty" (III.3).

⁴ *Ranger's...Felix:* Comic characters whom Garrick portrayed. Ranger is the rakish hero of Benjamin Hoadly's *The Suspicious Husband*. Benedict (or Benedick) is a leading character in *Much Ado About Nothing*, and one half of Shakespeare's most famous love-hate relationship. Drugger is the greedy and foolish tobacco-dealer of Ben Johnson's *The Alchemist*. The abusive and roistering Brute is the titular provoker of John Vanbrugh's *The Provoked Wife*. Kitely from Johnson's *Every Man in his Humour* and Felix from Susanna Centlivre's *The Wonder* are both stereotypical jealous lovers.

"The heart he cheated of its woe,
"And made the poignant tear to flow:
"Lit up a joy in ev'ry eye,   70
"Or drown'd the soul in agony.
"He ever was to Nature true;—
"By no false arts did he subdue
"Th' attentive mind, the list'ning ear;
"In all the Drama's vast career,   75
"He ne'er outstepp'd th' unerring rule
"Which he had learn'd in Nature's school.[1]
"In ev'ry part he did excel;
"He aim'd at all, and all was well.
"In those good times none went to see   80
"The mere effects of scenery—
"The constant laugh, the forc'd grimace—
"The vile distortions of the face.[2]
"In those good times none went to see
"*Pierots* and *Clowns*[3] in Comedy;   85
"Men sought perfection to discern,
"And learned Critics went to learn.

  "Shakespeare, immortal Bard sublime!
"Unmatch'd within the realms of time!
"He did not, with Promethean aim,   90
"Attempt to steal ethereal flame;
"Rather to him the thoughts of Heaven
"Were by celestial bounty given.
"He read profound, in ev'ry page
"Of Nature's volume, ev'ry age   95
"And act of man![4] Each passion's course
"He traces with resistless force;
"And, with a more than mortal art,
"Gives unknown feelings to the heart;
"And doth the willing Fancy bear,   100
"Just as his magic wills—and where.

  "His page still lives, and sure will last
"Till Time and all its years are past.
"The Poet, to the end of Time,
"Breathes in his works, and lives in rhyme;   105

[1] **He ne'er outstepp'd...school:** A reference to *Hamlet*. Hamlet charges the players to "o'erstep not the modesty of nature" by acting in an exaggerated manner (3.2.19).

[2] **mere effects of scenery...face:** Syntax complains that modern theatergoers have lost the taste for good acting, instead delighting in gaudily painted backdrops and overdone performances. In a piece for *The Pic Nic*, a short-lived journal that Combe edited, he claimed that the root of the problem was the size of the theaters. The subtleties of the performance could no longer be seen or heard, and the "public are therefore habituated to look for the splendour of scenery, instead of fine acting; and to be satisfied with the buffoonery of farce" (*The Pic Nic*, No. 1 [3 Jan. 1803], 22).

[3] ***Pierots* and *Clowns*:** Stock characters in the Harlequinade, a genre of low-brow comic theater. In the basic plot, Harlequin runs off with the daughter of a man named Pantaloon, who pursues him with his two foolish servants, Pierrot and Clown.

This debate over scenery finds its way into the infamous private theatricals held at Mansfield Park. Mr. Yates, who introduces the theatrical bug, wants three or four separate "scenes" or painted backdrops. Maria, though, prefers to "make the performance, not the theatre, our object" (I.13). Maria is mainly concerned (for the moment) about practicality, but her choice of words suggests that dramatic principles are also at stake: flashy visual trappings might detract from the acting, the core of the performance. If so, the eventual hiring of a pricey London scene-painter is a sign that the Mansfield thespians have truly lost all sense of proportion, not just financially but aesthetically.

"Mr. Grimaldi as Clown,"
Piercy Roberts?, 1822.
The Met.

[4] **He read profound...man:** Combe is echoing the standard praise of Shakespeare as "the poet of nature," the artist who best captures human nature in all its rich variety.

In the nineteenth century, Austen was often celebrated as the "prose Shakespeare" for her wide cast of realistic and finely differentiated characters (Wilkes, 29-50).

"But, when the Actor sinks to rest,
"And the turf lies upon his breast,
"A poor traditionary fame
"Is all that's left to grace his name.
"The Drama's children strut and play,   110
"In borrow'd parts, their lives away;—
"And then they share the oblivious lot;
"*Smith* will like *Cibber*,[1] be forgot!
"*Cibber* with fascinating art
"Could wake the pulses of the heart;   115
"But her's is an expiring name,
"And darling *Smith's* will be the same.
"Of *Garrick's* self e'en nought remains;
"His art and him one grave contains;
"In others' minds to make him live   120
"Is all remembrance now can give.
"All we can say—alas! how vain!
"We ne'er shall see his like again."

   Just as this critic speech was o'er,
The coach stopp'd at his Lordship's door: 125
But my good Lord was gone to bed;
So Syntax to his chamber sped—
Where, with his pipe, and o'er his bottle,
He chew'd the cud of Aristotle,
Till, stretch'd upon his bed of down,   130
Sleep did his head with poppies[2] crown;
And well he slept, until a voice
Desir'd to know if 'twas his choice
Still to sleep on? And then it stated
His Lordship and the breakfast waited.   135

   "Well," said my Lord, when he appear'd.
"I hope the play your spirits cheer'd.
"*Falstaff*, the morning critics tell,
"Was never surely play'd so well."[3]
"These critics," Syntax smiling said,   140
"Are wretched bunglers at their trade:—
"One sat beside me in the Pit,
"No more a critic than a wit.

[1] *Smith…Cibber:* Two famous actresses who lived a couple generations apart. Susannah Cibber was a contemporary of Garrick and, for a time, the most highly paid actress in England. Sarah Smith, better known today by her married name Bartley, was at the height of her popularity in the early 1810s.

Austen had the opportunity to see Smith act alongside the great tragedian Edmund Kean on 5 March 1814 at Drury Lane in London. Austen was wowed by Kean and thought Smith's acting very good, but added that "she did not quite answer my expectation" (5-8 Mar. 1814). While Austen was an eager theatergoer, she was not one who was easily impressed.

"Miss Smith," unknown, 1812. University of Illinois Theatrical Print Collection.

[2] **poppies:** Flowers associated with sleep since ancient times.

[3] *Falstaff…play'd so well:* The fat knight Sir John Falstaff featured in several of Shakespeare's plays and was his most popular comic character. At this time, he was being played at Covent Garden by George Frederick Cooke. Cooke was a decorated actor, but he was also an alcoholic and by 1810, when Combe was writing, his career was in steep decline. If Combe had a particular actor in mind here, it was likely Cooke.

Austen likely saw Cooke in better times. During Austen's years in Bath, her mother wrote in a letter that Cooke was enjoying packed houses (Byrne, 40). We do not know if Jane herself saw one of these performances, but it seems likely. If the somewhat hypochondriacal Mrs. Austen was attending plays in Bath, then it was probably Jane, who relished the theater, who was dragging her to them.

"Between the acts we both exprest
"Or what was worst, or what was best;   145
"And whil'd those intervals away
"In changing thoughts upon the play;
"And, tho' both form'd to disagree,
"Nought pass'd but perfect courtesy.
"Perhaps it may your fancy suit   150
"To hear our classical* dispute:
"I think, my Lord, 'twill prove a treat,
"If you'll allow me to repeat
"All that this criticising sage
"Knew of the humours of the stage: 155
"For, as to what should form a play,
"How Actors should their parts convey,
"What are the Drama's genuine laws,
"The source from whence true Genius draws
"Such scenes as when, to Nature shown,   160
"She loud exclaims—They are my own—
"He knew no more, it will appear,
"Than the tea-urn that's boiling here;
"Like that he did no more than bubble,
"And without any toil or trouble.   165
"They felt the trouble who sat near him,
"And, sure enough, 'twas toil to hear him.
"After some gen'ral trifling chat
"On the new playhouse,[1] and all that,
"The scenes that pass'd before our eyes   170
"Produc'd the questions and replies:
"In short, I'll state our *quids* pro *quos*[2]
"Just in the order they arose."

CRITIC.
"Oh, what a *Falstaff!*—Oh, how fine!
"Oh, 'tis great[3] acting—'tis divine!"   175

SYNTAX.
"The acting's great[3]—that I can tell ye;
"For all his acting's in his belly."

[1] **new playhouse:** The Theatre Royal, Covent Garden had recently been rebuilt following a fire.

[2] *quids* **pro** *quos:* Exchanges of opinion; literally, this's for that's.

[3] **great:** Syntax puns on the word, using it to mean *large* instead of *excellent.*

2

296

CRITIC.

"But, with due def'rence to your joke,
"A truer word I never spoke
"Than when I say—you've never been   180
"The witness of a finer scene.
"Th' admir'd actor whom you see
"Plays the fat Knight most charmingly:—
" 'Tis in this part he doth excel;
"*Quin*[1] never play'd it half so well."   185   [1] ***Quin:*** English
actor of the early
18th c. who excelled
in the role of
Falstaff.

SYNTAX.

"You ne'er saw *Quin* the stage adorn;
"He acted ere your sire was born.
"The critics, Sir, who liv'd before you,
"Would have disclos'd a diff'rent story.
"This play I've better acted seen   190
"In country towns where I have been.
"I do not hesitate to say,
"I'd rather read this very play
"By my own parlour fire-side,
"With my poor judgement for my guide,   195
"Than see the actors of this stage,
"Who make me gape[2] at Shakespeare's page.   [2] **gape:** Yawn.
"When I read *Falstaff* to myself,
"I laugh like any merry elf;
"While my mind feels a cheering glow   200
"That Shakespeare only can bestow.
"The swagg'ring words in his defence,
"Which scarce are wit, and yet are sense;
"The ribald jest, the quick conceit,
"The boast of many a braggart feat;   205
"The half-grave questions and replies,
"In his high-wrought soliloquies;
"The obscene thought, the pleasant prate,
"Which give no time to love or hate,
"In such succession do they flow,   210
"From no to yea—from yea to no—
"Have not been to my mind convey'd
"By this pretender to his trade.

"The smile sarcastic, and the leer
"That tells the laughing mock'ry near—   215
"The warning look, that, ere 'tis spoke,
"Aptly forebodes the coming joke—
"The air so solemn, yet so sly,
"Shap'd to conceal the ready lie—
"The eyes, with some shrewd meaning bright,   220
"I surely have not seen to-night.
"Again, I must beg leave to tell ye,
" 'Tis nought of *Falstaff* but his belly."

CRITIC.
  "All this is fine—and may be true;
"But with such truths I've nought to do.   225
"I'm sure, Sir, I shall say aright,
"When I declare the great delight
"Th' enraptur'd audience feel to-night.
"It is indeed, with no small sorrow,
"I cannot your opinions borrow   230
"To fill the columns of to-morrow.
"My light critique will be preferr'd;[1]
"The public always take my word.
"Nay, the loud plaudits heard around
"Must all your far-fetch'd thoughts confound: 235
"I truly wonder when I see
"You do not laugh as well as me."

SYNTAX.
  "My muscles other ways are drawn:
"I cannot laugh, Sir—while I yawn."

CRITIC.
  "But you will own the scenes[2] are fine."   240

SYNTAX.
  "Whate'er the acting, they're divine,
"And fit for any pantomime.
"Of this it is that I complain;
"These are the tricks which I disdain:
"The painter's art the play commends;   245
"On gaudy show success depends.

[1] **My light...
preferr'd:** The
major theaters often
paid newspapers for
reviews, which led
to many flattering
puff-pieces. In
1803, Combe edited
a paper called *The
Pic Nic* which began
to challenge this
system, refusing
such payments and
offering genuinely
independent theater
reviews.
[2] **scenes:** Painted
backdrops.

"The clothes are made in just design—
"They're all well character'd, and fine.
"The actors now, I think, Heav'n bless 'em,
"Must learn their art from those who dress 'em.   250
"But give me actors, give me plays,
"On which I should with rapture gaze,
"Tho' coats and scenes were made of baize:[1]   [1] **baize:** A coarse
"For, if the scene were highly wrought—   woolen cloth
"If players acted as they ought—   255 (OED).
"You would not then be pleas'd to see
"This heavy mass of frippery.
"Hear Horace, Sir, who wrote of plays
"In ancient Rome's Augustan days:—
"*Tanto cum strepitu ludi spectantur, et artes,*   260
"*Divitiæque peregrinæ: quibus oblitus actor*
"*Cum stetit in Scena, concurrit dextera lævæ.*
"*Dixit adhuc aliquid? nil sane. Quid placet ergo?*
"*Lana Tarentino violas imitata veneno.*"†

CRITIC.

"Your pardon, Sir; but, all around me,   265
"There are such noises they confound me:
"And, tho' I full attention paid,
"I scarcely know a word you said.
"To say the truth I must acknowledge
" 'Tis long since I have left the College—   270
"Virgil and Horace are my friends,
"I have them at my finger's ends—
"But Grecian Lore, I blush to own—
"Is wholly to my mind unknown.—

---

† For what voices have ever succeeded in drowning out the noise that echoes around our theatres? You would think it was the roaring of Garganus' woods or the Tuscan sea, **so great is the din that accompanies the viewing of entertainment, of works of art and foreign wealth, and when some actor stands on stage, tricked out in this gear, right hand clashes with left. "Has he said anything yet?" Nothing at all. "Then why is he going down so well?"** It's his woollen cloak with its Tarentine dye resembling violet.

Horace, *Epistles* II.i.200-208. The particular lines quoted by Combe are in bold.

"I therefore must your meaning seek—   275
"Oblige me, Sir,—translate your Greek.[1]
"But see, the farce[2] is now begun,
"And you must listen to the fun.
"It sure has robb'd you of your bile;
"For now, methinks, you deign to smile."   280

    SYNTAX.
  "The thing is droll, and aptly bent
"To raise a vulgar merriment:
"But Merry-Andrews,[3] seen as such,
"Have often made me laugh as much.
"An Actor does but play the fool   285
"When he forsakes old Shakespeare's rule,
"And lets his own foul nonsense out,
"To please th' ill-judging rabble rout.[4]
"But when he *swears*, to furnish laughter,
"The beadle's whip[5] should follow after.   290
"There's *Terence*, Sir, and then there's *Plautus;*[6]
"They've both a better lesson taught us."

    CRITIC.
  "*Terence*, I know, he wrote in Latin,
"Just as a weaver makes his satin.
"He well deserv'd the comic bays;   295
"For *Westminster*[7] he wrote his plays:
"And *Plautus* was a fellow famous,
"Who wrote a play call'd *Ignoramus;*[8]
"Where lawyers, by profession bold,
"In Latin and bad English scold."   300

  "At length, my Lord, the parley ended:
"I'm sure you think it can't be mended.[9]
"You well may laugh so loud, but I
"Feel myself more dispos'd to cry,
"When thus I see what asses sit   305
"In judgment upon works of wit.

  "I own, my Lord, I love a play:—
"When some performer's turn'd away,

[1] **translate your Greek:** The joke is that Syntax wasn't quoting in Greek at all, but in Latin.

[2] **farce:** After the main play, theatrical evenings often concluded with a short, comic playlet or "afterpiece." Combe himself wrote such a piece early in his literary career.

[3] **Merry-Andrews:** People who entertain by engaging in foolish, comedic acts.

[4] **An Actor...rout:** Hamlet complains that, in order to score easy laughs, some comic actors improvise during the performance instead of speaking their actual lines, in the process distracting the audience from the main focus of the play.

[5] **beadle's whip:** The beadle was a parish or town officer with the authority to punish minor offenses.

[6] *Terence... Plautus:* The two most famous comic playwrights of ancient Rome.

[7] **For *Westminster:* ** Every year, the boys of Westminster School put on a Latin play, usually by Terence. Of course, Terence, who lived during the Roman Republic, did not write his plays "for" this school; once again the critic has betrayed his ignorance of literature and history.

[8] *Ignoramus:* Another blunder on the part of the critic. *Ignoramus* was a 1615 play by George Ruggles partly written in Latin and only distantly associated with Plautus (it was an adaptation of an adaptation of Plautus). Occasionally the Westminster school play was *Ignoramus*, which may be why the critic mentions the two together. One begins to suspect that all his knowledge of classical drama comes from catching the occasional schoolboy performance.

[9] **mended:** Improved. In other words, the dialogue with the critic is already perfect—as a piece of comedy.

Farcical afterpieces were an important influence on Austen as a child. The Austen children put on two such afterpieces at Steventon—Henry Fielding's Tom Thumb *and Garrick's* Bon Ton—*and Austen likely read and saw many others. The burlesque humor of these playlets is everywhere evident in her juvenilia, especially the earliest pieces, which, like Elizabeth Bennet (PP), "delight[...] in any thing ridiculous" (I.3).*

Robert Ferrars (SS), whom Irene Collins memorably dubbed "the prize ass of the novels," is an alumnus of Westminster School (60). It is not hard to imagine the preening, self-important Robert making every effort to hog the spotlight in the annual school play.

"By Green-room tyrants,[1] from the boards
"Of London stage, our town affords   310
"To tempt or her or him to stay
"For a few nights, upon their way:
"Then Doll and I are seen to sit
"Conspicuous, in our country Pit."

   Thus as he spoke, with frequent bows,   315
And fifty whens, and wheres, and hows,
Vellum appear'd, with solemn look,
To talk about the Doctor's book.
He said, " 'Twas true a learned friend
"The manuscript did much commend:—   320
"He thinks it is a work of merit,
"Written with learning, taste, and spirit.
"The sketches too, if he don't err,
"Possess appropriate character.
" 'Tis to the humour of our age,   325
"And has your Lordship's patronage;
"I therefore wish the work to buy,[2]
"And deal with liberality.
" 'Tis true that paper's very dear,[3]
"And workmens' wages most severe.   330
"The volume's heavy, and demands
"Th' engraver's[4] and the printer's hands.
"Besides, there is a risk to run:
"Before the press its work has done
"New taxes may, perhaps be laid   335
"On some prime article of trade;
"And then the price will be so high;—
"The persons are but few who buy
"Books of so very costly kind:
"But still the work is to my mind.   340
"I'll try my luck, and will be bound
"To give, my Lord, three hundred pound."[5]

   After some little tricks of trade
The bargain was completely made—   } 345
The work transferr'd—the money paid.

[1] **Green-room tyrants:** Directors. The Green-room is a lounge in the theater where performers can relax between performances.

[2] **I therefore wish the work to buy:** Vellum is offering a new publishing arrangment. The original plan was to publish Syntax's book on commission. Vellum would advertise, print and distribute the book, and Syntax would repay the costs associated with these activities out of the book's sales, as well as a commission of around ten percent. If the book did not sell enough to cover costs, Syntax, or in this case Lord Carlisle, would have been required to make up the difference. Given Carlisle's wealth and standing, this was a risk-free proposition for Vellum. After consulting with a friend, however, Vellum is more confident the book will sell, and therefore would rather buy the copyright. Now, if the book fails, Vellum will have to eat the costs, but if it succeeds, he will be entitled to all the profits.

[3] **dear:** Expensive.

[4] **engraver's:** Vellum needs to hire an engraver to etch Syntax's drawings onto copper plates for printing—a significant added cost.

[5] **three hundred pound:** $43,200 in 2024 money, and quite a lot for a book by a first-time author.

Austen used both these modes of publication, though not always with the best discretion. Preferring the bird in the hand, she sold the copyright of Pride and Prejudice *for just £110 ($15,840). The work sold very well, but she never saw any of the profits. With her next two novels,* Mansfield Park *and* Emma*, she was determined to hold onto her copyrights. At first this worked out well:* Mansfield Park *made her more money than any of her other works. With* Emma*, though, she overshot the mark: the large first edition did not sell out, and after deducting the cost of publication Austen made only a small profit. Of course, if Austen had lived longer, her decision to retain her copyrights would have been vindicated. Even if she had never written again, residual sales of her novels likely would have earned her a decent income.*

For comparison, in 1833 the publisher Richard Bentley acquired the copyrights of all six of Austen's novels for just £250 ($36,000)!

"Tho'," said my Lord, "I think your gains
"By no means equal to your pains
"(For *Vellum* will a bargain drive
"As well as any man alive);
"The work will give my friend a name,   350
"And stamp his literary fame:
" 'Twill *Paternoster-row* command,
"And keep old *Vellum* cap-in-hand:[1]
"And, when a name is up, 'tis said
"The owner may lie snug in bed.   355
"Write on—the learned track pursue—
"And booksellers shall cringe to you."

Much pass'd upon his Lordship's part,
Which shew'd the goodness of his heart;
While Syntax made his full replies,   360
Not with his tongue—but with his eyes.

[1] **cap-in-hand:** Humble and subservient.

CANTO XXV.

EDITOR'S NOTE:

Readers will find Canto XXV much easier to follow if they first read the following introductory note. The map on p. 326 is another helpful resource.

Canto XXV is the only one that did not appear in *The Poetical Magazine* as part of *The Schoolmaster's Tour*, the original title of the poem. Instead, Combe added it for the first book edition, published in 1812. To keep the poem current, he selected as his theme a recent event: the opening of the new premises of the London Institution.

The London Institution was founded in 1805 by a number of prominent merchants in the city's commercial district (called the "City of London" or "City" with a capital C). The Institution offered courses of lectures and expansive reading rooms, but its primary purpose was to create a library of "Works of Intrinsic Value" for the benefit of those who lived or worked in the City. The Institution chose the great classical scholar Richard Porson to be its first librarian, and its library quickly gained a reputation for its fine collection of Greek and Roman authors. As the library's holdings grew, its original premises in Old Jewry proved inadequate, and in February 1812, the Institution rented larger ones a short walk away in Coleman Street.

Combe immediately spotted the satirical possibilities of this event. Here was one of the best stocked, most eminently staffed libraries in London sprouting up not in some genteel part of town, but in the City itself—home (supposedly) to underbred traders and vulgar profiteers. In Canto XXV, Combe, taking a page from the satirist Jonathan Swift, renders this clash as a "battle of the books." Syntax dreams that the classics, with the owl of Pallas Athena at the helm, are marching into the City to take up residence at the London Institution. As they approach, though, they are met by the armies of "Trade," made up of various commercial documents, who reject their mission and deny them entry. The conflict escalates into full battle, with the classics emerging victorious before settling peacefully into their new shelves. Readers might consider whether this outcome represents a triumph of learning over trade, as Syntax thinks, or something more reciprocal. After all, if trade and learning are mortal foes, what do we make of the fact, as the owl points out, that this new bastion of the classics, the London Institution, was founded, funded, and chiefly used by "Sons of Trade"?

MY Lord retir'd—the Doctor too,
As he had nothing else to do,
Thought he would take a peep and see
His noble Patron's Library.
So down he sat, without a care,   5
In a well-stuff'd Morocco chair,
And seiz'd a book; but Morpheus[1] shed
The poppies o'er his rev'rend head;
While Fancy would not be behind;
So play'd her tricks within his mind,   10
And furnish'd a most busy dream
Which Syntax made his pleasant Theme,
Soon as he met my Lord to dine,
Or rather while they took their wine.

THE DREAM.

That I was in the Strand[2] I dream'd,   15
And o'er my head methought there seem'd,
A flight of volumes in the air,
In various bindings gilt and fair.
Th' unfolded leaves, expos'd to view,
Serv'd them as wings on which they flew.   20
In the 'mid air they pass'd along
In stately flight a num'rous throng,
And from each book a label fell,
Form'd ev'ry author's name to tell:
Nor was it long before I saw   25
With a fond reverential awe
The celebrated Bards and Sages
Which grac'd the Greek and Roman Ages,
All headed by a solemn fowl
Which bore the semblance of an Owl.   30
'Twas Pallas' Bird[3] who led them strait
Thro' Temple-Bar's expanded Gate.[4]
—Year-Books, Reports and sage, grave Entries,
At either Temple-gate stood centries:
While Viner his Abridgment[5] shows   35
In sixty well-arm'd Folios.

[1] **Morpheus:** The ancient Greek god of dreams.

"St. Clement Danes," Thomas Boydell, 1751. YCBA.

[2] **the Strand:** A major thoroughfare in the City of Westminster, London. The Strand was also the location of Rudolph Ackermann's Repository of Arts, which published *Doctor Syntax.*

[3] **Pallas' Bird:** The owl is the symbolic bird of Pallas Athena, the ancient Greek goddess of wisdom (called Minerva by the Romans).

[4] **Temple-Bar's expanded Gate:** Grand entrance to the City of London from the City of Westminster. The gate derives its name from the adjacent Temple area, home to the Inns of Court, where lawyers were trained. Combe was a member of the Honorable Society of the Inner Temple for two years, but his engagement with legal practice was minimal and he promptly left his chambers at the Inner Temple after his guardian's death (Hamilton, 17).

[5] **Viner his Abridgment:** *A General Abridgment of Law and Equity* was a vast collection of English legal texts edited by Charles Viner, a legal scholar and Middle Temple resident.

Lydia Bennet (PP) and Mr. Wickham are married at St. Clement Danes, located on the Strand. No doubt Lydia is proud to have been married at such a grand church in such a fashionable part of town. She may have wished, though, that she had had more guests to fill the huge building. St. Clement's likely had a hollow, cold feeling on that poorly attended nuptial morning.

While those residing at the Inns of Court were supposed to be studying the law, many of the residents were, like Combe, idle gentleman. Mr. Wickham (PP) may have had chambers at one of the Inns for a while, but Darcy says "his studying the law was a mere pretence" (II.12). Mr. Elliot (Pers.) also spends time at the Temple without, it seems, any serious intention of becoming a barrister.

The Lamb, it baa'd, and the horse[1] neigh'd
In rev'rence of the cavalcade.
Near Clifford's Inn[2] appear'd to stand
Of *Capiases*[3] an ugly band,   40
For when their Parchment flags appear'd,
Instant, the crowded street was clear'd;
And the procession pass'd along,
Untroubled by a pressing throng.
St. Dunstan's savages[4] were mute,   45
But still they gave their best salute;—
Disdaining eloquence and Rhymes,
They 'woke their Bells to speak in Chimes.
Erskine's fam'd Pamphlet[5] Cap-a-pee,[6]
With many an *I* and many a *Me*,   50
Issued from Serjeant's-Inn,[7] and made
A speech to grace the grand parade.
The Stationers came forth to meet
The Stranger Forms in Ludgate-street,
Each one upon his brawny back,   55
Bearing a large, sheet Almanack.[8]
For a short time the Learned train
Stopp'd before Ave-Mary-lane,
That *Galen* might just view the College,[9]
The seat of medicinal Knowledge.   60
Nor did they fail awhile to tarry
Before Saint Paul's learn'd Seminary:
Where *Lilly's Grammar* did rehearse
Propria quæ Maribus[10] in verse.
At Cheapside[11] end there seem'd to stand   65
A Pageant rather huge than grand.
Ream upon Ream of Quire Stock[12]
Appear'd like some vast, massive rock:
On its firm base a figure stood,
A composite of brass and wood: 70
The months and weeks around it stand,
With each a number in its hand
Of Bibles, Hist'ries and Reviews,
And Magazines from every Muse,
With coverlids of various hue,   75
Pea-green and red and brown and blue.

[1] **Lamb…horse:** The symbol of the Middle Temple is a lamb bearing a flag, while that of the Inner Temple is a winged horse.

[2] **Clifford's Inn:** One of the Inns of Chancery, subordinate institutions to the Inns of Court. Clifford's Inn was a satellite of the Inner Temple.

[3] *Capiases:* Arrest warrants.

[4] **St. Dunstan's savages:** A pair of giant automata designed to strike the bells of St. Dunstan's Church on Fleet Street.

[5] **Erskine's famed Pamphlet:** Thomas Erskine, a prominent legal and political figure from around 1780 to 1810. Erskine was a staunch defender of freedom of political speech. His speeches on the subject in court were often printed and distributed in pamphlet form.

[6] **Cap-a-pee:** Literally, head to foot, a term used to describe a fully armed and armored knight. Erskine was, indeed, a formidable adversary in court.

[7] **Serjeant's-Inn:** A legal inn restricted to serjeants-at-law, an order of barristers (lawyers who argued in court) with exclusive privileges.

[8] **The Stationers…Almanack:** The Stationers Company, located at Stationers Hall, Ludgate Hill, oversaw the publishing industry in England. It kept track of copyrights and enjoyed a monopoly on publishing certain books, including almanacs, a major source of revenue for the Company.

[9] **Stopp'd before Ave-Mary-lane…College:** As the classics march down Ludgate Hill, they stop at the intersection of Ave Maria Lane. Peering down it, Galen, the ancient Greek physician and father of Western medicine, can see the Royal College of Physicians on Warwick Lane.

[10] **Saint Paul's…*Maribus:*** Lily's Grammar, as it was popularly known, was the official Latin textbook of England (by royal edict). It was written in the early 16th c. by William Lily, first headmaster of St. Paul's Cathedral School. *Propria quae Maribus*—or, "that which is proper to the male gender,"—is an early lesson on identifying the gender of nouns that all English schoolboys would have learned. It is also the shortened title of a popular 1650 adaptation of the Grammar by Charles Hoole.

[11] **Cheapside:** After crossing St. Paul's Churchyard, the classic army arrives at a fork. To the right is Cheapside, home to middle-class merchants and tradespeople, and to the left is Paternoster Row, chiefly occupied by booksellers. This is the neighborhood in which Combe grew up, a fact he concealed for the majority of his life. Despite his education and literary success, Combe never felt entirely secure in his status as a gentleman, and did his best to hide his "vulgar" origins in trade.

[12] **Quire Stock:** Paper that has been folded and prepared to be bound into books or pamphlets.

The Bennets's (PP) relatives the Gardiners live on Gracechurch Street, near Cheapside. The Bingley sisters sneer at the Bennets for this. Darcy, while less scornful, still thinks it will lessen the daughters' chances of marrying "men of any consideration," (I.8) i.e. gentlemen. Of course, he proves himself wrong by marrying a Bennet himself!

The shape was clad in Livery-Gown,
The face had neither smile nor frown,
While it held out a monstrous paunch
As fat with many a ham and haunch.   80
Two Printer's Devils[1] o'er his head
A crimson canvas widely spread,
Whereon was writ in gilded show,
GENIUS OF PATER NOSTER ROW.[2]
The mighty Giants of Guildhall,[3]   85
Urg'd by a sympathetic call,
No sooner heard the clock strike *One*,
Than from their stations they came down,
And in Cheapside they took their stand,
In honour of the Classic* Band: 90
But, when they heard the clock strike *Two*,
March'd back as they were wont to do.

  Now as they came near the Old-Jewry—[4]
Like Dulness, work'd into a Fury,[5]
A vulgar shape appear'd,[6] who flew   95
On pinions mark'd with ONE and TWO,
And other items which denote,
That four-pence is well worth a groat.
It seem'd to lead a num'rous train
Who render'd further passage vain.   100
Strait he came forward to produce
A *Blank Sheet* as a Flag of Truce.
By him, two flutt'ring *Pamphlets* bore
Standards, with figures cover'd o'er:
A gilt *Pence-table*[7] grac'd the one,   105
The *Price* of *Stocks* on t'other shone.
A picquet guard[8] of valuations,
And Int'rest tables took their stations
Around their leader, who drew nigh,
To make his bold soliloquy,   110
But, ere he speaks, my proper course is
Just to describe the city forces.
  Bill Books and *Cash Books* form'd the van,[9]
An active and a numerous clan:

310

¹ **Printer's Devils:** Apprentices in a printing office.

² **GENIUS OF PATER NOSTER ROW:** Paternoster Row was a street near St. Paul's Cathedral that served as the home of the London publishing industry. The "Genius," or spirit, of the Row bears a strong resemblance to Vellum, the corpulent bookseller we meet in Canto XXII.

³ **Giants of Guildhall:** Statues of the legendary giants Gog and Magog located outside the administrative building Guildhall. The giants were said to have been captured by Brutus, grandson of Aeneas, during his conquest of Britain to guard what would become London.

⁴ **Old-Jewry:** A street in London that turns off Cheapside. The classics need to take this turn in order to reach their destination: the new premises of the London Institution in Coleman Street.

⁵ **Fury:** The Furies were ancient Greek goddesses of revenge, usually depicted as part bird, part human.

⁶ **A vulgar shape appear'd:** This figure, who leads the armies of Trade, later reveals himself as the arithmetician Edward Cocker (1631-1676), author of a ubiquitous arithmetic textbook that went through 130 editions. Cocker's treatment of the subject was practical rather than theoretical, adapted for the daily use of merchants and tradespeople. Syntax apparently sees Cocker's approach to mathematics as dull, simplistic, and overly concerned with money.

⁷ **_Pence-table:_** An arithmetical table used for converting a given number of pence into shillings and pounds (OED).

⁸ **picquet guard:** A group of soldiers arrayed in a defensive line.

⁹ **the van:** The foremost part of an advancing army.

Austen was aware of this legend. She may even have told stories about Gog and Magog to her nieces. In a letter to her sister (2-3 Mar. 1814), she says she has not seen anyone in London "quite so large as Gogmagoglicus," intentionally garbling the names of the giants. This is a strange comment to make to an adult sister; probably it was intended for "little Cassandra," her five-year-old niece, whom she mentions just before and with whom she might have shared a private joke.

Engraving of Edward Cocker, Unknown, mid-17th c. National Portrait Gallery.

The *Journals* follow'd them, whose skill 115
Was exercis'd in daily drill.
On either side appear'd to range
Unpaid Accounts, Bills of Exchange
And Files of *Banker's Checks:*—these three
Manœuv'red as light infantry:— 120
While ev'ry other trading book
Its regular position took;
And Quires of *Blotting Paper* [1] stood
To suck up any flow of blood.—
The *Ledgers* the main body form, 125
Arm'd to resist the coming storm;
Whose pond'rous shapes could boldly show
A steady phalanx to the foe.

   Discord appear'd with base intent
The hostile spirit to foment. 130
Not *Discord* [2] that precedes the car
Of Mars whene'er he goes to war,
But of a different rank and nation,
Known by the name of *Litigation;*
Born on some foul attorney's desk; 135
Bred but to harass and perplex:
Whose appetite is for dispute,
And has no wish but for a suit.
She rose upon a Gander's wing, [3]
And round about began to fling, 140
Pleas, Declarations, and each bit
Of Parchment that could form a Writ.

   The *News-papers* with pen in hand,
In the balconies took their stand;
Waiting with that impartial spirit, 145
Which all well know they all inherit,
To make the hurry of the Battle
Thro' all the next day's columns rattle;
And, with one conscience, to prepare
The Hist'ry of this Paper war. 150

[1] **Quires of Blotting Paper:** Here, quires are stacks of 25 sheets of paper. Blotting paper is used to absorb wet ink from a page so it does not smear or bleed.

[2] ***Discord:*** The Greek goddess Eris (or Discord) was a fomenter of strife and war—including the famous Trojan War.

[3] **Gander's wing:** Traditionally, legal documents were written with a goose quill (a gander is a male goose).

The Herald now the silence broke,
'Twas mighty COCKER'S self[1] that spoke;
And thus to Pallas' Bird address'd
The solemn purpose of his breast.

"I state my claim to ask and know   155
"From whence you come and where you go:
"And by what licence you appear
"With all your foreign Pagans[2] here.
"Come you with all this Cavalcade
"'T' insult the Vehicles of Trade;   160
"And our dear, home-bred right invade?
"A mighty force awaits you here
"To check and punish your career.
"And I am order'd by my masters,
"Who fear disturbance and disasters,   165
"To bid you quickly turn about
"From London streets to take your rout,[3]
"Or we shall bravely turn you out.
"My name is COCKER which is known
"In ev'ry Counting-House in Town.   170
"Nay, such my use and reputation
"I am respected through the nation.
"Yes, I'm the Father, I who speak
"Of Mercantile Arithmetic;
"Source of a race that far outvies   175
"Your Greek and Latin progenies:
"And now I hope that in a crack
"You'll send an humble answer back
"Or else expect a fierce attack.
"I'll count twice two and then add four,   180
"That time I'll give but give no more.
"One, two, three, four, five, six, seven, eight.—
"I've done, and will no longer wait."

The Bird of Pallas who could speak,
In English or in Attic Greek[4]   185
As suited best—did not prolong
His answer in the Vulgar Tongue.

[1] **COCKER'S self:** See note 6 on p. 311.

[2] **foreign Pagans:** The ancient Greek and Roman authors were not, of course, Christians.

[3] **rout:** Retreat, especially a disorderly or panicked one.

[4] **Attic Greek:** The dialect of Greek spoken in Athens, which was also the main literary language of the classical period.

" 'Twas a petition duly made
"By certain of your Sons of Trade,[1]
"To beg my Mistress would permit
"That they should buy a little wit;
"And here import, though in defiance
"Of common rules, a little Science*.
"I ask not, if 'twas their intent
"To gain a name—or *ten per Cent.;*[2]
"Whether 'tis wisdom or misdoing,
"Whether 'twill prove their good or ruin;
"Or the result of common sense,
"Or a shrewd, mercantile pretence.
"Whether 'tis Interest or Pride
"That turns them from old rules aside;
"That urges them to tax their trade
"For off'rings to th' immortal maid;—[3]
"These self same matters, to be free,
"Are, *Mister Cocker*, nought to me.
" 'Tis by Minerva's high command,
"That I conduct this Classic* Band,
" 'Tis she commands, and we obey;
"Nor shall you stop us on our way,
"Whether it does or does not suit
"Your pleasure—to the Institute[4]
"We'll go, you calculating brute.
"Say will your low born volumes dare
"With these brave vet'rans to compare?
"What's all this bustle, all this fuss?
"Think you they can contend with us?
"They who are slaves, so base and willing,
"Of any pound and pence and shilling.
"As the pen gives they're forc'd to drink
"The venal dips of any ink;
"And when they're fill'd their lives expire,
"Consign'd to light a kitchen fire;[5]
"Or sent away to such vile use
"As Chandlers or as Hucksters[6] chuse.
"If they oppose our stated way;
"We'll sweep them from the face of day.

[1] **a petition… Trade:** The owl
190 alludes to the founding of the London Institution (see Editor's Note on p. 305).
195 [2] **I ask not… Cent.:** The owl does not care whether the founders of the
200 Institution had high-minded motives, or whether they merely wanted to make money
205 from subscriptions.
[3] **th' immortal maid:** Athena/ Minerva.

210 [4] **the Institute:** The London Institution.
[5] **And when…fire:** The owl taunts the army of Trade by
215 declaring that it will wind up as kindling or waste paper.
[6] **Chandlers… Hucksters:**
220 Candlemakers and dealers in small goods. Both used waste paper in their trades, for instance
225 to wrap their merchandise.

"At the same time we wish for peace,
"And that your saucy threats may cease.
"We do not mean to mock the city
"With any hope of being witty;   230
"We do not bring our learned pow'rs
"To vex its speculating hours:
"Or with poetic visions cross
"Your schemes of Profit or of Loss.
"We did not first suggest the deed,   235
"To bring you books, you cannot read.
"Meetings were form'd and speeches made,
"And all by weighty men of trade,[1]
"To frame the unforeseen request:
"And surely we have done our best,   240
"When we each Classic did provide,
"With a Translation by its side.[2]
"—Dryden is ready to rehearse
"All Virgil's Works in English verse,
"And Grecian Homer rests his Hope,   245
"Of being understood by Pope.
"Leland will give you if ye please,
"The speeches of Demothenes:
"And Northern Guthrie will bestow
"The Eloquence of Cicero.   250
"To Thomas Styles and John a Nokes,
"Carr will repeat old Lucian's Jokes.
"While Juvenal's sharp satire shines
"In William Giffard's rival Lines.
"Coleman and Thornton will convey   255
"Right notions of a Latin Play.
"Whate'er the ancient Critics wrote,
"You now may in plain English quote!
"And drink Pye's health, when o'er the bottle,
"For Anglicising Aristotle.   260
"Nay, all the Ancient Bards have sung,
"You now may sing in Vulgar Tongue.
"What could we more?—so cease your riot,
"And let us pass along in quiet.
"Dismiss your Counting-house parade;   265
"Send off these cumbrous tomes of trade;

[1] **weighty men of trade:** Most of the founders of the London Institution were prominent London merchants.

[2] **a Translation by its side:** The owl backs up this claim by listing a number of classical authors, together with their primary English translators. The owl sees this as an act of generosity: Athena is sending the classics in a form that tradespeople, few of whom would have known Latin or Greek, can understand.

"Back to their counters let them roam,
"And sip their ink and stay at home;
"Nor e'er again their threats oppose
"To Grecian and to Roman Foes."   270

COCKER.

"Fools may be found, I do not doubt it,
"Within this city as without it.
"This truth, indeed, is very clear,
"For they were fools who brought you here.
"I pray thee tell me what has wit   275
"To do with any plodding cit*?
"Of wit we know not what is meant
"Unless 'tis found in *cent. per cent.*[1]
"Learning a drug has always been;
"No Warehouseman will take it in.   280
"Should practic'd Mercers quit their satin,
"To look at Greek and long for Latin?
"Should the pert, upstart Merchant's boy
"Behold the Tower, and think of Troy?[2]
"Or should a Democratic Hatter   285
" 'Bout Old Republics[3] make a clatter?
"Should City Praters[4] leave their tools,
"To talk by Ciceronian rules;[5]
"And at our meetings in Guildhall
"Puzzle the mob with classic* brawl?   290
"No, to such things they've no pretence,
"No—let them stick to common sense.
"You may your ancient bards rehearse,
"But there's no common sense in verse.
"Not all the Classics at your tail   295
"Would weigh an ounce in Reason's scale.
"I treat the name of *Rome* with scorn,
"Give me the Commerce of *Leghorn*.[6]
"From Italy's prolific shore,
"The wond'rous science was brought o'er,   300
"The bright invention which convey'd
"Such vast facilities to trade.
"The DOUBLE ENTRY[7] far outvies
"All pictur'd, sculptur'd fantasies:

[1] *cent. per cent.:* One hundred percent, or a doubling of one's investment.

[2] **the Tower… Troy:** For Cocker, trade and learning have no more to do with each other than the Tower of London and the towers of Troy, setting of the *Iliad*.

[3] **Old Republics:** Such as the Roman Republic.

[4] **City Praters:** Unpolished speechifiers.

[5] **Ciceronian rules:** Cicero wrote several essays on the art of oratory.

[6] *Leghorn:* Livorno, Italy, a Tuscan port city.

[7] **The DOUBLE ENTRY:** Double-entry bookkeeping, developed in Renaissance Italy, greatly improved the accuracy of merchant accounts.

"And sure I am his honour'd name
"Deserves a brighter wreath of Fame,
"To whose keen mind the scheme occur'd,
"Than e'er was won by Conqu'ror's sword.
"What did the Greeks, pray, know of trade?
"Ulysses, as I've heard it said
"Was full *ten months* oblig'd to roam,
"Before he brought his cargo home:[1]
"A voyage in that self-same sea,
"Our coasting brigs would make in three.
"The INSTITUTION was display'd,
"As a mere trump'ry trick of trade
"Deck'd out, 'tis true with great parade;
"While you are coming, as a bribe,
"To make our purse-proud* cits* subscribe;
"And aid the primary intent
"Of dividends of *ten per cent.*—[2]

305

310

315

320

[1] **Ulysses... home:** In Homer's *Odyssey*, the hero Odysseus (or Ulysses) seeks to return home after the Trojan war. His journey actually takes ten *years*, not months.

[2] **INSTITUTION ...*cent.*:** Cocker tells the classics that they are being exploited as devices for profit by the Institution, and as mere status symbols by its wealthy but ignorant subscribers.

p. 314.

"We have our pedant tradesmen too,
"Who talk as if they something knew,
"And Learning's cud pretend to chew.
"Who get cramp words,¹ and court the Muse 325
"In Magazines and in Reviews.
"Yes we have those whose priggish rage is,
"Not to read books, but title-pages:
"Who spare no cost in drink and meat
"To furnish out a tempting treat 330
"That may attract an Attic train
"To *Mincing* or to *Philpot-lane;*²
"Who snatch the feast, and go away
"To mock the patron of the day.³
"There are who strive to have it thought, 335
"That they have minds with Learning fraught;
"Though if they have so small discerning;
"To interrupt their trade with Learning;
"The day will come, when they'll be found
"With *certain shillings in the pound.*⁴ 340
"But to be brief—consult your fame,
"And go back gravely as you came:
"Or we shall send you somewhat faster;
"Nor for your wounds afford a plaister*.
"—Look at that form which soars in air, 345
"And shines like a protentous⁵ star;
"It is the armorial symbol bright
"Of a renown'd, commercial Knight,⁶
"Who ask'd no other, higher fame,
"Than doth befit a Merchant's name. 350
"See how his ensign is unfurl'd
"O'er the Emporium of the world,⁷
"And does with threat'ning aspect view,
"Your Owlish worship and your Crew.
"While in its motions we decry 355
"The sure presage of Victory.
"Yes, on success I calculate,
"As sure as four and four make eight.
"Thus I have clearly stated the amount,
"*Errors excepted*, of my just account." 360

¹ **cramp words:** Long, obscure words used to appear intelligent.

² **To *Mincing* or to *Philpot-lane:*** Mincing Lane was associated with the tea and spice trades. Philpot Lane was home to a variety of well-to-do merchants.

³ **Who spare...day:** In other words, some wealthy merchants try to buy their way into intellectual circles by hosting lavish dinners for artists and scholars, but to no avail. Their learned guests eat the food but still look down on them.

⁴ **There are who...*pound:*** Cocker claims that those who subscribe to the London Institution are neglecting their business interests out of a foolish desire to appear learned. Instead of imitating the educated classes, they should take pride in their identity as tradesmen and focus on making money.

⁵ **protentous:** Portentous, presaging the future.

⁶ **renown'd, commercial Knight:** Sir Thomas Gresham, 16th-c. English merchant and founder of the Royal Exchange.

⁷ **See how his ensign...Emporium of the world:** Cocker points to the grasshopper-shaped weathervane atop the Royal Exchange ("the Emporium of the world"), which he sees as a presage of victory. The grasshopper was the symbol of the house of Gresham.

Cocker, who scoffs at the idea of a tradesman having intellectual interests, likely would have seen Elizabeth's uncle Mr. Gardiner (PP) as one such pretender. Though he takes his business seriously, Mr. Gardiner is also described as a man of "taste"— "intelligent" and "educated." In Austen's work those terms always imply, among other things, a love of books. One can easily imagine Mr. Gardiner paying £20 ($2,880 and the cost of a life subscription) for the privilege of enjoying the London Institution's vast library and commodious reading rooms—all of it a short walk from his house in Gracechurch Street.

"A View of the Royal Exchange," Daniel Havell after Thomas Hosmer Shepherd, c. 1820. YCBA.

THE OWL.
"Good *Mister Cocker* I have heard,
"All that your wisdom has preferr'd;
"And I entreat you'll turn your head
"In which such numbers have been bred,
"And see an Eastern wind prevail,
"To make your grasshopper turn tail;[1]
"From which my wise soothsayer draws
"An Omen fatal to your cause,
"And you may hear his tongue proclaim,
" 'Your boobies* will all do the same.'
"But talking is of little use—
"Therefore at once I break the truce."

As Critics now when call'd to duel,
Disdainful of the common fuel,
No more with shot or bullet vapour,[2]
But wound with ink, and kill with paper,
Both sides for conflict dire prepare—
And thus commenc'd the threaten'd war.

Euclid[3] at *Master Cocker* flew,
Whom, by one stroke, he overthrew,
Then with a knotty problem bound him;
And left him struggling where he found him.
Cæsar with all his Latins pounc'd
On the light parties, whom they trounc'd,
And soon a dreadful havoc made
Of bills that never would be paid:
While Banker's Checks made quick retreat,
And huddled into *Lombard-street*.[4]
With equal force the Greeks attack,
And drove the heavy legions back:
Ledgers and *Journals* lay all scatter'd;
Bill-books and *Cash-books* were bespatter'd.
Short was the contest; struck with dread,
Confus'd the City forces fled.
For aid on Stationers[5] they call,
But they were busy at their hall:

---

[1] **Eastern wind... turn tail:** In an eastern wind, the grasshopper weathervane of the Royal Exchange would face east, away from the confrontation in Cheapside. The owl sees this as an omen that the army of Trade will similarly "turn tail."

365

370

[2] **vapour:** Storm and fume.

375

[3] *Euclid:* Greek mathematician.

380

385

[4] *Lombard-street:* Street adjoining Cheapside and known for banking.

390

[5] **Stationers:** See note 8 on p. 309.

395

THE DOCTOR'S DREAM.

And this same hall their trade-craft found
To be a kind of neutral ground.
For they conceiv'd the havoc made,
Might serve the paper-making trade.   400
To side with either they were loth,
In hopes to profit from them both.

The Postman now his clarion[1] blew;
His blasts were vain—they would not do;—
The *Letter-books* disorder'd flew: 405
While *Pindar* from Bow-steeple[2] clock
Look'd down, and, as he view'd the shock
Chaunted, nor did he chaunt in vain,
A loud, and animating strain.
Forth from the Bank a troop was sent   410
Of threes and fours and fives *per cent.;*[3]
But they ran off, nor struck a blow;
For stocks that day were very low.
The *Policies* [4] remain'd secure,
Waiting for arms of signature: 415
For what brave spirit, e'er would fight 'em,
When nobody would underwrite 'em.

And now, these doughty cits* were beat;
Down ev'ry lane, up ev'ry street;
But met to form each broken rank,   420
Before the Portals of the Bank:[5]
There they a solemn council hold,
Whether, by added strength grown bold,
To a new contest they should come,
Or sneak away disbanded home.   425

Thus the old Classics having beat
The vulgar foe, sought *Coleman-street;*[6]
But as they pass'd, a numerous host
At *Coopers'-hall,*[7] had taken post.
Two blue-coat urchins play'd the fife   430
Which call'd them to the martial strife,
When, stead of pointed darts and lances,
They pelted the Antiques with *Chances.*[8]

[1] **clarion:** Military trumpet (OED). Postmen of this period actually used a bell, not a trumpet; Combe is exaggerating for mock-epic effect.

[2] *Pindar...*Bow-steeple: Pindar was an ancient Greek poet known in part for his "victory odes" celebrating the winners of athletic contests. A rival to the postman and his trumpet, he shouts encouragement to the classics from the steeple of St. Mary-le-Bow, a church in Cheapside whose bells could be heard, it was said, all over London.

[3] **Forth from the Bank...fives *per cent.*:** One of the functions of the Bank of England was to sell various types of government debt to the public. These securities usually payed between three and five percent interest, and were considered safe investments. Still, the market for them rose and fell as it did with all securities, and on this particular day, the market for government debt was apparently low.

[4] *Policies:* Insurance contracts. They do not take part in the battle because nobody is willing to underwrite them (sign them and take on their risks).

[5] **the Bank:** The Bank of England, located a stone's throw away on Threadneedle Street.

[6] *Coleman-street:* Location of the London Instution, the classics' destination.

[7] *Cooper's-hall:* Headquarters of the Company of Coopers, or barrelmakers, located almost next door to the London Institution. Drawings for government lotteries were held at Cooper's Hall.

[8] *Chances:* Lottery tickets.

When Austen speaks of characters, especially women, as having a "fortune" or lump sum of money, she is probably referring to investments in these sorts of safe government funds. The owner of the fortune would not spend the principal except in an emergency, but rather would live on the interest. In Austen's fictional world, the rate of interest is generally assumed to be 5%. Thus, John Dashwood (SS) estimates that each of his half-sisters, with a fortune of £1,000, can count on an annual income of £50 ($7,200). Mr. Bennet (PP) uses the same formula when calculating the annual interest of Lydia's £1,000 inheritance.

But Fortune who is ever blind,
Turn'd short and left her bands behind:—   435
Their Leader lost, away they steal,
And hide their numbers in *the wheel*.[1]

   At length the Classic* sages greet
Their Parthenonian retreat:[2]
But while the echoing walls around   440
With *Io Pæans*[3] loud resound;
Again the vengeful foes appear'd,
Again their angry standards rear'd.
"Must we once more," the Ancients said,
"O'ercome these frantic imps of trade?   445
"Is there no power will save our race
"From war, when conquest is disgrace?"
The Greeks then call'd on PORSON's name:[4]
The Latins echo'd back the same;
And straight in Grecian stole[5] array'd,   450
Appear'd the venerable Shade.
Homer went down upon his knees,   }
And so did Tragic Sophocles,[6]   }
With all the names that end in ης.[7]   }

   "Hail sacred tomes!" he said, "to you   455
"I grateful ow'd whate'er I knew:
"From you I gain'd my mortal fame;
"The honours of a scholar's name:
"To you the immortal power I owe,
"To give the aid I now bestow.   460
"I come from that Celestial Hall
"Where they all dwell, who wrote you all."
He spoke—and lo! a *Volume* came
Of size immense and rueful name.
Its back no verbal title bore;   465
But num'rous dates of times long o'er;—
While on its letter'd sides appears,
"LONDON GAZETTES[8] for FIFTY YEARS!!"
Strait to the foe that, all aloof,
Flutter'd about each neighb'ring roof,   470

¹ *the wheel:* Lottery wheel.

² **Parthenonian retreat:** The London Institution.

³ *Io Pæans:* Prayers of gratitude addressed to Apollo, particularly after battle.

"Richard Porson," Richard Sharp after John Hoppner, 1810. National Portrait Gallery.

⁴ **PORSON's name:** Richard Porson, famous English classical scholar and first librarian of the London Institution.

⁵ **stole:** A long robe (OED).

⁶ **Sophocles:** Ancient Greek tragic playwright.

⁷ **all the names that end in ης:** The Greek letters ης were pronounced "ease" in the 18ᵗʰ and 19ᵗʰ centuries. Porson was especially well known for his studies of Greek drama, and several ancient Greek playwrights happen to have names ending in those letters (Sophocles, Euripides, Aristophanes).

⁸ **LONDON GAZETTES:** *The London Gazette* published, among other news, accounts of bankruptcies—the ultimate fear of the commercial classes. Its appearance routs the armies of Trade once and for all.

After his bank failed, Henry Austen, Jane's brother, had the humiliation of appearing in The London Gazette. *The 16 Mar. 1816 issue announced his bankruptcy and those of his partners. The event had consequences for Jane's finances, too. Henry had been contributing £50 ($7,200) a year to the support of Jane, Cassandra, and their mother, but the bankruptcy put an end to that expression of familial generosity. Francis, another brother who was invested in the bank, had to pull his support as well. Fortunately, Jane was earning her own money as an author at this point, which somewhat softened the blow.*

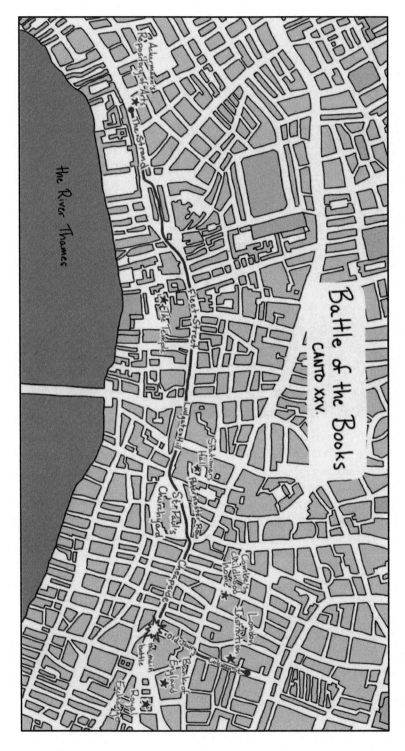

It did full many a page unfold,
And show'd 𝖂𝖍𝖊𝖗𝖊𝖆𝖘,[1] and cried, "behold!"
While that same word, upon the walls
Blaz'd forth in flaming Capitals.
𝖂𝖍𝖊𝖗𝖊𝖆𝖘, a thousand voices rung,
And on the wing there upwards sprung
A flight of *Dockets,* who were join'd
By dire Certificates[2] *unsign'd.*
These saw the foes, and, chill'd with dread,
Trembled and shriek'd aloud, and fled.

  The Ghost now vanish'd from the view;
The Bird of Pallas vanish'd too.
And then I thought the classic* elves
Instinctive sought their proper shelves,
Where undisturb'd each learned Tome
Might slumber to the Day of Doom.
I 'woke and felt a real glee
At this same fancied victory.
Nor would I change my Classic* lore,
Poor as I am, for all the store,
Which plodding anxious trade can give,
In constant doubt and fear to live.
My treasures are all well secur'd,
I want them not to be insur'd—
My Greek and Latin are immur'd
Within the Warehouse of my brain;
And there in safety they remain.
My little cargo's lodg'd at home
Where storms and tempests never come.

  Learning will give an unmix'd pleasure,
Which gold can't buy, and trade can't measure.
But each within his destin'd station:——
Learning's my pride and consolation.
That high-form'd inmate of the soul,
Which, as the changing seasons roll,
Acquires new strength, preserves its power
And smiles in Life's extremest hour.

[1] 𝖂𝖍𝖊𝖗𝖊𝖆𝖘:
Bankruptcy
announcements in
the *Gazette* began
475 with this word, as
in, "Whereas a
Commission of
Bankrupt is
awarded and issued
480 forth against Henry
Thomas Austin
[sic]…" (16 Mar.
1816, 519).
[2] **Certificates:**
Certificates of
485 Discharge,
documents which
allowed a person
who had gone
bankrupt to resume
490 trading. These
certificates, though,
are unsigned, and
therefore imply
ongoing
495 bankruptcy.

500

505

The learned man, let who will flout him,
Doth always carry it about him:
And should he idly fail to use it;   510
Though it may rust, he will not lose it.
Fortune may leave off her caressing,
But she can't rob him of that blessing.
Full many a comfort money gives;
But ask him who for money lives,   515
Whether he other pleasures shares,
Than sordid joys and golden cares?

How oft I've pass'd an evening hour
Within an hawthorn's humble bower,
And read aloud each charming line,   520
That doth in Virgil's Georgics[1] shine.
Though wealth pass'd by in stately guise,
I felt no rankling envy rise;
Nor could the show my mind engage
From the Immortal Poet's Page.   525
When homeward as I us'd to stray,
Along the unfrequented way;
Enraptur'd, as I stroll'd along,
With Philomela's[2] evening song.
I felt what worldlings never share,   530
Oblivion of all human care.
Such hours are few, but well we know,
That Learning can those hours bestow.

My Lord continu'd the debate:—
And time pass'd on in pleasant prate   535
Till night broke up the Tête-à-tête.[3]

[1] **Virgil's Georgics:** The great Roman poet's second major poem, which focuses on agriculture.

[2] **Philomela's:** Philomela was a figure in Greek mythology who was turned into a nightingale. The nightingale was famously associated with the writing of poetry in this period.

[3] **Tête-à-tête:** Intimate conversation.

CANTO XXVI.

CROWN'D with success the following day
The Doctor homeward took his way;
And on the morrow he again
Was borne by Grizzle o'er the plain.
But Grizzle, having liv'd in clover,[1]   5
Symptoms of spirit did discover,
That more than once had nearly thrown
Her deep reflecting master down;
Nor, till they'd travell'd half the day,
Did he perceive he'd lost his way: 10
Nor to that moment did he find,
That Grizzle, by some chance unkind,
Had left her ears and tail behind.
"Ne'er mind, good beast," he kindly said:
"What tho' no ears bedeck your head;   15
"What tho' the honours of your rump
"Are dwindled to a naked stump;
"Now rais'd in purse as well as spirit,
"Your master will reward your merit."
Another day they journey'd on;—   20
The next, and, lo! the work was done.

[1] **liv'd in clover:** Lived in comfort and plenty.

Some days before (I had forgot
To say), a letter had been wrote,
To tell how soon he should appear,
And re-embrace his dearest dear: 25
But not one solitary word
Of his good fortune he preferr'd.

  "Yes, home is home, where'er it be,
"Or shaded by the village-tree;
"Or where the lofty domes arise,   30
"To catch the passing stranger's eyes."
'Twas thus he thought, when, at the gate
He saw his Doll impatient wait;
Nor, as he pass'd the street along,
Was he unnotic'd by the throng;   35
For not a head within a shop
But did through door or window pop.
He kiss'd his dame, and gravely spoke,
For now he brooded o'er a joke;—
While she to know impatient burn'd   40
With how much money he return'd.
"Give me a pipe," he said, "and ale,
"And in due time you'll hear the tale."

He sat him down his pipe to smoke,
Look'd sad, and not a word he spoke; 45
But Madam soon her speech began,
And in discordant tones it ran:—

"I think by that confounded look,
"You have not writ your boasted book:
"Yes all your money you have spent, 50
"And come back poorer than you went:
"Yes, you have wandered far from home,
"And here a beggar you are come:
"But bills from all sides are in waiting,
"To give your Reverence a baiting.[1] 55
"I do not mean to scold or rail;
"But I'll not live with you in jail.
"So long a time you've stay'd away,
"That the Town-Curate[2] you must pay;
"For, while from home you play'd the fool, 60
"He kindly came to teach the school;
"And a few welcome pounds to earn
"By flogging boys to make them learn:
"But I must say, you silly elf,
"You merit to be flogg'd yourself; 65
"And I've a mind this whip shall crack
"Upon your raw-bon'd lazy back.

[1] **a baiting:** A series of harassing attacks. The image is of a tied bear or bull being attacked by dogs.

[2] **Town-Curate:** As opposed to a country curate like Syntax. There may have been a perception that the pastoral duties of town curates were lighter, and that they were thus more available to take on odd clerical jobs (*Advice to the Universities of Oxford and Cambridge*, 100).

p. 338

"Yes, puff away—but 'tis no joke
"For all my schemes to end in smoke.
"What, tongue-ty'd booby*! will you say   70
"To Mrs. Dress'em:—Who will pay
"Her bill for these nice clothes?—Why, zounds*!
"It borders upon twenty pounds."

Thus, as she vehemently prated,
And the delighted Doctor rated,[1]   75   [1] **rated:** Rebuked,
From a small pocket in his coat   scolded.
He unobserv'd drew forth a note.
And, throwing it upon the table,
He said, "My dear, you'll now be able
"To keep your mantua-maker[2] quiet;   80   [2] **mantua-maker:**
"So cease, I beg, this idle riot: Dressmaker.
"And, if you'll not make such a pother*,
"I'll treat you with its very brother.
"Be kind—and I'll not think it much
"To shew you half a dozen such."   85

She started up, in joys alarms,
And clasp'd her Doctor in her arms;
Then ran to bid the boys huzza,
And give them all a holiday.

"Such is the matrimonial life,"   90
Said Syntax;—"but I love my wife.
"Just now with horse-whip I was bother'd;
"And now with hugging I am smother'd.
"But wheresoe'er I'm doom'd to roam,
"I still shall say—*that home is home!*"   95   [4] **fatted calf:** A

                                                       metaphor for a
Again her dear the dame caress'd,   lavish welcome
And clasp'd him fondly to her breast.   given to one who
At length, amidst her am'rous play,   has returned from a
The Doctor found a time to say—   long absence,
"The fatted calf[4] I trust you've slain,   100 derived from the
"To welcome Syntax home again."   parable of the
"No," she reply'd, "no fatted calf;   Prodigal Son (Luke
"We have a better thing by half: 15:11-32).

"For, with fond expectation big
"Of your return, we kill'd a pig; 105
"And a rich *Haslet*,[1] at the fire,
"Will give you all you can desire:
"The sav'ry meat myself will baste,
"And suit it to my deary's taste."
"That dish," he cry'd, "I'd rather see 110
"Than *Fricandeau* or *Fricasee*[2]
"O," he continu'd, "what a blessing
"To have a wife so fond of dressing;
"Who with such taste and skill can work
"To dress herself—or dress the pork!" 115
She now return'd to household care,
The dainty supper to prepare.

  Whoe'er has pass'd an idle hour,
In following Syntax through his Tour,
Must have perceiv'd he did not balk 120
His fancy when he wish'd to talk:
Nay more—that he was often prone
To make long speeches when alone;
And, while he quaff'd th' inspiring ale,
Between each glass to tell a tale: 125
Or, as he smok'd with half-shut eyes
Now smiling, and now looking wise,
He'd crack a joke, or moralize:
And when this curious spirit stirr'd him,
He minded not tho' no one heard him. 130
This he did now—as 'twill appear;
He talk'd tho' there were none to hear.
When the whiffs paus'd, he silence broke,
And thus he thought, and puff'd, and spoke:—

THE SMOKING SOLILOQUY.

  "That man, I trow*, is doubly curst, 135
"Who of the best doth make the worst;
"And he, I'm sure, is doubly blest,
"Who of the worst can make the best.

[1] **Haslet:** A pork meatloaf made with a plentiful amount of herbs.

[2] **Fricandeau** or **Fricasee:** Lighter dishes of chopped meat served with flavorful sauces. Here, as elsewhere, Syntax prefers solid, homely fare to fancier cuisine.

"To sit and sorrow, and complain,
"Is adding folly to our pain.   140

    "In adverse state there is no vice
"More mischievous than cowardice:
" 'Tis by resistance that we claim
"The Christian's venerable name.
"If you resist him, e'en old Nick   145
"Gives up his meditated trick.[1]
"Fortune contemns the whining slave,
"And loves to smile upon the brave.

    "In all this self-same, checquer'd strife
"We meet with in the road of life,   150
"Whate'er the object we pursue,
"There's always something to subdue;
"Some foe, alas! to evil prone,
"In others' bosoms, or our own.
"That man alone is truly great,   155
"Who nobly meets the frowns of Fate;
"Who, when the threat'ning tempests lower*,
"When the clouds burst in pelting shower,
"When lightnings flash along the sky,
"And thunders growl in sympathy,   160
"With calmness to the scene conforms,
"Nor fears, nor mocks the angry storms:
"He does not run, all *helter-skelter*,
"To seek a temporary shelter;
"Nor does he fume, and fret, and foam,   165
"Because he's distant far from home;
"For well he knows, each peril past,
"He's sure to find a home at last.[2]

    "If petty evils round you swarm,
"Let not their buz your temper warm;   170
"But brush them from your mind away,
"Like insects of a summer's day.

    "Evil oppose with Reason's power,
"Nor fear the dark or threat'ning hour:

[1] **If you resist…trick:** A paraphrase of James 4:7: "Submit yourselves therefore to God. Resist the devil, and he will flee from you." Old Nick is a nickname for the devil.

[2] **home at last:** That is, in heaven.

335

"Combat the world;—but, as 'tis fit,   175
"To the decrees of Heav'n submit.

    "If Spite and Malice are your foes,
"If fell Revenge its arrow throws,
"Look calmly on, nor fear the dart;
"Virtue will guard the honest heart: 180
"Nor let your angry spirit burn
"The pointed missile to return.

    "The good man never fails to wield
"A broad and strong protecting shield,
"That will preserve him thro' the strife   185
"Which never fails to trouble life;
"And, when he meets his final doom,
"Will form a trophy for his tomb.

    "*Bear* and *forbear*—a dogma true
"As human wisdom ever drew.   190
"If you would lighten every care,
"And every sorrow learn to bear,
"To be secure from vile disgrace,
"Look frowning Fortune in the face;
"And, if the foe's too strong, retreat,   195
"But not as if you had been beat:
"Calmly avoid th' o'erpow'ring fray,
"Nor fight when you can stalk away;
"For you can scarce be said to yield,
"If, when you slowly quit the field,   200
"You so present yourself to view,
"That a wise foe will not pursue.¹

    "I, who have long been doom'd to drudge,
"Without a patron or a judge;
"I, who have seen the booby* rise   205
"To dignified pluralities,²
"While I his flock to virtue steer,
"For hard earn'd thirty pounds a year;

336

Detail from "The Clerical Alphabet" showing a pluralist with one living on his head and two more tucked under his arms, Richard Newton, 1795. British Museum. The caption reads, "P Was a Pluralist ever a craving."

¹ **if the foe's too strong...pursue:** The general meaning is that people ought to adopt an attitude of dignified resignation in the face of misfortune. The metaphor of the honorable retreat, however, is rather cryptic. Syntax may be alluding to his practice of walking away from quarrels and ignoring insults and jeers, rather than stooping to the level of his persecutors by arguing back.

² **pluralities:** Additional church livings. Some clergymen were fortunate enough to hold multiple livings, a significant financial benefit. In most cases, "pluralists" would do the work of one of their livings and hire a curate or curates to serve the others. While pluralism certainly contributed to the divide in the Anglican clergy between the haves and the have-nots (as satirists were quick to point out), not all pluralists were rich. Some church livings paid very little, and a clergyman might need more than one to cobble together even a middling income.

For her part, Austen seems to have been untroubled by the practice of pluralism. Catherine Morland's (NA) father, a respectable man, has "two good livings" (I.1), and Edmund Bertram (MP), a model clergyman, eventually comes into a pair of livings himself. Austen's tolerant attitude is not surprising given that she and her family benefited from the practice: her father held the adjacent livings of Steventon and Deane.

"A flock, alas! he does not know,
"But by the fleeces they bestow;—[1]
"I, who have borne the heaviest fate
"That doth on Learning's toil await;
"For, when a man's the sport of Heaven,
"To keep a school the fellow's driven;
"(Nor when that thought gay Lucian spoke,
"He did not mean to crack a joke[†];—)
"I still man's dignity maintain'd,
"And tho' I felt, I ne'er complain'd.

"If life's a farce, mere children's play,
"Let the rich trifle it away:
"I cannot model mine by theirs;
"For mine has been a life of cares.

"Men with superior minds endow'd
"May soar above the titled crowd,[2]
"Tho' 'tis their humble lot to dwell
"In calm Retirement's distant cell:
"Or by Dame Fortune poorly fed,
"To call on Science* for their bread—[3]
"To lead the life that I have led.
"Tho' neither wealth nor state is given;
"They're the Nobility of Heaven.

"In its caprice a Sovereign's pow'r
"May make a Noble ev'ry hour:
"A King may only speak the word,
"And some rich blockhead struts a Lord:
"But all the scepter'd pow'rs that live
"Cannot one ray of genius give.
"Heaven and Nature must combine
"To make the flame of genius shine;

210

215

220

225

230

235

[1] **A flock...bestow:** Syntax's rector has no dealings with his parishioners other than to collect their tithes (fleeces).

[2] **titled crowd:** Those with aristocratic titles.

[3] **call on Science for their bread:** Rely on their intellectual toils to earn a (scant) living.

[†] Lucian says, that, when the gods make a man the object of their sportive persecution, they turn him into a schoolmaster. Such an one as Doctor Syntax was may think that the sarcastic Greek is in the right; but the Masters of Eton, Westminster, and Winchester, are, probably, of a different opinion. [Combe's note. Eton, Westminster, and Winchester were elite schools for the sons of gentlemen. For more on Lucian's joke about schoolmasters, see note 2 on page 271.]

"Of wealth regardless, or degree,[1]
"It may be sent to shine on me.

"Learning, I thank thee;—Tho' by toil
"And the pale lamp of midnight oil
"I gain'd thy smiles; tho' many a year
"Fortune refus'd my heart to cheer;
"By the inspiring laurels crown'd,
"I oft could smile while Fortune frown'd.
"Beguil'd by thee, I oft forgot
"My uncomb'd wig and rusty coat:
"When coals were dear, and low my fire,
"I warm'd myself with Homer's lyre:[2]
"Or, in a dearth of ale benign,
"I eager quaff'd the stream divine,
"Which flows in Virgil's ev'ry line.
"To save me from domestic brawls,
"I thunder'd Tully[3] to the walls.
"When nought I did could Dolly please,
"I laugh'd with Aristophanes:[4]
"And oft has Grizzle, on my way,
"Heard from me Horace smart and gay.

"Tho' with the world I struggl'd hard,
"Virtue my best, but sole, reward;
"When my whole income would but keep
"The wolf from preying on the sheep;[5]
"Ne'er would I change my classic* store
"For all that Crœsus had, or more;
"Nor would I lose what I have read,
"Tho' tempting Fortune, in its stead,
"Would show'r down mitres* on my head.[6]

"*Bear* and *forbear*,—an adage true
"As human wisdom ever drew.
"That this I've practis'd through my life,
"I have a witness in my wife;
"For, tho' she'd sometimes snarl and scold,
"I never would a parly[7] hold;

240 [1] **degree:** Social rank.

[2] **When coals...lyre:** When Syntax had no
245 money even for coal, he took comfort in the works of Homer.
[3] **Tully:** Cicero
250 (106-43 BCE), Roman statesman and orator.
[4] **Aristophanes:** Athenian comic playwright (446-386
255 BCE).
[5] **keep...sheep:** Keep the wolf from the door, that is,
260 barely ward off starvation.
[6] **When my whole income...head:** "Even when I barely made enough
265 to avoid starvation, I still prized my learning over wealth or advancement." Crœsus was an ancient king
270 legendary for his wealth. The mitre was symbolic of a bishop's office.
[7] **parley:**
275 Discussion.

"And when she, tho' but seldom swore,
"I check'd the oath, but said no more,[1]
"And all returning taunts forbore.
"I dress'd my spirit from the pages
"Of learned Dons* and ancient sages: 280
"But my lean form was never smart
"From barber's skill or tailor's art;
"So that my figure was a joke
"For all the town and country folk.
"But this my feelings never griev'd 285
"And I with smiles their smiles receiv'd:
"I ne'er retorted, like a fool,
"Their inoffensive ridicule.

    "So that my Dolly's clothes were fine,
"She never car'd a doit* for mine: 290
"So that, on ev'ry Sabbath-day,
"She could appear in trappings gay,
"And in a pew her form display,
"She'd let me walk about the town,
"Till my black coat was almost brown. 295
"But she was, as I can't deny,
"The soul of notability.[2]
"She struggled hard to save the pelf*;
"And, tho' she might except herself,
"I do believe, upon my word, 300
"To all things Syntax was preferr'd.

    "*Bear* and *forbear*, I've thought and said,
"Is part of ev'ry Parson's trade;
"And what he doth to other's preach
"He should by his example teach.
"Whene'er the scoffer trotted by, 305
"I ne'er have turn'd an angry eye:
"Nay, when of Wealth I've been the jeer,
"When petty Pride let loose a sneer,
"I never fail'd the joke to join, 310
"And paid them off in classic* coin.[3]

[1] **when she…no more:** Syntax would not reply when his wife scolded him, except to rebuke her for swearing (which she rarely did).

[2] **notability:** Competence and efficiency in household matters (OED).

[3] **classic coin:** As a kind of private joke, Syntax would sometimes reply to his taunters with a garbled allusion to antiquity, and then laugh to himself when they betrayed their ignorance by failing to detect the error. On the next page he gives two examples of this.

"My Rector, fat as fat can be,
"With prebend stall,[1] and livings three,
"Once told me if I kept my riches
"Within the pockets of my breeches,
"To make them of materials stout,
"Or else the weight would wear them out.
"O, with what base irrev'rent glee
"He chose to mock my poverty!
"Yet I did not my cloth* disgrace
"By squirting spittle in his face;
"But answer'd, from St. Paul, in Greek,
"And bid him the quotation seek
"In Pliny:—When the purse-proud* brute
"Nodded assent—and then was mute.[2]

"The Oilman[3] there, in that fine house,
"Who boasts th' escutcheons[4] of his spouse,
"Soon after he had left off trade,
"Lov'd some great, noble Lady's maid,
"Who by my Lord had been betray'd:[5]
"To Hymen's Fane the fair he led,
"And gave the claim to half his bed.
"She talks of Duchesses by dozens,
"As if they were her cater-cousins.[6]
"He once said, 'Doctor, do you see?
"Let's hear what is your pedigree;'—
"When I, with rev'rence due, reply'd,
"I am not to the great allied;
"But yet I've heard my grandame say,
"(Tho' many a year has pass'd away
"Since she is gone where all must go,
"Whether they are or high or low,)
"That one of our forefathers bore
"A place of state in days of yore;
"That he was butler, or purveyor,
"Or trumpeter to some Lord Mayor,
"When *Carthaginian Hannibal*
"Din'd with his Lordship at Guildhall:
"That great man being forc'd to come
"By order of the Pope of Rome,

[1] **prebend stall:** A cathedral position that offered high pay in exchange for little work.
[2] **But answer'd... mute:** In other words, the rector, who should be well-educated, cannot even tell Greek from Latin (the language in which the Roman author Pliny [d. 79] wrote).
[3] **Oilman:** Seller of lamp oil.
[4] **escutcheons:** Coat of arms, here used ironically to refer to the social pretensions of a mere Lady's maid.
[5] **by my Lord... betray'd:** The oilman's wife was seduced by her master, who, to hush the matter up, likely arranged her marriage to the oilman.
[6] **cater-cousins:** Intimate friends.

315
320
325
330
335
340
345
350

341

"To end some quarrel 'tween the houses
"That bore the pale and crimson roses.'
"The oilman said, 'It might be so:
"And 'twas a monstrous while ago.'[1]

    " 'Tis thus I give these fools a poke,   355
"And foil their tauntings with a joke;
"For that man has no claim to sense,
"Whose blood boils at impertinence.
"Were I to scourge each fool I meet,
"I ne'er must go into the street;   360
"I ne'er my bearded chin must pop
"Into the chatt'ring barber's shop.

    "*Bear* and *forbear*—a maxim true
"As erring mortals ever knew.
"But things are chang'd; new scenes appear,   365
"My mind to soothe, my heart to cheer,
"The Pow'rs above my fate regard,
"And give my patience its reward.
"But while I trod Life's rugged road,
"While troubles haunted my abode,   370
"With not an omen to protend[2]
"That toil would cease, that things would mend,
"I did to my allotment bow,
"And smok'd my pipe as I do now.

    "Hail, social tube![3] thou foe to care!   375
"Companion of my easy chair!
"Form'd not, with cold and Stoic art,
"To harden, but to soothe, the heart!
"For BACON, a much wiser man,
"Than any of the Stoic clan,   380
"Declares the pow'r to controul
"Each fretful impulse of the soul;
"And SWIFT has said (no common name,
"On the large sphere of mortal fame)
"That he who daily smokes two pipes   385
"The tooth-ach never has—nor gripes.[4]

[1] **But yet I've heard my grandame say… ago:**
A reference to the War of the Roses and another instance of Syntax paying his mockers back in "classic coin." The "great man" sent by the Pope to negotiate an end to the conflict was the Italian prelate Francesco Coppini (d. 1464). Hannibal (c. 247-183 BCE), the ancient Carthaginian general, obviously had nothing to do with the matter. The mix-up goes unnoticed by the oilman, showing that, for all his pride in his wife's (illusory) pedigree, he really knows nothing of history.

"A Smoking Club," Henry William Bunbury, 1792. Lewis Walpole Library.

[2] **protend:** Portend.
[3] **social tube:** Tobacco pipe—here called social because it promotes kindly feelings in Syntax toward his fellow humans.
[4] **Form'd not…gripes:** The stoic philosophers of antiquity taught that humans should adopt a stern toughness in the face of adversity. Syntax, on the contrary, turns to his creature comforts—especially smoking. As support for his approach, he cites the natural philosopher Sir Francis Bacon (1561-1626), who wrote that "Tobacco comforteth the Spirits" (*Sylva Sylvarum*, X.927). He also refers to a comment on smoking supposedly made by the satirist Jonathan Swift (1667-1745), though we have not been able to trace that reference.

Austen offers a hilariously condensed account of the War of the Roses in her satirical History of England: "There were several Battles between the Yorkists and Lancastrians, in which the former (as they ought) usually conquered." Her purpose, she says, is not to give information but "to vent my Spleen against, and shew my Hatred to all those people whose parties or principles do not suit with mine" (Juv. 178). Austen's joke about the War of the Roses is a good deal more layered than Combe's. Is she making fun of prejudiced historians? The foolish quarrels of kings and nobles? Her own tendency to form fiery opinions?

Edward IV (1442-83), a key player in the War of the Roses, imagined as a lout by Cassandra Austen in *The History of England.*

"With thee, in silence calm and still,
"My Dolly's tones, no longer shrill,
"Tho' meant to speak reproach and sneer,
"Pass in soft cadence to my ear.   390
"Calm Contemplation comes with thee,
"And the mild maid, Philosophy!
"Lost in the thoughts which you suggest
"To the full counsel of my breast,
"My books all slumb'ring on the shelf,   395
"I thus can commune with myself;
"Thus to myself my thoughts repeat,
"Thus moralize on what is great;
"And, ev'ry selfish wish subdu'd,
"Cherish the sense of what is good.   400

  "While I thy grateful breath inhale,
"I see the cheering cup of ale,
"Benignant juice! Lethean stream!¹
"That aids the fond, oblivious dream,
"Which fits the freshen'd mind to bear   405
"The burden of returning care

  "Let Pride's loose sons prolong the night
"In Bacchanalian delight;²
"I envy not their jovial noise,
"Their mirth, and mad, intemp'rate joys.   410
"The luscious wines that Spain can boast,
"Or grow on Lusitanian coast,
"Ne'er fill my cups:—† Repast divine!
"The home-brew'd beverage³ is mine.
"Thus, cheer'd with hope of happier days,   415
"My grateful lips declare thy praise.

¹ **Lethean stream:** Syntax compares ale to the river Lethe, one of the four rivers of Hades, which grants forgetfulness to those who drink from it.

² **Bacchanalian delight:** Drunken revelry.

³ **home-brew'd beverage:** Syntax declares his preference for simple home-brew'd ale over fine wine.

---

† ———Mea nec Falernæ
  Temperant vites, neque Formiani
      Pocula colles.   HOR. L. i. Od. xx.

[Combe's note. In English: "my goblets hold no flavor of wine from the vines of Falernus or Formia's hills." (Horace, *Odes* 1.20.)]

"How oft I've felt, in adverse hour,
"The comforts of thy soothing pow'r!
"Nor will I now forget my friend,
"When my foul fortune seems to mend;— 420
"Yes, I would smoke as I do now,
"Tho' a proud mitre* deck'd my brow.

   "Hail, social tube! thou foe to care!
"Companion of my easy chair!
"While, as the curling fumes arise, 425
"They seem th' ascending sacrifice
"That's offer'd by my gratitude.
"To the great Father of the good."

   More had he spoke; but, lo! the dame
With the appointed Haslet came: 430
When Syntax having bless'd the meat,
Sat down to the luxuriant treat.
"And now," he said, "My dear 'twill be
"As good as Burgundy¹ to me,
"If you will tell me what has pass'd 435
"Since we embrac'd each other last."
"O," she replied, "my dearest love,
"Things in their usual order move.
"Pray take a piece of this fine liver:—
"The Rector is as proud as ever. 440
"I'll help you, dear, to this or that:
"Let me supply your lean with fat.—
"I thought the oilman's wife would burst
"When in this dress she saw me first.
"It was at church she show'd her airs: 445
"My bonnet spoil'd the woman's pray'rs.
"Your knife is blunt; here, take the steel:
"Cut deep, the haslet cannot feel.—
"There's Lawyer Graspall got a beating,
"As you may well suppose, for cheating: 450
"Our honest butcher trounc'd him well,
"As the Attorney's bones can tell.
"He order'd home a rump of beef;
"And, when it came, the hungry thief,

¹ **Burgundy:** A fine French wine.

345

"Having shav'd off a pound or two,   455
"Return'd it, for it would not do.
"The fraud discover'd, words arose,
"And they were follow'd soon by blows:
"When, as he well deserv'd, the sinner
"Got a good threshing, for his dinner."   460

 Said Syntax, "If I had a son—"
"Pooh!" she reply'd, "you have not done:—
"You still, I hope, can pick a bit,[1]
"And no excuse will I admit.
" 'Tis long since we've together been,   465
"Since we've each other's faces seen:
"And, surely, I'm not such a fright
"To make you lose your appetite."
"But," he continu'd, "if a boy
"Were, my dear Doll, to crown our joy,   470
"I'd sooner far the stripling see
"The heir of dire Adversity
"Than to an attorney bind him,
"Where old Nick is sure to find him."
She added, "Yes, with naked feet   475
"I'd sooner have him pace the street:
"But ere you let your Choler[2] burst,
"Let's have the little Urchin first."

 The Doctor thought his jolly wife
Ne'er look'd so handsome in her life.   480
Her voice he thought grown wond'rous sweet—
To him a most uncommon treat:
So much in tune, it made him long
To hear it quaver in a song.
"Come, sing, my charmer," Syntax said,   485
And thus the simp'ring* dame obey'd:—

 SONG.

 Haste to Dolly! haste away!
 This is thine and Hymen's day!

[1] **You still...can pick a bit:** Mrs. Syntax appears to be expressing confidence in her husband's potency.

[2] **Choler:** Bodily humour associated with anger.

Bid her thy soft bondage wear;
Bid her for Love's rites prepare.   490
Let the nymphs with many a flower
Deck the sacred nuptial bower:
Thither lead the lovely fair,
And let Cupid too be there.
This is thine and Hymen's day!   495
Haste to Dolly! haste away!¹

Thus pass'd the time; the morrow came,
And Mrs. Syntax was the same:
But when (for 'twas not done before)
She heard the Doctor's story o'er,   500
With all the hopes he had in store,
By joy, by vanity, subdu'd,
Her warm embraces she renew'd;
While he, delighted, fondly kiss'd
Those hands which, form'd into a fist,   505
Had often warn'd his eyes and nose
To turn from their tremendous blows.

At length, of golden ease possest,
No angry words, no frowns, molest;
No symptoms of domestic strife   510
Disturb'd their very alter'd life,
For she out-dress'd the oilman's wife:
And he could now relieve the poor,
Who sought his charitable door.

Tho' to each virtue often blind,   515
The world to wealth is ever kind;
For, lo! a certain tell-tale dame,
Yclep'd² and known as *Mistress Fame*,
Had told to all the country round
That Syntax, for a thousand pound,   520
Had sold a learned book he wrote;
That now he was a man of note,
By Lords protected; and that one
Would make him tutor to his son;

¹ **Haste…away:**
Mrs. Syntax's song
calls on a husband
to tend to his bride
on their wedding
night (Hymen is the
Greek god of
weddings). The
invitation to Syntax
here is clear.

² **Yclep'd:** Named.

347

So that, whenever he went forth,   525
All paid their homage to his worth;
While it became the fond desire
Of ev'ry neighb'ring rural 'Squire
To send his hopeful boys to share
The favour of the Doctor's care.[1]   530

   But all these views soon found an end;
A packet came, and from a friend;
From 'Squire Worthy, who resides
On Keswick's bold and woody sides.
The wond'ring postman made it known,   535
As he pass'd on, to all the town:
For such a letter ne'er had been
Within his little circle seen:
Nay, by the fiat of the post,
It more than seven and six-pence[2] cost.   540
The Doctor star'd—while Ma'am, unwilling,
Slowly dealt forth each ling'ring shilling.
"Ne'er mind your silver," Syntax said,
"The postman, Deary, must be paid:
"And now these papers I behold,   545
"I see they're worth their weight in gold.
"Come, sit you down, and take good heed
"To what I am about to read.

  "*My Rev'rend Sir,*
               "Our Vicar's dead;   *549*
"And I have nam'd you in his stead.   550
"I often wish'd his neck he'd break,
"Or tumble drunk into the Lake;
"So, you must know, the poaching hound
"Fulfill'd one wish—for he is drown'd.
"Unfit for preaching or for praying,   555
"His merit lay in cudgel-playing:[3]
"And he preferr'd, to saying prayers,
"The laying springes[4] for the hares.

  "You will perceive I keep my word,
"And to this church you're now preferr'd: 560

¹ **While it… Doctor's care:** Tutoring the sons of the gentry would be a step up for Syntax, both in pay and prestige. His current pupils, as he reveals in Canto XXIII, are the sons of tradesmen.

² **seven and six-pence:** Seven-and-a-half shillings, about $54 in 2024 money. The postage is high because the letter has traveled far and because it contains a large packet of papers. This cost falls on the Syntaxes because recipients, not senders, typically paid for postage.

The gentry are eager to send their sons to Syntax in part because of a rumor that a lord intends to do so. As it happens, the tutoring career of the Rev. George Austen, Jane's father, may have benefited in a similar way. His second pupil, John Charles Wallop, was the eldest son of the Earl of Portsmouth (Hussain, 8- 9). Though the boy did not stay long, his high status may have helped George Austen attract other pupils from among the gentry.

³ **cudgel-playing:** Fighting or dueling with cudgels.
⁴ **springes:** Traps.

The Edinburgh and London Royal Mail, John Frederick Herring, Sr., 1838. Berger Collection. This is likely the route Squire Worthy's letter would have taken.

"By ev'ry legal act and deed,
"To Parson Hairbrain you succeed.
"The papers which you now receive
"A right and full possession give.
"You, Sir, may make the living clear   565
"Above three hundred pounds a year;
"And if you will but condescend
"To my son's learning to attend,—
"If you'll direct his studious hour,
"I'll add some fifty pounds or more: 570
"And soon we hope that you will cheer
"The parish with your presence here.
"Miss Worthy and her sister join
"Their kindest compliments to mine;
"And to your prayers I recommend   575
"Your faithful and admiring friend,
            "JONATHAN WORTHY."

The dame exclaim'd, "My Grecian boy,[1]
"I know not how to tell my joy.
"This is the height of my desire: 580
" 'Squire Worthy is a worthy 'Squire."

[1] **My Grecian boy:** In other words, "My darling scholar."

"Ha, ha!" said Syntax, "O, the fun!
"Why, Dolly, you have made a pun.
"But still a pun I do detest,
" 'Tis such a paltry, humbug jest;   585
"They who've least wit can make them best.
"But you may frisk and pun away;
"I'm sure I cannot teach to-day;
"So tell the boys to go and play.
"Thank Heav'n, that toil and trouble pass'd,   590
"My holidays are come at last!"

At length, the busy school resign'd,
They both prepar'd to leave behind
A place, which little had to give
Than the hard struggle how to live.   595

For the long journey to prepare,
Syntax had bought a one-horse chair,
With harness for the grizzle mare.
Ralph would not from his master part,
But trudg'd beside the farmer's cart   600
That bore the Doctor's books and chattels,
With Madam's clothes and fiddle-faddles.[1]
The cook upon the baggage rode,
And added to the weighty load;
For she, kind maid, was fully bent   605
To go wherever *Ralpho* went.
The Doctor walk'd about to tell
The day, when he should say farewell.
And they who had disdain'd before
To pass the threshold of his door;   610
When Syntax gave his farewell treat,—
Sought that same door to drink and eat.
The neighbours now, who never yet
Knew his great worth, his loss regret:
And Madam, on whom no good word   615
Had been throughout the town preferr'd,
Was now a most delightful creature,
Of temper mild,—of winning feature.
The ringers, who, for many a year,
Refus'd his natal day to cheer;   620
Now made the bells, in woeful zeal,
Chime forth the dumb, lamenting peal.[2]
The time soon came, when, quite light-hearted,
The Doctor and his spouse departed;
And as they journey'd on their way,   625
They did not fail to pass a day
With the good Doctor's early friend,
The kind and learned *Dickey Bend:*
Nor did he think it a delay,
The Christian Vicar to repay,   630
And 'neath his roof a night to stay;
To add for former kindness shown,
His Dolly's greetings to his own.
At York they form'd the pleasant party,
For a whole week, of *'Squire Hearty.*   635

[1] **fiddle-faddles:** Trifles, trinkets.

[2] **The ringers… peal:** The village bell-ringers never rang the bells on Syntax's birthday, but they ring them now to mourn his leaving.

351

A few more days, and, lo! the Lake[1]
Did on th' enraptur'd vision break:
And, rising 'mid the tufted trees,
Syntax his sacred structure sees,
Whose tow'r appear'd in ancient pride,   640
With the warm Vic'rage by its side.
"At length, dear wife," he said, "we're come
"To our appointed, tranquil home."

   The courteous people lin'd the way,
And their rude, untaught homage pay: 645
The foremost of th' assembled crowd,
The fat Exciseman,[2] humbly bow'd.
"Welcome," he said, "to SOMMERDEN!"[3]
The Clerk[4] stood by, and cry'd "*Amen!*"
Grizzle dash'd boldly through the gate,   650
Where the kind 'Squire and Ladies wait,
With kind embrace, with heart and hand,
To cheer them into CUMBERLAND.[5]
The bells rang loud, the boys huzza'd;
The bonfire was in order laid: 655
The villagers their zeal display;
And ale and crackers close the day.

   Syntax, whom all desir'd to please,
Enjoy'd his hours of learned ease;
Nor did he fail to preach and pray,   660
To brighter worlds to point the way;
While his dear spouse was never seen
To shew ill-nature or the spleen;
And faithful Grizzle now no more
Or drew a chaise*, or rider bore.   665

   Thus the good Parson, horse, and wife,
Led a most comfortable life.

¹ **the Lake:** Presumably Derwentwater, on whose banks the town of Keswick lies.

"View of Skiddaw and Derwentwater," Joseph Farrington, c. 1780. YCBA.

² **Exciseman:** Official responsible for collecting the excise tax.

³ **SOMMERDEN:** Syntax's fictional parish.

⁴ **Clerk:** The clergyman's lay assistant.

⁵ **CUMBERLAND:** The county that contains Keswick.

If Cumberland is Syntax's ideal county, then Derbyshire, home of Pemberley and its environs, must be Elizabeth Bennet's (PP). Both characters have a keen appreciation for the picturesque, and both are blessed with an ending that allows them to live amidst natural beauty. More practically, both endings, and the endings of all Austen's novels, see the main character established in a new and financially secure home. This was a blessing that Austen, who experienced years of transience, and Combe, who wrote most of this poem from debtor's prison, could both appreciate.

DOCTOR SYNTAX Taking Possession of his Living.

SUGGESTIONS FOR FURTHER READING

The introductory materials and annotations in this book treat a wide range of topics and draw on an equally wide ranges of sources. The reader will find a full list of those sources in the bibliography. We thought it would be useful, however, to offer the reader a much smaller list of suggestions pertaining to the major topics of the book. Each of the works discussed below will provide a thorough introduction to one of those topics, and will open up many avenues for further exploration as well.

- **William Combe:** There is only one full-length biography of William Combe, but thankfully it is an excellent one: Harlan Ware Hamilton's *Doctor Syntax: A Silhouette of William Combe, Esq.* **(Chatto & Windus, 1969)**. Combe, a rather secretive man, was a very difficult subject for early sketchers of his life. Their accounts tend to be riddled with errors and inaccuracies (for instance, that he was born in Bristol or that he attended Oxford—both untrue). Many of these inaccuracies continue to be recycled in modern biographical snippets. Hamilton's account corrects a great deal of the record and is the proper starting point for any serious study of Combe. The "Biographical Essay" in this volume is another valuable resource. While deeply indebted to Hamilton's work, it also builds on it in several important ways.

- **Thomas Rowlandson:** There is a robust body of work on the illustrator of *Doctor Syntax*. The book we found most helpful was *Regarding Thomas Rowlandson, 1757-1827* **(Hogarth Arts, 2010)**, by Matthew and James Payne. In addition to a deeply researched account of Rowlandson's life, the book contains well over a hundred illustrations, thirty two of them in full color.

- **Rudolph Ackermann:** John Ford's outstanding biography, *Rudolph Ackermann & The Regency World* **(Warnham Books, 2018)**, is an absorbing exploration of the Regency's most entrepreneurial publisher. Ackermann's interests and acquaintance were so wide ranging that his biography reads like a history of the entire age. Ackermann is most famous today for the high-quality prints he published: our sense of what the Regency *looked* like—its fashions, buildings, modes of transportation, amusements—is largely thanks to him. It is appropriate, then, that his biography is one of the most beautifully illustrated we have seen, not just of Ackermann, but of anyone. Ford's book is, however, hard to find. If you have access to a university library, you can probably acquire it through an interlibrary loan service, even if your university does not own a copy.

- **The Picturesque:** In this case, we recommend going back to the source. Combe's and Rowlandson's satire is focused on the writings of William Gilpin—early theorist and popularizer of the Picturesque. Jane Austen herself was "enamoured" of Gilpin, according to her brother, and her work shows a thorough familiarity with his theories. We offer an overview of those theories in the Contextual Essay in this book, but if the reader wishes to learn more, we recommend starting with Gilpin's *Three Essays: On Picturesque Beauty; On Picturesque Travel; and On Sketching Landcape* **(R. Blamire, 1792)**. It is a quick read and freely available on Google Books.

- **Curates and the Church of England:** Doctor Syntax is a *curate* who serves a rural *parish,* the *benefice* of which is held by an absentee *rector* who is also a *pluralist.* In the end Syntax becomes a *vicar* after being *preferred* to the *living* of Sommerden. As those two sentences show, Regency church language can be difficult for non-experts to follow! In our opinion, the best introduction (by far) to church matters in Austen's day is Brenda Cox's *Fashionable Goodness: Christianity in Jane Austen's England* **(Topaz Cross Books, 2022).** Cox covers the organization of the Church of England, the work of the country clergy, and the major religious movements and controversies of the day, drawing illustrations and examples from Austen's life and work along the way.

NOTE ON THE TEXT

The text of the poem in this book is drawn from the third edition of *The Tour of Doctor Syntax in Search of the Picturesque*, published by Rudolph Ackermann in 1813. We chose this edition for two reasons. First, it was the largest and fastest-selling edition published during Combe's lifetime, and thus, one assumes, the most widely read. Second, it was the last edition to which Combe made any significant changes. To fellow Janeites, we will add: this is the edition Austen was most likely to have read, though any of the first five are possibilities.

The tale of Doctor Syntax first appeared in print from 1809-1811 in Ackermann's *Poetical Magazine* under the title *The Schoolmaster's Tour*. For most of the periodical run, Combe was writing by the seat of his pants: Ackermann would send an illustration or two to Combe's rooms in King's Bench debtor's prison, and Combe would dash off some verses to accompany them, without knowing what illustrations would come next. There was no revising with the benefit of hindsight; no adjustment of the earlier parts of the story to square them with the later parts.

When Ackermann decided to bring out a book edition of *Doctor Syntax* in 1812, Combe undertook a substantial revision of the whole, especially of the first few cantos. He also added a canto near the end (Canto XXV). He made further changes for the second edition, and added a few final adjustments for the third. For example, in the third edition the hero is introduced as "Good Syntax" instead of "Old Syntax"—a change that signals the final consummation of Combe's vision of Doctor Syntax, developed gradually over the periodical run, as a kind-hearted eccentric rather than a curmudgeonly and pedantic nincompoop. Changes introduced in the 4th through the 9th editions consist mostly of small-scale stylistic tweaks and corrections of errors.

In editing the text, we have preserved Combe's spelling and punctuation as much as possible and confined ourselves to the correction of clear errors. When possible, we used the ninth edition to correct the third. When the error persisted in the ninth edition, we corrected it on our own. On very rare occasions, we made a change simply to improve the sense or style of the line, but only if the change was already reflected in both the second and ninth editions, which would suggest that it was Combe's intent all along, and that the difference in the third edition was a printer's error.

In the text, a left-facing brace (}) indicates a group of three rhyming lines (in general, the poem is in rhyming couplets). This notation was used in every edition of the poem published during Combe's lifetime.

LIST OF EMENDATIONS

Editors' Note: Emendations marked with an asterisk (*) were made with the editors' best judgment. All other emendations were made using the 9th edition (see Note on the Text).

*p. 3: jocosins → jocosius
I.123: IT" → IT
II.72: "He said → He said
*II.91: sketch? → sketch?"
II.138: will, → will
*III.162: purlieu → purlieus
IV.44: lay. → lay!"
IV.69: Sytax → Syntax
IV.71: SYNTAX → SYNTAX.
IV.84: enormons → enormous
IV.107: toast. → toast."
IV.133: tail? → tail?"
V.46: disgrace, → disgrace.
VI.45: you'd → "you'd
VI.67: so → to
VI.92: day. → day."
*VI.149: *aqua-tint'* → *aqua-tint*
VI.205: away," → away."
VI.222: twould → 'twould
VII.46: great. → great."
VII.103: starves, → starves.
VII.215: spash'd → splash'd
VII.271: Thetis → Thetis'
VII.274: faculties → senses did
VII.295: good → so good
VIII.111: pound. → pound."
IX.29: rhe → the
*IX.99: e'er → ere
IX.174: Ghost → Ghosts
IX.179: view. → view."
IX.189: chamber → chambers
X.110: *more.* → *more."*
X.150: mind. → mind."
X.157: Grizzles' → Grizzle's
X.204: Zounds → "Zounds
XI.7: chequer'd → checquer'd
XI.29: writ → write
XI.114: fashion, → fashion

XI.167: confouud → confound
*XI.176: e'er → ere
XII.229: you → your
XII.242: on. → on."
XIII.69: fortnne → fortune
XIII.124: empty. → empty;
XIV.34: kite, → kite
XIV.54: growing → glowing
XIV.92: Sooths → Soothes
XIV.121: eye's → eyes
XIV.223: SQUIRE → 'SQUIRE
XV.144: "The → The
XV.252: ostler, → ostler
*XVI.38: feign → fain
XVI.60: I → "I
XVI.115: rout. → rout,
XVI.127: and with, → and, with
XVI.157: school. → school,
XVI.182: tell → "tell
XVI.212: wages → wagers
XVI.255: Sir, → Sir,"
XVI.255: distress'd → "distress'd
XVI.291: bare → bear
XVI.293: must → "must
XVII.39: keeps → kept
XVII.65: flow. → flow."
*XVII.147: villains → villain's
XVII.246: Sir, → Sir,"
XVII.276: minstresly → minstrelsy
XVIII.175: way: → way:"
XVIII.179: business → bus'ness
XVIII.212: "And → And
XVIII.235: Iu → In
XIX.20: the → th'
XIX.61: groupe → group
XIX.81: was → what
XIX.84: dock. → dock;
*XIX.167: e'er → ere

XIX.217: councell'd → counsell'd
XIX.221: He'll → "He'll
XIX.222: And → "And
XIX.240: builds → "builds
XIX.253: Livorpool → Liverpool
XIX.340: do → no
XIX.344: same? → same?"
*XIX.360: I know → "I know
XIX.370: useful, → useful
*XIX.378: Lorship → Lordship
XX.8-9:
While the gilt spur on either heel
In equal rounds, their points reveal.

↓

While the gilt spur, well-arm'd with steel,
Was [corrected from "Is" in 9th ed.] seen
    to shine on either heel.
XX.73: By all → Among
XX.127: there's → "there's
XX.128: it's → its
*XX.184: him. → him."
XX.218: straw, → straw.
XX.219: is → "is
*XX.247: try'd → try'd;
*XX.253: carry'd:— → carry'd:—"
XXI.152: tranquil, → tranquil
XXI.153: Tis → 'Tis
XXI.231: Bur → But
XXI.250: lost. → lost,
XXI.263: loftiest, → loftiest
XXI.271: should, → should
XXI.319: bare → bear
XXI.325: bare → bear
XXI.367: SQUIRE → 'SQUIRE
XXII.80: Or → Of
XXII.81: gives → gives,
XXII.182: on's → our
*XXII.308: "To → To
XXII.309: here:— → here:"
XXII.323: *Row.* → *Row.*"
*XXII.356: dont → don't
XXIII.74-5:
But truth alone my patron moves,
Whose gen'rous deeds his friendship
    proves.

↓

Truth can alone my patron move,
Whose gen'rous deeds his promise
    prove.
XXIII.103: ghaftly → ghastly
XXIII.119: pockot → pocket
XXIII.178: lot → lot,
XXIII.246: tradesmens' → tradesmen's
XXIII.298: need, → need
XXIII.303: rest, → rest.
XXIII.305: be blame → be to blame
XXIII.363: to-morrow, → to-morrow?
XXIII.379: gold. → gold;
XXIII.382: vaccilating → vacilating
XXIII.441: write. → write,
XXIII.512: Now → Now,
XXIII.515: and → "and
XXIV.9: hear'd → heard
XXIV.12: sacred → sacred head
*XXIV.120: other's → others'
XXIV.135: waited, → waited.
XXIV.171: produced → produc'd
XXIV.201: Shakespear → Shakespeare
XXIV.220: shrew'd → shrewd
XXIV.263: *adhue* → *adhuc*
XXIV.280: smile. → smile."
XXIV.313: sit. → sit
XXV.19: The → Th'
*XXV.111: e'er → ere
XXV.148: days → day's
XXV.174: Arithmetic. → Arithmetic;
XXV.214: compare. → compare?
XXV.235: do → did
XXV.309: Greeks → Greeks,
XXV.313: self → self-same
XXV.462: all. → all."
XXVI.91: Syntaz → Syntax
*XXVI.154: other's → others'
XXVI.242: thee? → thee;
*XXVI.260: me from → from me
XXVI.292: trapping → trappings
XXVI.412: grown → grow
*XXVI.477: e'er → ere
XXVI.488: day? → day!

NOTE ON THE ILLUSTRATIONS

This edition of *The Tour of Doctor Syntax in Search of the Picturesque* brings together, for the first time, both sets of illustrations that accompanied the poem in the nineteenth century: the original hand-colored aquatints based on pen-and-ink designs by Thomas Rowlandson, and the later wood engravings of Alfred Crowquill.

The aquatints are certainly the more important of the two. They give us the original Syntax, the one dreamed up by Rowlandson. Indeed, so central were Rowlandson's designs to the tale that Combe's verses were produced to accompany them, not the other way around. In this book, as in the original, each of them occupies a full page.

The specific processes used in the 1810s to create these images mean that, much to the delight of collectors, no two *Doctor Syntax* aquatints are exactly alike. If you were to lay a second and a third edition side-by-side and

---

WHAT IS AN AQUATINT?

Aquatinting is a method of etching copper plates that produces the effect of shade or tone in the paper prints (called aquatints) taken from them. Unlike manual shading techniques, such as hatching (small lines) or stipple (dots), aquatinting creates smooth, even regions of tone that resemble a wash of diluted ink—thus the name, **aquatint**.

Were you to examine those regions of tone more closely, you would see, not solid gray, but instead a fine, irregular network of black lines. This network is created by treating the original copper plate in a particular way. After the main design is etched onto the plate, the parts to be shaded are sprinkled with a powdered resin, which is then heated to make it adhere. The whole plate is then submerged in acid. The acid bites into the copper in the tiny gaps between grains of resin, creating a network of minuscule channels. The resin is then scraped off and ink applied. The ink will collect in the channels and, when stamped onto a sheet of paper, will create (to the naked eye) a field of even gray tone.

Some aquatints were left black and white while others, like the ones in this volume, were colored in by hand. When the aquatinting was done well, coloring was quite easy. One could paint over a stretch of forest with a single shade of green watercolor, and the aquatinting would naturally express the lights and darks.

---

turn to the frontispiece, for example, you would notice some marked differences. The times on the clock differ. The bow of Syntax's fiddle is hung in two different ways. In the second edition, the pamphlet at Syntax's feet is inscribed "Every Man his own Farrier" (Syntax is poor and has to economize wherever he can); in the third, that text is gone.

These differences exist because of the relatively short life span of the copper plates used to print illustrations in the period—about 2,500 copies per plate. The original plates, etched by Rowlandson himself, lasted through the periodical run of *The Schoolmaster's Tour* and the first two book editions of *Doctor Syntax*. The third edition required a fresh set of plates, which, though skillfully executed, inevitably differed in subtle ways from the first set. The third edition was so large that the plates wore out again, and new ones had to be etched for the fourth. The sixth edition called for yet another set of plates—with the ultimate result that, during the Regency, there were at least four (sometimes five) printed versions of each *Doctor Syntax* illustration.

Even among prints taken from the same plate, there could be great diversity. The illustrations for the sixth and seventh editions, printed when the copper plates were fresh, are sharp and well-defined. Those of the ninth edition, meanwhile, printed when those same plates were on their last legs, are badly faded. And then, of course, there was the fact that each print was coloured by hand. Some colourists stayed inside the lines; others were messier. Some chose pink for this or that dress; others chose yellow, or left it white to save time.

Given this diversity, we decided not to draw all the images published in this book from the same edition or copy of *Doctor Syntax*. No single one, after all, is representative. Instead, we tried to find the best images from among the ten copies of the book, spanning eight editions, which the Bowes Art and Architecture Library at Stanford generously made available to us. We freely admit that our choices were subjective: sometimes we decided based on the quality of the etching or the aquatinting; sometimes we were struck by the precision or brilliancy of the colouring. Nevertheless, our guiding wish throughout was to give readers a sense of the heights which Regency-era copper-plate printing could reach when a draughtsman of genius like Thomas Rowlandson joined forces with a premier publisher like Rudolph Ackermann. The provenance of the individual images is as follows:[1]

---

[1] The exact copies used, by Stanford catalogue number, were: NC1479 R8 A1 C6 V.1 (1st ed.); NC1479 R8 A1 C62 1812 (2nd ed.); NC1479 R8 A1 C62 1813A (4th ed.); NC1479 R8 A1 C6 1813 V.1 (5th ed.); NC1479 R8 A1 C62 1817 (7th ed.). One

- **1ˢᵗ edition (1812):** *Stopt by Highwaymen; Bound to a Tree by Highwaymen; Copying the Wit of the Window; Loses his Money on the Race Ground at York; Made Free of the Cellar; Drawing after Nature; Rural Sport; Taking Possession of his Living*
- **2ⁿᵈ edition (1812):** *Mistakes a Gentleman's House for an Inn; & Dairy Maid*
- **4ᵗʰ edition (1813):** *Losing his Way; Pursued by a Bull; Meditating on the Tombstones; At a Review; With My Lord; With the Bookseller*
- **5ᵗʰ edition (1813):** Frontispiece; Title Page; *Setting out on his Tour to the Lakes*; Disputing his Bill with the Landlady; Entertained at College; At Liverpool; Reading his Tour; Preaching; At Covent Garden Theatre; The Doctor's Dream*
- **7ᵗʰ edition (1817):** *Tumbling into the Water; Sketching the Lake; Robb'd of his Property; Sells Grizzle; Returned from his Tour*

The second group of illustrations in this volume are the wood engravings supplied by the Victorian comic illustrator Alfred Henry Forrester (pen name Alfred Crowquill) for Ackermann and Co.'s 1838 edition of *Doctor Syntax*. Readers will find them scattered throughout the text, providing light and amusing visual commentary on the action. In the original, they generally appeared near the bottom of the page, with a couplet from the poem serving as a caption. We have tried to preserve their original placement as much as possible, but formatting constraints often required us to move them slightly.

Crowquill's images are largely forgotten today, but they are worthy of inclusion—both on their own merits and for the light they shine on the Victorian reception of *Doctor Syntax*. Syntax fever, which had run high from 1812 into the early 1820s, was little more than a memory when Victoria took the throne in 1837. The most recent edition was almost ten years old, an 1828 "pocket" volume at a bargain price designed to squeeze a few more sales out of the Syntax phenomenon. Ackermann and Co. attributed the decline more to Rowlandson than Combe: "the taste for his broad, luxuriant, but too exaggerated caricature" was out, they thought, but Combe's verses might still have life in them. The recent success of Charles Dickens' *Pickwick Papers* (1837), a work very much in the vein of *Doctor Syntax*, may have provided further encouragement.

Crowquill was brought on board to usher Syntax into the new, more

---

illustration, marked with an asterisk in the list above, was drawn from NC 1479 R8 A1 C62 1813B, another copy of the 5ᵗʰ ed.

serious Victorian era. Crowquill's wood engravings show a milder, more respectable Syntax—usually engaged in conversation or contemplation, rather than in the scenes of chaotic action which were Rowlandson's bread-and-butter. As the Preface punningly put it, while Syntax would always appeal to the gay, he was now also "adapted for the graver."[2]

The experiment was a success. At least four high-quality editions of *Doctor Syntax* with the Crowquill illustrations appeared between 1838 and 1866. Judging from the many copies which are still available in antique book stores, these print-runs were apparently quite large. Interest in Rowlandson's original illustrations would revive toward the end of the nineteenth century, but Crowquill deserves credit for helping to keep the good Doctor trotting along through the century's middle decades.

p. 145.

---

[2] "Graver" has a double meaning—more serious people, of course, but also the tool used for engraving wood.

LIST OF ABBREVIATIONS

Em.: *Emma* (Austen)

FS: *Remarks on Forest Scenery, and Other Woodland Views, Relative Chiefly to Picturesque Beauty* (Gilpin)

Juv.: *Juvenilia* (Austen)

LM: *Later Manuscripts* (Austen)

The Met: The Metropolitan Museum of Art

MP: *Mansfield Park* (Austen)

NA: *Northanger Abbey* (Austen)

OCW: *Observations, Relative Chiefly to Picturesque Beauty, On Several Parts of England; Particularly the Mountains and Lakes of Cumberland and Westmoreland* (Gilpin)

ONSE: *Observations on Several Parts of the Counties of Norfolk, Suffolk, and Essex. Also on Several Parts of North Wales; Relative Chiefly to Picturesque Beauty* (Gilpin)

OW: *Observations on the River Wye, and Several Parts of South Wales, Relative Chiefly to Picturesque Beauty* (Gilpin)

OWP: *Observations on the Western Parts of Engand, Relative Chiefly to Picturesque Beauty* (Gilpin)

RA: *Repository of Arts, Literature, Commerce, Manufactures, Fashions, and Politics* (periodical published by Rudolph Ackermann)

Pers.: *Persuasion* (Austen)

PP: *Pride and Prejudice* (Austen)

San.: *Sanditon* (Austen)

SS: *Sense and Sensibility* (Austen)

TE: *Three Essays* (Gilpin)

Wat.: *The Watsons* (Austen)

YCBA: Yale Center for British Art

CITATIONS

Doctor Syntax in Search of the Picturesque: All quotations of *Doctor Syntax* use the text as it appears in this book, and are cited by canto and line.

Austen's works: All quotations of Jane Austen's literary works are taken from *The Cambridge Edition of the Complete Works of Jane Austen* (2005-2008), edited by Janet Todd. Austen's novels are cited by volume and chapter; all other works are cited by page number.

Austen's letters: Austen's letters are cited by date and quoted as they appear in the fourth edition of *Jane Austen's Letters* (Oxford UP, 2011), edited by Deirdre Le Faye.

The Bible: All biblical quotations are taken from the 1769 text of the Authorized Version of the Bible, also called the King James Version.

Shakespeare: All quotations of Shakespeare are taken from *The Oxford Shakespeare: The Complete Works* (2005), edited by John Jowett et al., and are cited by act, scene, and line.

MONETARY CONVERSIONS

Whenever we mention sums of money in this book, whether in our notes on the text or the introductory materials, we provide a conversion to 2024 US dollars in parentheses, using a multiplier of 144. We derived that number by combining data for the year 1800 from the "Retail Prices Index: Long run series: 1800-2024," published by The Office for National Statistics, with data for 1 June 2024 from Exchange Rates UK. It is important to remember, however, that there is no perfectly accurate way to convert early nineteenth-century pounds into modern currency. Some things were more expensive back then, such as books and manufactured goods, while other things were cheaper, like labor. Our conversions are intended merely to give readers a rough sense of what the sums mentioned in this book were worth.

BIBLIOGRAPHY

Adolphus, John. *Memoirs of John Bannister, Comedian* (London: Richard Bentley, 1839).

Advice to the Universities of Oxford and Cambridge, and the Clergy of Every Denomination (London: G. Kearsley, 1783).

Armstrong, Patrick. *The English Parson-Naturalist: A Companionship between Science and Religion* (Leominster, UK: Gracewing, 2000).

Austen, James. *The Complete Poems of James Austen, Jane Austen's Eldest Brother*, edited by David Selwyn (Chawton, Hampshire: Jane Austen Society, 2003).

Austen, Jane. *Emma*, edited by Richard Cronin and Dorothy McMillan (Cambridge UP, 2013).

——. *Jane Austen's Letters*, 4th edition, edited by Deirdre Le Faye (Oxford UP, 2011).

——. *Juvenilia*, edited by Peter Sabor (Cambridge UP, 2013).

——. *Later Manuscripts*, edited by Janet Todd and Linda Bree (Cambridge UP, 2013).

——. *Mansfield Park*, edited by John Wiltshire (Cambridge UP, 2013).

——. *Northanger Abbey*, edited by Barbara M. Benedict and Deirdre Le Faye (Cambridge UP, 2013).

——. *Persuasion*, edited by Janet Todd and Antje Blank (Cambridge UP, 2006).

——. *Pride and Prejudice*, edited by Pat Rogers (Cambridge UP, 2013).

——. *Sense and Sensibility*, edited by Edward Copeland (Cambridge UP, 2013).

Austen-Leigh, William and Richard Arthur Austen-Leigh. *Jane Austen, Her Life and Letters: A Family Record*, 2nd edition (London: Smith, Elder & Co., 1913).

Bacon, Francis. *Sylva Sylvarum* (London: W. Lee, 1627).

Bentham, Jeremy. *The Works of Jeremy Bentham*, edited by John Bowring (Edinburgh: William Tait, 1843).

Byrne, Paula. *Jane Austen and the Theatre* (London: Hambledon, 2002).

Byron, Lord (George Gordon). *English Bards and Scotch Reviewers: A Satire*, 3rd edition (London: James Cawthorn, 1810).

Campbell, Thomas. *Life of Mrs. Siddons* (London: Effingham Wilson, 1834).

Cervantes, Miguel de. *Don Quixote*, translated by Tobias Smollett (New York: Barnes and Noble, 2004).

Coleridge, Samuel Taylor. *The Complete Poetical Works of Samuel Taylor Coleridge*, edited by Ernest Hartley Coleridge (Oxford: Clarendon Press, 1912).

Collins, Irene. *Jane Austen and the Clergy* (London: The Hambledon Press, 1994).

Combe, William. *The Devil Upon Two Sticks in England*, 3rd edition (London: Logographic Press, 1791).

———. *The Diaboliad* (London: G. Kearsly, 1777).

———. *A Historical and Chronological Deduction of the Origin of Commerce* (London: J. Walter, 1789), Vol. 4. (The first three volumes of this edition of *The Origin of Commerce* were by Adam Anderson).

———. *Letters to Marianne* (London: Thomas Boys, 1823).

———. *The Philosopher in Bristol* (Bristol: G. Routh, 1775).

———. *The Philosopher in Bristol, Part the Second* (Bristol: G. Routh, 1775).

———. *The Thames; or, Graphic Illustrations of Seats, Villas, Public Buildings, and Picturesque Scenery, on the Banks of that Noble River* (London: Vernor, Hood, and Sharpe, 1811).

Cowper, William. *The Task, a Poem in Six Books* (London: J. Johnson, 1785).

Cox, Brenda. *Fashionable Goodness: Christianity in Jane Austen's England* (Tucker, GA: Topaz Cross Books, 2022).

Duncan, Andrew. *A Study of the Life and Public Career of Frederick Howard, Fifth Earl of Carlisle, 1748-1825*, doctoral dissertation (Oxford University, 1981).

Ewing, Jennifer S. "As the Wheel Turns: Horse-Drawn Vehicles in Jane Austen's Novels," *Persuasions On-line*, Vol. 40, No. 1 (Winter, 2019).

Ford, John. *Rudolph Ackermann & The Regency World* (Warnham Books, 2018).

Gilpin, William. *Observations, Relative Chiefly to Picturesque Beauty, Made in the Year 1772, On Several Parts of England; Particularly the Mountains and Lakes of Cumberland, and Westmoreland* (London: R. Blamire, 1786).

———. *Observations on the River Wye, and Several Parts of South Wales, Relative Chiefly to Picturesque Beauty*, 2nd edition (London: R. Blamire, 1789).

———. *Observations on Several Parts of the Counties of Cambridge, Norfolk, Suffolk, and Essex. Also on Several Parts of North Wales; Relative Chiefly to Picturesque Beauty* (London: T. Cadell and W. Davies, 1809).

———. *Observations on the Western Parts of England, Relative Chiefly to Picturesque Beauty* (London: T. Cadell and W. Davies, 1808).

———. *Remarks on Forest Scenery, and Other Woodland Views, Relative Chiefly to*

Picturesque Beauty (London: R. Blamire, 1791).

———. *Three Essays: On Picturesque Beauty; On Picturesque Travel; and On Sketching Landscape: with a poem, on Landscape Painting. To these are now added Two Essays, Giving an Account of the Principles and Mode in which the Author Executed his own Drawings*, 3rd edition (London: T. Cadell and W. Davies, 1808).

Grose, Francis. *A Provincial Glossary, with a Collection of Local Proverbs, and Popular Superstitions* (London: S. Hooper, 1787).

Guarini, Giovanni Battista. *The Pastor Fido of Guarini in English Blank Verse* (Adam Black, 1809).

Gully, Anthony Lacy. *Thomas Rowlandson's Doctor Syntax*, doctoral dissertation (Stanford University, 1972).

Hackwood, Frederick. *William Hone: His Life and Times* (London: T. Fisher Unwin, 1912).

Hamilton, Harlan W. *Doctor Syntax: A Silhouette of William Combe, Esq.* (London: Chatto & Windus, 1969).

Hart, Tindal. *The Curate's Lot: The Story of the Unbeneficed English Clergy* (London: John Baker, 1970).

Horace. *The Odes and Epodes*, translated by Joseph P. Clancy (U of Chicago P, 1960).

———. *Satires and Epistles* [including the *Ars Poetica*], translated by John Davie (Oxford UP, 2011).

Hotten, John Camden. "The Life and Adventures of the Author of *Doctor Syntax*," *Doctor Syntax's Three Tours: In Search of the Picturesque, Consolation, and a Wife* (London: John Camden Hotten, [1868]), v-xxxiv.

Howard, George (Viscount Morpeth). "The Lady and the Novel," *The Keepsake*, edited by Frederic Mansel Reynolds (London: Longman, 1835).

Hussain, Azar. "The Boys at Steventon: Mr. Austen's Students, 1773-1796," *Persuasions On-line*, Vol. 44, No. 1 (Winter, 2023), 1-43.

Jacob, W.M. *The Clerical Profession in the Long Eighteenth Century 1680-1840* (Oxford UP, 2007).

Lockhart, J.G. *Memoirs of the Life of Sir Walter Scott* (Paris: Baudry's European Library, 1837).

Lucian, *Lucian in Eight Volumes*, translated by A.M. Harmon (London: William Heinemann, 1925).

Pool, Daniel. *What Jane Austen Ate and Charles Dickens Knew* (Touchstone, 1994).

Pyne, William Henry. "Mr. Ackermann's Repository of Arts," *Somerset House*

Gazette and Literary Magazine, No. XLI (1824), 221-2.

Report: Pauper Lunatics in Middlesex (House of Commons, 1827).

The Rich Old Bachelor: A Domestic Tale (Canterbury: Ward, 1824).

Robert, Paul and Isabelle Taylor. *Racecourse Architecture* (Turnberry Consulting and Acanthus Press, 2013).

Roe, F. Gordon. *Rowlandson: The Life and Art of a British Genius* (Leigh-on-Sea, UK: F. Lewis, 1947).

Rousseau, GS. "Review of *Doctor Syntax: A Silhouette of William Combe, Esq. (1742-1823)*," *Eighteenth-Century Studies*, Vol 5, No. 2 (1971), 353-6.

Scott, Sir Walter. "Art. XI [Review of *Emma*]," *Quarterly Review* (Oct. 1815), 188-201.

Shakespeare, William. *The Oxford Shakespeare: The Complete Works*, 2nd edition, edited by John Jowett et al. (Clarendon: 2005).

Smith, Horace. "Biographical Preface," *Memoirs, Letters, and Comic Miscellanies in Prose and Verse, of the Late James Smith, Esq.* (London: Henry Colburn, 1840).

Smith, Leonard. *Private Madhouses in England, 1640-1815* (Palgrave Macmillan, 2020).

Sterne, Laurence. *The Florida Edition of the Works of Laurence Sterne. Vol. 7: The Letters: Part 1: 1739-1764.* Edited by Melvyn New and Peter de Voogd (UP of Florida).

———. *A Sentimental Journey through France and Italy* (Dublin: G. Faulkner, 1769).

Timbs, John. *English Eccentrics and Eccentricities* (London: Richard Bentley, 1866).

Wilkes, Joanne. "Jane Austen as 'Prose Shakespeare': Early Comparisons," *Jane Austen and William Shakespeare: A Love Affair in Literature, Film and Performance*, edited by Marina Cano and Rosa Garcia-Periago (Palgrave Macmillan, 2019), 29-50.

Woolf, Virginia. "Jane Austen at Sixty," *The New Republic*, Vol. XXXVII, No. 478 (30 Jan. 1924), 261.

GLOSSARY

Booby: Fool.

Cit: An urban tradesperson, especially one living in the City of London. The term is mildly opprobious, implying a lack of cultivation or breeding.

Chaise: A carriage.

Chaise and pair: A carriage pulled by two horses.

Classic/classical: Having to do with the literature or culture of the ancient Greeks and Romans.

Clerk: Antiquated term for a clergyman.

The Cloth: The clergy, so named for their distinctive black garb.

Common: A piece of open land available to the community for foraging, grazing, and other purposes.

Cot: Cottage.

Doit: A tiny sum of money, literally a small coin.

Don: A scholar, especially one associated with Oxford or Cambridge.

Low'r/lour/lower: To scowl or threaten; often used figuratively to describe the sky when a storm is brewing.

Mitre: Headdress worn by bishops during official ceremonies, often used as a symbol of a bishop's rank or office.

Nag: A small riding horse.

Ostler: A stableman at an inn.

Pelf: Worldly goods, sometimes with an additional sense of "ill-gotten gain."

Plaster/plaister: Bandage spread with a medicinal substance.

Pother: Fuss.

Pound: An enclosure for detaining stray or trespassing livestock.

Purlieus: Borders, confines.

Purse-proud: Vulgarly arrogant on account of one's money, despite lacking other claims to status such as birth, breeding, and education.

Rill: A brook or rivulet.

Science: Knowledge of any kind gained by scholarly study, and not, as now, the study of the material universe specifically.

Simpering: Smiling in a coy or mischievous way. Often used in the context of flirtation.

Trow: Believe—an antiquated word mainly found in poetry.

Vale: Valley.

Wight: Person, sometimes with an undertone of pity or contempt.

Zounds: A mild oath, formed by contracting "God's wounds."

INDEX OF AUSTEN REFERENCES

Printed in Great Britain
by Amazon

50422092R20235